# Praise for
# YOON HA LEE

'Powerful. Unforgettable.
This is another amazing piece of work, and I have the
feeling I need to read it again to get it fully!'
**Stephen Baxter**

'A fiercely original and enchanting new fantasy.'
**Adrian Tchaikovsky**

'A smart, thought-provoking book, and one which
feels incredibly timely.'
*ScFiNow*

'A story of art, love, human connection,
the power of creation, colonialism, and the roles
we all have to play in fighting oppression.'
**Paul Weimer**

'The story is dense, the pace intense, and the East
Asian setting might make it seem utterly alien to many
readers—yet metaphors for our own world abound.
A breathtakingly original story.'
**N. K. Jemisin,** *The New York Times*

'I love Yoon's work! Solidly and satisfyingly full of
battles and political intrigue, in a beautifully built setting
that manages to be human and alien at the same time.'
**Ann Leckie**

'Yoon Ha Lee has arrived in spectacular fashion.'
**Alastair Reynolds**

'A density of ideas and strangeness that recalls the works of Hannu Rajaniemi, even Cordwainer Smith. An unmissable debut.'
**Stephen Baxter**

'Sheer poetry. Every word, name and concept in Lee's unique world is imbued with a sense of wonder.'
**Hannu Rajaniemi**

'Pushes the frontier of science fiction. A must-read.'
*Kirkus Reviews*

'Thoughtful, intricate, and completely human.'
*Tor.com*

'Readers who don't mind being dropped in the deep end will savor this brilliantly imagined tale.'
*Publishers Weekly* **Starred Review**

'Lee's prose is clever and opulently detailed; the worldbuilding is jaw-droppingly good.'
*Ars Technica*

'Rather than aping the generic clipped-and-grim style so often employed by other, less talented writers, Lee leans in the other direction, finding a sumptuous beauty in physical moments and complexity in thought and motivation.'
*NPR*

'Daring, original and compulsive. As if Cordwainer Smith had written a *Warhammer* novel.'
**Gareth L. Powell**

'For those itching for dense worldbuilding, a riproaring plot, complex relationships, and a deep imagination, it'll do just the trick.'
*Tor.com*

'Lee's ability to balance high concept with a deep examination of character is nigh unprecedented.'
**B&N Sci-Fi & Fantasy Blog**

'*Phoenix Extravagant* marks a different way of looking at Empire and power and living within, under, and against that than Lee's first novels, but no less a powerful one. A fantastic, brilliant undertaking.'
**Waterstones Bookseller's Review**

'Ambitious. Confusing. Enthralling. Brilliant. These are the words I will use to describe Yoon Ha Lee's utterly immersive, utterly memorable novel.'
***The Book Smugglers***

'For sixteen years Yoon Ha Lee has been the shadow general of science fiction, the calculating tactician behind victory after victory. Now he launches his great manoeuvre. Origami elegant, fox-sly, defiantly and ferociously *new*, this book will burn your brain. Axiomatically brilliant. Heretically good.'
**Seth Dickinson**

# Phoenix
# EXTRAVAGANT

388 3727

First published 2020 by Solaris
an imprint of Rebellion Publishing Ltd,
Riverside House, Osney Mead,
Oxford, OX2 0ES, UK

*www.solarisbooks.com*

ISBN: 978-1-78108-794-7

10 9 8 7 6 5 4 3 2 1

A CIP catalogue record for this book is available from the
British Library.

Designed & typeset by Rebellion Publishing
Watercolour cloud stock art by White Snow on Shutterstock

Printed in Denmark

# Phoenix
# EXTRAVAGANT

SOLARIS

This book is for Stephanie Folse
for her support in matters artistic and creative,
and for her own beautiful artwork,
which has been an inspiration for years.

# Chapter
# ONE

GYEN JEBI STROVE to keep their hand from shaking as they dipped their brush into the paint they'd mixed from pigments, a part of every artist's training. *Remember,* they reminded themself, *you're good at art. There's no reason to be nervous.*

That didn't do anything to soothe their nerves. They sat in a large room along with eleven other painters taking the Ministry of Art's examination, light filtering in through paper-covered windows, which gave everything a dreamlike aspect. The other painters varied in age, but most of them looked like they were in their twenties. Jebi themself would turn twenty-six on the New Year, when everyone grew a year older.

They'd already completed the first three parts of the examination, which tested the artist's ability to paint the most important subjects: first bamboo (easy), then landscape (mostly easy, unless you were ambitious and tried to outshine that famous painting of the Diamond Mountains), figure painting (a girl greeting a bird, in case the examiners were feeling sentimental). The last, hardest part of the exam was flower painting.

Jebi had mixed feelings about flowers. Even in past eras, choosing the wrong flower could indicate political opinions or innuendo; such games were even more dangerous now. The land of Hwaguk had been conquered and renamed Administrative Territory Fourteen by the Empire of Razan six years ago, although the Razanei presence went back years before that. And every flower had a meaning, and Razanei and Hwagugin associations were sometimes, but not always, the same.

*I will be conventional,* Jebi decided. Cowardly, but they needed this job. They were tired of eking out an existence painting crude tigers and frogs for collectors of folk art, even if it weren't for the trifling matter of that debt. Jebi yearned for a chance to paint *real* art, to spend time with a community of like-minded artists—even if that meant working for the Razanei government.

Their sister Bongsunga wouldn't understand, never had. Bongsunga had said that Jebi was welcome to stay with her as long as necessary. But Jebi knew what they made selling folk art, they knew what they owed the moneylender, and they knew what the Ministry of Art paid its staff artists. They didn't understand why the Razanei were so eager to recruit Hwagugin artists, but they didn't care. With any luck, they'd secure a comfortable position painting portraits of scowling officials, making them less scowly in the process. They could soothe their aching conscience by painting the moonscapes and native birds that called to them in their off hours.

If they dithered any longer, the paint would dry on the brush, and then where would they be? Jebi bit their lip, then settled on a peony, inoffensive in both Razanei and Hwagugin symbolism. Either way it represented romance and prosperity.

With deft strokes, Jebi finished the painting, depicting the peony with a single petal curled as though about to fly away. It was in the looser, impressionistic style that the Westerners had made popular among the Razanei. Jebi had mixed feelings about foreigners adulterating a tradition of art going back centuries, but even they had to concede that fashions changed, whether or not foreigners were involved.

Like everyone in the examination room, Jebi had come dressed in the modern clothes that the Razanei had introduced. For all her complaints, Bongsunga owned similar outfits. In parts of the former capital—now styled Administrative City Fourteen; at least the Razanei made things easy to remember— wearing native clothes wasn't safe. Easier to put on shirts and slacks, also styles imported from the West, and fit in.

Jebi's only concessions to Hwagugin tradition were two knotted mae-deup charms under their shirt, one bought from a charm-seller just yesterday. People had divided opinions on whether luck was like wine or flowers: that is, whether magic charms grew in power over time, or withered and had to be replaced. Jebi had split the difference by borrowing one from their sister and picking up a new one in the same style. One in red cord, one in blue, together suggesting the flow of yang and yin.

They didn't wear the charms openly. Most Razanei scoffed at Hwagugin superstition, although charms were usually reliable as far as magic went. But the red and blue specifically evoked the yin-yang taegeuk symbol of old Hwaguk.

Besides waiting for the paint to dry—something it did rapidly on the absorbent hanji paper—they had to do one final thing before they could consider themself done with the exam. They'd done it three times before; they could do it once more, even if guilt pricked at their heart.

Jebi bit their lip, then dashed out a signature in Razanei script, making sure it was legible: *Tesserao Tsennan.*

It was a Razanei name, not a Hwagugin one. Tsennan meant *bud*, which appealed to Jebi's sense of irony. Hwaguk meant *flower land*, which either referred to the spectacular springtime displays of azaleas and forsythias and plum blossoms or to the beauty (or seductiveness) of its people, depending on how bawdy you liked your poetry.

Like a growing proportion of Hwagugin, Jebi was fluent in Razanei. And like a small but significant number of their people, they sometimes found it convenient to go by a Razanei name. The two peoples resembled each other to a strong degree, after all: both black-haired and brown-eyed, with tawny skin, not too tall and slight of build. The Razanei administration encouraged the name changes and had set up a Registry of Names for Fourteeners, as they referred to their subjects. Jebi had lost no time in signing up, although they'd waited until their sister was at the market to get this done because they hadn't fancied a quarrel, especially over the registration fee.

*Tesserao Tsennan.*

As the paint dried, Jebi thought wistfully that they wouldn't *mind* signing their own name to their paintings. But if wishes were wings, all the world would fly. In the meantime, they needed the job.

They washed the brush out in the provided ceramic container, quotidian stoneware rather than the nicer white porcelain cup they used at home. The examiners did permit people to bring their own brushes. Privately, Jebi thought this was likelier to be a cost-cutting measure on the government's part than a concession to artistic quirks.

The examiner at the head of the room sat with an open book, gazing imperturbably at all the examinees. Jebi stared frankly at him, wondering why he had brought the book if he wasn't going to read it. Since nobody was allowed to leave early, Jebi entertained themself by imagining how they would draw a caricature of the man. Definitely exaggerate that unseemly beak of a nose, plus the gray hairs sprouting out of his ears. Maybe compare him to a tiger, cliché as it was? A balding white tiger, with a ferocious but comical roar.

With a start, Jebi realized that the man was staring back at them, with ill-concealed hostility. Hastily, Jebi jerked their gaze away and looked down at their four paintings, neatly arrayed on the table before them. Surreptitiously, they checked out the competition, cataloging faults, from sloppy brushstrokes to wobbly composition. Their confidence grew; their paintings were clearly among the best.

By the time the gong rang from outside, signaling an end to the examination, Jebi's head was throbbing. They had eaten only a light breakfast of rice porridge with a few shreds of chicken in the morning. They couldn't wait to get some food into themself.

"Please leave your paintings in place and exit the room single-file," the examiner said in a gravelly voice. "The results of the exam will be posted on the Ministry of Art bulletin board in three days."

Jebi gathered up their coat in anticipation of the cold outside. It was early enough in the winter that they had worn a lighter coat. The heavier one had a prominent ink stain that Jebi and their sister hadn't been able to remove despite hours of scrubbing.

Jebi was the second-last to leave the room, following the other hopefuls through the hallway and out of the building. From the outside, it looked like any other ministry building, with its peaked roof and roof-tiles sporting stylized plum blossoms. But the old signs in Hwamal, the language Jebi had grown up speaking, had been replaced by new ones in Razanei script.

*It doesn't matter,* Jebi thought. The Ministry of Art was still the Ministry of Art, no matter what language it was labeled with.

One of the other examinees fell in step with Jebi as they headed east toward a street with food carts. She was a drab young woman, her earlobes elongated by long earrings that jingled distractingly. Jebi wondered for a moment if they'd paint her ears faithfully, or exercise some aesthetic judgment and paint them without the stretching.

"How many of us do you think they'll accept this round?" the woman asked breathlessly. She couldn't have been older than sixteen or seventeen years, fresh-faced, her plump cheeks already reddening in the chill air.

Jebi fought down an irrational surge of jealousy. "I'm sure

the Ministry has plenty of positions," they said with false cheer. Did the Ministry even accept youths? "If you'll excuse me, I need to get something to eat."

The woman's face fell, and Jebi lengthened their stride, leaving her behind in the afternoon crowd of people with government business, couriers, and, most unnerving of all, automata.

Jebi's heartbeat sped up when they spotted the automata. From a distance they resembled ordinary people. They even wore clothes and smart black boots like ordinary people, to the extent that their blue uniforms were 'ordinary,' down to the golden Sun in Glory badges upon their chests and the vicious curved swords any Hwagugin would have been arrested for carrying. But the masks—their wooden masks showed blank visages with cut-outs for eyes, no nostrils, no mouths, only peculiar painted motifs.

Intellectually, Jebi knew that the automata would not harm them. Jebi hadn't *done* anything. Unlike human police— whether Hwagugin collaborators or Razanei occupiers—the automata were impartial. They didn't pick on drunks out of spite, or demand bribes, or beat up people who looked at them crosswise. But neither did they understand mercy, and they didn't *talk*.

A patrol of automata and their human interpreter, who could be identified by her necklace and bracelets of wooden beads, marched past as Jebi got in line in front of a food cart selling fried pancakes stuffed with jujubes, nuts, and melted brown sugar. Jebi did not have as much of a sweet tooth as their sister, and they should save money until they *knew* they had passed the Ministry of Art examination—the Razanei had a positive *obsession* with paying on time—but they were so hungry. Their stomach growled as they inhaled the rich smells of the frying pancakes.

*It'll be all right,* Jebi thought as they counted out the money for two pancakes. They had spent all their life practicing painting, even before the Razanei invaded; had scrimped for lessons from the best teachers they could find. Bongsunga hadn't understood, exactly, but she had made her own sacrifices to help Jebi in their pursuit of art. And Jebi had seen the others' paintings. There was no way they had failed the exam.

The pancake-seller made an especial production of Jebi's pancakes, flipping the dough ostentatiously and juggling their circular spatula. Jebi smiled back, although they didn't intend anything more than a harmless friendliness. Behind them, two people were talking about the latest Razanei troop movements as they continued to harry the rebels. The Army had recently secured an ancient Hwagugin observatory; Jebi was only middling educated in the ways of astrology, but their sister had a passion for it. They doubted the Razanei cared about stars and celestial cycles. It was probably about securing the high ground, one of the few military principles Jebi had any familiarity with.

When the two pancakes were done, the seller tucked them into a paper packet and handed them over. Jebi amused themself trying to figure out where the paper came from. Outdated examination papers were the usual source, but sometimes people used unclassified documents. This packet appeared to have been cut from a shrill essay on the encroachment of Western styles in pottery. Jebi had no strong feelings about the subject, but it made for entertaining reading, to the extent that reading was possible while weaving between the passers-by.

By the time Jebi arrived at their sister's apartment across town, they had devoured the first of the pancakes and were seriously considering eating the second as well. They wouldn't, of course. The whole point of having a sister was to *share*, and that included sharing your fried pancakes even if one was very hungry after a tense day of sitting exams.

In this part of town, people lived in family houses that had been converted to rental units. These particular houses had been confiscated from people who had put up a fight when the Razanei administration was consolidating its hold on the city. Jebi and Bongsunga had had a screaming argument before they moved into the apartment. Bongsunga had wanted to stay in their mother's old rental, even if the roof leaked and it had been broken into twice and they couldn't afford to replace the iron grilles over the windows, since the landlord refused to do it. (The price of metal had gone up precipitously since the Razanei commandeered the output of the famed Hwagugin mines both for their automata and their war engines, from tanks to battleships.) Jebi had pointed out that they'd be less miserable moving into a less dilapidated place, and Bongsunga had finally given in.

This particular rental was one of the nicer ones, not that you could tell from the outside. Bongsunga, who never did anything by halves, had insisted on seeing all the available units and haggling down the price. Now, to hear her talk, the whole thing had been her idea in the first place. Jebi didn't mind. They liked keeping their sister happy.

Jebi unlocked the door and entered, calling out, "Are you home, Bongsunga?" They spoke in Hwamal; there was no need for pretenses here. They slipped off their shoes and added, "I brought you a—"

"Sit down," Bongsunga said coldly. "We need to talk."

Bewildered, Jebi set the remaining fried pancake on a table and began taking off their coat. "What's the—?"

"Sit down."

Bongsunga was already sitting cross-legged on a cushion in the middle of the floor, a folder in her hands, next to the baduk set. The game in progress, with its black and white stones, changed every few days even though Jebi never met Bongsunga's opponents. Perhaps she was playing herself, or working strategy puzzles.

Her hair remained cropped short the way it had been ever since her wife Jia died in the war with Razan six years ago. Bongsunga had never grown it out once the mourning period passed, even though Jebi chafed at having to cut it every time it strayed far from its current severe bob. Bongsunga had taught Jebi to cut her hair when they were small, to save money, even before their mother died. Looking at it now, Jebi wished that their sister would get over Jia's death—it had been *six years*, after all—then winced inwardly at their own insensitivity.

Jebi let their coat fall in a crumpled heap, which would ordinarily have occasioned a lecture. They retrieved a floor cushion of their own from the stack by the wall, then arranged themself on the floor, also cross-legged. A sudden wild panic seized them: "The landlord didn't jack up the rent, did they?"

Or worse, what if Bongsunga knew about Jebi's debt?

Bongsunga's scowl faltered. "You think this is about something as petty as *rent?*"

That was when Jebi knew how badly they'd fucked up. In the ordinary course of things, Bongsunga took money very seriously. "Then what?"

Bongsunga opened the folder with tight, controlled motions, like she was close to ripping it in half. "I found this in your room," she said, and held up a sheet of paper.

The first thing that surged through Jebi was irritation. They weren't *ten* anymore; their sister, even an older sister who liked being the responsible one, shouldn't be going through their room. And never mind that the two of them could afford two separate rooms, which allowed Jebi plenty of space for splashing ink about and storing art supplies, instead of sharing like so many of their neighbors did.

The second thing—

"Where did you find that?" Jebi blurted out, which was *stupid*, their sister had just *told* them. The red stamp of the Citizens' Bureau faced outward, clearly visible to them.

In answer, Bongsunga's eyes narrowed. "'Tesserao Tsennan,'" she read, although she stumbled over the pronunciation; the sound *ts* didn't occur in Hwamal words. Unlike Jebi, Bongsunga had only learned the bare minimum of Razanei words—what she called 'Rassanmal,' the Hwamal term for the language—necessary to survive. "Whose idea was this?"

As if they'd been conned into getting a name certificate by some feckless friend over drinks. "It was *my* idea," they said loudly.

Bongsunga tugged at a lock of her hair, white-lipped. She closed her eyes, breathed in and out. Opened them.

"If that's all—" Jebi said, daring to hope that they could get this argument over with and slip off to the kitchen for a proper dinner. Maybe Bongsunga didn't realize what a name certificate cost. After all, she considered the whole business distasteful; might not have paid attention to the bureaucracy involved.

"I'm not finished," Bongsunga said. She put the certificate back in the folder. "You could have gotten into—this could get you into trouble with patriots. I'll burn this, and we'll have no more of this nonsense."

Jebi's temper flared. "What do you mean, 'burn this'? I spent good money on—"

They realized the admission was a mistake the moment the words left their mouth.

"Money," Bongsunga repeated slowly. "What money?"

Jebi gritted their teeth. There was no way Bongsunga would understand taking out a loan for something like this, so they had to lie to her. "I took odd jobs. Painting posters, the endless pictures of tigers to sell in the markets, you know. Believe it or not, people will pay *something* for good art. And I'm good at what I do."

"Then why do you need this—this—?" Bongsunga indicated the offending document.

"Listen," Jebi said, "could we at least discuss this after dinner? Because I'm famished after—" They clamped their mouth shut. *Stupid.* They'd meant to tell Bongsunga—*after*. Only *after* they'd passed the exams and it was a done deal.

Bongsunga's voice took on what Jebi always thought of as her Mom But Not Mom Voice. "After what?" she asked with deceptive calm.

In Jebi's earliest memories, their mother had yelled occasionally—not malice, just an uncertain temper after the tribulations of raising two children with her husband dead. Of course, she hadn't lived long. Bongsunga had sworn once that she would never yell. And for the most part she succeeded. Jebi often wished she *would*, because yelling—even throwing chopsticks—would have been more endurable than this deadly coldness.

"Let's talk about this after dinner," Jebi repeated, and looked down. Their hands were shaking.

"I told you that you should have had more breakfast," Bongsunga said, as if that mattered right now.

Jebi loved their older sister, even when she was mad, but sometimes she acted like she was still the only grown person and Jebi was still a teenager. "Never mind," they said, "I'm not hungry after all." They got up to go to their room—*hide* in their room, if the truth be told, until this blew over, and maybe they were acting like a teenager after all. Unfortunately, their stomach betrayed them by growling loudly. At any other time, it would have been funny.

Bongsunga rose as well, leaving the folder next to her cushion on the floor. She caught Jebi's arm. "Listen to me."

Jebi froze.

"Whatever it is you did that you think is so clever"—she said the word with no particular inflection—"you might as well share it now. We'll get through it together. We always have."

Jebi's heart ached, because they didn't think *together* was what their sister would be feeling once they admitted where they'd been all day. "It's not trouble," they said, trying to buy time. "I haven't gone down to the gambling parlors and lost the month's rent, if that's what you've been thinking." The moneylender had given them until the end of the month to come up with the money. And the Razanei paid on time. The problem was going to go away.

Bongsunga's brow furrowed. Whoops; bad joke, bad time, and even when she was in a good mood, Bongsunga had no sense of humor when it came to money. "If it isn't trouble," she said, "why are you avoiding telling me?"

An excellent question, and one whose answer would only infuriate her. Fine, then; better to get the explosion over with so the two of them could resume an ordinary existence. Besides, Bongsunga would come around once Jebi started bringing in more money. After all, she'd wanted to replace the floor cushions with nicer ones. Their current set was starting to look threadbare. Jebi liked how their sister's face glowed when she was able to afford things without worrying about money, especially since they were painfully aware how tightly she budgeted so that Jebi could have the art supplies they needed. Bongsunga spent all day out of the house, hustling at tasks she refused to talk to Jebi about, and worked half the night on top of it. Jebi wanted her to be able to lead an easier life.

Jebi squared their shoulders and bowed slightly, as though presenting a petition to someone close to their age. "I took the Ministry of Art examination today," they said. "I did well. It'll be a steady job. I'll bring in more money than the scribal stuff and cheap pictures I've been doing."

Bongsunga let go of their arm, and for a moment Jebi thought she wasn't mad anymore. "What name," she said, "did you register under?"

"I don't see why that's—"

"Exactly. You *don't* see." Bongsunga's mouth crimped. "*Answer the question.*"

Jebi lifted their head and looked their sister directly in the eye, which caused her eyes to narrow. After all, Jebi was the younger. They might push her, they might defy her, but open disrespect from a younger sibling was another matter.

On the other hand, at this point, etiquette was the least of Jebi's problems.

"I registered as Tesserao Tsennan," they said into Bongsunga's hostile silence. They couldn't help themself: they made a point of pronouncing the foreign name perfectly, as they had practiced so carefully in the markets and at the downtown districts when Bongsunga wasn't around to overhear. The words spilled out of them in a tumble. "You know what it's like for Hwagugin these days. The Rassanin"—they used the Hwamal term for Razan's people with the ease of long practice—"give preference to their own when they hire."

Whoops. They'd revealed more than they'd meant to.

"It's bad enough," Bongsunga said flatly, "that you think it's necessary to bow to the conquerors—"

Jebi made a frantic shushing motion; there were things you didn't *say*, even within your own apartment.

But Bongsunga didn't care about that. She continued, "—and even worse that you're impersonating them."

"It's not impersonating, really," Jebi protested, "I'm just letting them make whatever assumptions they want to—"

"You know perfectly well that Rassanin don't live in this part of town. Even the lower-ranked ones have no trouble turning decent people out of their houses so they can loll about in luxury. The truth about your heritage will come out eventually, and then where will you be?"

"I just thought—"

Jebi might as well have been trying to argue with a monsoon. Bongsunga's voice rose just slightly, like a string tuned too taut. "You know how Jia died!"

They did, although Bongsunga rarely spoke of it. Her wife had gone to war against the Razanei; had been cut down by a Razanei duelist wearing flamboyant Hwagugin red and blue— except the witnesses had seen the Sun in Glory armband, and she'd wielded a curved Razanei sword. If it hadn't been the duelist, it would have been artillery shells or bullets, anyway. Hwaguk's old-fashioned military, wielding swords and spears, had been no match for the Razanei with their tanks and modern rifles, technology reputedly stolen from the Westerners. Jebi still remembered the awful day when the messenger from the Hwagugin army had brought the news and recounted the whole thing in detail, and how Bongsunga hadn't spoken for a week afterward.

*I should have anticipated this,* Jebi thought, fighting to keep their face from crumpling. They'd wanted Bongsunga to be happy. If only she hadn't found the name certificate, everything would have worked out all right. Why had their luck charms failed them so badly?

Bongsunga was shaking. "Jia would have been appalled— appalled—" Then, to Jebi's horror, their sister began to cry.

Jebi reached out instinctively. "Bongsunga, I—"

"Get *out*," Bongsunga snapped. "Since you're so keen on working for the conquerors, you might as well rely on them for your housing too. I'm not going to share my roof with a collaborator." She thrust the name certificate at Jebi.

They stared at her. "You can't mean that." But they snatched the precious certificate anyway.

Bongsunga's chilly stare was answer enough.

Numbly, Jebi walked to their room, all the while aware of Bongsunga watching, and packed their money, clothes, and most essential art supplies as quickly as they could. They didn't want to linger one second longer than necessary. Not with their sister in this mood.

It wasn't until they were out the door that they realized that they had left behind the fried pancake.

# Chapter
# TWO

JEBI PULLED THEIR coat more tightly around themself as they walked away from their sister's apartment. *She'll cool down,* they thought miserably as the evening's chilly wind skirled up their sleeves and cut past their scarf. *I'll come back tomorrow, and we'll have breakfast, and everything will be all right.*

They had the sinking feeling that reconciliation was the last thing on Bongsunga's mind. She rarely mentioned Jia by name; that she had done so was a testament to how upset she was.

Jebi could think of several friends they could stay with for a few nights, but not a long-term solution. Money was going to be a problem until the end of the month, unless they took out another loan, which they didn't want to do. They shivered, sinking further into misery, and to top things off, they were really hungry.

They walked the half-hour to Hak's place. Hak worked as a low-level clerk for the Citizens' Bureau, on account of her beautiful calligraphy, in addition to brokering art sales on the side. In an earlier era, she would have been a poet, renowned for her graceful turns of phrase and ability to quote from the Huang-Guan classics. As it stood, she entertained herself in her off hours translating Razanei poetry into Hwamal. There was an underground market for the stuff, and Hak was a practical woman.

Most collaborators were less obvious about it, but Hak was a gumiho, a shapeshifting fox spirit. The Hwagugin didn't want to cross her. The gumiho were known for seducing travelers and eating their livers. The general sentiment was that Hak was welcome to hang around the Razanei and eat *their* livers, if they were so foolish as to offend her. The one time Jebi had asked about the topic, Hak had laughed and said that she was a modern gumiho, not a traditionalist, with better ways of obtaining food.

Getting the name certificate had been Hak's suggestion, so Jebi could count on her sympathy. Just as importantly, Hak had a generous spirit and wouldn't mind hosting a down-on-their-luck artist for a couple nights. Jebi hated to inconvenience her, but of their friends, Hak was the best prospect.

*I'll make it up to her later,* Jebi thought as they passed beneath the street lights. A lone automaton was igniting the lanterns one by one, although the sun was still a red-orange disc on the horizon. Jebi had no doubt that, by sundown, all the lights would be on, and timed perfectly, too.

That was one thing they liked about Razanei rule, although they'd never have admitted it to their sister. The Razanei had cleaned up the streets, hired street-sweepers, wired the central portion of Administrative City Fourteen for electricity. No electricity out here, of course—the street lights were ordinary lanterns—but they sometimes caught themself wishing for it in their home district. The streets felt *safer* with good lighting, even if violent crime was a rarity in most parts of the city thanks to the automata patrols. After all, automata didn't care about day or night, or need to sleep at all.

While they were daydreaming, they wouldn't mind electric lamps in a spacious art studio. Bongsunga—as much as it hurt to think about her—had originally given Jebi the larger room, not just so they could have the space for their supplies, but because it had a wonderful north-facing window. The other room was in the shade most of the time, thanks to a profligate wisteria that attracted hornets in the summertime. Being able to work whatever hours they pleased with good light, instead of being bound by the rising and setting of the sun, sounded like an impossible luxury.

Perhaps the best way to proceed would be to—and Jebi sighed—bring a small gift. It was the polite thing to do, even if they had to hoard their money carefully until the job came through. Still, the best way to ask for a favor was to do a favor, wasn't that how the world worked?

With that in mind, Jebi detoured to a book-seller's stall. There were always book-sellers, many of them trading in old Hwamal books and the occasional import from the great land of Huang-Guan to the north of Hwaguk's peninsula. Increasingly they sold books in Razanei, too. The Razanei government attempted to regulate the trade in books, but so far their efforts had been half-hearted and not terribly successful, unless the book-seller was stupid enough to pass around openly seditious literature.

This one-armed book-seller sat on a stool that had seen better days, hunched over a ledger as they cataloged their stock. The two of them exchanged nods of recognition: they both wore their hair in asymmetrical haircuts, like geu-ae currently did in the capital. The Razanei seemed baffled by geu-ae, people who chose to live not as men or women at all, or who sometimes dressed and spoke as one and sometimes as the other. But they left them alone, for which Jebi was grateful.

"Do you have any poetry?" Jebi asked, using a moderately respectful form of the verb. One thing they'd learned from Bongsunga—their heart clenched—was that speaking sweetly to shopkeepers was a great way to open a round of haggling.

"What sort are you looking for?" the book-seller asked, reciprocating the formality level.

"Whatever's new," Jebi said. "Rassanmal, if you have it."

"Any poet in particular? Kiiam is very popular lately."

"That works for me," Jebi said, eager to get going before the sun sank below the horizon. Hak kept late hours, but best not to push their luck.

"It's for a friend," the book-seller said knowingly. "You're not into poetry at all, are you? I bet you've never even heard of Kiiam."

"Got it in one," Jebi said. "Doesn't bother you, does it?"

The book-seller shrugged. "Your money's just as good either way. I don't care if you're going to draw doodles all over the pages, or use them to wipe your ass. They're just books."

"If you say so," Jebi said, appalled in spite of themself, and haggled over the price before handing over the money.

The sky darkened as Jebi kept walking. They paused for a moment in spite of their haste, and gazed up at the jewel-sash of glittering stars, the blade-slash of the moon. Bongsunga used to take Jebi up to the roof at night and name the constellations for them, and tell them all the old stories of celestial attendants. Hwaguk's astrologers had observed the celestial beings directly since the invention of telescopes, although the meanings of their movements often puzzled people, and were a frequent source of gossip.

By the time they arrived at Hak's place, a modest house located in what was euphemistically known as the Virgins' District, it was not too far past sundown. Bongsunga had hang-ups about the Virgins' District—so called because "everyone's a virgin if you pay them to be"—and Jebi hadn't figured out why until they learned that Jia had, before the marriage, dallied from time to time with the prostitutes there. But prostitutes had to make a living, too.

The first thing that told Jebi that they'd arrived at an awkward time was the fact that the gate was propped open by a weathered kimchi pot. People milled about the courtyard. Beyond the laughter and buzz of conversation, Jebi heard— was that musicians? A bamboo flute and a drum, and they bet there was also a zitherist to complete the trio, although the instrument was too quiet for a party of this sort.

*I should head back, or bother someone else,* Jebi thought, hesitating. But they'd come all this way, with a gift no less, and besides, they could smell the food from within. The rich aromas of barbecued meat and sauces and sliced fruits made their mouth water.

What the hell. At worst they'd be kicked out and they could

try some other friend. Jebi ducked behind the wall just long enough to comb their fingers through their hair, then strode into the courtyard.

Almost everyone was speaking Razanei, which explained why Hak hadn't invited Jebi. While Jebi was fluent and rarely had problems passing on casual contact, Hak knew Bongsunga's opinion of the Razanei. For that matter, Bongsunga didn't think highly of Hak, either, or foxes in general, but that didn't matter anymore.

A few people turned at Jebi's entrance, then dismissed them as nobody of note. The rucksack crammed full of their possessions looked out of place here, where the guests were dressed in finery. Jebi didn't bristle at the assessment. As much as Bongsunga resented Razanei governance, hierarchy had always been a part of Hwaguk's society. Having Razanei at the top of the pecking order wasn't all that different from having the old government's scholar-aristocrats in charge. But Bongsunga would never see it that way.

Jebi spent several minutes dodging through the crowd. Where was Hak? They should say hello, explain the situation to her. But there were so many people, and they didn't spot her anywhere.

What the hell, maybe they could at least get a little food in their belly, then resume the search. Jebi inched toward the food. The tables showed a staggering spread, only half-eaten. The meat had not been as popular as Jebi had expected. They sniffed again, suspicious this time. Was that *liver*? Must be Hak's idea of a joke.

"I don't recognize you," a sharp voice interjected just as Jebi reached for a skewer.

Jebi glanced sidelong at the woman, whose brocade silk jacket declared her wealth. Among other things, Jebi hadn't seen fabric of such a rich indigo in this part of town in forever. "Excuse me," they said at their most polite. "The host is a friend of mine. I didn't catch your name?"

The rich woman raised her eyebrow as she looked Jebi up and down, gaze lingering on the ink stain. Jebi was regretting not wearing their best coat for the visit, but they hadn't wanted to risk getting it soiled. If only they'd known about the party and its judgmental guests beforehand.

Maybe this hadn't been such a great idea after all. "I'll be going," Jebi said, sliding the skewer back onto the tray with a longing look and turning around.

Jebi almost collided into Hak in their haste to leave. "Tsennan!" Hak said, smiling brightly.

Hak was small even for a Hwagugin, and indecently chubby at a time when the only people who were eating well were, not to put too fine a point on it, collaborators. Even her clothes were fine, although her fox-red coat was less showy than the other woman's brocade jacket. But Hak was also generous, and Jebi figured they had a lot to learn from her adroitness in navigating recent politics.

"I'm so sorry I didn't think to invite you," Hak went on. "It must have slipped my mind."

Jebi knew why they hadn't gotten the invite; no sense in taking offense. "It looks like a lovely party," they said. At least Hak had addressed them by their Razanei name; they appreciated her attention to detail.

"Chiaza, have you met my friend Tsennan?" Hak said, snagging the skewer that Jebi had just returned and casually handing it back to them, bless her. "They're an artist."

"An artist, really," Chiaza the rich woman said, still looking skeptical. "What school of calligraphy do you subscribe to?"

"I was originally trained in Flowing Salamander," Jebi said truthfully, wishing they'd prepared a better lie. Even they knew that Flowing Salamander was considered eccentric among the Razanei, although at least it was a recognized school. "But these days I've adapted to Four Friends." And *that* was respectable to the point of being stodgy. It referred to four plants: bamboo, plum blossom, orchid, and chrysanthemum. But if forced to demonstrate, especially with cold-numbed fingers, it was the other style they could pull off easily.

"I suppose that's acceptable," Chiaza said, as if her acceptance meant anything to Jebi.

"Chiaza deals in antiquities," Hak said, patting Jebi's hand in warning: *Don't react.* As if Jebi would do anything foolhardy in a courtyard full of Razanei. "That's why we're gathered here. Chiaza, don't let me keep you, I just want to show Tsennan around."

Jebi chomped down the meat with unseemly haste, and put down the skewer. They kept from glancing back over their shoulder at the mouth-watering food. At least Hak had fed them one skewer, which was better than none. "Antiquities?" they asked in a low voice as Hak ushered them toward the house.

"Oh, yes," Hak said, "it's the latest rage among collectors back in Razan."

*I hadn't heard,* Jebi almost said; but best to keep quiet about their ignorance.

Hak's next smile was less forced. "Very profitable, if you know the right people. Granted, *my* business isn't direct. I introduce people to each other, in exchange for a consideration. One has to take care of oneself when the pickings are lean, you know."

"I do," Jebi said. Outdated attitudes still lingered even in Administrative City Fourteen. In the old days, while a professional painter or calligrapher could make a respectable living, people reserved their respect for amateurs—usually aristocrats or poets or courtesans who practiced the arts on the side. The Hwagugin aesthetic preferred honesty and spontaneity over strict technical proficiency. Jebi had mixed feelings about this, but they kept their opinions to themself. No sense in offending one's clients, after all, or other artists of whatever stripe.

Once inside, both Hak and Jebi slipped off their shoes and left them on the low shelf reserved for that purpose. The common room had been transformed, aglow with paper lanterns in what Jebi identified, cynically, as a compromise design that could be interpreted as either Hwagugin or Razanei: round, ribbed, decorated inoffensively with the symbol for long life in black calligraphy.

Tables and artfully placed screens turned the common room into a miniature labyrinth displaying the artifacts that Hak had mentioned. The first to catch Jebi's eyes was—it had to be a counterfeit. But it *looked* real, gleaming in the flickering glow of the lanterns: an antler-crown of one of Hwaguk's old dynasties, its delicate prongs covered in gilt and dangling comma-shaped jade beads. Or anyway, if it wasn't real jade, it looked damn close.

"That's right," Hak said, noticing Jebi's hesitation. "That's genuine, according to the scholars I consulted. Priceless, and wasted in the shrine where it was moldering away."

Jebi scarcely heard her. They drifted among the tables, marveling at the treasures showcased. Brittle greened daggers of bronze with the peculiar mandoline-shaped blades that sometimes turned up in the junk markets. Vases, some pure white, others of the blue-gray celadon that was so prized even today, still others painted with elaborate scenes of cloud and crane. Lacquered boxes for cosmetics, decorated with abalone inlay. Silk scrolls from which bodhisattvas of ages past stared, serene to the point of stiffness, skin depicted in gold and robes in red.

"This is remarkable," Jebi said, because they had to say something. They'd grown up with art like this, to the extent that everyone did. The riches of ages past, brought here for the delectation of foreigners.

*These foreigners rule us,* Jebi thought, determined to recognize the reality of their situation—everyone's situation, no matter what people like their sister might think.

Hak chattered brightly about the provenance of various items, pointing at a golden incense-holder here, a carved wooden duck there. Apparently the Razanei had sent expeditions to the tombs, the temples, the ancestral halls. Why should items of such charming and primitive beauty be left where no one could appreciate them, after all?

Except 'no one' meant the people who had made this art, and left it where they wanted it, for reasons of their own—reasons which had almost certainly not included pillage by Razanei.

Jebi breathed in and out, reminding themself to stay calm. It wasn't any of their business, and it wasn't their problem to solve, either. So what if Hak wanted to broker some deals? She had a right to make a living.

They became aware of other people circulating in the common room. Some of them weren't even paying attention to the priceless artifacts in front of them. Snatches of conversation drifted toward Jebi:

"...need a sterner hand, is what," a baritone was saying. "There's no way the Governor-General would have ordered such extreme actions unless there was a full-scale insurrection."

*Insurrection?* Jebi wondered, heart beating more rapidly. Sure, they'd heard of rebels, people who put up crude posters only to have them taken down by the patrols of automata, or else hid in the mountains and carried out ineffectual raids.

Someone with a higher voice answered the first: "But in an out-of-the-way place like Parugan-Namu? Barugan-Namu? I swear, I keep practicing, but those complicated Hwamal"— they *almost* said the word correctly—"consonants keep defeating me. I'll get it right one of these days."

*Thank you,* Jebi thought ironically. Nice to know someone was trying. By the sound of it, the speaker was referring to some place called Ppalgan-Namu, which meant Red Tree; they were used to teasing out Hwamal words from Razanei mutilation. Jebi had never heard of the place, but that didn't mean anything. Hwaguk was full of settlements, from as small as three or four households clinging to hard-fought terraces of rice to whole sprawling towns. Most of them had descriptive names like Red Tree or Big Boulder, if you dug through the etymology.

Hak was still talking, and the people discussing the massacre had moved away. Jebi put it out of their mind. If it affected ordinary citizens here in the capital, which they doubted, they'd be able to scrape up the news elsewhere.

"...to the moon," someone else was saying. "If celestials can live up there, then so can ordinary human beings. It's just a matter of arranging transport."

"Even the Ministry of Technology hasn't figured out how to invent a flying machine," a bored voice responded. "And who cares about a bunch of louche celestials and their pets? There's nothing interesting in the sky unless you want to catch moon rabbits."

"...want some tea?" Hak gestured at the rucksack's straps, and Jebi gave up on the intriguing astrological conversation. "I can find you a safe place to put that down. Your back must ache."

"Yes, of course," Jebi said, smiling their gratitude. Besides, they hadn't had anything to drink all day, and dehydration was giving them a headache.

The two of them drifted into the kitchen, which was absurdly small considering the bounty of food outside. "If you ever need a caterer, I can absolutely recommend the Kim family that lives next to the statue of Nongae," Hak said with a wry smile as she poured for both of them. She was still speaking in Razanei. "They're used to, shall we say, accommodating odd tastes."

"Really," Jebi said, eyes crinkling. "That looked like ordinary food." They weren't going to mention the livers if Hak wasn't going to. At a nod from Hak, Jebi eased the rucksack off their shoulders and leaned it against a counter. Then they took the proffered teacup and drained it in one gulp, too thirsty to be decorous.

Hak lowered their voice confidentially. "Nothing's as spicy as it usually is! They used the absolute weakest pepper paste they could get away with, for appearances' sake. I didn't want anyone to go away with their mouth on fire."

Jebi grinned. "You're always the thoughtful host. Speaking of which—I realize this is not the best time, but could I trouble you for a spot to sleep for the next week or so?"

"Oh," Hak said, her face screwing up in sympathy. "Let me guess. Things with your honored sister finally came to a head?" She nodded wisely at the rucksack. "At least you come prepared."

"Something like that," Jebi said, and grimaced. "I hate to impose—"

"Nonsense," Hak said briskly. "What are friends for? As long as"—and she grinned—"you don't mind helping me clean up after everyone's gone home."

"Of course, of course."

"How did the examination go, by the way?"

Jebi brightened. "I did good work. You know how my sister frets about money all the time. Once I bring home the signing bonus"—*and pay off my debt*—"and start drawing that salary, she'll come around."

"She'd better," Hak said. "I know your sister's set in her ways, but she should appreciate that art is work too!"

Jebi laughed, uncomfortable with the old argument. Hak had never quite understood Bongsunga's feelings about art. Bongsunga had never been anything but supportive of Jebi's vocation, but Jebi was always itchingly aware of the sacrifices that Bongsunga made, when she must have dreams of her own.

By all rights, Bongsunga should have remarried, or at least adopted a child to carry on the family name. She was the elder, after all. Their parents had died young, of disease, leaving Bongsunga to raise Jebi. And Jebi was an artist, married, as tradition would have it, to their art. They might take lovers—had done so in the past—but marriage was out of the question. They'd only known a few artists who had attempted that path, and they'd rapidly become irrelevant. Unfair, perhaps, but not something Jebi had any power to change.

The hard truth was, finding someone willing to marry the widow of a Hwagugin soldier—and one who'd died fighting the Razanei, at that—posed a difficulty. And beyond that, children cost money. (According to an old saying, children *ate* money. Not a saying that Bongsunga had ever repeated in front of Jebi, who was always aware of the eight-year difference in their ages, but one Jebi thought about nonetheless.)

"It'll blow over," Jebi said at last. "I just need a place to stay for a few nights, until the examination results are released and my sister's temper cools down."

"It's no problem." Hak smiled. "Still, I think I should put your bag somewhere safer, in case someone mistakes it for an artifact! I'll set it in my bedroom. Will that do?"

"Thank you," Jebi said. "Besides, you have to talk to people, don't you? That's the whole reason you threw this party. Just as long as you don't mind me availing myself of your food..." The more of this feast they enjoyed, the less of their own money they'd have to spend. A mercenary way to use a friend, but they didn't have any better options.

"Eat, eat," Hak said. She lifted the rucksack. "I'll take care of this. You can find me later."

Jebi waved her off, then returned to the common room, leaving the empty teacup behind. They slowed down just in time to avoid colliding into a knot of three Razanei, one of them in the blue-and-gold uniform of Razan's military. The Razanei didn't so much as glance at them, instead gesticulating at a wooden sculpture and talking in a hushed voice. Jebi gave up on trying to understand them once they switched to a thick dialect Jebi didn't recognize. *That*, they could tell, was on purpose, so they might as well give the three their privacy.

*It's not* my *art that's being sold to foreign collectors,* Jebi thought, to ease the traitorous pang that stabbed through their heart. They'd stopped in front of a painting of two hawks circling in a way that evoked the blue-and-red taegeuk yin-yang symbol featured on Hwaguk's old flag.

*It could be worse,* Jebi consoled themself, moving on to the next painting. This one wasn't, strictly speaking, an artifact. They could almost smell the newness of the paints, in the pastel style that some modern artists preferred. Depicted were shelves and books using the Western innovation called *perspective*, which had become a fad among some of Jebi's generation—introduced by Western philosophers visiting both Huang-Guan to the north and the islands of Razan. While the former government of Hwaguk had forbidden Western visitors, the influences had trickled in anyway.

The unsettling geometrical realism both fascinated Jebi and made them uneasy. Surely what mattered was an artist's ability to capture the inner spirit of the subject, and not the minutiae of its exterior appearance? At least Hak—who had, in days past, pronounced herself charmed by the technique—wasn't standing here to argue with them over it.

*I should pay more attention to the important things in life, like food,* Jebi thought, shaking their head. They slipped on their shoes and headed back out into the courtyard with its temptation of dishes.

On the third morning of their stay with Hak, Jebi woke early enough to catch her before she left. Hak had already prepared a lunchbox, as she had the previous mornings; when did she sleep? "We'll celebrate tonight," Hak said, smiling as she slid the lunchbox across the table to Jebi. "My treat."

"Oh, I can't," Jebi protested, "not after all your generosity."

"Nonsense," Hak said. "You'll have plenty of opportunities to return the favor in the days to come." She winked, her eye gleaming fox-amber before returning to its usual brown. "Maybe we can even invite that sister of yours."

"Maybe," Jebi agreed, despite a twinge of resentment. They didn't *want* to share their triumph with Bongsunga, even though they owed it to her just as surely as they did to Hak.

Jebi and Hak headed out together, although their paths diverged after just a couple of blocks. The autumn chill had let up today, although that was only temporary; according to the almanacs issued by the government, the first frost was right around the corner. Jebi had dressed respectably for the occasion, bringing a minimum of necessities. They doubted the Ministry would ask them to start painting on the spot. There was, they'd heard, an orientation period over the course of two weeks.

Although they'd set out early, a small crowd had gathered around the bulletin board by the time they arrived. Mostly curious onlookers, Jebi figured, since there were easily twice as many people as had taken the exam. Chest tight, Jebi elbowed their way through the crowd so they could get close enough to the bulletin board to read the results.

*ACCEPTED APPLICANTS*, said the first sheet, with a list of five names. Jebi read and reread the list with a growing sense of unreality, then the official signature at the bottom of the sheet certifying the results. *This can't be happening.*

Five names, and theirs—Razanei or Hwagugin—wasn't one of them.

# Chapter
# THREE

JEBI DIDN'T REMEMBER how they'd ended up at the shabby parlor three buildings south from the One-Armed Warrior. The statue had not lost its limb during the Razanei invasion, as some claimed; rather, some vandal had taken a chisel to it ten years earlier. Jebi had a great view of it from the second floor balcony of the parlor. Its mutilation echoed Jebi's mood. They felt as though someone had chopped off their right arm, or cut out their heart.

Blearily, they stared at the cup of rice wine, then sipped it. What they wanted to do was down the whole thing at once, but the taste was so terrible that even in this mood they couldn't bring themself to do it. Getting drunk was difficult when one didn't *like* alcohol. But if they kept at it long enough, inebriation would ensue.

The sun highlighted the roof-tiles of the nearby buildings, most of them sporting the faces of dokkaebi goblins or legendary warriors. Under other circumstances, Jebi would have doodled their own versions of the familiar motifs, recognizable even from a distance. But the last thing they wanted to do right now was *draw*.

How could they have failed the exam? Had the examiners discovered their Hwagugin origins? Because those had been some of their finest paintings. They'd been so sure that the examiners would be impressed.

Preoccupied, they almost didn't notice Hak and another person had slid into the seats across from them until Hak spoke.

"You have no idea how long it took to chase you down," Hak said, cheeks pink and a little breathless. She must have been running.

Jebi blinked slowly. "What are you doing here?" Then they realized how ungracious that sounded. "I mean, I thought you were busy."

Jebi glanced at Hak's companion, a slender person dressed daringly in a sleek masculine beige coat, and a shockingly vivid purple scarf embroidered with nesting birds, a feminine motif. Aniline purple must be popular right now. "I don't believe we've met," the stranger said in Razanei. Their voice was low and warm. "I heard from Hak what happened. So sorry."

"I can't figure out what I did wrong," Jebi said dully, not caring that Hak had brought a stranger along to witness their failure. After all, the results had been posted in public. Everyone who cared would know.

Even Bongsunga would know. They were sure of it, and just as sure that they couldn't go back to her, not without rekindling the argument that had led her to kick them out in the first place.

The moneylender too. If he hadn't found out yet, he would soon. Jebi needed to find a source of income before the end of the month. They only had twelve more days to come up with the money.

"The examiners are mercurial," Hak said, reaching out to pat Jebi's hand. "You can try the next time they have openings, surely? I bet it was close."

Hak's sympathy only made Jebi want to lash out, but their friend deserved better. "Who knows when that will be? And in the meantime, I either have to patch things up with my sister or find alternate living arrangements." They knew better than to assume that they could stay with Hak indefinitely.

"Yes, that's why I brought Ren along," Hak said, nodding at the stranger.

Ren leaned forward, flipping the ends of their scarf fetchingly over their shoulders. "Some of my friends work at the Ministry of Armor," they said. "I wasn't sure this would be the best time, but Hak said you might be interested in any leads, even uncertain ones."

"Mmm," Jebi said, not sure what this had to do with them. They already knew that they'd rather avoid designing propaganda posters for Armor. Among other things, the posters didn't *work*. Nobody had ever looked at the awkward attempts to make the automata look *cuddly* and stopped making warding symbols, or scurrying for cover when a patrol marched by.

"They're hiring," Ren said, confirming Jebi's fears. "I heard someone mention that they're specifically looking for painters. What could it hurt to knock on their door and find out?"

*I mustn't be rude,* Jebi thought. Hak was trying to help, preposterous though the job was. "Thanks for the thought," Jebi said, "but I'll try my luck elsewhere." They weren't that desperate—not yet.

Ren shrugged. "Well, keep it in mind." They rose in one fluid motion and bowed to Hak. "I'll see you another time."

After Ren had slipped downstairs, Hak frowned at Jebi. "You should have heard them out."

Jebi regarded her with surprise. "I'm not out of options yet. I just have to look harder."

"It's just that opportunities are thin on the ground these days," Hak said, the closest she would come to naming the Razanei presence as an influence on the arts scene. "I wanted to help, that's all."

Jebi forced themself to smile. "I appreciate it, Hak."

What they wanted to ask was, *Are those slender opportunities why you've ingratiated yourself with the Razanei and their art collectors?* But it wasn't something they could say out loud, not if they wanted to preserve the friendship. Besides, it wasn't any different than what they'd tried to do in applying to the Ministry of Art.

"Well," Hak said briskly, straightening, "I'll keep an ear to the ground in case anything else turns up. But don't wait too long, all right? The sooner you pick yourself up and get moving, the less it will hurt. You'll see." And with that, she, too, departed.

\*     \*     \*

OVER THE COURSE of the next week, as the twelve days trickled away, Jebi became comprehensively familiar with the number of doors that were shut to them.

They stopped by their sister's house several times and stood in front of the gate for the better part of an hour, listening. The first two times, they heard voices from within, Bongsunga's voice, and those of strangers. The third time, despite the unfamiliar voices, they nerved themself up and banged on the door. But Bongsunga didn't answer, and after half an hour of knocking, they gave up and went away.

They'd worked in the past with a broker who offered folk art by anonymous artists—one of the parts that Jebi detested most about the business, although they were ashamed to have their name associated with these pieces anyway. They visited him to inquire as to whether he was interested in more work. His shop remained dismal, poorly lit and crowded with the usual stereotyped images. Jebi counted no less than eight tigers, all of them in the crude, bold style that the market currently favored, and six of them all but indistinguishable despite—probably—having been painted by completely different people.

The broker caught them looking. "No more room for tigers," he said, almost in a grunt. "There's talk that tigers are seditious."

Jebi swallowed an incredulous laugh. Tigers, *seditious?* They'd featured in Hwagugin art for hundreds of years, if not longer, as mountain guardians and mercurial sages as well as the buffoonish subjects of folktales in which clever peasant children outwitted the beasts who had eaten their grandparents. (Why the grandparents never managed to save themselves the same way, Jebi couldn't figure out.)

Then again, tiger-sages had also served as the patrons of warriors, and maybe the Razanei administration feared that the resistance would take inspiration from them. Never mind that tiger-sages made chancy allies at best.

"I should keep track, huh," Jebi said, swallowing their bitterness. They had grown bored of painting cartoonish tigers, but they could do it in their sleep. Truth to tell, they were horrified at themself for resenting the sudden uselessness of a skill they hadn't even enjoyed picking up in the first place.

"You didn't bring anything, did you?" the broker said, still gruff.

He named a figure; the percentage had gone down.

*That's*—Jebi clenched their teeth, took a deep breath. It wouldn't do to let him see their outrage.

He noticed anyway. "Nothing personal," he said, "but the local interpreter is asking for bigger bribes. You know how it goes."

"I see," Jebi said with a sigh. They shouldn't have bothered coming here anyway. The folk art had only ever been an uncertain source of income. "Thanks."

The man didn't even look up as Jebi made their way out of the shop.

Jebi had no better success at the other places they checked. How had they never noticed how few good jobs there were, and how many artists competed for the ones that existed? In the past, Bongsunga's support had insulated them from the ups and downs of having to scramble for money.

They inquired with several schools of portraitists, but portraits had fallen in popularity since Hwaguk's conquest. The few portraitists who commanded high prices had adapted to the trends that the Razanei had set—not a surprise in itself, but Jebi also gathered, from the oblique comments they heard, that bribery and connections helped in securing one's place. One of the schools offered them a membership, which they would have considered if they'd been able to afford the fee. The school promised access to clients, although it took a cut of any commissions. But the fee—for a full year, up-front— was too high.

They also looked into the rent at communal houses, because sooner or later Hak would start hinting that they needed to move out. Jebi hated the idea of living with strangers, but they weren't going to find a room as luxurious as the one their sister had kicked them out of, either. Maybe they could find a hostel, pay by the week, in the hopes of going back home soon.

None of this helped with the immediate problem of finding work. Jebi regretted not making more connections with printmakers or sign-painters, people with their own cliques. They'd never break in unless they made contacts, which would involve bribes, or drinks, or gifts. It all came to the same thing.

*This is what I get,* Jebi thought glumly as they stopped by a food cart to haggle over fish cakes in spiced sauce, *for playing high-and-mighty while I studied traditional art.* Some of the ministries outsourced their posters to printmakers. Jebi preferred painting, but the printmakers had jobs, and they didn't. It was too late to change fields, anyway.

The seller only gave Jebi a scant serving of fish cakes. Jebi almost argued about it, then thought better of it. After chasing leads all day, they were too tired to quibble, and Hak had fed them well the past few days.

That evening, and the next, and the next, Jebi walked all the way to the Ministry of Armor's complex before heading back in indecision. *I'm not that desperate yet,* they kept thinking. But none of the other jobs they applied for panned out, and in the meantime Jebi found it harder and harder to face Hak during their brief encounters.

*I'm not that desperate yet*—but they only had five days left before the moneylender came after them.

ON THE EIGHTH day after the exam results were posted, the day dawned gray and misty, smothering the entire city. Even the smells of rotting leaves and waste were muted. With Jebi's luck, it would rain today.

In spite of themself, Jebi's feet led them down to District One, once known as the Government District. They passed alongside the Old Palace, which the Razanei had rehabilitated for various administrative buildings, and stopped in front of the Ministry of Armor.

*Why not?* Jebi thought, staring dubiously at the building. *It doesn't hurt to look around.* Armor occupied the western wing of the palace. In the old days, it had sported a banner with the White Tiger of the West, which was associated with autumn. Now, it simply featured a wooden sign saying *ARMOR* in the Razanei character.

Jebi had faint childhood memories of the Old Palace and

its gardens. The Razanei had lost no time relandscaping. The pigeons, crows, and magpies that pestered people for scraps didn't care, and some of the Razanei bureaucrats had taken to feeding the birds themselves. Jebi felt the familiar ambivalence when they looked at the imported cherry trees, so emblematic of Razan. They'd shed most of their leaves already, but they'd bloom gloriously in the spring, beautiful and alien.

Unsurprisingly, more automata patrols marched along the streets around the Old Palace. Jebi tried not to gawk too obviously as one group passed them. They'd never seen automata with masks with marks that color before, a weird shimmering... orange? Green? They couldn't tell for sure, and that bothered them. Some new paint? *That* intrigued them.

The interpreter didn't take notice of Jebi, or at any rate, not *more* notice than anyone else in the street. Still, Jebi clutched their bag, since it contained the precious name certificate. It wouldn't fend off a Razanei determined to take offense, of course; they just had to keep matters from getting to that point.

Like all the ministries, Armor had a bulletin board. Say this for the Razanei: they were *organized*. Despite all the stereotypes about the artistic soul, Jebi appreciated this. One could always expect the Razanei to put things where people could find them.

This late in the afternoon, only a few other people lingered near the bulletin board. A functionary in white and gray was pulling down older notices. Jebi glimpsed some of them: cryptic lists of numbers and names, something about the cafeteria, a reminder not to feed the birds. A woman in crutches and a child who resembled her were feeding the birds, and no one bothered them about it.

"Do you mind if I have a look before you take the rest of those down?" Jebi asked the functionary in moderately deferential Razanei.

The functionary shrugged. "Suit yourself," she replied. "No one's going to notice if some of these linger for another day anyway." With that, she strolled away.

It didn't take Jebi long to locate the call for staff artists. *Why can't they borrow them from the Ministry of Art?* they wondered.

It was only when a mild voice answered from next to them that they realized they had spoken aloud. "What's your interest?"

Jebi bit their tongue by accident as they whirled. "I'm an artist," they blurted out, too wrung out by their fruitless search to dissemble.

The speaker was a man in the same white and gray as the woman who'd been clearing the board, slim of stature, balding. He leaned on the oddest wooden cane Jebi had ever seen. It was topped by a rifle stock, if its barrel had been replaced with polished wood. "I haven't seen you around the Ministry of Art," he said, still mild.

"Oh, no," Jebi said, heat rising to their face, "I'm independent." A nice way to say *unemployed.*

The man raised his eyebrows. "Well, don't let me keep you from your reading." He smiled.

That was awkward, but Jebi couldn't think of a polite way to excuse themself. And it would be a shame to have come all this way only to be driven off. Since they were here anyway, they might as well scrutinize the postings.

Jebi continued reading. When they got to the mention of starting pay, their jaw dropped. *How* much? And what was the catch? There had to be a catch.

"You're wondering what the catch is," the man said.

"You're very good at reading minds," Jebi observed, more bemused than resentful.

The man chuckled. "You weren't making any effort to hide your expression."

"Well, all right," Jebi said, "if you work here, or even if you don't, what *is* the catch?"

They hadn't been expecting an answer, but he said, "Everyone's jumpy because the head of the artists' workshop died under mysterious circumstances."

Jebi started. "I hadn't heard." They wracked their brains. They'd had a vague awareness that Armor, like most of the ministries, used artists in some capacity, but who *had* been the head of the workshop?

To Jebi's dismay, a cold skittering rain began to fall. While a freestanding roof protected the bulletin board, the wind picked up as well, causing the notices to flutter like trapped birds. At this rate, they were going to get drenched on the way home. Well, 'home.'

"That tiny umbrella isn't going to do you much good," the man said, craning his head back to study the sky critically. "Tell you what, I've got an office—I can tell you more about the job there."

*He's not going to do anything to me,* Jebi told their thumping heart. They wavered.

"At the least," the man added, "you can wait out the squall and head back to wherever you were going after it's passed. I can tell you from experience that this roof isn't going to offer much protection."

"Thank you," Jebi said in surrender.

The man led the way to Armor's main building. He walked with a subtle limp, but at a decent clip. Jebi imagined he didn't want to stay out here to get wet, either.

Two human sentries and two automata in blue-painted masks guarded the entrance. They let the man and Jebi pass with only nods of acknowledgment on the parts of the former and that inhuman stillness from the latter. Not for the first time, Jebi wondered what the world looked like to an automaton. If they worked for Armor, maybe they'd find out.

*If the Ministry of Art didn't want you,* Jebi chided themself, *what makes you think Armor would?* Worse, would they want to be the kind of person who worked for Armor? Despite their falling out with Bongsunga, Jebi felt it was one thing to paint harmless commemorative portraits or landscapes, and another to work with a branch of the military.

Inside, functionaries and servants bustled through the halls. The interior of the building looked disconcertingly mundane, with ceiling beams painted in the five cardinal colors—red, yellow, blue, black, and white—and portraits hanging on the walls. The depicted figures wore old-fashioned Razanei lamellar armor, not the robes of Hwaguk's aristocrat-scholars of old, and all the signs were in Razan's script. Jebi tried to imagine the halls as they might have looked during Hwaguk's last dynasty, the reign of the Azalea Throne; but Razan's living presence overwhelmed their attempts to repaint the halls in their head.

When they headed up the stairs to the second story, Jebi almost made a comment about how the man should ask his boss for a first floor office, then thought better of it. After all, the limp didn't impede his progress any.

They arrived at a door with no sign and a plain door. Automata stood at either end of the hall, taking no notice of either of them. The man slid the door open and preceded Jebi into the office.

"Forgive the Western furniture," the man said with a hint of irony that Jebi didn't understand. "It's easier on my hip, you see."

He took a seat behind an ornate desk whose rococo ornamentation sported several dents, in a chair just as elaborate. Uneasily, Jebi sat on the other side. An awful realization was dawning on them.

"You're not just another bureaucrat," Jebi said slowly. They'd switched to a very formal mode of speech, and a very polite *you*.

"I didn't mean to deceive you," the man said. "I thought you already knew, until it became clear you didn't. But yes, you're correct. I'm Girai Hafanden, Deputy Minister of Armor."

Jebi resisted the urge to close their eyes and reach for the mae-deup charms they'd bought last week. "I can't imagine," they said, "that it's usual for someone of your stature to speak with random passersby."

"'Random' is a matter of opinion," Hafanden returned. "You've been lingering around the Ministry; the patrols noticed. So naturally I took an interest. That sort of thing is my job now."

"Why," Jebi couldn't resist asking, "what did you do before?"

"I was a sniper once," he said. That explained the peculiar rifle-shaped cane. "It was a long time ago. In any case—" And, sounding a little apologetic, he proceeded to list the times when his people had observed Jebi approaching Armor.

A cold lump settled at the pit of Jebi's stomach. That couldn't be the whole story. After all, if the deputy minister considered them a *threat*, he'd simply have had them arrested and flung into some dank prison cell, and then Bongsunga would never hear from them again. No; he wanted something from them, and Jebi had the feeling that the murdered artist had something to do with it.

"Yes," Hafanden said in response to whatever expression he saw on their face, "I am in need of artists, as the notice said. You happen to be ideal for my purposes, even if the Ministry of Art didn't find a use for you."

Jebi winced, then regretted it. But hell, it wasn't as if he didn't have them cornered already. "What kind of use?" they asked warily. What if Hafanden had kept them from the coveted position, all so he could force them to take this job? But given what he was paying, why weren't people lining up to apply? Something smelled off.

"We have," Hafanden said delicately, "something of a difficulty retaining artists. People don't like working with the automata, which is exactly what we require. The violent death of the former person we had on one particular project, Issemi, has made it all the more difficult to recruit. All of our current hires are—occupied with projects of their own. To be blunt, we need fresh blood."

This sounded like a *terrible* job. "It's very kind of you to think of me," Jebi said, "but—"

"I know you're looking both for housing and a source of income," Hafanden continued, "and that you owe a certain moneylender a considerable sum. We could arrange to pay that off for you, as part of the deal."

*This* wasn't casual interest. He'd had Jebi followed, or set spies on them. Jebi thought back to their meeting with Hak's friend Ren. Had Ren ratted them out to Hafanden?

"I should get going," Jebi said, more desperately. From the drumming on the roof, the rain was pouring down worse than ever. But they didn't like the prospect of being trapped here any longer, and they'd survive a little damp.

"You'll want to hear me out," Hafanden said, still polite, but with a hint of steel in their voice. Jebi was reminded of the difference between their stations. "I took a look at the paintings you did for your examination, and the fact that you have a name certificate... expedites certain other matters. You're quite suitable for my purpose."

Jebi stood, shaking.

"Sit down, please," Hafanden said. He tapped the surface of the desk. "Your sister, Gyen Bongsunga. She has revolutionary connections, you know."

Jebi went cold all over. Was it true—? But it didn't matter. The accusation alone, made by a Razanei official, and a high-ranking one at that, could ruin Bongsunga. And even among their own people, there were informers happy to turn in suspected rebels.

Besides, anyone who knew Bongsunga would find the allegation believable. Hell, Jebi believed it themself. They thought of all the hours they'd spent painting while Bongsunga went out to run errands, or her unnamed visitors. Jebi had never asked her to account for herself, and why should they have? She was the elder, and the head of the household. But that meant she could have tangled herself up with any number of things, including revolutionaries or radicals.

"Please tell me clearly," Jebi said, still deferential, "what exactly you are proposing. So that we are honest with each other about what this is."

"I'm so glad you're being reasonable about this, Tsennan," Hafanden said. Naturally he used their registered Razanei name.

Jebi did not feel reasonable, either about the situation or about the damned name certificate, but they knew better than to interrupt.

"We offer a signing bonus and an extremely competitive monthly salary, in addition to dealing with the moneylender," Hafanden said. He named the figures; Jebi's eyes widened. "You will be required to live onsite, with some restrictions to your movements, but rest assured that you'll be able to leave from time to time, with guards. You won't be a prisoner. You'll work with a project requiring a security clearance. In exchange, we won't arrest your sister. She will stand surety for your good behavior."

For a second Jebi thought about turning their back and walking out. After all, they still hadn't patched things up with their sister. A monstrous petty part of them wanted to punish her for evicting them.

But the choice was no choice.

Jebi hadn't said any of these thoughts aloud, but Hafanden nodded. "It's settled, then."

Miserably, Jebi sat back down, defeated.

# Chapter
# FOUR

AFTER SIGNING A small infinity of papers, none of which they bothered to read, Jebi followed Hafanden out of the office. "I cleared my morning," he said in response to Jebi's bewildered look. "I'll get you settled in." This did not inspire confidence.

Jebi found the courage to ask about their art supplies, which they'd left at Hak's. "I should fetch them, if you want me to—"

"I had a servant retrieve them from your friend's residence," Hafanden said. "Your belongings will await you in your new workshop."

Once, the prospect of a workshop of their own would have excited them. Under the circumstances, however, Jebi could only work up a kind of pale resignation. "I imagine this is dangerous work, if people die doing it," Jebi said. Since they were stuck with the job, they might as well gather what information they could.

They admitted to a certain morbid curiosity as to how their predecessor—Issemi—had perished. People didn't ordinarily think of art as a dangerous profession, but artists died of toxins in paints, or inhaling too many particulates. And that was before factoring in automata.

"We know what precautions to take," Hafanden said, also not confidence-inspiring. "Vei will talk you through that."

"Vei?" Jebi asked, careful to attach a suitable honorific to the name.

"Dzuge Vei. She's the Ministry's duelist prime. She'll be your supervisor."

Jebi puzzled over that. How did dueling relate to art? But then, they'd never understood the intricacies of Razanei administration, including the fact that every ministry had a duelist prime to defend its honor. Hwagugin didn't practice the barbaric art of dueling, given the choice. Of course, sometimes an offended Razanei duelist didn't *give* a Hwagugin that choice.

"You will have figured this out," Jebi said as they headed back down the stairs, since it wouldn't do to take Hafanden for a fool, "but I'm a painter, not a sculptor or a smith. I don't know anything about metallurgy."

"That won't be part of your duty," Hafanden said. The tap-tapping of his cane made a distracting counterpoint to his words, although if Jebi was honest with themself, the whole situation was already distracting in its own right and the noise didn't make that much difference. "Your job will be dealing with masks."

*I'm not a mask-maker either,* Jebi almost retorted. But then they thought of the automata and the bizarre colored marks on their masks. "It's something to do with those painted symbols, isn't it? That's how you bring them to life."

"*That's* not a state secret," Hafanden said dryly. "It's not difficult to figure out."

"Then—?"

"I'll have Shon give you a demonstration."

*I'm sure,* Jebi thought.

They reached the ground floor and cut across the building to another staircase behind a contingent of human and automaton guards. This one, however, led down.

At this point, Jebi balked. "How old is this section?" they demanded. The shakes returned. Granted, it wasn't as though they'd ever entered this building before, but they'd never heard of anything *underground.* And the air—the air that wafted up from the stairwell had an ominous smell of metal and fire.

"You're quite correct," Hafanden said, pausing on the first step. "This is a newer addition. We needed additional space for certain experiments. Since we couldn't go *up,* and the other ministries had already claimed the other buildings, we went *down.*"

Jebi had never thought of themselves as possessing much in the way of phobias, but they discovered that they didn't enjoy the sensation of walls closing in on them. From time to time people dug up or traded the bones of ancient animals, preserved in the earth. They'd never before known that the ground beneath the Old Palace contained so many of them, exposed in the passages' walls. They tried to imagine what the creatures had looked like in life, and couldn't quite get there.

They hurried after Hafanden, not wanting to be left behind. At least the stairs were well lit, and electrical lights at that, at what must be considerable expense. Jebi had only the haziest idea of how electricity worked, but they did know that artificial lighting didn't come for free.

Besides that, the electrical light had a chilly aspect, without the warmth of sunlight. And it didn't bring any significant heat with it. The air here was uncomfortably cold, although not as bad as the outdoors, and dry in comparison with today's damp. Like a cave, probably, if Jebi had known anything about caves but what they'd heard in stories about bandits' hideouts and tiger-sages' lairs.

"There's an elevator," Hafanden added, as though the stairs inconvenienced Jebi more than himself, "but it's used for freight, and the security precautions are a hassle. Besides, I wanted to mention a few things to you before we meet Vei and Arazi."

*Arazi,* Jebi thought, mentally translating the name: *storm.* An inauspicious name by Hwagugin standards. But who could say how a Razanei thought of it?

"You may be having qualms about helping your conquerors," Hafanden said. "I wish to assure you that your work will be an act of the highest patriotism."

Besides the fact that this was an uncomfortable topic even among friends, Jebi had to suppress an incredulous laugh. *Patriotism?* For Razan, presumably, since they couldn't see how this benefited Hwaguk. Especially if they were going to be helping create more automata for the patrols in the streets.

"I can't see your expression," Hafanden said with a half-sigh—he was still in the front—"but I can imagine you're skeptical. Let me put it this way, then. Disorder does no one any favors, Hwagugin or Razanei."

Jebi made an involuntary noise, and Hafanden slowed, turning back toward them.

"I prefer not to use the term 'Fourteener,'" he said. "Your people have an identity of their own, one that is valuable in its own right. You have your doubts, and you're not entirely wrong, but—look at it this way. You've seen the encroachment of Western arts, Western books, Western ideas."

Jebi shrugged.

"We can only stand against that encroachment," Hafanden said, with a fervor that surprised them, "if we stand together. The means may be regrettable, but the cause justifies it."

"I'm not political," Jebi said, trying to devise a tactful way out of this topic. For all they cared, Hwaguk had been doing just fine by forbidding Western traders and diplomats and philosophers from entering the country. They couldn't deny, however, that it hadn't taken long for their people to adopt Western technologies and comforts, like electrical lighting and automobiles. Those who could afford them, anyway.

"Forgive me," Hafanden said, inclining his head. "The truth is, you don't need to be, not for your role. But I always feel that my people work better if they understand the Ministry's mission."

Jebi shuddered inwardly at the matter-of-fact possessiveness of *my people*. Maybe they should have read more carefully before they signed all those papers. Not that it would have made any difference. They'd still be here, and Bongsunga was still a hostage for their good behavior.

They arrived at last several levels down. Jebi had lost track of the number of stairs, and they cursed themself for not keeping count. They passed more guards, again in the common pattern for the Ministry: two humans accompanied by two automata.

*I should keep track of the patterns on the automata's masks,* Jebi thought halfway down the hallway, after they'd left the automata behind. Rattled as they were, they couldn't bring the image to mind. They'd have to do better in the future. Of course, they might soon know more about the masks than they wanted to.

Next came a hallway that meandered at uncomfortable angles for which Jebi could see no logic, and which gave them a nagging headache when they tried to examine them too closely. Doors opened off the hallway to either side, not the sliding doors that were common to Hwagugin and Razanei wooden buildings, but hinged, with numbered metal plaques, no names or words.

The end of the hallway led to double doors of metal, and more guards. Jebi had the inane desire to strike up a conversation with one of the humans, ask them about their favorite novel or what they ate for lunch, anything to ease the dungeon-like atmosphere of the underground complex. But they knew better than to do so in front of Hafanden.

The guards parted for Hafanden, giving Jebi a clear view of the snaking symbols etched into the doors. A colored enamel of some sort filled the symbols. Jebi thought at first that it was purple or brown, but it more closely resembled the murky colors of a new bruise. Trying to memorize the shapes only worsened their headache.

Hafanden pressed his hand directly against a bare section of the left door, then the right. The doors opened silently, and he passed the threshold. After a worried pause, Jebi hurried after him.

They both emerged into an immense cavern, its planes and hard angles betraying its artificial origins. The sight of all that space was so disorienting that Jebi tripped over their own feet. Hafanden reached out just long enough to steady them, and Jebi blurted out a mortified thank-you. As much as they disliked the liberty, they didn't want to fall flat on their face, either.

Several people stood at the cavern's edges. All of them wore gray and white with the particular black armbands that singled them out as belonging to Armor. Jebi couldn't tell what, if anything, they were doing. Perhaps only watching.

The light here differed from the cold, clear radiance out in the stairwell and the hallways. For one thing, it had no visible source. And it had a peculiar sea-torn quality, as though it had passed through turbulent water. Jebi had known something like it during their childhood, before their mother had died: she'd taken them and Bongsunga to the nearest lake, a journey of four days out of the capital. Jebi had fretted about bandits, all the while secretly longing to be kidnapped by some so they could have an adventure. Bongsunga assured them that bandits stayed away from well-traveled roads, spoiling the fun. In their mind's eye, the ocean was like that lake, but bigger in all directions, and wilder too.

What made the breath stick in Jebi's throat, however, was not the light, or even the harsh cold whisper of air circulating through unfathomable passages, but the dragon.

They'd only seen automata in human form, had assumed that was the only kind. It should have occurred to them that, just as a sculptor could hew bear or badger from the same piece of jade, the artificers could create automata in whatever shape they pleased. Metal was malleable, after all.

Jebi had drawn dragon-horses, a common good-luck motif in folk art, with their smoky manes and talons. But the mechanical dragon that dominated the cavern, three times Jebi's height at the withers, didn't resemble a horse, not in motion. The wedge-shaped head, adorned by a mask of painted wood, was surrounded by a frill of wire coils and gutting spikes. Phoenix-colored light burned behind the eye holes of the mask, like fire and fire's yearning. Serpentine articulations gave it the look of a suit of armor gone wrong, grown beyond any hope of taming, and its great tail ended in four wicked spikes. It rippled in a circular path, or something that would have been a circle if geometry admitted such subtly wrong curves. Only then did Jebi see the chains, which struck melodies of restraint, a percussion of imprisonment, against the glassine rock floor.

The dragon was too tall to be contained by any ordinary fence, and for whatever reason, its keepers had declined to put it in a cage. Admittedly, constructing a large enough cage would have been a nontrivial proposition. But someone had painted a circle on the cavern floor in virulent green paint. Jebi guessed that one wasn't supposed to cross the circle.

"Arazi," Hafanden said.

The movement stopped. The dragon stood like a predatory statue, one forelimb poised as though to strike despite the chains.

*Storm,* Jebi thought again. A fitting name for a dragon, now that they knew.

Dragon-spirits inhabited lakes and clouds and mists, stories that the people of Huang-Guan, Razan, and Hwaguk held in common. Most beloved by Hwaguk was the Dragon Queen Under the Sea, who protected sailors in exchange for their tribute, and who sent her children to bring the rains necessary for rice cultivation. Dragons were *benevolent*.

Looking at Arazi, Jebi wondered how much the usual rules could be expected to apply to *mechanical* dragons. Had it been responsible for Issemi's death?

Hafanden raised his voice. "Vei, if you would greet our guest—?"

*Guest,* Jebi thought; but they weren't about to interrupt.

One of the gray-and-white figures detached itself from the far wall of the cavern and approached them. She was a tall woman with arresting predator's eyes, her brown skin marked on one side by an asymmetrical abstract tattoo. Her nightfall of hair swept down past her waist, surely impractical for dueling, but perhaps she bound it up to fight. Jebi itched to paint her. At the same time, they had no desire to offend this woman with her raptor's mien.

"You sent word," Vei said, coming fully into view, her voice like smoke and supple leather.

*I should have noticed earlier,* Jebi thought when they spotted the duelist's sword hanging at Vei's side. Hafanden hadn't hidden the nature of Vei's work from them, after all. The sword sported a gilded guard and a hilt covered in some kind of braidwork, and a sheath of lacquered wood that gleamed pitilessly in the turbulent light. Jebi, whose feelings about dueling ever since their sister-in-law's untimely death were mainly negative, identified it as a curved Razanei cavalry sword, from the days when their soldiers rode to war against each other. Bongsunga had once remarked, in private, that it was a pity they hadn't killed each other off instead of emerging from the bloody wars of unification stronger than ever. Then again, Jebi also had no intention of bringing up such a volatile topic with a warrior good enough to secure a position as duelist prime.

"I'm Dzuge Vei," the woman said, turning to Jebi and inclining her head. "You are—?"

"Tesserao Tsennan," Jebi said, a touch defiantly. They weren't going to insist on using their Hwamal name in this place.

"The new artist." Vei nodded coolly at Hafanden. Interesting: Jebi got the notion that the two did not enjoy each other's company. "I can take it from here, Deputy Minister."

"Thank you," Hafanden said, just as chilly. "Inform me immediately if—"

"I can take it from here," Vei repeated.

The dragon, perhaps losing interest, resumed its pacing.

Hafanden didn't persist, but left. The tap-tapping of his cane reverberated oddly in the cavern, forming a counterpoint to the sound of the dragon's chains striking the floor.

Vei studied Jebi with interest, and they wondered, suddenly self-conscious, what she saw. Her clothes were more finely tailored than that of the average bureaucrat, and—interesting. Jebi, examining Vei in turn, caught a glimpse of something that looked suspiciously like a mae-deup good-luck charm, of yellow cord, tucked beneath her collar. Jebi's mood darkened. *Good enough to collect as souvenirs, but not good enough to show off?* But they wouldn't say so out loud.

"You must have questions," Vei said. She spoke, not informally—they'd only just met—but certainly less formally than Hafanden had. "The deputy minister is not always as forthcoming as he could be."

Jebi was wary, but they had to start somewhere. "I've never seen an automaton chained up before," they ventured. "We're always told that they're—safe. I assume there's a story there."

"Good, you have a sense of self-preservation," Vei said. "You've noticed how we're all standing outside the circle."

"That had occurred to me, yes."

Vei's sudden smile flashed at them. "Well, you've volunteered to be one of the few people who gets to go inside, where the dragon can reach. It will be one of your duties."

Wonderful. "You still haven't mentioned why it's in chains."

"Yes, about that," Vei said. She craned her head to look back toward the pacing dragon. "How much have you heard about what happened in Ppalgan-Namu?"

Vei's pronunciation was perfect, with just a hint of one of the dialects common in the Virgins' District. Jebi told themself that Vei's extracurricular activities were none of their business, and at least they wouldn't struggle to understand her if she needed to say something in Hwamal.

But that mention of Ppalgan-Namu... Jebi wracked their brains. They'd heard that name recently, but where? "It sounds familiar," they said reluctantly, "but I can't place it." Ppalgan-Namu, *Red Tree*. Some village? A shrine?

"Maybe you've heard the rumors," Vei said, with a hint of bitterness. "They tried to suppress all word of the massacre, and I *told* the deputy minister it wouldn't work."

Involuntarily, Jebi backed up a step. "*Massacre?*" they said

73

incredulously. Looking at the dragon with its gleaming claws and brutal jaws, however, they could believe it. "Massacre how?"

No wonder Hafanden hadn't been able to find anyone to fill this job. Especially if everyone else had already known about whatever had happened at Ppalgan-Namu. Jebi was surprised that they hadn't heard stories of a dragon-shaped monster on the loose. It wasn't the kind of thing that people forgot.

Vei's smile became crooked. "I don't blame you for your second thoughts. Arazi is an experimental war engine, more advanced even than the tanks. The Ministry has had high hopes for it. It was taken to a test site at Ppalgan-Namu, chosen because of its isolation. There used to be a Razanei garrison there."

*Used to be.* "You lost control of it."

"It's not entirely clear what happened," Vei said. "Issemi—the artist you're replacing—messed up somewhere. Understand, I wasn't present for the incident; I had duties elsewhere. The dragon killed the garrison. It took additional troops to subdue it, strip it of its mask, and bring it back to this complex, an operation complicated by the necessity of secrecy."

Jebi laughed incredulously. "How do you keep something that size *secret?*"

"It wasn't," Vei said with a gesture that reminded Jebi of a parry that their sister-in-law had once demonstrated, "constructed in one piece. They took it apart, transported it in pieces, and reassembled it down here."

That almost made sense. The Razanei logisticians were always transporting supplies in and out of the city. No one would have batted an eyelash at yet more parcels.

"Why did you put the mask back on?" Jebi added, glancing up at the dragon's head.

"It's not the same mask," Vei said. "But we felt it would be beneficial to have it active for study until its grammar could be corrected."

"What's *your* connection to this incident?" Jebi said, worrying as they spoke that they would alienate their new supervisor. They might not like her—or more accurately, it was too early to tell, prejudices against duelists or no—but their survival depended on her goodwill. Besides, if Arazi went rogue again, it might be good to have a warrior on their side.

That crooked smile again. "You're wondering why your supervisor is a duelist with nothing better to do than practice forms, and not an artificer or paper-pusher."

"Something like that," Jebi said, taken aback.

"I asked for the assignment," Vei said. Her gaze was disturbingly direct. "Issemi was a friend of mine. Granted, I don't think it's meaningful to seek vengeance against an automaton. I'm told they only do what we instruct them to do. It was a horrible accident, not malice.

"At the same time, I want to make sure that we avoid another massacre. And I spent a lot of time with Issemi; I might be able to offer insights into her thought processes, things she didn't leave in her notes." Vei grimaced. "It's a pity her assistant was so rattled by the whole affair that she fled. I can't honestly blame her. There's a price on her head now, which is regrettable—but she had access to classified information. It can't be helped."

Jebi frowned. "I assume there are established artificers and artists in this workshop," they said, and Vei nodded. "Why haven't you tasked one of them with this?"

"I suggested it to the deputy minister," Vei said. "But each of the existing artists, besides being deeply affected by their colleague's death, is working on their own projects, which are critical to the war effort. We were already understaffed. Bringing in someone new was inevitable."

Jebi didn't buy the story. It *almost* sounded plausible—if one didn't think too hard about it. But why bring in a complete newcomer, one who would have to start at zero, on a project this important? Something didn't add up.

*I have to do this for Bongsunga,* they reminded themself, taking a steadying breath. It didn't matter if Hafanden and Vei were keeping secrets. After all, the two didn't have a lot of reason to trust Jebi with security matters, either. *Just do the job and worry about it later.*

"I assume some of the notes still exist, since you've mentioned them," Jebi said.

"Indeed," Vei said. "I'll show you your quarters, and then the studio where you'll be doing most of your work. You might find a demonstration of how the automata are given their instructional grammars edifying."

Jebi nodded their assent.

The dormitory was distressingly close to the dragon's cavern, to the point where Jebi could hear the faint echoes of its movements when they concentrated. Each door displayed a simple paper sign with its inhabitant's name, and someone had already put one up for them. The room itself, while austere, had good lighting—Vei showed Jebi the switch for turning the lights on and off, and demonstrated its use—and a luxurious amount of space to recommend it. It already sported a sleeping mat and quilts, two small tables of lacquered wood and tasseled floor cushions, and a small bookshelf with three books crowded up against the left side. Jebi itched to investigate the books, but Vei had already led them back out of the room and toward the studio.

To Jebi's relief, the studio looked normal, with screens dividing it into separate workspaces. There were closets and cabinets in the back for supplies, and some shelves for reference materials as well. They caught sight of some of the other artists, but none emerged to greet them, not yet. "They're busy," Vei said. "You'll see them at lunch."

Issemi's old workspace had been tidied recently, the piles of notebooks and papers neatly arranged. Jebi spotted their rucksack and its supplies set next to the table. They bet it had been searched, not that the Razanei would have found anything more incriminating than the occasional halfhearted caricature.

Most interestingly, the wall contained a display of masks hanging by their ribbons, all of them intended for human-type automata. Both the markings and their colors varied. Jebi wondered if any prototypes remained of the dragon's mask, and asked Vei.

"They were destroyed as a safety precaution," Vei replied. "Not my decision, and done before I could protest."

The more they learned, the more Jebi's qualms about their unwanted new job multiplied. They pointed to the small jars of pigments. "What are those?"

"Paints," Vei said. Jebi's relief at a mundane, straightforward answer evaporated as Vei continued speaking. "The secret to the automata's animation. The paints imbue them with the illusion of life, and the particular qualities we want them to display—loyalty, courage, that sort of thing." She raised her voice. "Shon, our new painter is here. I need you to give a demonstration."

A balding Razanei man emerged from behind one of the screens. Dust covered his smock. "Come this way," he said to Jebi, then gave Vei a jerky nod.

Curious now, Jebi drifted after Shon to his workspace. Several mortars and pestles of different sizes rested on his bench, along with a number of jars sporting cryptic labels. A pile of paintings rested to the side, haphazardly stacked. Jebi longed to snatch the paintings up and put them away more carefully.

Shon removed the topmost painting and squinted at it. "This one will do," he said. "Probably test out as Dragon's Labyrinth. We can always use more of that."

*Test out as?* Jebi wondered. *Dragon's Labyrinth?* But they might as well watch the demonstration before asking their questions.

"Wait a second," Jebi burst out when they got a better look at the painting. "That looks like *South Gate of the Tiger-Sage's Temple.*" One of the most famous works from the dynasty before the Azalea Throne, by the artist Nyang, and one that Jebi admired tremendously. Their favorite part was the tiger partly camouflaged in the shrubs just to the side of the gate. They'd made copies of copies of the piece during their studies, though never one this fine.

"Who's the copy by?" Jebi asked. Hwaguk must be awash in renditions of the thing. This one had masterful brushwork, despite the badly faded paints, almost as though...

"It's the original," Shon said, his face creasing in a broad smile. "That Fourteener Hak came through for us again."

Before Jebi had time to register the significance of this—it wasn't as though Hak's dealings were a *surprise*, after all—Shon took the priceless painting, almost a thousand years old, and ripped it in half. Jebi let out a cry and lunged, only to be restrained by Vei.

"*Watch*," Vei said, and her grip tightened just enough to warn Jebi not to struggle.

Jebi watched, sick with horror, as Shon shredded the painting, then grabbed an indiscriminate handful of the pieces and dumped them into one of the mortars. Grinding paper shouldn't have worked like this, except the mortar and pestle gave off a faint grayish glow, and the incoherent sound of distant voices. Magic.

When Shon finished grinding, nothing remained of the paper but a fine yellowy sediment. Jebi fought back nausea as he continued the process. He mixed a vehicle consisting of gum arabic, honey, and water, plus some other ingredients that they didn't recognize, and then added the sediment—pigment, presumably. Looking at the resulting paint made Jebi's eyes water.

"Hard to look at, isn't it?" Shon asked, as casual as if he hadn't just destroyed one of Hwaguk's most famous architectural paintings. "I was right."

"You always are," Vei said, inclining her head. "Different artworks produce pigments with different magical properties." She still hadn't let go of Jebi. "Shon's expertise in identifying which ones are suitable for Ministry use is why he has this job."

*That's it,* Jebi thought morosely. *Now that I've witnessed this, they'll never let me leave, not without a guard at my back.*

For the first time, they wondered if they'd failed the Ministry of Art exam after all, or if the whole thing had been set up by Armor so Hafanden could pressure them into this position. Maybe they'd done *too* well, convinced the Razanei of their suitability for the work. Betrayed by their own talent.

"What you're doing here is monstrous," Jebi whispered before they could help themself. They thought of the antiquities collectors and dealers that Hak had hosted at her party, gathering around Hwagugin vases and paintings like vultures. Thought of the hours they'd spent studying copies of masterpieces. How many paintings now existed *only* as copies, if at all?

Vei let them go, and faced them. "*Your* job will be to use these pigments and the existing mystical symbols to write a new grammar for the dragon, one that allows us to use it in combat without it going berserk."

Jebi recognized the continued warning and shut up. They finally understood why their supervisor was the Ministry's duelist prime. Because *her* job was to cut them down if they tried to escape like Issemi's assistant had. And Jebi had no doubts that, if they ran, Vei would chase them to the world's end and slice them head to toe.

# Chapter
# FIVE

I'M LIVING UNDER *the Old Palace,* Jebi thought, with a sense of unreality. They wondered if Bongsunga or Hak had missed them yet; kept wondering, in the days to come. Would Armor tell Jebi's family and friends what had happened, or make excuses?

One of the first things they learned about life in a secret underground complex, especially one where no one ever turned off the lights in the hallways and shared areas, was how time crystallized around them. The studio and their room both included clocks, the former on the wall and the latter tucked away on top of the shelf. The studio also featured a large wall calendar with cryptic abbreviations, presumably reminders. Also doodles of gears, sprockets, and malformed genitalia, because artists were artists.

Nevertheless, Jebi requisitioned, and received, a small calendar of their own. It was printed on cheap paper, and the ink had already smeared, but it would let them track the passing days.

Vei introduced them one by one to the other artists (not many) and artificers, who ranged from experts in clockwork mechanisms to metallurgists, sculptors (for casting prototypes) to scholars. The scholars, Jebi gathered from Vei's comments, researched the provenance of the artwork and artifacts that the Razanei intended to destroy. *How do you live with yourselves?* Jebi wanted to ask.

The only artist who seemed inclined to welcome Jebi was Shon. Jebi rapidly figured out that they'd associated themself with the one other artist that nobody else liked, although Vei treated him with a certain distant courtesy. When Jebi asked about this in private, Vei sighed and looked sideways, then said, "Shon argues with his orders too much. It's bad for everyone when he does that, but the deputy minister puts up with it because he's so excellent at pigment manufacture."

The two of them were going over Issemi's papers in Jebi's room, mainly because Vei professed herself unwilling to distract people in the studio. Given how much the other painters gossiped while working, Jebi doubted one more conversation would make much of a difference. But they didn't mind the chance to study Vei, either.

Despite their better judgment, Jebi had conceived a fascination with her. She smelled of salt and sweat and cedar-sandalwood incense. Jebi longed to run their hands through her hair and find out if it was as smooth as it looked, a wholly inappropriate response that they tried not to think about;

but being around her made it hard to suppress their growing attraction.

"I notice that you always mention the deputy minister, but never the minister," Jebi said cautiously as they frowned over a cryptic muddle of writing in what looked to be a personal shorthand or cipher.

Vei, who was sitting across from them, looked surprised for a moment, then laughed ruefully. The expression made her look less like a sword-saint out of Razanei legend and more like a human being with quirks and questions of her own. "I forget that you don't know all the ins and outs of the Ministry. For all intents and purposes, the deputy minister *is* the head of Armor—within Administrative Territory Fourteen. The Minister of Armor lives in Razan proper; it's from her that the deputy minister receives his directives. People in Territory Fourteen sometimes elide the difference."

"I had no idea," Jebi said, looking awkwardly down at their hands.

"There's no reason why you should have known. Even people who work here sometimes slip and call Hafanden the minister." Vei flipped to the next sheet in her own pile. "Aha—this is a schematic. Useful to you?"

"I suppose," Jebi said, accepting the page and unfolding it carefully. Their eyes throbbed as they attempted to focus on the diagram; no such luck. "What on earth—?"

"You too?" Vei grimaced. "Issemi told me once that it was a countermeasure. She'd taken the most critical of her notes in an ink called Dragon's Labyrinth. You've now experienced its effects."

So this was what Shon had showed them on their first day.

Jebi eyed the rest of their pile with dismay. "There's no way to undo it? Like looking at the diagram through a special lens?"

"If any such device existed," Vei said, "she never told anyone about it, and we didn't find it in the remaining items."

"Remaining." Jebi remembered that Issemi's assistant had fled. "Do you know how much of Issemi's materials she made off with?"

"We think she left most of the documents behind, if that's what you're worried about."

Jebi sighed. Their hopes of staying out of convoluted Ministry politics were steadily diminishing, the more they heard about their predecessor. Since they had Vei's attention anyway—"I think you'd better tell me more about this assistant."

"Her name," Vei said, her tone brisk, "is Mirhai. The deputy minister hired Issemi and Mirhai together; she'd originally been Issemi's apprentice. The two of them produced rapid results, which the deputy minister appreciated. But Mirhai's very closeness to Issemi proved a liability after the latter's death."

"Did she disappear immediately?"

"We're not altogether certain of the timing," Vei said. "Things were chaotic leading up to the experiment with Arazi. We had pressure from the Ministry back in the homeland."

*Homeland,* Jebi thought. Not *home.* An interesting distinction.

"It was a full week before people realized that Mirhai wasn't holed up in the city in some gambling den or taking solace in the arms of a lover. The deputy minister's agents found reliable reports from the city guard that she'd headed out the West

Gate just before curfew the night that we received word of the massacre."

Jebi was starting to realize that Vei's cool, almost glacial tones hid a persistent anger. "You knew her well?"

"Not well, no," Vei said with a slight pause that made Jebi wonder if she was telling the truth. "But she owed her loyalty to Armor. It was cowardice for her to run."

*I'd better not do the same,* Jebi thought, alarm prickling down their spine. They resolved never to forget that, for all her austere beauty, Vei was a trained killer.

THE FIRST THING Jebi did during their visits to Arazi was to sketch it from various angles. The dragon usually stopped to loom over them during their visits, and they took advantage of its statue-like stillness. They marveled at its articulations, the fiendish scythe-like claws and spiked tail. According to Vei, the dragon, with its superior mobility and magical abilities—currently disabled—had been designed as a tank-killer.

"Who has tanks but Razan?" Jebi asked. Surely everyone would have heard if Hwaguk's rebels had managed to liberate such weapons of war.

"The Westerners do," Vei said. "They're the threat Hafanden fears."

Jebi almost asked why the Westerners would show up in Hwaguk, then reconsidered. They might never have seen one of the foreigners, but even foreigners had to have uses for Hwaguk's mines. Too bad Razan seemed determined to pick a fight with the Western nations.

Jebi also asked about the massacre at Ppalgan-Namu. To

their frustration, no one wanted to talk about it. *This isn't morbid curiosity,* they wanted to shout at the other artists and Armor's own soldiers, although there was, if they were honest with themself, some of that too. They didn't see how they were supposed to fix the dragon's grammar without finding out what *exactly* had gone awry.

Arazi, for its own part, paced in those endless circles when it wasn't looming, dragging the chains after it. It never, so far as Jebi could tell, made any attempt to escape. It might as well have been nothing more than an immense kinetic sculpture, like a bigger version of the clockwork toys that they'd seen at an exhibition a few years ago. Jebi was almost tempted to let down their guard—but they knew better.

Jebi devoted themself to studying the lexicon of mystical glyphs that, used in conjunction with the magical pigments, could be used to generate an automaton's grammar. The grammar gave it a set of instructions to follow. A simple grammar could result in an automaton that merely walked in circles, like Arazi often did, or stood in place; more complex ones almost simulated life.

"You should always run your grammars by Nehen," Shon told Jebi once. "They've got the most expertise, and you don't want to accidentally program an automaton to attack you or something."

Jebi shuddered. "Thanks for the warning." After that, they spent the rest of their time constructing potential grammars based on the elliptical instructional manuals.

"You've got a knack for this, especially for a Fourteener," Nehen said the fifth time Jebi came to them. The two of them had just gone over Jebi's latest proposed correction to

Arazi's grammar, the first time they'd incorporated combat instructions.

Jebi stiffened. "I don't know what you mean."

Nehen's hand flew to their mouth. "Oh, sorry, that just slipped out. Your accent's so good, I almost wasn't sure at first. I won't tell anyone."

"Thank you," Jebi said, dubious. In all honesty, they were surprised no one had figured it out earlier. The servants probably had, by observing Jebi's preferences in food. The cafeteria served a mixture of what was apparently Razanei food and more familiar Hwagugin fare, and Jebi wasn't strong enough to resist the latter.

"Let's get back to the grammar," Nehen said hastily. "You have a contradiction between the instruction to *defend the base* and *defer to authority* right here." They pointed with their pencil to the columns of glyphs. "If there's a contradiction, it gets a choice. You see? So we do our best not to incorporate any paradoxes, so we can completely predict the automaton's actions."

"So we're eliminating the possibility of choice wherever we can," Jebi said, thinking not just of the automaton's constricted existence, but the choices that had been taken away from them, and their people in general.

Nehen beamed at Jebi. "Yes, that's it exactly."

At other times, Jebi visited the artificers, who were willing to answer any questions Jebi had about the inner workings of automata. Unfortunately, they had no explanation for why a dragon automaton had gone rogue while human automata built using the same techniques remained obedient. Nehen confirmed that the grammar given to Arazi, while unusually complex, had been tested on smaller, more easily subdued automata first.

Based on their studies and those of Issemi's papers they'd deciphered, Jebi had one of the artificers start manufacturing more masks to fit Arazi. The artificer obliged them with nary a word of complaint. Jebi dreaded having to paint and use the masks according to their proposed grammars, but they'd worry about that later.

A couple weeks in, Jebi started spending more time in the studio despite their distaste. The pigment-grinder Shon continued to warm to them, discussing how he selected artwork and how to determine the properties of the paints he made from them. Swallowing their revulsion, Jebi allowed him to tutor them in the methods. Paintings weren't the only items to be vandalized. Shon had them practice on a damaged wooden cosmetics box, frail with age.

"We prefer originals in good condition," Shon remarked, "but for your first attempt we should use something expendable."

Jebi bit the inside of their mouth so they wouldn't say something regrettable. "Surely some artifacts are easier to reduce"—Shon's term—"than others," Jebi ventured as Shon gestured for them to sit by him.

"Special tools blessed by the priests of old," Shon said in his usual rough manner. He pointed to his mortars and pestles. "Sometimes blunt reduction is required first."

A fancy way of saying that one smashed the art, or ripped it into pieces, whatever was necessary to render it into particles. Jebi wondered if the mortars and pestles had had some other purpose at first. They couldn't imagine that even Razanei priests had invented some ritual expressly to get rid of art, even art they didn't like. "Show me," Jebi said faintly.

Shon chose one of the mortars and slid it toward them, along with the pestle. "Break off a piece," he said. "You might want gloves." He offered a pair of those as well, although they were comically too large for Jebi's hands; Shon was not a small man.

Jebi demurred, thinking, *It's supposed to hurt.* Destroying something ought to make you bleed, even if it was a damaged piece, and not especially rare. Even Razanei collectors, as Hak had told them ages ago, had standards—however confusing— as to how much wear and tear was "charming," and how much devalued an object.

Some long-ago crafter had labored over this box. Someone had owned it, or received it as a gift. Someone might have prettied themselves up using the cosmetics within, some of which remained as a faint residue. Someone might have danced afterward, or written poems, or met a lover.

This box might be the repository of any number of stories. Jebi thought about that as they tensed their hands, then broke off a splinter. It took less effort than they'd braced for, but the splinter pierced their hand. Blood welled up.

"You should have taken the gloves," Shon said. "Bandage?"

"Does the blood make a difference?" Jebi asked: more morbid curiosity.

"Not that I've ever noticed."

*So you've experimented.* Which made sense, although it repulsed them. They'd heard that the Razanei cared more about purity than Hwagugin, or anyway they cared *differently.* But if people beneath the Old Palace bothered with cleansing rituals, they did so in private, where Jebi couldn't observe them.

Under Shon's watchful eye, Jebi ground down the splinter. The faint gray glow returned. They disliked being involved with Razanei magic, although they couldn't deny its efficacy. Even rickety old wood shouldn't have gone to *powder* that easily. And the splinter produced far more powder than it should have.

"There's the pigment," Shon said, satisfied. "This one should prove out as Allure. Not one that we have much call for, in our line of work. We don't make automata to be *pretty*."

"You're not always sure what pigment will be the result?"

"Just like ordinary pigments, there's some variation in effect," he said. "It's why securing adequate supplies is—a matter of some concern."

*I just bet.* "And the rest of the process is as I saw before?"

"Indeed. Refining, mixing the paint, the usual."

*He's hiding something.* But what? And more importantly, would they get in trouble for inquiring further?

Jebi said, with pretended diffidence, "I suppose painting on wood and painting on silk aren't so different after all."

That was calculated to inspire a lecture. Every artist Jebi had ever known was happy to rant about the ineluctable differences between media. But Shon merely nodded, tight-lipped.

Something occurred to Jebi. "Do you ever reduce—living artists' work?" That might be the source of the others' distaste for Shon.

"Oh, no, no," Shon said, shaking his head for emphasis. "No point in that."

"Why not?"

"Ineffectual, so no point in it."

He hadn't said that the artist might object. Jebi doubted such considerations occurred to him. So the process depended on the artist being dead. "So you can tell that Issemi's apprentice isn't dead in a ditch somewhere?" After all, if Mirhai had left any artwork behind, Shon could have reduced it and seen if it turned into working pigment or not, settling the question of whether she was alive or dead.

Shon's mouth compressed, then he nodded. "Don't do that anymore," he said. "We tried it in the early days, art made to order, living artists handsomely compensated. Never worked. And figuring out whether people are dead isn't what this is for, you know. The point is art, not fortune telling. And Mirhai would have hated having her sketches torn up like that, good Razanei work that it was."

It didn't surprise Jebi that the workshop only destroyed Hwagugin artwork, when surely Razanei works would have been easier to obtain. The whole enterprise made them queasier the more they learned about it. "Still," they pressed, "if it's so urgent to capture Mirhai and bring her back here—"

"Can't find out anything beyond that," Shon said. "Dead or alive, that's it. Not like diviner's smoke, to lead you in a direction."

"Thank you," Jebi said. They were certain that they wouldn't get the answers they wanted from him, but that didn't mean the answers couldn't be found.

DZUGE VEI CONTINUED overseeing Jebi, meeting with them at least once a day—sometimes more often. It was from Vei that Jebi learned the origin of the underground complex's nickname: the Summer Palace.

Vei had brought Jebi dinner, because Jebi was mired in Issemi's papers and had missed the call to the cafeteria where the artists dined. The kitchens were theoretically open at all hours—whoever had set the place up had a realistic notion of artists' schedules—but while Jebi didn't like to take breaks when they were engrossed in something, it was more hassle for the servants if they went in at odd hours, and as a fellow Hwagugin, Jebi didn't want to make their lives harder than necessary.

"Is it that interesting?" Vei said mildly as she watched Jebi alternating mouthfuls of rice and acorn jelly with scribbling notes on the notes. "I suppose there's not much to see in the Summer Palace."

It wasn't the first time Jebi had heard the term. "Why do you call it that?" they wondered. "People say it sometimes, and then look awkward. There must be some story behind it."

Vei laughed wryly. "No one's told you yet? It isn't anything profound. It's Issemi's fault, which is why I suppose it's an uncomfortable subject. When she took up residence, she painted a triptych during her off hours. A summer garden. Someone thought her yearning for real weather was funny, hence the name."

Jebi could relate. Electrical lighting lacked the warmth and variety of natural lighting. They went up to the surface every few days, always accompanied by a guard, and stood in the courtyard drinking in sunlight, the smells of damp and rotted leaves, the magpies' raucous calls.

"Where's the triptych now?" Jebi asked. They would have liked the additional insight into Issemi's work, however unrelated it might seem.

Vei shook her head. "I don't know. I think it was destroyed."

*You don't know?* Jebi almost asked, then thought better of it, remembering the fact that they were a prisoner and some questions were better left locked behind their teeth. At times it was almost easy to forget that they couldn't trust her.

Vei always treated them with courtesy, and, if Jebi was honest with themself, they loved watching her at her morning exercises, which she did in the common room, brushstroke-lithe, her slim figure perfectly balanced. They hadn't asked for permission to sketch her—not because they thought she'd say no, but because they were afraid she'd say yes. For Vei's part, if she'd noticed Jebi's attraction, she was kind enough not to mention it.

After Jebi had finished dinner, Vei reached for the tray, and Jebi reached out on impulse to stop her. Their hands met; Jebi flushed and snatched their hand away. *I've done it now,* they thought miserably.

Vei caught their gaze, held it. Smiled. "You don't need to be afraid of me," she said. "We may not be friends, but I am not your enemy either."

"Do you say that to all your opponents?" Jebi asked. For the first time, they wished they knew something of the duelist's art so that they could spar with Vei, meet her in the dance of blade against blade, understand the way that she tensed and flexed and flowed in her own terms rather than the academic manner of a student of the human form.

"Is that what we are?" Vei's smile widened fractionally. "As long as you deal honorably with the Ministry's tasks, I have no quarrel with you."

What a peculiar way to put it, *honorably*; but Jebi supposed they couldn't expect any different from a duelist, of all people. They'd never thought about art in terms of *honor*. The traditional schools emphasized expression of the subject's inner nature, or the feelings it provoked in the artist. Lately, the Western schools stressed accurate depictions, so that realism mattered more than any sense of visual poetry. Neither group cared much about *honor*.

Perhaps sensing Jebi's discomfort, Vei changed the subject. "What progress have you made?"

"Let's take another look at Arazi," Jebi said. "I want to compare the notes we did decipher"—a process involving much squinting and tea for headaches—"with the actual mask." They gathered up the papers.

"Sounds good to me." Vei led the way to Arazi's cavern.

Inside, the dragon Arazi continued its pacing. The painted circle that separated it from the rest of the cavern had not changed, nor the percussive clattering music of its chains. Jebi couldn't help but wonder if the dragon meant to wear out the metal. How much patience did an automaton have? After all, it didn't *age*, in the way of flesh.

Jebi called out, in a voice that quavered more than they would have liked, "Lower your head." They weren't a translator, but they'd learned over the past weeks that the dragon responded to simple commands. They thanked whoever had written the current grammar to make the creature easier to work with.

The dragon halted before Jebi. Its head snaked down until it came to a stop in front of them. Jebi studied the mask, wondered how heavy it was. The ones in the workshop were deceptively light. "Wait a second," they said slowly. They held up the copy they'd made of one of Issemi's diagrams. "That's not good."

Vei inhaled sharply. "Oh?"

"I think Issemi hoodwinked everyone."

"Speak carefully," Vei said. "She was my friend."

Jebi studied Vei's face, worried by her lack of expression. They still found Vei beautiful, despite the unfashionable narrowness of her face and the pointed chin, so unlike the moon-visaged women that the Razanei favored. The ability to hide one's inner thoughts would be an advantage in dueling.

*Stop staring and start talking.* They couldn't afford to let their infatuation distract them. "There's a difference," they said carefully, "between the designs that she left behind, and what's actually painted on the dragon. I never noticed it before, but now that I have them side by side—"

Now Vei's expression did shift: narrowed eyes, a tautness around her mouth. "Explain."

"You're a duelist," Jebi said after the doors had closed behind them, "so I assume you have a good eye."

"It's one of the requirements of the profession, yes."

"Then you'll see it." Jebi held out the diagram. "This is from the grammar that Issemi got approved to paint on the dragon." They indicated Nehen's signature, and the deputy minister's seal below it. "I've talked to Shon about the pigments Issemi used. Phoenix Extravagant for destructive power, as befits an engine of war. Blood Circle, for loyalty to the Empire." They could not bring themself to say *Razan.* "Lion's Breath, for courage. And some others, but those are the dominant pigments."

Vei studied the diagrams. "And?"

Jebi brought out a series of enlarged diagrams. "This is what Issemi drew—" They pointed. "This is a different grammar than whatever it was wearing at Ppalgan-Namu, but some of the fundamentals telling the dragon how to move are the same on this newer mask. Look at the blue glyphs on the mask."

Vei held her hand out, and Jebi passed over the sheaf of papers. Her brow furrowed as she looked through the diagrams, then at the mask. "How is it that no one noticed this before?"

Vei didn't sound *surprised*. Had she already known? Especially if she'd been friends with the late Issemi—but that was another of the long list of questions they couldn't ask.

"Because paper is two-dimensional," Jebi said, "and the mask is three-dimensional. Its surfaces are curved, so there's a certain amount of distortion involved. If you're not familiar with how that works, it's easy to overlook that."

"I've had training in calligraphy and I'm familiar with the underpinnings," Vei said. "You needn't explain the glyphs to me."

Jebi bit their lip as they considered the dragon's motionless head. "So the dragon's grammar isn't what Issemi told the deputy minister it would be," Jebi concluded.

"It's tragic that her disobedience resulted in her death," Vei said, with much less sympathy than Jebi expected of a grieving friend.

"No, that's the part I don't understand," Jebi said. They looked at the papers in Vei's hands. "If Issemi painted this grammar, there *was* no massacre. Or anyway, the massacre wasn't the dragon's fault." They indicated a series of glyphs. "*Devotion to peaceful solutions.* It's a pacifist."

Vei's face gave nothing away. "So our war-engine is useless, is what you're saying."

"That's exactly what I'm saying. Are you sure the massacre at Ppalgan-Namu happened as the reports say?"

Instead of answering, Vei stared at the dragon for a long time. "I must tell the deputy minister of your findings."

Jebi hadn't expected to get the pages back, but no matter. They had an accurate eye for detail, and they could replicate the grammar as long as they still had ink and brush and paper. "Of course."

Someone was lying about the dragon, about Issemi, about the massacre. But who, and why?

# Chapter
# SIX

JEBI THOUGHT THAT some form of action would result from the untidy revelation that Issemi had sabotaged the project. An investigation into her lovers, perhaps, or a formal ceremony severing her from Razan. Something dramatic.

Instead, for the next several weeks, nothing happened that they could see—or, perhaps more accurately, that they were *allowed* to see. They showed up for breakfasts on the days that they got up on time. On occasion they traipsed up the stairs—excellent exercise—and stood in the courtyard, marveling anew at snow, or the color of light caught in ice, or the smell of roasted chestnuts from the street vendors.

Jebi investigated the three books in their room and discovered that one of them was an excruciatingly boring but well-regarded set of essays on the topic of ethics and governance from Huang-Guan, *The Classic of the Orderly State*. They took to marking each passing day—or each tolling of the 'morning' gong, anyway—in the back with a pencil. During their excursions outdoors, they asked passers-by the date. The passers-by usually gave them odd looks, but the answers reassured them.

In the old stories, the Dragon Queen Under the Sea brought worthy mortals to live with her in that watery realm. It was a mixed blessing, because such people returned to find that hundreds of years had passed, and the people they had loved were long buried. Jebi started having nightmares in which they watched from the window, helpless to speak or move, while their sister Bongsunga aged and withered and died alone, with no one to make offerings of food and rice wine at her grave.

Jebi did not mention these dreams to Vei. They didn't think she would understand. Or if she did, she would only look inscrutable and offer exquisitely courteous sympathy, which would only make them feel worse.

They did, however, finally get up the courage to ask Vei if the Deputy Minister had anything to say about their findings about Issemi's work. Jebi was grinding pigments. By now Jebi had almost gotten used to the idea of destroying artwork, whether old and decrepit or old and *irreplaceable*, for the Razanei project. Vei had entered, looking slightly perturbed.

Jebi gestured to the space next to them, careful not to knock over the mortar full of earth-colored powder. "I was wondering," Jebi said before Vei could speak, and faltered, then started over. "Have you found out why Issemi sabotaged the dragon?"

"It's being investigated," Vei said in a tone that made Jebi think nothing of the sort had happened.

*Here goes nothing.* "It wasn't that she had gambling debts and someone bribed her? Or a fox spirit ate her liver?" Jebi pressed. "Or she fell into bed with a crime lord?" That was another thing about Razanei rule—between their regulations and all the automata, violent crime was at an all-time low. "Or maybe she thought the experiment would make her immortal?"

Vei blinked. "Is that even possible?"

Jebi was sorry they'd mentioned that. "No," they said with more confidence than they felt. "I've never heard of anyone succeeding in their attempts to communicate with the celestials, not in recent memory. But I was thinking of those old stories about the Eight Immortals and the peaches, or maybe it was the Eight Peaches and the immortal, I always lose track." They wished they'd paid more attention to their mother's stories while she'd still been alive. Bongsunga would have known—but. "I don't mean to insult your late friend. It's just that there had to be some *reason*. People don't do things at random."

"Indeed they don't," Vei said. She reached up to twirl a loose lock of hair around one finger, then abruptly put her hand down. "The deputy minister will take care of it."

*She's nervous,* Jebi thought in surprise. But why? And would it be better to ask, or leave her alone?

Vei saved Jebi from having to make a decision. "I wanted to tell you," she said. "I'm going to be absent tomorrow."

"Oh," Jebi said blankly. "Only one day?" They chided themself for their childish sense of abandonment. They weren't

six years old anymore. Vei didn't owe them anything. She was
Armor's duelist prime, for crying out loud, not—not a friend.

For all her amicable manner and polished courtesy, Vei
wasn't here because she *liked* them. Vei had *duties*. And Vei
was still the person who would cut them down if they stepped
out of line.

Vei's hands tautened, then stilled, another nervous tic Jebi
hadn't seen before. "Well, that depends," she said with a hint
of wry humor. "I will be facing someone in a duel."

"Oh," Jebi said again. "You'll win, won't you?" It came out
sounding more plaintive and less confident than they'd meant.

"I always hope so," Vei said, her expression grave, "but in
this business one should never *assume*. I thought it would only
be fair to let you know, so you didn't wonder."

Jebi shoved the mortar and pestle away from them, and
looked sidewise at Vei. She'd been about to say *worry*. They
were sure of it. Perhaps Vei didn't regard them merely as an
assignment after all.

Pointing that out would be discourteous, and Vei had made
no overtures—no obvious ones, anyway. Ordinarily Jebi didn't
mind flirtations, and they couldn't deny that they had come to
look forward to her company, either. On the other hand, they
didn't want to distract her on the eve of a duel.

*Maybe she* wants *a distraction*, Jebi thought, and hesitated.
By the time they'd made up their mind to say something, or
reach out for her hand, however, the moment had passed.

"If something happens to me," Vei said, now brisk, "my
successor will have all my notes."

"Of course," Jebi said. They almost hesitated again, then
thought, *What the hell.* They reached inside their collar and

pulled out the two knotted mae-deup luck-charms that they carried, the same ones they had worn during the artists' examination they'd flunked. "Red or blue?"

For a second they wondered if Vei knew the charms' significance. Not all Razanei did. Then they remembered that Vei had been wearing one herself, partly concealed, the first time they met her.

"Red for blood, blue for luck," Vei said in a low voice. Vei's eyes crinkled in the truest smile that Jebi had seen from her yet, although it didn't touch that serene mouth. Then she pressed her fingers against Jebi's palm, the most fervent kiss they'd ever had, and picked the red one. "A duelist could not choose otherwise," she said. "Save the luck for yourself."

JEBI SLEPT POORLY that night, tormented by the memory of Vei's touch. They had never slept with a duelist—not that they sought to 'collect' professions, of course—and they couldn't help but think of those strong, flexible fingers touching them in places secret and pleasurable. Their longing for the simple complexity of sex collided with anxiety over the duel.

*She must be good,* Jebi thought, *or the Ministry of Armor wouldn't retain her.* But even good duelists could suffer bad luck, especially if the spirits willed it. It wasn't like *art,* where bad luck had less fatal consequences. One might offend a powerful patron and have to give up the profession or go into exile, or land in prison, but artists didn't brave the physical threat of death in the same way.

At last Jebi rose and dressed. They withdrew their last weeks' pay, which servants delivered without comment. They'd even gotten out of the practice of counting the printed notes to make sure that they hadn't been shorted, a bad habit. But it was so hard to care when they didn't have much to spend the money on but street food. The Ministry provided everything they needed, to the point where they felt smothered.

*What the hell,* they thought, *I don't have anything else to do with this.* They grabbed half the sum and put it in a purse.

Then they slipped out of their room on soft feet, too embarrassed to let the other artists know they cared. They glanced at the clock in the great hall: only half an hour until the morning bell.

Jebi made no secret of their approach. The guards were used to their comings and goings by now. "Greetings," they called out to the guards, or at least to the human ones. Two humans and two automata, four total; a warning of sorts, given that *four* and *death* sounded almost the same in Hwamal.

"You're not thinking of going out today of all days, are you?" the squatter of the two human guards said, squinting at Jebi. He didn't seem overly concerned about their proximity, although in all fairness, Jebi's late sister-in-law had pronounced their punches *too weak to harm a butterfly.*

"You're not adequately dressed for it," the guard went on. "It's the dead of winter out there."

"I'll survive," Jebi said. They patted their purse suggestively. "Please, I'd really like to go out to—you know."

"No, I don't know," the guard said. The other one frowned sternly at Jebi.

Jebi pulled out a wad of bills without looking at it. In a lowered voice, they said, "It's been a while since I've had a chance at any frolics, hmm? No offense, but I have a rule that

I never sleep with colleagues." This wasn't true, but it wasn't as if the guards would care. "And since the duelist prime has other matters on her mind, it's a good opportunity."

"I'll assign you a watcher," the guard said, resigned. "But the crowds are going to be a problem."

The guard named the price, and Jebi paid both guards their bribes. That was the nice thing about Razanei. When they told you how much they wanted, they meant it literally. With a fellow Hwagugin, Jebi would have been left guessing how much extra to pay on top.

"Very good," the guard said after he'd counted the money twice. "Zakan will be your watcher this time." Zakan emerged from the office where she'd been waiting, and nodded at Jebi.

With that, Jebi headed upstairs.

ON THE GROUNDS that money was a tool for getting things done, Jebi took a cab most of the way to the dueling site, the plaza in front of the Old Gardens, paying the extra for Zakan as a second passenger. Riding in an automobile was a ridiculous luxury, one they'd only indulged in once before. They spent the entire ride staring out the window marveling at the simple fact of sunlight, which had a surreal quality after it was filtered through the winter clouds. Even the chill—the cab wasn't heated—did nothing to dilute Jebi's pleasure.

The crowd had grown so thick, even two hours in advance of the duel, that Jebi disembarked at its edge and spent more money so they could watch from the balcony of a nearby house. Zakan rolled her eyes but made no objection. Jebi guessed it wasn't the first time the enterprising homeowner, a thick-bodied Hwagugin woman, had earned some extra cash this way. At least the woman was a pleasant host, bringing out snacks and tea. The warmth was especially welcome in the winter chill.

"Who's dueling, anyway?" Jebi ventured to ask the woman, feeling stupid for not knowing.

The woman blinked. "You paid to watch a Rassanin duel and you don't even—?"

Jebi shrugged, despite the heat rushing to their face. "I like watching duels, but I lose track. Terrible memory. It embarrasses my family all the time."

"Oh, there he is," the woman said eagerly, pointing toward the platform. "His opponent must be late."

The balcony provided them a splendid view. Jebi, with their superior vision, could almost pick out the individual charms decorating the priest officiating over the duel. The priest's silken robes, of white and red, looked woefully inadequate for the cold. But then, maybe Razan's gods fortified their priests against the mere vicissitudes of weather.

"The one in the green and indigo robes is *the* Chuora Kyovin, from the House of Chuora," she went on.

Jebi nodded. They wondered at the woman's evident adulation of a Razanei, but maybe it was nothing more than a simple crush. They watched as the priest anointed Chuora with water or oil, impossible to tell at this distance. Too bad it was so cold; they could sketch with gloves on, but it made for a clumsy process. Still, they wanted to jot down their impressions, so they pulled out a pocket sketchbook and a pencil, and made gesture sketches to capture the poses.

The woman sighed as wistfully as any maiden and fished

out a miniature portrait from her coat pocket. Its frame was painted a yellowy green that clashed horrendously with the cooler green of the painted clothes. The former was probably some cheap mixture of blue and yellow pigments, but the latter's vividness made Jebi think it was copper arsenite.

"See?" she asked, practically shoving the portrait under Jebi's nose while Zakan caught Jebi's eye and looked heavenward. "I bought this at his first duel in Territory Fourteen. I can't imagine why he isn't married yet."

"He's very handsome," Jebi said, which might or might not have been true. The lopsided face of the portrait made it appear as though Chuora had a double chin. "Is he the favorite?"

"Of a certainty," the woman said. "You can see him out there, can't you? Such a dashing figure." She sighed again.

*I don't care about him,* Jebi thought, not that they would have dreamed of saying so to their host. "And his opponent?" They didn't do as good a job of pretending diffidence as they would have liked. Zakan was snickering behind her hand.

Luckily, the woman was too caught up in fervor for the coming duel to notice. "Oh, *her*," she said, her nose wrinkling. "I suppose it was inevitable, really." She lowered her voice conspiratorially. "People say they were lovers once, but *I* don't believe Master Chuora would have such terrible taste."

Jebi made an effort not to clench their teeth, because their host *would* notice that, to say nothing of Zakan. "Why, what's her name and what has she done?"

Vei struck them as singularly unlikely to involve herself in scandal... but then, Jebi didn't know anything about her personal life. Just because they'd spent the past couple months working with her didn't mean Vei didn't have secret vices. What could they be? Gambling? Opium? The Razanei hated opium, even though the modern painkillers they'd introduced to Hwaguk didn't work nearly as well. Maybe an unfashionable fondness for kimchi?

"Oh, her name is Dzuge Vei," the woman said with considerably less enthusiasm. She mangled the *dz* sound, perhaps deliberately, given that she hadn't had any trouble pronouncing Chuora's name. "It's a wonder she's allowed to duel at all. *You* know."

Jebi counted to three. "No, I don't," they said, smiling at the woman in an attempt to coax her into an answer. They leaned forward; Zakan's amusement only increased. "Tell me the dirt."

*That* worked, although Jebi almost wished it hadn't. "Her father could have served Razan honorably," the woman said. "He was duelist prime for Razan's embassy, decades ago, during the reign of the Azalea Throne. He's apparently the one who taught Dzuge how to duel, for all the good it'll do her. But he took up with not one but two Fourteeners! Dzuge is half and half."

Jebi grimaced. So that explained Vei's accent when she spoke Hwamal. She must have learned the language from her other parents. It wouldn't be the first time a Razanei soldier fell for one of the prostitutes in the Virgins' District, although most of them didn't formally acknowledge their offspring. Jebi couldn't imagine that Vei had had an easy time growing up, considering the prejudices that some Hwagugin and Razanei had against children of mixed heritage, like this woman.

The woman misinterpreted Jebi's expression. "So you see what I mean," she said, with a disdain that they found repulsive. "Dueling is in the nature of a ritual, you know. It's sacred. It will be just as well when Master Chuora cuts *her* down and the Ministry of Armor can look for a proper duelist prime."

Zakan shook her head, but kept her opinions to herself. She, like Jebi, would have seen Vei training.

Jebi made the mistake of asking, "Who does Master Chuora work for?" Calling him 'master' galled them, but they had spent the last several years using honorifics for people they didn't like. This was no different, and Jebi didn't want to lose this spectacular view by antagonizing their host.

Nevertheless, their plan backfired: "*Oh,*" the woman said, her entire face pulling down in a scowl, as she finally looked at Jebi's sketchbook. Jebi realized they'd been doodling a monstrous caricature of Chuora with a bulbous head and comically huge ears. Zakan started to laugh. "That's not what he looks like at all!" She lunged.

What she couldn't have known was that Jebi had long practice defending their sketchbooks from offended subjects. (Their habit of caricature had gotten them into trouble before.) They snatched it out of reach and shoved it into their pocket, then rose precipitously and backed away. "I'd best be going," they said. Maybe it wasn't too late to join the crowd outside, even if they had every expectation of being squashed. "Bye!"

The crowd was so thick, especially this close to the dueling platform, that it took them forever just to open the door. That accomplished, they shoved and elbowed fiercely until they came to rest at a suitable viewing spot.

"Nice job," Zakan said sarcastically from next to Jebi, having kept up with them during the whole ridiculous interlude. "We could have been watching the duel from a nice comfortable spot, but you had to ruin that."

"Sorry," Jebi lied.

Just their luck, they were squeezed next to a vendor selling noodles supposedly sponsored by Master Chuora. Given the number of supporters in Chuora's green-and-indigo armbands, Jebi kept their skepticism to themself.

So distracted were they by the business of breathing in the suffocating crush that they didn't notice at first that Dzuge Vei had ascended the platform. But the murmuring and gossip caught their attention, Vei's name in hundreds upon hundreds of mouths. Notably, no one called her *Master* Dzuge, although as a duelist she merited it.

Jebi looked up, and their heart stopped in their chest.

Vei was resplendent in her own duelist's finery, a red jacket over wide blue pants, a white sash holding her sword's lacquered scabbard. The red and blue, homage to Hwaguk's forbidden national emblem, could not be denied.

That wasn't what shocked Jebi, though. Rather, they recognized the costume, for all that they'd never seen it before. The duelist in red and blue who'd cut down their sister-in-law Jia.

*Bongsunga. Bongsunga needs to know.*

"It's her," Jebi breathed. They doubted any other Razanei duelist in Hwaguk matched that description. They'd never made the connection before—and how could they have? They didn't follow dueling; found the profession distasteful and barbarous, for all the beauty of its forms.

And Vei—Vei had never practiced in her formal dueling clothes. All this time they'd been falling for her, she was the one who'd cut down Bongsunga's wife. Jebi struggled with a sense of betrayal, although one of the few things they did know about dueling was that the clothes had a ceremonial purpose and were not for casual wear. Surely Vei hadn't known about this part of Jebi's past.

Jebi tried to sort out their inconvenient feelings about Vei as they watched the priest anoint Vei with that same clear liquid. Vei and Chuora took up their positions several paces apart, each poised with their hands above their swords' hilts. The priest raised their hands.

"Here we go," Zakan mouthed, her eyes bright. "Don't you worry."

The crowd roared Chuora's name, chanting it until the syllables blurred.

The priest spoke—or anyway, their lips moved; Jebi couldn't hear a word.

Forever after Jebi would remember how Vei looked: her long hair swept up into a chignon so it wouldn't get in the way, her brow marked with red paint, her jacket whipping about her slim, poised form. The sun had gone behind a cloud, and the murkiness of the light made her into a phantasm of a bygone spring. *I could paint you,* Jebi thought, *and my sister would kill me for it.*

Jebi didn't have the space to pull out their sketchbook again, but it didn't matter. The image had already burned itself into their brain.

Then the priest brought their arms down, slicing through the air like an executioner's stroke.

Both duelists leapt forward. Jebi's eyelids felt as though they had frozen open. Not that it made a difference. They didn't know what to look for; couldn't follow motions that swift.

Two blades flashed in the winter sunlight, so quick that they were visible only as blazing crescent blurs.

Jebi's throat ached. Only then did they realize that they had, damningly, screamed Vei's name. Not *Dzuge* or *Master Dzuge*, which would have been proper, but her personal name: *Vei*.

They held their breath, wondering. Then Vei was on the other side of the platform, as though she had simply translated across the intervening space. Blood dripped from her blade. Jebi swore they could hear it hitting the platform, impossible as that was.

Then they saw Chuora. Vei had slashed him from hip to collarbone, nearly cleaving him in two. Jebi was suddenly glad they hadn't rented the balcony long enough to down more than one or two of the cookies, because they would have vomited it all up. Oh, they'd seen dead people before—everyone had, who had lived through the consolidation—but not like this. Not *freshly* dead people.

And not over... at this point Jebi realized that they had no idea *why* Chuora and Vei had dueled each other. And it was a little late to ask. A matter of honor, they presumed, since the Razanei cared about such things. And never mind that Vei was only—'only'—half-Razanei.

As the crowd keened its grief for the beloved Master Chuora, Jebi stood numbly, wondering if they had wanted Vei to live or die.

# Chapter
# SEVEN

ZAKAN TACTFULLY DIDN'T attempt to engage Jebi in conversation on the way back to the Summer Palace. Jebi wasn't making any secret of their mood. At first they fretted that they wouldn't be able to return before Dzuge Vei did, but they needn't have worried. The rituals of the duel, to say nothing of the combination of mourning and celebration—a few people had in fact supported Vei, outnumbered though they were—meant that Vei was unlikely to extricate herself from the crowd anytime soon.

The rest of the day passed in a haze, as did the ones following it. Jebi wished they'd stayed out longer. It might have been nice to see the night sky again, and lose themself in the study of the winter constellations. The stars reminded them of their sister and her fascination with stories of the celestials.

Jebi longed to ask around and find out if Bongsunga missed them yet. Unfortunately, even though they went up topside again to indulge in roasted chestnuts and buns stuffed with sweet red bean paste, they had no luck shaking their watcher. Frustrated, Jebi fantasized about the things they would say to Bongsunga, even though they knew everything would end in her telling them *I told you so.*

By the time Vei returned to the Summer Palace, Jebi had thrown themself back into studying Issemi's notes to double-check their work. They had a solution in mind, but not one that they dared show to Nehen. Since they wouldn't have the usual safeguard of a second pair of eyes on the new grammar they planned on giving Arazi, they had to make absolutely certain that nothing would go wrong.

The artisans of the Summer Palace remained reluctant to discuss the Ppalgan-Namu incident with Jebi. But Jebi knew of one more witness, if they could only coax it to talk: the dragon itself. After all, who knew better what Arazi had done than Arazi itself?

Jebi remembered what Nehen had told them about contradictions and choices, and attempted to communicate with the automata that guarded the cafeteria. The human guards in their blue uniforms gave Jebi carefully neutral looks as Jebi approached. "You just missed the last of the extra desserts," the taller one said.

"Oh, I don't mind that," Jebi said, although they wouldn't have minded the flower-shaped cookies that the kitchens had been producing lately, in lopsided imitation of Hwagugin sweets. "Can I talk to the automata?"

The other guard, a squat fellow with a birthmark along the

side of his face, shrugged. "Doesn't matter to us one way or the other. They're not exactly great conversationalists."

"Thanks," Jebi said, turning to face the automata. "Do you understand me?" they asked.

The automata stared blankly back at them.

"Can you nod, or sign?" Jebi tried. Some of the vendors at the market that Bongsunga frequented had been deaf, and communicated by signing. Jebi didn't know the details, but surely the automata would have come up with the solution for themselves even if they didn't have voices.

The automata didn't move.

One of the servants cleaning up dishes in the cafeteria pointed at the spectacle Jebi was making of themself and grinned. Another, speaking in Hwamal, whispered back something unflattering about Rassanin and their airs. Jebi flushed, but didn't react. They *knew* they looked ridiculous, and besides, they didn't want to get the servants in trouble if the guards didn't understand them.

"It was worth a try," Jebi said. The grammars of standard automata hadn't allowed for that kind of intelligence or reactivity, but they'd wanted to be sure.

But they'd studied the initial grammar Issemi had given Arazi. Not only had the grammar involved more advanced glyphs—enough, Issemi hinted, to give the dragon intelligence equivalent to a human's—she had also used the rarest pigments, such as Phoenix Extravagant. The pigment Jebi needed the most, though, was fortunately extremely common: Chirping Cicada, which represented the desire to communicate one's ideas—a motive shared by many artists. They thought they saw a way to modify certain glyphs so the two of them could share thoughts without speaking them aloud, a device they had seen in one of Bongsunga's adventure novels and one that would be handy to avoid being overheard by the guards.

"Sorry it didn't work out," the squat guard said. "Like I told you, they're no good for witty banter."

"You did warn me," Jebi agreed, and retreated to the workshop. They opened up their sketchbook, in which they'd written in deliberately terrible handwriting to reduce the chance that anyone would spy on their notes. In fact, that probably made their scribblings look more suspicious, but no one had commented on it—yet. They kept hesitating over the matter of *contradiction* and *choice*. If they forced the dragon to *always tell the truth*, it would just as easily reveal Jebi's questioning to anyone who asked. If they gave it a choice, the dragon might lie to them.

*I have to take the risk,* Jebi thought, circling the relevant glyphs. *To tell the truth* and *to exercise discretion*, two conflicting directives. Which would, according to Nehen, mean that the dragon could *choose*.

A DAY AFTER her return, Vei checked in with Jebi. She knocked on the door to the workshop before entering, a peculiar quirk given that she had the key and all the artists were in the habit of leaving the door ajar. Ordinarily Jebi liked that about her, that ingrained courtesy. But now all they saw when they looked at her was that red-and-blue outfit, and their sister-in-law Jia's face on the last day before she went off to the war.

"Is something the matter?" Vei asked as she approached Jebi's workstation.

Jebi hastily smoothed their expression. "Just worried," they said. They had no intention of telling Vei that they were going to question Arazi. "Any word on the investigation?"

"Issemi?" Vei shrugged one shoulder. "Nothing new from the deputy minister. He does want to know, however, if you'll be able to restore the dragon's function."

"About that," Jebi said, both grateful that Vei hadn't pried into their unease and nervous about the current topic. "What is the timetable for this?"

Vei's face stilled.

"I realize there are security implications," Jebi said, picking their words with care. They glanced down, saw that their hands were tapping nervously on the work bench, made them stop. "But I can be of more use to you if I know how fast I need to work, and what to prioritize."

"I can't answer that question," Vei said, to Jebi's surprise. "But the deputy minister can. He's been wanting to talk to you anyway. Come with me."

"I was working on—"

"Come with me." Because she was Vei, she rose and waited for Jebi to follow suit, rather than striding off and expecting them to catch up.

Jebi's hopes for an aboveground excursion were dashed when Vei led them to a corridor they hadn't explored before. They smiled at the guards, even the silent automata, out of pure nerves. The guards saluted Vei and did not challenge her right to enter.

Vei stopped in front of the only unlabeled door down this hall. "Deputy Minister," she called out. "I've brought the artist."

"Come in," Hafanden said, and Vei did. "I've been expecting you."

Jebi waited until Hafanden gestured impatiently at the seat across from his desk to sit down. They'd assumed that Vei would take it, but apparently not.

Jebi's gaze was arrested by the immense map that covered the wall behind Hafanden, one that had not been present in his aboveground office. It took them a couple of seconds to spot Razan's home archipelago, and then Administrative Territory Fourteen, and the immense land of Huang-Guan to the north of the Territory. But the map depicted lands beyond the three that they knew, with unfamiliar names and shapes, as well as notations for existing colonies and—most worrying of all—planned conquests.

Hafanden said, "It's time to get a progress report directly from you. Vei, you may leave us."

"Of course," Vei said, and slipped out as quietly as she had come.

*Danger,* Jebi's senses whispered to them, a cold hole at the pit of their stomach. "I had thought that the duelist prime was reporting on my doings," they said, careful to speak deferentially.

"Yes," Hafanden said, leaning forward, "she had mentioned that you'd spotted sabotage. How close are you to finding a solution?"

At least Jebi had an answer to this. "The design work is straightforward," they said, their voice trailing off uncertainly because they didn't know how much Hafanden wanted them to explain. But Hafanden nodded and turned his hand over, indicating that Jebi should continue. "The problem is supply."

"Supply of what?" he asked sharply.

"Pigments," Jebi said. "I've been talking to Shon about it. We are almost out of the enchanted pigment known as Phoenix Extravagant. I asked him if it was possible to obtain more, but he said that this will take time because of the rarity of suitable source artworks."

"You needn't concern yourself with that," Hafanden said. "A supply will be obtained."

"*Be obtained,*" Jebi thought: passive voice, with no indication of who would do the obtaining. "I'd understood that the project was urgent," they said.

"That it is," he said, and for the first time his face sagged into weary lines.

Jebi gathered their courage and ventured, "I hadn't thought that the Empire anticipated any difficulty in the Administrative Territory? The dragon Arazi is an impressive achievement, but I'd been told it was intended to defeat tanks, and surely I'd have heard even here if we were under that kind of threat."

Hafanden's smile lacked humor. "Not here, no. I don't expect an artist to keep track of international relations"—insulting, but in Jebi's case, true—"but the Western powers have been circling Razan and Huang-Guan like hungry sharks. It is only a matter of time before their navies show up to annex us the way they have annexed other lands."

"I had no idea," Jebi said blankly. Like many of their people, they had only a vague idea of geography beyond Hwaguk's nearest neighbors. "So Arazi is intended to be our defense against the Westerners." They'd almost said *your*, but caught themself in time.

"Correct." Hafanden folded his hands together, his face stern. "You will have guessed that the advantage of automata is that they can be manufactured in whatever quantities our resources permit. We have secured sources of metal, and we have built factories."

*Hwagugin metal,* Jebi thought. They did know that one of Razan's motivations for invading mountainous Hwaguk had been its wealth of ores and minerals. Bongsunga had always complained that they should have built more guns and swords to arm their soldiers before the war; but it was too late now.

"So you'll secure more of the pigment?" Jebi asked, frowning.

"Don't worry about it. It's my problem." Hafanden straightened. "I want you to document everything about the fix, and hand it in to Vei once you've unriddled the notes completely. Understood?"

"Understood," Jebi said, more certain than ever that they didn't dare tell Hafanden—or Vei, for that matter—that they already knew how to fix the problem. The question was, did they trust the Razanei to use weapons like Arazi against foreigners, instead of Hwagugin rebels? And the answer to *that* was obvious.

# Chapter
# EIGHT

JEBI'S PLANS RAN aground on an unexpected shore: sickness. They woke up coughing in the middle of the night, their nose runny and their throat sore. They almost called out for Bongsunga before remembering where they were.

*I hope she's far away,* Jebi thought. Surely by now she would have noticed Jebi's disappearance and drawn her own conclusions—none of them good—about Razanei involvement.

The next day, they woke to find Vei at their door with a tray of food. "I have to work," Jebi protested when Vei told them the time.

"You need to get better," Vei replied. "I hope you'll eat what you're able. Stay in bed, and call for a servant if you need anything." And she left the tray on the table next to Jebi's bedroll.

*She's so thoughtful,* Jebi thought at Vei's retreating back. *Too bad she killed Jia.*

Resentfully, Jebi choked down half the porridge, horrified by how drained even that little effort left them. *I just need a little rest,* they thought, and lay down. Their eyelids drifted shut.

Jebi was appalled to wake up hours later. Scraps of dream clung to them: a squad of clockwork dragons parading through the city's streets, along with patrols of the more common human-shaped automata. They'd woken when the dragons started to leak fire from between their articulated joints, setting the city alight.

Jebi almost wept with sudden fury at the way the light in the hall didn't tell them anything about the hour. It could have been morning, or midnight, or anything in between. *Time,* they thought. *What I need is time, and that's what I don't have.*

They stood with an effort, swaying, and considered that Vei was probably right and they should stay in bed. But they didn't know how long it was safe to delay, if at all. They pressed their ear to the door, struggling to hear anything—anything at all. The Summer Palace's passages carried sound quite a distance, both a blessing and a curse.

The strokes of a hammer came to them, and animated chatter. People were still up, then. Jebi ground their teeth and made their way back to the bed. They couldn't risk lying down; they'd only slide into sleep again.

To keep themself awake, they grabbed a book off the shelf and began paging through it. *The Classic of the Orderly State,* with their hash marks in it. They'd stopped keeping track of the days after Vei's duel. Jebi started yawning within the first ten pages. The dense, flowery text was difficult to understand, and they'd never cared for philosophy. The author was concerned about ways for the citizenry to give voice to their opinions, and ways for the government to act on their righteous desires, and how to tell righteous desires from selfish desires, all of which Jebi agreed with in principle, but did it have to be so *wordy*?

*Fuck this,* Jebi thought, and pulled out a pencil. Maybe the reading would go better if they *illustrated* it. While they normally didn't approve of marking up books, it wasn't as if there weren't a zillion copies of *The Classic of the Orderly State* floating around, in Razan, Hwaguk, *and* Huang-Guan, and probably beyond. Besides, they'd already written in this copy.

Jebi doodled cartoon bureaucrats and animal magistrates in robes that started out as traditional Hwagugin judges' outfits and steadily became more and more fanciful, with tassels and lace and elaborate headpieces. Soon they lost the thread of the text entirely. The doodles became more intricate textured drawings of a civilization on the moon where people and automata could live in peace, with domed colonies and more friendly animals. They drew their imaginary automata with wide, smiling mouths.

With a start, they looked up. How much time had passed while they were lost in their reverie of drawing? They rose, tucked the much-abused book under their arm and—feeling even more feverish—tottered to the door.

This time they heard nothing more than a few laughs and the enthusiastic thrashing of lovers. That would be Tia and

Mevem again; no one else quite had that same luxurious laugh as Tia. Jebi flashed on an image of Vei, wondered what she would look like as she disrobed. *You need to get over this.* Flushing, they nudged the door open and crept out.

It took all their self-control to walk as though they belonged here. *I do,* Jebi thought despite their growing sense of alarm. *No one has any reason to suspect anything if I don't* act *suspicious.*

That did nothing for the rapid patter of their heart. If it beat any faster, it would burst out of their chest. Taking deep, calming breaths didn't help, either.

Jebi made it to the workshop without their heart exploding. Unfortunately, when they slipped through the door, they saw Shon at his workbench, patiently sorting artifacts. They bit back a groan of dismay. Should they sneak away and try again another night? But there was no guarantee that he wouldn't be there then; or someone else, for that matter.

The matter was decided for them when Shon looked up, alerted by a clattering noise. Jebi had been trying to walk quietly, but someone had discarded an old, splayed brush on the floor and they'd kicked it by accident. Jebi cursed their own carelessness, to say nothing of people who couldn't be bothered to dispose of old brushes properly. To the extent that old brushes ever needed to be disposed of; like many artists, Jebi found even completely dead brushes to be of use for spatter effects. What kind of person just left a brush on the floor for people sneaking around to trip over?

"You look dreadful," Shon said, blunt as always. Although Vei had been likewise blunt, so maybe they did look as sick as they felt. "I'll escort you back to bed."

Jebi hated themself for what they were about to say, but they needed him *out of the way* as quickly as possible. "I didn't know *that* was what you were after," they snapped, crossing their arms and backing away from him.

Guilt flashed over Shon's face, then was gone so quickly that Jebi almost thought they'd imagined it. "I don't mean any discourtesy," he said, his voice gruff. "If you'll excuse me—"

"I came here because I think better in the quiet," Jebi said, still rudely. That part was almost true. Of course, their own coughing was more disruptive than any amount of grinding or hammering or water-splashing could be, but they weren't about to admit that.

"I'll leave you to it, then," Shon said. He stalked out of the workshop, his back stiff.

Jebi winced as they watched him go. There must have been a better way to coax him into leaving, but they were so damn tired and achy, and nothing else had come to mind. *It's done now,* they thought.

Still unsteady, they walked over to their own workbench. They were still carrying the defaced book; they hadn't meant to, but maybe it could serve a purpose. *Voice of the people,* Jebi thought, wondering what the connotations of the phrase had been in the original Huang-Guanmal text. It dovetailed with what they planned, now that they thought of it.

Jebi already had several blank masks made to fit the dragon Arazi's head, a whole box full of them. Tia had made them to Jebi's specifications. Jebi had never had a chance to try them on Arazi earlier, but it couldn't be helped. Besides, they trusted Tia's insistence on precision.

"I'm sorry I thought you were stuffy and boring," Jebi said to the anonymous author of *The Classic of the Orderly State*. "I should appreciate your ideas even if your translator is terrible."

They still didn't have a source of Phoenix Extravagant, but that wasn't why they'd come back.

*This could be a terrible idea,* Jebi thought as they ripped out a handful of pages. The tearing noise made them cringe, but then, some of the other artists had a habit of shredding their sketches whenever they were having a bad day. With any luck, anyone listening in would think it was just someone having a tempestuous night.

What if the dragon chose to stay silent, after all the trouble Jebi had gone to? What if, instead, it wanted to *eat* them? Not that automata had ever evidenced hunger that they'd heard of, but they couldn't rule out the possibility that they'd missed something in the new grammar.

Or worse, maybe the dragon would want to talk *too much*. Jebi couldn't imagine what it would have to say, after it had spent most of its existence pacing in a circle. Maybe it had gone mad, or as mad as a machine ever could. That thought didn't inspire confidence, either.

Grimly, Jebi applied the miraculous mortar and pestle to the pages they'd shredded. *Sorry about the cartoons,* they added silently. Maybe the dragon would be an *art critic*. That would be hilarious.

The pigment that took shape in the mortar was powdery and had a slightly bitter smell, like oversteeped green tea. Jebi had experienced more noxious things in the service of art, however. They kept grinding. They wanted to make sure they had plenty of pigment from the same batch. Better to overprepare.

When Jebi judged that they had enough, they mixed in a conventional pigment so they could see what they were doing, something Shon had taught them. Some mystical pigments had variable visibility, which made them inconvenient to work with. Jebi didn't want to mess this up because the paint was *invisible*. After a moment's thought, they chose carbon black. Of the five traditional colors, black signified water and wisdom, both of which an incendiary weapon of destruction could benefit from.

*Do I have time to make a preliminary sketch?* Jebi wondered. They couldn't afford not to. By now they had most of the glyphs memorized; their excellent memory for visuals served them well.

Every chance noise, every murmur that drifted into the workshop caused Jebi to tense. *I have to ignore the distractions,* Jebi thought, even if the 'distractions' might be their only warning of intrusion—or danger. They would paint poorly if they jumped at every sound.

Jebi took another few precious moments to meditate, something they'd never been particularly good at. Even Bongsunga hadn't pressed them to do it much, given how chancy *her* temper was. Thinking of their sister caused Jebi's rhythm to stutter, and they spent more moments taking deep breaths until they calmed.

*Now I'm ready,* Jebi thought, and took up the pencil again. With quick, deft strokes, they sketched the initial design on the surface of the mask. Their hand slipped once, smudging the gray marks. They grabbed a kneaded eraser and lifted the worst of the smudges, then returned to work.

Jebi fetched a small bowl of water from the sink in the back, and their favorite brush. This one needed replacement; the bristles no longer came to quite as fine a point as they had when Jebi first obtained it. But they would rather work with a familiar brush than try to break in a new one on a project of this importance.

In the past, Jebi had not been particularly aware of painting as a ritual. Oh, they'd learned from their first teachers the work of grinding pigments, measuring out binders, mixing paints, cleaning brushes. But it had all struck them as something to get out of the way, part of the price one paid for the joy of expressing the inner heart of things on paper or silk.

This time, however, the ceremonial aspect of their work impressed itself on them. It no longer seemed surprising that the strange magic of the glyphs and these paints had been discovered by a priest. Jebi was only middling religious as Hwagugin went, making small offerings or relying on charms as the situation required, instead of frequenting shrines or fortunetellers; the larger ancestral offerings, while a necessity, were Bongsunga's duty as the eldest.

At last Jebi finished painting the mask. They stared down at the black lines and curves, the glyphs that sometimes resembled clouds, sometimes waves, sometimes—and how had they not noticed this during the act of creation?—the phases of the moon. The paint glistened wetly, with an unearthly luster as of dark pearls, or perhaps abalone shell.

A memory returned to Jebi: a conversation they'd overheard at Hak's party, the Razanei bureaucrats whispering of a plan to colonize the moon. The moon! Did Hafanden intend for the dragon to fly? Arazi had no wings, but neither did the dragons in the folktales and paintings, and that never stopped them. Too bad they'd never thought to ask him about *that*. If cavalry thundering over the hills was terrifying, surely flying war machines would be even more so.

It took all of Jebi's patience to wait for the paint to dry. If they'd had access to a *window* and daylight, they'd have put the mask in the sun to hurry the process along, even if it risked fading. They didn't think it would matter in the time they had left, anyway.

Jebi's heart nearly seized when the door swung open more widely and one of the artists ambled in: Tia, singing softly off-key. *How didn't I hear her coming in?* Jebi berated themself.

"What're you working on?" Tia asked, too loudly for Jebi's comfort.

"Things," Jebi said, repositioning themself to block Tia's view of the painted mask. Of all the times...

Tia made a face. "I thought you were a normal person, but here you are, trying to make us look bad again by working while you're *sick*." She was smiling as she said it. "*I'm* going to work on a personal project for once. Are you going to snitch on me?" She belched, with great enthusiasm.

Jebi couldn't help but grin. "No," they said. All the same, they worried that Tia was going to report on them anyway. Just because she was acting friendly *now* didn't mean she wasn't also reporting odd behavior to Hafanden. At least, in Hafanden's place, Jebi would have informers, instead of relying on the guards. And of course the automata *couldn't* report what they saw or heard.

*I'm going to change that,* Jebi thought. For Arazi, anyway.

Once they had satisfied themself that Tia was, indeed,

working on... what the hell *was* that? The painting she'd pulled out didn't resemble any work of representational art Jebi had ever seen. A bunch of abstract paint splotches in fierce reds and yellows. Maybe the abstraction was the point. It wasn't a vision they understood. Under other circumstances, they would have liked to talk to Tia about it, but they had another mission.

Jebi carefully touched one of the painted lines with a fingertip—good, it was dry—then wrapped it up in hanji paper so they could carry it. After a moment's thought, they added a mortar and pestle, and the jar of pigment for good measure.

Nobody interrupted them on the way to Arazi's prison, not even Vei. *And why am I thinking about her anyway?* Jebi thought, annoyed with themself.

The guards eyed Jebi sourly. "At *this* hour?" one of them demanded.

Jebi spread their hands apologetically. "Inspiration, you know." Their favorite excuse. They'd heard the other artisans using it to wheedle special treatment out of the guards, too.

The guard sighed and made a notation on their clipboard. "If you insist."

"I need to concentrate," Jebi added. "It's *very important*. The guards inside need to wait outside or they'll disrupt my focus. They can go back in after I'm done."

It was a stupid bluff, but the guards either believed them or didn't mind letting Jebi incriminate themself. Jebi tried not to think about the latter.

Jebi hurried past once the guards inside had filed out, pretending it was eagerness rather than terror. The doors scraped shut behind them, leaving them alone with Arazi.

The dragon still paced, but Jebi fancied they detected tension in the lines of its body. Did it, too, sense what was to come, a change in its routine?

"Arazi," Jebi said after a deep breath. "Come here. I just want—I just want to talk."

They didn't know what they would have done if the dragon had kept pacing, because their skills didn't include wrestling giant war machines into submission. Something they should have thought of earlier.

Arazi slowed, and came to a halt before Jebi, and lowered its head, as gracious as any aristocrat. The beauty of its design struck them all over again. What would it be like to see something this glorious come to end your life?

*Stop that.*

"This is for you," Jebi said. "So we can talk. And I do mean 'we.'" They held the mask up.

Arazi craned its head forward.

Jebi unfastened the previous mask and placed it carefully on the ground. Then they placed the new one on the dragon's head. The mask fit perfectly—thank goodness for Tia's skill—and clicked almost imperceptibly as it settled into place.

Jebi screwed the mask in. A soft murmuration filled Jebi's ears, as of the far-off sea.

"Arazi?" Jebi asked, uncertain.

Through the mask's eye holes, Jebi saw the dragon's eyes glow sea-blue, sea-black. Arazi stared back. For a terrible moment, Jebi thought they had done all of this for nothing; that they'd have to return to their room empty-handed, and submit to Hafanden's questions, and maybe Vei's too.

Then the dragon spoke in their head. It had a mind-voice

like softly ringing metal, with overtones of sea-crash and wind-cry. *{You must have given me a voice for a reason. Ask your questions.}*

Jebi's heart sang. The grammar had worked, at least as far as giving the dragon the ability to speak. They had indeed mastered the glyphs and pigments.

Could they reply in the halls of their mind, too? They hesitated. *{My name is Gyen Jebi.}* Not *Tesserao Tsennan*, not with the questions they were about to ask. *{I have heard several conflicting stories about what happened at Ppalgan-Namu, the massacre. But you were there. You know what happened. And you're the only one I haven't heard from.}*

The dragon's unblinking gaze held them fast. *{Of course you haven't heard the truth,}* Arazi said. *{There was a massacre at Ppalgan-Namu.}* Its pronunciation of the Hwagugin name was flawless. *{But it wasn't my doing.}*

That wasn't news, given Issemi's sabotage. "Tell me," they whispered, forgetting and speaking aloud.

*{The deputy minister and his soldiers took me to the village to test my capabilities,}* Arazi said. *{But I had no desire to kill, especially not for a war I never agreed to. What harm had the villagers ever done me?}*

*{Then—?}*

*{First Hafanden asked Issemi, who was the one who made me, why she had failed him.}* Arazi's voice was quiet, controlled; but the dragon's eyes burned more brightly, more darkly. *{He had her killed first. She, too, was not interested in murdering people, or making tools for murder; and so she had to die. Since she was no longer useful to him, he planned on using her art for the next supply of Phoenix Extravagant.}*

Word choice mattered. *Murder*, it said. Jebi had preserved the part of Issemi's grammar that suggested *seek peaceful solutions*, but they hadn't ruled out violence entirely. Nevertheless, the dragon clearly had a memory; perhaps, once woken, it retained opinions and an intelligence of its own, despite the restrictions placed by the change in masks.

Jebi had opened their mouth to ask what had happened next, but the dragon beat them to it. *{Hafanden did not want his superiors to know just how the experiment}*—had they imagined its sarcasm?—*{failed, or the local population, either. So he ordered all the witnesses killed.}*

Jebi's mouth went dry. *{How many?}*

*{A few hundred,}* Arazi said. *{He had other automata under his control, along with the human soldiers. They could not say no; their grammars were not designed for it. But even one death would have been too many.}*

*{We have to get you out of here before Hafanden forces another mask on you and uses you against my people,}* Jebi said softly. *{But how?}* They looked at the chains wrapped around the dragon's limbs. If it could have escaped before, it would have done so by now.

Arazi shook itself with a light clattering of metal against metal. *{Where would we go?}*

As far away as possible, was Jebi's first thought. And what could be farther than the moon? *{I know where we can go,}* they said instead. *{If we can get out. Go back to your pacing— are you willing to wait, while I work on a plan?}*

*{Yes,}* Arazi said. *{But hurry.}*

Jebi hesitated at the threshold of the great chamber, wondering if the new mask would be discovered, but shook their head and hurried out. No-one had noticed Issemi's deception, after all.

When had they gone from artist-candidate to revolutionary? Jebi wasn't sure. But they knew they couldn't stand by and let Hafanden massacre more people.

# Chapter
# NINE

AT THE NEXT meal, Jebi lingered after everyone else had dispersed back to their work or projects of their own. One of the servants, a thin woman with a smallpox-scarred face, crept in to clear the dishes and wipe down the tables. Jebi beckoned her closer.

The servant didn't look them in the eye. "What do you need?" she asked in awkward, accented Razanei.

Jebi lowered their voice and spoke in Hwamal. "The guard named Zakan. Does she have any vices?"

The servant blanched. "I wouldn't know about that."

"I just want to slip the leash a bit," Jebi said. They disliked confiding in the woman, even if they were both Hwagugin. They didn't have any illusions that she would cover for them if questioned, and for that matter, Jebi didn't want to get her in trouble. Carefully, they grasped the woman's hand and slipped a generous sum into it. "It's a simple enough question."

The woman's face went blank. Then: "I've heard that Zakan likes music. Sometimes she talks about going to performances in the Virgins' District."

"Where?"

The woman listed several bars.

"Thank you," Jebi said.

When they signed out that evening, they requested Zakan. The guards looked at each other, then shrugged. "There's a fee for special requests," one of them said.

Of course there was. Jebi haggled, not because they cared but because it would have looked suspicious if they hadn't.

"Where are we going this time?" Zakan asked.

Jebi chose one of the bars at random, the Lucky Cat. "I haven't had much chance for entertainment," they said, which had the benefit of being true.

Zakan brightened. "Oh, I know that place! I can show you the best items on the menu."

{*Are you planning on getting her drunk?*} said a curious voice in Jebi's head: the dragon.

Jebi nearly jumped. {*Can you... hear through my ears?*} they asked tentatively.

{*Yes,*} said Arazi. {*Sorry, am I being rude?*}

{*No, it was... just a surprise.*}

{*So, are you?*} the dragon asked. {*Going to get her drunk, I mean.*}

{*If necessary, yes,*} they said.

{*I have never seen anyone drunk, although the guards talk*} *about it,}* Arazi said. *{It's not permitted down here, and Hafanden's people are very strict. This will be exciting!}*

'Exciting' wasn't the word Jebi would have chosen, but then, maybe ordinary human drunkenness offered some entertainment to an imprisoned automaton.

Jebi was impatient to reach the Lucky Cat, but the Virgins' District wasn't far, only about an hour's walk. Besides, even though their legs ached from all the stairs, they wanted to savor the outside world. Zakan seemed content to walk at their elbow, so Jebi occupied themself describing their surroundings to Arazi. Bare-limbed sycamores and maples with a few last leaves clinging to their twigs, the slush underfoot, the magpies arguing over fallen snacks in the streets. The way that Jebi's fellow Hwagugin gave them a wide berth, since they were accompanied by a uniformed watcher.

The Virgins' District had its own charm, despite the occasional presence of a blue-uniformed soldier. The late afternoon sun slanted through the clouds and splashed gray light across the roof tiles of the brothels with their ornate statues and gates. A taffy-seller clacked his oversized scissors as he advertised his candy. Jebi's mouth watered at the thought of the treat, which they hadn't tasted in some time.

"Need to catch your breath?" Zakan asked, mistaking the reason Jebi had slowed down.

Jebi stared longingly at the taffy. Duty came first.

*{I want taffy,}* Arazi said. *{You can tell me all about it. No one has ever shown me taffy before.}*

Jebi caught themself smiling. "I want a snack," they said aloud, and went to buy the taffy. The seller cut off an extra long piece for them. Jebi immediately stuffed it into their mouth, struggling to bite off a manageable amount.

Zakan gave up trying to converse with Jebi while their mouth was full, which gave Jebi ample opportunity to mentally describe the burnt-sugar taste of the stuff to Arazi. *{Do you even have a sense of taste?}* they demanded partway through.

*{Not exactly, but I have an imagination,}* Arazi said serenely. *{Eating sounds so fun. You must taste all the things for me.}*

*I am going to be very round at the end of this adventure,* Jebi thought. They liked the idea of sharing their experiences with Arazi, though. Its enthusiasm was infectious.

By the time they arrived at the Lucky Cat, Jebi's fingers and chin were quite sticky, something else that Arazi found delightful. *Just wait until someone gums up your joints,* Jebi thought; but no need to spoil its fun yet.

The receptionist, a refined young man in a woman's hanbok, raised an eyebrow at the evidence of Jebi's taffy malfeasance. At least, he had his hair cropped short, instead of in a geu-ae's style. "A bowl of water?" he inquired delicately.

"Yes, please," Jebi said, too happy to be embarrassed.

At a gesture from the receptionist, a long-haired woman glided toward Jebi with a bowl of scented water and a towel. Jebi cleaned up while Zakan negotiated over the fee for a performance by the house ensemble. They described the smell to Arazi—a complicated floral essence—and the welcome heat of the water, warm enough to restore feeling to their cold-numbed fingers.

*{It's always cold where I am,}* Arazi mused, *{but it's not unpleasant the way it must be for you.}*

*{If I'm ever reborn, perhaps I'll ask to be an automaton,}* Jebi agreed, a little dubiously.

Zakan made Jebi pay for the performance, an extortionate sum, which Jebi put up with mainly because they planned to ditch her later in the evening. The gliding woman led them both to a private room. Paper screens with restful if inexpert paintings of frolicking cats divided the room into two. The musicians were tuning behind the screens, which hid them from visitors' eyes.

"I've never understood that," Zakan said with what Jebi interpreted as genuine regret. "I'd love to see them playing. But I don't want to intrude upon the tradition, either."

*{What tradition?}* Arazi asked, and then: *{I can hear the music, a little, through your senses. It's not what I thought it would be.}*

Jebi knew the reason for the practice, even if Zakan hadn't figured it out. *{Entertainers who are available for sleeping with show their faces,}* Jebi explained. *{Entertainers who aren't hide them.}*

Zakan, emboldened by Jebi's willingness to pay for the experience, ordered two cups of rice wine. Jebi wondered if Zakan thought Jebi was going to sleep with *her*—the kind of escapade some bars and brothels facilitated. She wouldn't be the first person to think of artists as willing lovers. Or maybe she really was that keen on Hwagugin music.

The performance began. Jebi found the music, slow as it was, frankly soporific.

*{Really?}* Arazi said. Jebi was distracted by the distinct sensation that, in its prison underground, the dragon was swaying to the plaint of the zithers. They caught themself

doing the same. Zakan winked at them, to their discomfiture, likely taking it as being caught up in the music, albeit with an abysmal sense of rhythm. *{I think the sea would sound like this, if I'd ever been to the sea.}*

That raised the question of how much Arazi knew about the outside world, and from where. *{Where did you hear of the sea?}*

*{I am a dragon,}* Arazi said, *{even if I don't come from the weather or the water.}*

Jebi drank the wine, and listened to the music. In between numbers, Zakan insisted on discussing the music with them. To Jebi's dismay, Zakan cared *very much* about music theory, which Jebi only knew about because one of their lovers four years ago had been an aspiring composer. Every time Jebi made a half-hearted remark, Zakan took great pleasure in correcting them.

Midway through the performance, a calico cat sauntered in and made a beeline for Jebi's lap. Jebi attempted to shoo it away, with little effect. The cat began to purr, and Jebi helplessly scritched it behind the ears. They should have realized that the Lucky Cat would have an actual cat or three in attendance. It was a plump little creature, with glossy fur.

Zakan continued to order more wine. Jebi pretended to drink theirs, much to Arazi's disappointment. *{If you want to see me properly drunk,}* Jebi told it, *{you'll have to wait for another occasion. We need to get you out of there, remember? Besides—}* And they spared a few moments to describe Zakan's slurred speech and increasingly loud laughter. It wasn't entirely clear to Jebi how much of the scene Arazi could take in directly, through the connection between them, and how much it relied on their descriptions. They were starting to suspect that Arazi simply enjoyed having someone talk to it, whatever the topic, and who could blame it, given its isolation?

Once Jebi judged that Zakan was drunk enough, they shoved the little calico out of their lap, not hard. The cat immediately made for Zakan's lap instead, its tail lashing in affront. "Gotta piss," Jebi said. Zakan waved them off without taking her eyes off the shadows moving across the screens.

Jebi did avail themself of the outhouse, in fact, before slipping out while the receptionist was busy placating a belligerent Razanei.

*{Damnation,}* Jebi thought, squinting at the dark sky. It was past sundown, and curfew would be in effect. Without Zakan as escort, they risked being picked up by the city guard. *{At least I won't get mugged,}* Jebi added to Arazi. *{If I can get to my sister Bongsunga, she'll be able to help me figure out how to get you out of the complex.}*

*{I didn't realize you had a sister,}* Arazi said, and lapsed into silence.

Jebi lost no time putting distance between themself and the Lucky Cat, winding up in a distressingly pristine alley while attempting to avoid the patrols. It reminded Jebi of the Razanei insistence on cleanliness. The Razanei patrols wouldn't hesitate to beat or imprison—or execute—people caught pissing against buildings or vomiting onto the streets.

The heavy tread warned Jebi that automata were approaching. The streets here were swept clear of snow, with only gray piles to either side, and the patrol came right up to Jebi before they could unpuzzle an escape route. The automata surrounded them in a half-circle.

"You are violating curfew," the interpreter said, fingering her necklace of wooden beads.

An idea occurred to Jebi. Maybe this wasn't a complete loss after all. "I'm prepared for the penalty," they said, trying not to sound too eager. They wished they'd worn another layer, but it might have tipped Zakan off that they had planned to stay out.

The interpreter looked askance at them. "I'm going to have to send you to a holding cell overnight, and in the morning you can pay the fine."

"That's going to be a problem," Jebi lied—they had the money right now—"but my sister will be good for it." They smiled as unctuously as they knew how, and the interpreter's eyes clouded with distaste. They gave Bongsunga's name and address, neither of which were secrets to the Ministry of Armor. Even if Bongsunga had gone into hiding, as indeed they hoped she had, someone would hear and get word to her.

"Oh, a Fourteener," the interpreter said dismissively. "You lot are always getting into scrapes, aren't you? Well, come along, and maybe next time you'll have the good sense to pay heed of laws that are set in place for your own good, and the rest of us besides."

Wonderful. They'd found a *philosopher*, and one determined to educate them. Jebi nodded and made penitent noises as the automata surrounded them, ignoring the urge to bolt. After all, the interpreter thought them an ordinary feckless Fourteener. Being locked up in one of the overnight cells, however unpleasant, might be safer than wandering around at night. They doubted that Hafanden would look for them there.

The interpreter passed them off to another patrol, who passed them to another, until Jebi arrived at the nearest lockup. The bored magistrate's assistant on duty misspelled Jebi's Hwagugin name, and they didn't bother correcting him. With any luck, the Razanei would be looking for Tesserao Tsennan, and not Gyen Jebi.

*See, there's a practical use for this business of two names after all,* Jebi wanted to tell their sister. Granted, they knew that Bongsunga would retort that this sort of duplicity was a business for spies or... revolutionaries? Suddenly they weren't sure what she'd say after all.

Jebi was flung into a cell with five other people, two finely dressed, three in rags. The cell reeked of alcohol fumes, vomit, and piss, and even the straw bales that served as makeshift seats smelled moldy. Jebi resigned themself to an unpleasant stay standing up.

Nevertheless—Jebi pressed against the bars of the cell and waved at the guard. "Please, if you have a moment—"

The guard didn't glance in their direction, or give any indication that they'd heard Jebi.

Jebi fished surreptitiously in their purse for a coin of appropriate denomination, not so large as to attract unwanted attention, but not so small that it would offend someone looking for an honest bribe. This time they held it out, turning it this way and that so it caught the flickering light of the lantern. "Please, honored guard—"

Someone beyond Jebi guffawed at the obsequious address, but they ignored them. The guard yawned ostentatiously, then strode forward and snatched the coin. "Speak your piece," they said in a gruff voice. "And make it quick."

Jebi wondered how much drunken oratory the guard had to endure on any given night, but it would have been rude, or unwise, to inquire. "My sister will pay to have me let out early," they said, servile in their own turn. "Her name's Gyen Bongsunga." They gave her address.

The guard looked pleased at the prospect of another bribe. "I'll see what can be done. You'd better not be wasting my time." They called to one of their fellows and conferred briefly with him before he stomped out, presumably to send someone to fetch Bongsunga.

"Of course not," Jebi said despite the unease pooling in their gut. Now that they'd escaped, the number of things that could go wrong weighed on them. The guard might not be honest. Or Bongsunga might not be willing to bail Jebi out after all. Or worse, maybe Hafanden had lied to them from the beginning, and Bongsunga was already rotting in a cell of her own, or—

*She can't be dead,* Jebi thought. They would have felt it if she had died—wouldn't they?

*{I am looking forward to meeting her,}* Arazi said.

For a second Jebi resented having it in their head. Then they reminded themself that they'd set up the connection in the first place. Besides, the dragon was trying to be comforting. It would be unfair to spurn its kindness.

The Summer Palace wasn't the only place where time lost meaning. The jail didn't have any windows, just the one flickering lamp. Jebi longed for clear sweet electric lights, then hated themself for it. *{Sunlight is best,}* Jebi told Arazi.

*{I remember it,}* the dragon said, its tone wistful. *{And the light of the half-moon, too, the way everything looks different at night. But the lantern light is interesting, too. The flickering*

*sounds very different from the steady light we have in the Summer Palace.}*

*{What about the light in your cavern?}* Jebi asked, remembering the storm-torn quality of it.

*{A gift of the Dragon Queen, I heard Issemi say once,}* Arazi said. *{Storm-light for one of her children. It's a pretty story, but the light there is an artifact of one of the pigments. They would have liked to use it elsewhere to save on the cost of fueling the electric lights, but they ran out.}*

Just as Armor had run out of Phoenix Extravagant.

One of the other prisoners sidled closer to Jebi while they were engrossed exchanging stories of the dragon spirits with Arazi. "You have any money for me?" she asked in a wheedling voice, reaching toward Jebi's pouch.

They shrank back. They should have realized the guard wouldn't be the only person interested in their coin. The problem was, where could they go? If they backed up any more, they'd be stepping in a puddle of old vomit.

*{I confess I'm glad I'm not in there with you,}* Arazi observed. *{You have a very vivid sense of smell.}*

*{You wouldn't fit anyway,}* Jebi said, briefly distracted by the image of an immense dragon squished into the lockup.

"Hey," the guard called out, finally paying attention again. They scowled at the woman bothering Jebi. "None of that."

The woman slunk away, and Jebi breathed a quiet sigh of relief. Bless the guard for their straightforward corruption. For the moment, the coin—and the promise of more—had bought Jebi a bit of protection.

The hours trickled by. Come the morning, a servant came in and emptied the waste pail—Jebi had had to avail themself of it once—and after that, two of the prisoners were released. Jebi realized, with a dismal sense of failure, that the guard's greed meant they were trapped in here until Bongsunga showed up, or Jebi themself revealed that they had more money.

Jebi was so ravenous that by the time the servant returned with some plain, stale rice, they wolfed down their share with their fingers. No utensils were provided. *{It must be nice not to get hungry,}* Jebi said to Arazi.

*{Issemi said once that masks can wear away and reduce automata to motionless husks,}* Arazi replied. *{It sounds unpleasant. I like being able to move, even if it is only in circles.}*

Jebi flinched. *{I should have thought this plan through more carefully.}* They were almost starting to wish that Zakan would show up and liberate them, furious though she must be.

Jebi had given up hope that Bongsunga would ever appear and that they'd be stuck in this pit forever when the second guard returned with her in tow. She was bundled up in the neatly patched coat that Jebi knew so well, and gloves, and beyond that a scarf that Jebi didn't recognize, of sensible undyed wool. Jebi's heart lit at the sight, despite Bongsunga's forbidding expression. Had her face always had those lines around the eyes and mouth?

*{She looks fierce,}* was Arazi's observation. *{Like a soldier.}*

Jebi had never thought of her in those terms, only Jia, but Arazi's words forced them to assess her anew. She did, in fact, have something of a soldier's manner. They wondered that they hadn't seen it before—wondered what it meant.

They wondered, too, what it meant that Arazi had gone from asking Jebi to tell them about the outside world to making comments on everything they saw or perceived. While they hadn't anticipated this level of intimacy with a giant war machine, they had to admit to themself that having a companion was nice. Especially since they couldn't imagine that learning about the disgusting conditions in a prison was all that enthralling.

{It's very enthralling,} Arazi commented brightly. {Sometimes I'm glad my sense of smell is purely imagined!}

"There they are," the first guard said to Bongsunga. They laid a threatening hand on their sword's hilt. "No one get any notions, hear?" Then they opened up the door and gestured brusquely for Jebi to emerge.

Jebi scurried out too quickly for dignity, all too aware that they stank. "Thank you, honored guard," they said, bobbing a bow.

The guard had lost interest and said instead to Bongsunga, "Take them and go."

Bongsunga must have made her payment earlier. She nodded curtly to Jebi and hustled them out of the jail. She didn't even wrinkle her nose at the stench, for which Jebi was disproportionately grateful.

The air outside, however bitterly cold, smelled so much better that Jebi choked down a sob of gratitude. Bongsunga gave them a moment to orient themself, then led the two of them not toward home, but down a route that Jebi didn't recognize. Jebi didn't protest. It was enough that their sister had come for them. Time enough, once they'd reached safety, to explain their dilemma to her.

Outside, the first silvery light of false dawn brightened the sky near the horizon. Jebi yawned hugely. Lack of sleep was catching up with them; they'd tried napping standing up, which hadn't gone well. They would have killed for a decent hot meal. They didn't say anything, though, too intimidated by Bongsunga's grim mien.

When the jail had disappeared behind them and they were lost in a warren of side streets, Bongsunga spoke at last. "Do you have any idea how long you've been gone?" she demanded.

*So you missed me after all.* "I'm not sure," Jebi said in their best penitent voice. It was even true. They hadn't kept up their tally of days in the Summer Palace. "It's complicated. Please, I need your advice on something urgent."

"More urgent than running afoul of curfew?" Bongsunga said, but her heart wasn't in it. "Let's get out of the cold. I know someone who runs—a safehouse of sorts."

Jebi hadn't realized what a relief it would be to speak their own language as a matter of course. Within the Summer Palace, they'd usually spoken Razanei. "Whatever you think is best," they said.

If Bongsunga wasn't taking them home, that meant home was compromised. Jebi longed to ask what she was up to these days, and who she spent her time with. But they wouldn't do so in the open, even if curfew wasn't over yet and few people traveled the streets.

Bongsunga took them through more side streets, past closed-up noodle shops and tailors and tenements with dented grilles over their windows, until they reached a door that Jebi almost hadn't spotted, so well did it blend in with the wall. She rapped three times, then once, then three times again. The door swung open, and an old, hunched man frowned at them from within.

"They're with me," Bongsunga said to the man without greeting him, and he stood aside to admit them.

Bongsunga and Jebi entered the second available room, and left their shoes by the door. Two people were sleeping on mats on the floor; one of them had a loud snore. "Don't mind them," Bongsunga said. "They're no threat to you. Like I said, this is a safehouse."

Jebi didn't have to ask how Bongsunga had gotten involved with this place, or what kind of people needed a safehouse to begin with. The deputy minister hadn't lied about her revolutionary connections. They'd never thought of their sister as the type, despite her obvious dislike of the Razanei administration, but maybe revolutionaries didn't have a type. Maybe, taken one by one, they all had their own varied reasons.

Bongsunga sat cross-legged on the floor and indicated that Jebi should sit across from her, which they did. Neither removed their coat; the room was chilly, and had a draft. "Now," she said, "tell me why you sent for me."

Jebi did. The words spilled out in a jumble, and they had to backtrack time and again to put the events in order. Arazi helped on occasion by offering prompts when Jebi faltered, and Jebi was grateful all over again to have the dragon as a lodestar presence in their mind.

Bongsunga listened intently, without interruptions, her face grave and thoughtful. Besides the mental link to Arazi, which Jebi didn't think she would believe in, the only thing Jebi left out was their inconvenient attraction to Dzuge Vei. They didn't think their sister would understand *that*, so best not to trouble her with it. Besides, what if she tried to exact revenge from Vei? Jebi had seen Vei dueling, and didn't want to lose Bongsunga to her blade.

At last Jebi had nothing else to say. They bowed their head, ashamed of the rush of emotion that had overcome them. "I've got to organize some kind of distraction so I can get Arazi out of the Summer Palace. I think I can finagle the keys off Vei if I approach her right, but that would mean going back in there. I'm going to be in a lot of trouble for running out on my watcher."

Bongsunga squared her shoulders. "There's something you could do that would be of great value to Hwaguk," she said. "If you are willing."

Jebi knew where this was going. Cold gripped their heart. "What?" they asked, because they needed to hear it.

"It would be dangerous for you to sabotage the dragon a second time," Bongsunga said.

"And pointless," Jebi said acerbically. Arazi was already useless to the Razanei.

"But I wonder," Bongsunga said, "since you've become knowledgeable in the ways of this Rassanin magic—can you turn the dragon *against* its Rassanin masters?"

Jebi stared at her. After an appalled moment, they said, "That's still sabotage."

{*I would like to have some say in what I do,*} Arazi said, its metallic voice turning discordant.

All the same, Jebi didn't want to explain that Arazi had objections, not least because they needed Bongsunga's help getting it out. If she didn't believe it was of use to her cause, she might not aid Jebi in smuggling it out of the city.

"I know it's asking a lot," Bongsunga said. "But think about it. If the Rassanin have such a weapon, they're not going to stop with just one, and they're not only going to use it to invade Huang-Guan for its resources. If anyone in Hwaguk rises up against the Rassanin, they'll use it to put the rebellion down."

Jebi's gaze slid toward the two sleeping figures. Did they have any guarantee that either was really asleep? Or that they weren't more of Hafanden's agents? *I should have thought of that earlier.* Now it was too late.

"And there's going to be a rebellion," Jebi said slowly. "You know what happens to rebels!"

Bongsunga caught and held their gaze; Jebi flinched. "Yes," she said, "I know what happens to rebels. The ones who get caught, like this Issemi"—she stumbled over the name—"did. She was a brave woman, even if she was Rassanin. Perhaps they're not all evil; all the same, we can't tolerate them in our country any longer."

"And what are you going to do once they're gone?" Jebi demanded. "The Razanei still control the local seas, and the shipping routes. It's their expertise that built the manufactories and brought us electricity."

"Do you think we haven't been learning from them?" Bongsunga retorted. "It was that one sage from Huang-Guan who said that your best teacher is your worst enemy, after all."

Jebi was silent for a moment. Then they said, "You know what you're asking of me." And of Arazi, who hadn't asked to be a war machine.

"I'm asking of you what I would ask of any of our people," Bongsunga said. "Except you're in a unique position, because of your—adventures. You could do us great good."

"But it means more coming from *you*," Jebi said, not a little bitterly. She was their sister.

"I'm not done asking for things," Bongsunga said. "If you had the materials, could you oversee the manufacture of more automata? Ones loyal to Hwaguk?"

{No,} Arazi said, even more discordantly. {*Don't give us the means to think and then take away our choices.*}

{*She has to believe that I'll help her,*} Jebi said, gritting their teeth. {*Let me tell her what she wants to hear. It'll buy time.*}

Once they wouldn't have hesitated to do as Bongsunga asked. They'd never considered things from the automata's viewpoint. It was different when the automaton could talk to them, and take delight in taffy, and keep them company. Jebi didn't want to be the kind of person who would condemn Arazi to servitude.

Arazi fell silent, and they were afraid that they had angered it.

"I could smuggle out the manuals and train people," Jebi said, because Bongsunga was still waiting for an answer. She was their *sister*. And she'd rescued them from the jail, despite their estrangement. She'd expect them to respond accordingly.

"It's settled, then." Bongsunga sat straight-backed, almost imperious in her certainty. "I will have my contacts smuggle word into the Summer Palace once they've figured out a way to get you to safety."

"'Safety'?" Jebi said. "Where's *that* to be found, in Territory Fourteen?" They used the Razanei term deliberately.

"It's true, we could make use of your information within Hwaguk," Bongsunga said. "But we have been cultivating allies in the lands outside our borders, including the West."

Jebi's blood chilled. They knew some of their people had gone into exile rather than face life under Razanei rule, but they didn't like the thought of involving even more foreigners in the fate of their country.

"You'd be asking me to go into exile myself," Jebi said slowly. The words tasted like poison.

"Or you could stay, and help us," Bongsunga said. "Your choice."

Some choice. They'd always known their sister to be hardheaded. They just hadn't expected that to be turned against them in quite this fashion.

"The first step is getting back into the Summer Palace," Jebi said after some furious thinking. "That's the only way I can do anything for you."

Bongsunga smiled. It did nothing to warm her face. "I'll make arrangements."

# Chapter
# TEN

THE GUARDS FROWNED at Jebi when they showed up at the entrance to the Summer Palace. "Zakan doesn't appreciate what you did," said the shorter one. "She's in a lot of trouble, and it's all because of you."

"It's my responsibility," Jebi said, resigned to having made an enemy. They'd prepared a lie with Bongsunga's help. "I went drinking and slept it off at an old friend's place." The 'friend' was one of Bongsunga's contacts.

A third guard emerged to escort Jebi down into the Summer Palace, and closeted them in a room for interrogation. Jebi repeated the story, keeping the details simple. They couldn't tell whether the guard believed them or not.

"All right," the guard said at last. "Your aboveground privileges will be revoked for the next month."

Jebi grimaced. That would make escaping harder, but not impossible. "That'll teach me to drink so much of the Lucky Cat's rice wine."

The first thing Jebi did after the guard released them was go to the baths and soak for a good hour. *{I will never take baths for granted again,}* they said to Arazi.

*{I always worry about rust,}* Arazi admitted, *{even with the enamel paints.}*

Jebi had to admit that this was one problem that hadn't occurred to them. *{We'll keep you out of the rain,}* they said, a promise they weren't sure they could keep.

After the bath, they returned to their room, fell onto their mat, and collapsed asleep. They had turbulent, inchoate dreams that might have involved dragons and fire and storms; or perhaps it was the last remnants of their illness. Whatever the case, they didn't wake until well into the next day.

Vei was sitting at their table, with a covered meal tray, when Jebi woke. "What—?" they began. They didn't remember her entering.

"I heard about your quarrel with Shon," Vei said. Her face was intent, almost stern. "Has he troubled you before?"

Jebi blinked, trying to figure out what Vei was talking about, when what they really wanted to do was attack the meal tray. Their appetite had returned—surely a sign that the worst of the sickness was over, right? Then the memory of the quarrel flashed before them, and they flushed.

"I was too harsh," they said. They hadn't meant for Shon to get into trouble. Although—"There's been no *impropriety*, if that's what you mean, but I should have asked myself why he's the only one who willingly interacts with me." Jebi realized what they'd just implied and said, "I mean—"

The corner of Vei's mouth crooked upward. "I'm not taking offense, unless it's on *your behalf*. If you think no action is warranted at this time—"

Jebi blanched. "Oh, no, no."

Vei nodded once, firmly. "Let me know if anything changes." She added, with a note of curiosity, "It would have been the same in the Ministry of Art, you know. Part of the duelist prime's duty is to ensure that the bounds of honor are enforced."

This was an aspect of working with the Razanei that Jebi had never thought much about. Oh, they'd known that each ministry *had* a duelist prime, as had the embassy, back before the conquest, but their distaste for the profession had prevented them from looking more deeply into the matter. If only they'd known...

Vei wasn't done. "You shouldn't have been adventuring topside, not without your watcher. Especially when you need your rest."

Shit. How could they have forgotten that Vei was *also* here to keep an eye on them? The guards would report directly to her. "I missed the sunlight so much," they said. They didn't even have to fake the miserable note in their voice. "Electric light isn't the same."

"It's an unfortunate consequence of our location, yes," Vei said. "I heard you'd been experimenting with a new mask for Arazi? Nehen says you didn't run the new grammar past them."

"I was so sure it would work," Jebi said. "But there's no change." They had to keep Vei from insisting that they return the old one. "I wanted to leave it on, see if there was a long-term effect."

*{Thank you,}* Arazi said.

A crease formed between Vei's brows. "I'd like you to run the new grammar by Nehen. They might have some insights."

Jebi desperately wanted to escape this line of questioning. *I need to distract her*—"I'm not the first member of my family that you've had dealings with," they blurted out.

Shit, what had led them to choose *that* particular distraction? But it was too late. They'd spoken; they were committed.

Vei's eyes widened. She leaned forward ever so slightly. "You don't look familiar, not in that way," Vei said. With no particular emphasis, she added, "I remember everyone I have ever dueled. I would have noticed a resemblance."

*Remember,* Jebi told themself, in a desperate attempt to avoid drowning in the shadows of those dark eyes, or to stop noticing the smell of incense that drifted from her skin and hair. *Remember that she could kill you as easily as scissors cut paper.*

Jebi swallowed once, twice. Their mouth had gone dry. "It wasn't a blood relative," they said, "she didn't look like people of my lineage. Her name was Jia."

Vei was utterly focused on them. "Then it was during the war," she said. "Those were the only opponents whose names I didn't know."

Jebi bit back their revulsion. They remembered the chaos of those early battles, and how they had hid with Bongsunga in the old apartment, hoping that no one would smash it open. Soldiers had, once; not even Razanei soldiers, but Hwagugin deserters. They raided what was left of the rice wine and cinnamon punch. Jebi had never forgotten the terror that the two of them would have their throats slit by *their own people*. Bongsunga had never spoken of it afterward, and Jebi had been too afraid to bring it up.

They didn't know why they'd expected Vei to blanch at the name, or show some reaction. But if they'd thought about it, they would have realized that, duelist or soldier, people wouldn't be standing around shouting their lineages at each other. At least not during an invasion, as opposed to a formal duel.

"It was war," Vei said, "but nevertheless, she was important to you. You're an artist—would you draw her?"

It wasn't an apology, quite. Jebi shivered. They remembered Jia vividly; remembered how she had always been showing off with fancy, wildly impractical sword-moves, to Bongsunga's delight. Bongsunga had laughed a lot more, in those days.

Silently, Jebi pulled out their sketchbook and flipped to an empty page. Picked up a pencil. They began sketching, starting with construction lines that they hadn't relied upon in a long time, then proceeded to fill in details.

They'd *intended* to draw Jia the way Vei would have met them. As a soldier, in her uniform, a little rumpled the way she'd always been despite all her complaints about her sergeant. With her sword, inadequate as it would prove against Razanei rifles—and, ultimately, a Razanei blade.

Instead, what emerged from their pencil was a depiction of Jia at home—and not just Jia, but also Bongsunga. The two of them embracing, Jia lifting Bongsunga. Jia's fiendish grin, Bongsunga's smile like sunrise.

When Jebi had finished, Vei reached out and touched an empty corner of the page, her narrow face taut with an emotion

Jebi couldn't name. Regret, perhaps. "That one's your sister," she said, pointing. It wasn't a question.

"Yes," Jebi said. "She goes by Gyen Bongsunga."

"I remember. From the deputy minister's report."

Well, at least Vei wasn't pretending she didn't know how Jebi had been blackmailed into working for Armor.

"We are not enemies," Vei said softly. It wasn't the first time she had expressed the sentiment. Then: "You should eat. I have been remiss."

*Bongsunga will never forgive me,* Jebi thought. At the moment they weren't sure they cared. After all, for all that their sister meant to them, the last time they'd seen her, she had turned them into a tool of the revolution.

*{I have to keep distracting her,}* Jebi told Arazi, not sure whether they were making excuses to themself or to the dragon. Did mechanical dragons have any insight into affairs of the heart?

*{Can I help?}* Arazi asked.

Jebi choked back a laugh at the thought of Arazi poking its head in the doorway and making suggestions for lovemaking. "It's not the food I'm interested in," they murmured to Vei, bowing to temptation, and reached for her hand.

They expected Vei to draw away, proper as ever. She did not. The strong fingers tightened around Jebi's own hand. She pulled Jebi into an embrace.

Jebi stiffened for a moment, not because they didn't want this, but because they *did*; because they hadn't thought their heart's desire might be theirs for the asking. And never mind that even this was artifice, a way to keep Vei from thinking about the all-important matter of Arazi's new mask. They relaxed, then, and pressed against her. Tilted their head for Vei's kiss, sweet and deep.

Vei's body was all wiry strength and sword-curves, subtle musculature and grace. The skin of her neck was unexpectedly delicate despite the sun-browning of her face and hands. She tasted of salt, of sweat, of a faint residue of incense smoke.

Months had passed since the last time Jebi had taken a lover, and they didn't know how long it had been for Vei. They tugged at Vei's buttons and laces, fumbled with clasps. Vei laughed deep in the back of her throat and helped them, more leisurely than she had any right to be.

"What's the hurry?" she asked.

In answer, Jebi kissed her again, and Vei laughed.

Vei had clever fingers, not unusual for a duelist, and an even cleverer tongue. For all her decorousness in her day-to-day life, she knew an astonishing variety of filthy poetry and ballads, which she quoted piecemeal as she kissed and licked and sucked her way along the lines of Jebi's body. Jebi, less articulate, marked the canvas of her skin in return with teeth and fingernails, savage kisses.

Thankfully, Arazi kept its observations to itself, although Jebi was tangentially aware of its presence in their mind. They didn't think they could have kept its comments secret if it had made any. They did think that it would probably quiz them about lovemaking at some later, inconvenient time.

Vei had so much hair, a thick nightfall of the stuff, only a little tangled. Jebi took great pleasure in making their way through handfuls of it, working the knots loose with their fingers and performing brushstroke gestures across their own skin and hers with the strands, like invisible calligraphy. Vei found this very entertaining; the way her muscles tensed and relaxed beneath her skin amused Jebi inordinately.

Much later, Jebi demanded, "Do you not get *tired?*", breathless and sated—or so they'd thought.

"Call it martial discipline," Vei said, and touched them again, in another way entirely. She had exquisite control; could wake whole new harmonies of pleasure with careful inflections of touch. Jebi wondered, a little dreamily, why they hadn't ever tried sleeping with a duelist before. And then, for another long span of time, thought became impossible again.

Once Vei had finished with them, she rose and dressed, as unhurried as before. "Your food is cold," she said. "I will have someone bring you a fresh tray, and take away the old." Jebi was too breathless to respond, but she seemed to take that as a compliment.

After Vei had left, Jebi stared up at the ceiling and thought, *What have I done?*

JEBI SPENT THE next several days in a whirl of confusion. People figured out rapidly that they'd slept with Vei—not that either of them had been making any attempt to keep quiet. Shon kept his distance, but given their last interaction, Jebi wasn't much surprised.

Jebi did find out, quite by accident, that duelists prime, by convention, were welcome to take whatever lovers they pleased, so long as it didn't conflict with their duty. A few of the artisans were gossiping about the matter in the common room when they thought Jebi couldn't overhear them from the hallway. Jebi was dying to ask whether, like Hwagugin artists, they were properly considered married to their profession. It would have fit with what they understood of Razanei notions of honor. The best person to ask would be Vei herself.

If it had been up to them, they would have luxuriated in the joy of a new lover. But they remained aware of the danger they were in, and Arazi as well.

Jebi spent a couple of late evenings preparing a plausible fake grammar to present to Nehen. It looked similar enough to the mask Arazi currently wore to pass on a superficial inspection, without the incriminating matter of glyphs to allow the dragon to talk to Jebi mind-to-mind. Arazi took great interest in the glyphs, and Jebi enjoyed working with its help.

They couldn't weasel out of pigment manufacture while doing this, though. Shon had offloaded part of the work onto them, now that they were back. Every time they reduced another artifact or painting or lacquered box, a little part of them shriveled up. The book hadn't been so bad, because there were hundreds if not thousands of copies of it. But even a student copy of a painting expressed a unique vision, one that disappeared forever when it was destroyed.

{*That means books would be the ideal way to mass-produce a source of pigment,*} Arazi commented in fascination. {*You can always print more of them.*}

Jebi blanched when the implications sank in. {*We are not telling Armor,*} they said faintly. Then they reconsidered. Why not trade a few easily replaceable books in order to save one-of-a-kind artworks and artifacts? Jebi had started to see value even in the ugliest, most worn-down necklaces and combs and scrolls. Nevertheless, they didn't like the idea of giving Armor an infinite supply of their precious pigments.

As Jebi worked with the mortar and pestle, they imagined someone tearing up one of *their* paintings, even one of the terrible tigers, and cringed. If they faced any of the dead artists in the afterlife, they would be in for an eternity of punishment. If only they'd thought of this earlier, acted sooner.

They emerged eventually from the workshop to fetch themself more tea. Other artisans stopped talking when Jebi neared them, or gave them sly glances. One even winked at them, presumably in congratulations. Jebi didn't know whether to find the gesture charming or grotesque.

One of the servants slipped and spilled a tray right in front of them. He apologized in an obsequious babble, bowing over and over in a way that made Jebi wince. Then they saw the slip of paper that he had left on the table: *When the duelist prime leaves, you should escape.* Jebi met the servant's eyes, held his gaze, and nodded. He palmed the slip of paper and stuffed it into his mouth, then scurried off.

The next day, Vei approached Jebi after a grueling session going over the fake grammar with Nehen. Despite her dedication to courtesy, a smile warmed Vei's dark eyes. "I thought I'd find you here," she said. "I wanted to let you know—I'm going to be gone for several days on Ministry business, starting two days from now. The deputy minister has some matters to see to, and I must, of course, accompany him."

This was probably duelist for *I have to act as bodyguard.* Jebi flashed on the memory of Vei's unlucky dueling opponent, slashed almost in two, the livid redness of the blood. "When will I see you again?" Jebi asked, fumble-tongued and awkward not because they were unable to disentangle themself from a new lover, but because they remembered the anonymous message. How much time would they have to spring Arazi and escape?

Vei shrugged expressively. "I can't predict the duration of the trip. I'll see you when I see you." She raised a hand to her collar and drew out the mae-deup charm that Jebi had given her before the duel. "I'm sure this will see me back safely."

She hadn't spoken in Hwamal, but Jebi smiled wanly. "Stay safe," they said.

VEI CAME TO them again that night, after everyone but Tia had gone to bed. Jebi almost lost themself in the exchange of caresses. But even as Vei left trails of bruising kisses across their thighs, they thought, *This is an opportunity to steal her keys. I will have no better.*

If only they could *ask* Vei—but Vei worked for the deputy minister. Jebi had no reason to believe her disloyal. And Vei's judgment—or Hafanden's—could prove lethal. Jebi was afraid that if they made Vei choose between the Ministry and them, the choice would be no choice at all. Better not to confront her with it at all.

Bongsunga would have said *I told you so.* Or something more scathing. Jebi could hear her in their head.

*This is what I get for entangling myself with a Razanei, even as a distraction.* Half-Razanei. And the woman who'd killed her sister-in-law.

{*She makes you happy and sad at the same time,*} Arazi said. {*I didn't realize it would be so complicated for you.*}

{*It's the nature of the situation,*} Jebi replied. {*If only I'd found a different distraction—*}

"Something's bothering you," Vei murmured into the nape of their neck.

Jebi laughed weakly. "You're not leaving for another duel, are you?" Another deflection. They didn't like how good they were getting at those.

"I hope not," Vei said, taking the question seriously, as Jebi had known she would. "But you never know. I can't assume that I won't."

"Come back tomorrow night," Jebi said, heart beating rapidly. They hoped that Vei would take it for desire, and drew their hand down between her legs, touching, teasing. It wasn't entirely a lie.

Vei laughed softly. "Oh?" She scissored her legs shut, trapping Jebi's hand; grazed their shoulder with her teeth.

Jebi shivered as pleasure unknotted at their groin. *Think about it later,* they told themself, and surrendered.


THE NEXT MORNING, Jebi woke with the thrumming awareness that they only had one more day to set their plan into motion. Wary of triggering Vei's suspicion, they did not visit Arazi that day. *{I'll make it up to you later, after we're free,}* they promised recklessly. *{I'll show you the yellow forsythias when springtime comes, and the pink and white azaleas for which our last dynasty was named.}*

*{I am glad I can see colors,}* Arazi said, which made Jebi blink. They'd always taken color for granted, although they'd heard once of people who couldn't distinguish certain hues. But then, if Arazi didn't have a sense of taste, there was no guarantee its sense of sight worked the same as a human's.

*{When I see something grass-green, do you see sea-blue instead?}* Jebi wondered.

*{How would I know?}* Arazi asked, reasonably enough.

During the day, they feigned devotion to the task of preparing and painting masks according to the proposed grammars that Nehen had hammered out with them. After all, the supplies were there; it would be a shame to let them go unused. Even if Hafanden would not have approved of Jebi's purpose.

"So devoted," Shon remarked as he glanced over at Jebi's workbench and the half-painted mask they were working on.

At least he was speaking to them again. "I'm doing my best," they said, trying not to let a waspish bite enter their tone.

"If I may—"

His almost mocking formality stung, but then, it was too much to expect anything but awkwardness between them right now. "Go ahead," Jebi said.

Shon pointed out an inconsistency in the pigment's saturation. "I don't know what you're doing," he said, which might or might not have been true, "but you'll want to see to that, all the same."

Jebi could have kicked themself for their carelessness. "Thank you," they said, wary but grateful.

Shon grunted and turned away. "I'm hungry," he announced to no one in particular, and stomped off.

Maybe that had been an invitation. Jebi glanced around and didn't follow him, even though they could have used a bite to eat. No one was watching them, which gave them the opportunity they'd been waiting for all morning.

Striving to make their motions as nonchalant as possible— difficult when they wanted to hyperventilate with nerves—

Jebi liberated an ancient bronze mirror, crusted with verdigris, from the bottom of Shon's pile. They'd been eyeing possibilities in his workspace all morning. Of the items that remained, the mirror looked the most promising.

*It doesn't have to be exact,* Jebi thought, willing their hands to stop shaking. The counterfeit they planned to create just had to be approximately the right shape and size and weight. The paint would take care of the rest.

Jebi mouthed an apology to the long-dead craftsperson who had forged the mirror. It had been fine work once. They could still see the scrollwork on the back through the layer of dull green, the depictions of cranes in flight and clouds. The kind of item an aristocrat would have owned.

They tested the mirror for weak spots, then used a saw to cut off five jagged strips of metal. The noise made them grit their teeth. The mirror was more fragile than it looked, but even so, the work took more time than they liked. With a drill they cut holes in the strips so they could put the fakes on Vei's keyring. It would take magic to make them pass as keys, but Jebi had that part covered.

Jebi was counting on the fact that Vei was going out of town. If she ended up needing one of the keys for *that*, the whole ruse would fail. Jebi was gambling that the keys were all for use in the Summer Palace, or the Ministry of Armor aboveground—or, hell, some swank apartment where she had a secret lover stashed.

*Stop that.* If anything, Jebi was the one keeping secrets, even if they had nothing to do with lovers—a topic neither of them had brought up. After all, Jebi had no claim on Vei, or the other way around, and—they were getting distracted again.

*{Do you always find lovers this distracting, or is Vei special?}* Arazi wanted to know.

*{It's pretty common where love is concerned,}* Jebi answered. *{If you're the kind of person who takes lovers at all, anyway.}*

*{Not something I've ever worried about,}* Arazi said dryly.

Shon had returned and was lingering in the hallway, talking in his curt way to one of the other artists. *I'd better hurry up,* Jebi thought. They hastily hid the metal bars behind some of the jars. Not very good concealment—it wouldn't stand up to a search—but one of the nice things about working with temperamental artists was that they knew not to invade one's space unless invited.

It wasn't until later that afternoon, after a snack break of their own, that Jebi finally returned to the counterfeits. On the way back to their workspace, they'd snagged some extra sketchbooks from the supply closet. No one had blinked, and no one had spotted Jebi slipping in a coil of copper wire between one of the books' pages, either.

Shon, miffed, had muttered something about coming back later, "when it's less noisy," even though the workshop had been quiet at the time, or as quiet as it ever was. Jebi had neither the time nor the patience for his delicate feelings. All they cared about, at this point, was getting him out of the way.

*Here goes nothing.* Jebi retrieved the five bronze rectangles— well, 'rectangle' was generous, but close enough—and arrayed them on the workbench. Next came the jars of pigment, specifically Crane in Winter and Moonlit Footsteps, both of which discouraged viewers from examining the painted object closely. Jebi wondered just how many automata were sneaking around the capital unnoticed, although Vei had assured them that Armor didn't have the resources for omnipresent patrols.

*{Would I notice them?}* Arazi wondered. *{All of your art assumes the viewer is human. Does that affect the way the pigments work?}*

*{I have no idea.}* Jebi was starting to think that Arazi was wasted as a war engine. Armor should employ it as a scholar or natural philosopher instead.

Jebi mixed the paints, dipped their brush, and began, trying not to think about the fact that they planned to deceive a woman they'd bedded.

Vei came again that night to say farewell, just as she had promised. "Stay," Jebi said, their voice husky with mingled dread and desire. If their heart beat any faster, it would fly free.

"I have to leave early in the morning," Vei said. Nevertheless, she allowed Jebi to draw her down to the pallet, as pliant now as she had been aggressive the previous nights.

"So you have something to remember me by," Jebi said in a whisper, wondering that they didn't choke on their own hypocrisy. The hell of it was that they wanted Vei; wanted to see those dark eyes heavy-lidded with pleasure, wanted to hear her laugh, wanted their skin bruised with a constellation of her kisses.

None of that changed the fact that they were about to betray her.

*Don't think,* Jebi told themself. *Loose yourself like an arrow from a bow.* And they caught Vei close in a crushing embrace, and for a time there were no more words, only heat and pressure and the poetry of skin on skin.

At last Vei drowsed. Jebi had forgotten her endurance. They slipped out the five counterfeit keys on their counterfeit ring from their place under the pile of blank sketchbooks. Again, not a particularly good hiding place, but the enchantment held.

Jebi searched Vei's clothes for her keyring, which she always wore at her waist. They were starting to panic when they finally located it under, of all things, one of her shoes. Their own fault, in retrospect. They had insisted on undressing Vei more untidily than she would have on her own.

*This is it. The point of no return.*

Jebi made the substitution, freezing once when the real keys clinked dully. Vei stirred, then began to snore softly. Under other circumstances, Jebi would have been charmed.

*I like you too much for my own good,* Jebi thought wretchedly, finally admitting it to themself. But they had to spring Arazi.

# Chapter
# ELEVEN

JEBI SCARCELY SLEPT that night, although Vei eventually roused and slipped out, pressing a last kiss to Jebi's brow. Feigning sleep was difficult. They wanted to grab Vei's arm and confess the truth about Arazi. But the impulse passed, and Jebi was left alone in the dark with the hallway's light creeping from beneath the door.

They overslept afterward, waking only when Mevem banged on their door. "You alive in there?" Mevem asked. "They've saved some of the breakfast porridge for you, but you should hurry or it's going to get cold."

"Thank you," Jebi muttered, feeling anything but grateful. It wasn't Mevem's fault, though, and they were right. Jebi needed to get up and shovel some food into themself, or hunger would make them even more cranky.

"No problem," Mevem said through the door. Their footsteps retreated.

Jebi paid a visit first to the baths, trying to scrub all traces of Vei's touch away. Not because they hadn't liked it—quite the contrary—but because they felt self-conscious. *I'm guilty,* they thought over and over as they examined the marks and bruises on their skin.

But it was one thing to be attracted to Vei, and another thing to ignore who and what she represented.

Jebi devoured the porridge without tasting it, which was a shame. It was oversalted, but the cooks had contrived to serve abalone porridge, one of their favorites, and a treat that they didn't indulge in often. But today Jebi had no attention to spare for mere food, or for the tea.

With each passing hour, Jebi's paranoia grew. Were the two artificers speaking in hushed voices about the spring-loaded mechanism they were working on, or about something else entirely? Were people looking at Jebi behind their back whenever they bent over their sketches? And most of all, had Hafanden captured Bongsunga after all? Jebi could only trust that their sister had had the good sense to leave the city—but then again, joining revolutionaries hardly counted as good sense, so who could tell?

Jebi gave up all pretense of doing useful work and started doodling moon rabbits. Some of them had great feathered wings, and others dragonfly wings, and still others soared through the sky upon kites. The constellations behind them didn't correspond to any night sky that Jebi was aware of, mainly because they couldn't be bothered to rummage through the shelves of reference materials to look at star charts and almanacs.

*So what if it isn't realistic?* Jebi thought as they added another few freckles of stars for reasons of composition rather than astronomical accuracy. It wasn't as though a telescope would do anyone good underground. They'd whispered wishes to the moon rabbits during the harvest festival as a child, staring up at the moon's coin-pale disc, but the only one of those to come true had involved an extra helping of honey cookies.

Well—they'd wished to become an artist, and that had come true, just not in the way they'd meant. Perhaps moon rabbits were fickle.

Jebi frowned at the page, realizing that they'd started stabbing the paper with their pencil, and hastily turned to the next page. The marks dimpled even the next sheet, and they grimaced at their outburst. Then again, the point of a sketchbook was that no one else had to see its imperfections. They'd generated their share of ugly, misshapen, hastily dashed-off sketches in the past.

In groups of two and three, the other artists headed out of the workshop. Shon was among the first to leave. The last one was Mevem again.

"Dinner," Mevem said, their smile faintly puzzled. "Whatever you're working on, it must be good. Are you ready to share?"

Jebi's face must have shown their dismay, for Mevem raised their hands in apology and backed off. "Never mind, forget I asked," they said. "But come on, you'll think better for having gotten some food into you."

"Did V—did the duelist prime put you up to this?" Jebi demanded. They couldn't think of any other reason for Mevem's newfound solicitousness.

Mevem made a moue. "How'd you guess?"

The two of them headed out of the workshop together, although Jebi brought their sketchbook with them, not wanting to leave it undefended. They weren't the only one paranoid about sketchbooks; Mevem had theirs too.

Jebi said, "I couldn't think of anything else. You don't need to look after me like I'm a child."

"Between you and me," Mevem said, then paused, their mouth crimping into a stubborn line. "Let me put it this way. I make it a rule not to piss off people who know how to use swords." They lowered their voice, then added, "I'd be careful around her. Honor means a lot to our duelist prime."

Was that a warning not to cheat on Vei? "I'll keep that in mind," Jebi said. Frankly, getting caught sleeping with someone else was the least of their concerns. Not that they thought Vei would take that well—who ever did?—but Jebi's betrayals were of a whole different order of magnitude. Vei's duty to the Ministry would supersede personal jealousies.

Dinner was a hushed affair, despite the usual complaints about the food. Jebi refrained from joining in, despite the fact that the oxtail soup was also oversalted. Some of the Razanei didn't like oxtail soup, although it was a Hwagugin delicacy, and another of Jebi's favorites.

*I usually don't talk to the servants,* Jebi thought as they slurped up the soup. They watched one silently wiping off a table after one of the artists had left a mess, scattering chopped green onions and splashes of broth on the surface. Jebi had avoided drawing attention to themself by talking to them, but they knew, despite the fact that the servants always spoke in careful Razanei, that anyone doing such menial work was Hwagugin. The Razanei had a keen sense of their own superiority, and while Jebi assumed that they had servants in their own land, no one except the rich and powerful would have bothered bringing Razanei servants with them when there was a plentiful supply of cheap labor in Administrative Territory Fourteen.

Maybe the oversalted food was a subtle revenge on the cook's part. Jebi couldn't tell whether it was deliberate or not; they'd assumed the cook was just trying to appeal to weird Razanei tastes, but maybe that wasn't it either. They'd never know for sure.

Nevertheless, the mindless sketching had done Jebi some good. This time they were able to concentrate on the food. Of a sudden they missed Bongsunga's cooking. Simple fare, but she would bargain hard over fresh or pickled vegetables and dried meat, and only select ingredients that met her standards for quality. It was probably nostalgia, but even her rice had tasted better.

More than Bongsunga's cooking, Jebi missed cooking with her. They didn't even have to discuss the division of labor, something they'd worked out during their lives together. Jebi didn't know if they'd ever share the simple tasks of chopping and mincing and boiling water again, and it saddened them.

At one point Jebi looked up to find Mevem watching them, not making any attempt to hide their surveillance. Jebi grimaced at them, and Mevem shrugged back, as if to say, *It can't be helped.* The last thing Jebi wanted to do was get someone else in trouble with Vei, so they'd just have to endure it.

Besides, it wasn't as though they'd have to put up with their snooping much longer.

After dinner, Jebi returned to the workshop, ignoring Mevem's mostly friendly jeer of "Spoilsport," as if they were working hard because they wanted to. Most people had retired for the evening, heading either to the common room or congregating in their own rooms. This gave them the opportunity to try something with less chance of getting caught.

Jebi drew out the remaining good-luck charm, the blue one that Vei had declined. Was the dye in this stuff going to be fast? They checked the inside of their collar and grimaced: there was a faint blue smudge against the fabric, and against their skin, where the dye had bled. But given what they'd paid for the charm, they shouldn't have expected proper use of mordants.

*You're just a good-luck charm,* Jebi said to the mae-deup, running their fingers over the artistically arranged knots. *No one is ever going to look at you*—no one Razanei, anyway—*and see anything but a bit of minor magic.* That had bothered them at times in the past, but today they meant to use it to their advantage.

A quick glance around confirmed that everyone in the workshop was occupied with their own projects, or in one case, with a borderline scandalous caricature of an automaton flirting with a Razanei official. Jebi wished they could join the others gawking at that one, but best not to be caught looking, even if Arazi wanted them to stare at the thing for its edification. They mixed up more of the Crane in Winter and Moonlit Footsteps.

There had to be a better way to do this than saturating the charm with the paint, but Jebi didn't have the time to experiment with using the pigment as a fabric dye, or ways to fix the color. *I need your virtue,* Jebi thought at the long-dead artists who had contributed the qualities of concealment and discretion. They didn't yet know if the magic would make *them* hard to notice, or just the *charm*, but there was only one way to find out.

Worse, they didn't know how long the effect would last, or whether there was someone else in the room who'd had the same idea, watching them unseen. But that train of thought led to paranoia. They would have to trust themself and carry this plan through the best they could.

As predicted, blue dye leaked into the paint, leaving a mess. But the stains were difficult for Jebi to focus their eyes on. Their heart rose: evidence that the paint was working as intended. They took long, deep breaths in a futile effort to meditate while it dried.

{*I want a coat of that paint,*} Arazi said in excitement. {*Imagine the pranks I could play!*}

The prospect of an enormous mechanical dragon sneaking up on people for fun alarmed Jebi. {*I don't have enough to coat your entire body,*} they pointed out, and it subsided.

Jebi had to feel around the table when they made the mistake of taking their eyes off the charm. Ah: there it was. Right where they had left it, except the magic had made it difficult to remember. The cord had dried to a stiff consistency, impregnated by the pigment. They worried that it would flake off, but it would have to do.

Jebi pinned the charm back to their collar. No one was watching them. Growing bolder, they dropped a metal container full of old brushes on the floor. It clattered as it rolled, and brushes fell out. Jebi stood over the can, tensed, waiting.

# PHOENIX EXTRAVAGANT

People looked around. Then their eyes clouded and they returned to what they had been doing. The caricaturist was making excellent progress. Jebi had no idea where she meant to hide the finished product, but that wasn't their problem.

*I have a chance,* Jebi thought, although their elation was tempered by the gravity of their mission, however self-imposed. They suppressed a smile out of sheer habit as they walked out of the workshop, their passage unmarked even by Mevem.

JEBI'S HEARTBEAT STUTTERED all the way to the dragon's cavern in the Summer Palace. Strange how the simple act of walking unseen could be so nerve-wracking. They would have felt better if someone had shown some sign of noticing their presence.

Guards, both human and automaton, stood at the junctures and at the ends of each hallway. The lights in the automata's masked eyes flickered as they passed, and Jebi had the uncanny sensation that the creatures marked their passing. But they did not raise the alarm, for which Jebi was grateful.

At last Jebi reached the doors and shoved them open, tensing as they did so. The doors scraped against the floor, but the guards showed no sign of noticing. Jebi left them open as they walked through the cavern to where Arazi awaited them.

*{I can see you, but your image wavers like smoke,}* came Arazi's observation. *{It must not work as strongly on automata as on humans. I wonder how it would affect birds or dogs?}*

Jebi ignored these musings, interesting as they would have been at any other time. The manacles ringed each of the

180

dragon's four legs. They pulled out the stolen keys, but their hands shook so badly that they dropped them with a clatter. One of the guards outside called out an inquiry. Shit, they hadn't known how fragile the charm's effects would be.

Still shaking, Jebi snatched the keys up and jammed the first one into the right forelimb's lock. No luck. Well, there were only five of them, how hard could this be? For the first time they wished they'd spent more time learning disreputable tricks from one of their former lovers. Jebi had dumped her upon learning that she'd stolen art supplies from one of the local merchants, because the only thing more despicable than stealing art was stealing art supplies when you were, as it so happened, the filthy rich scion of a venerable family. It had not been one of their better-thought-out affairs.

Jebi flashed inconveniently on a memory of Vei's lithe fingers entering them just as the fourth key turned in the lock. The manacle clattered free. Jebi jumped back so it wouldn't land on their foot.

They'd just gotten started on the second lock when the doors creaked again.

Hafanden's voice echoed in the cavern, not particularly loudly, but with the accustomed note of authority. "We know you're in there, Tsennan. We can do this the easy way or the hard way. Your choice."

Jebi's heartbeat raced. Fuck, they were trapped *underground*, they couldn't jump out a window. The key ring fell from their nerveless hand.

While they stood paralyzed, Hafanden entered with Vei, her face expressionless, at his side. Four automata flanked them, two on each side.

*{Can you free yourself of the other two locks?}* Jebi asked Arazi.

The dragon had already snatched up the fallen key ring with its talons and had twisted around in an effort to unlock its rear legs.

*I'm in for it now,* Jebi thought, and raced for the door, knowing that they had no hope of squeezing past. Sure enough, one of the automata clocked them on the side of the head, and then darkness rose up to swallow them.

# Chapter
# TWELVE

JEBI AWOKE IN a prison cell, cleaner if not more luxurious than the group cell they'd been stuffed into after they'd given Zakan the slip. They suffered a moment's confused terror thinking that someone had flung them toward the moon, there to be burned up by whatever embers lit its surface. Jebi was not clear on the details, in spite of Bongsunga's efforts. Astronomy had never been their strong suit.

Their eyesight was blurry, and a spike of panic hit them. Would they ever be able to see clearly again? Or would the effect wear off with time?

They blinked, and several figures came into focus through the metal grille that kept them trapped here. Automata—no lower-ranking human guards. Jebi's mouth went dry. Were they about to die, without anyone to witness it?

{*Did you make it out?*} Jebi asked Arazi.

{*I wasn't fast enough,*} the dragon replied, chagrined. {*I'm back where I started. But they have done me no harm, only a few scratches, and I don't have nerves the way you do. You're in a bad way, aren't you?*}

{*You might say that.*} Jebi rose with an effort and peered through the grille until their vision cleared.

Not just automata. Two humans: Girai Hafanden, leaning more heavily than usual upon his cane, and Dzuge Vei. It did not escape Jebi's notice that Vei's hand rested upon the hilt of her sword.

Jebi wanted desperately for Hafanden to shout at them, not because they relished the abuse but because the man's utter icy silence terrified them. They resisted the urge to make an obscene gesture at him; just because he was out there and they were in here didn't mean he couldn't send automata in to beat them up.

"Your behavior," Hafanden said, "is quite incriminating."

They glared hotly at Vei, trying to gauge her involvement. Had she known that Hafanden would return to check on the dragon? Or had the whole mention of a trip been a ruse to reveal Jebi's treachery?

*What did you expect?* they asked themself. They'd known about Vei's loyalties from the beginning, even if she had Hwagugin blood. Being intimate with Jebi didn't change her nature.

But they couldn't help wishing it were otherwise.

"Do you have anything to say about your attempt to free the dragon?" Hafanden said.

Jebi remained silent.

Hafanden sighed, his face creasing in exhausted lines. "I understand that your heritage may make things difficult for you at times," he said. "And that people of your profession have a reputation for being erratic."

*Erratic?* Jebi thought, more outraged by his pretense of sympathy than by his mention of their 'heritage.' What they really wanted was for Vei to say something, even if to repudiate them. But Vei stood still, as honed and intent as the weapon she carried.

"You could at least tell me what you hoped to accomplish. Did you really think you'd escape unnoticed?"

Jebi bit their lip. Anything they said would put Arazi in danger, and Bongsunga as well. They didn't have confidence in their ability to withstand torture, but it would be contemptible to blurt out the truth before things got that bad.

Hafanden had turned to give one of the automata an instruction when Vei finally spoke up. "I advise against torture," she said.

Hafanden's lip curled. "If this is because you are personally involved, Duelist—"

Vei didn't color at the note of distaste in his voice. "Hardly," she said. "Rather, the crude application of pain never inspires people to say anything but the fastest, most plausible lie that will get the pain to stop."

To Jebi's surprise, Hafanden let out a wry chuckle and shook his head. "You've been listening to the Deputy Minister of Ornithology, haven't you?"

Jebi's blood chilled at the mention of the Razanei spymaster. All this time they'd assumed that their warning had given Bongsunga a chance to vanish into... wherever revolutionaries went when they were evading the authorities. What if spies had followed Jebi to the so-called safehouse, raided it after they thoughtlessly exposed it?

*If something's happened to Bongsunga, and it's my fault—*

"Occasionally I talk to people about things that aren't sword techniques or art history," Vei said in a deceptively mild tone. "Besides, you forget. You already have leverage on Tsennan, don't you?"

"Fuck you," Jebi spat.

"Don't be crude," Hafanden said, "even if that *was* what you were doing."

Vei was staring intently at Jebi, as if they had said something more significant than a simple obscenity.

*Wait a second.* If Bongsunga could be held over their head as a threat, that meant—she was still alive? Or was this some elaborate trick that Hafanden and Vei were playing on them?

Jebi wouldn't put such deviousness past Hafanden. He had no reason to treat Jebi as anything but a Fourteener spy. But Vei—maybe Vei was giving them a gift. Maybe Vei had some sympathy for them after all.

*Or maybe I'm just seeing what I want to see.*

"But you're correct," Hafanden went on, unaware of Jebi's turmoil. "The sister is in a very precarious position indeed. Ornithology is very close to bringing her in." He smiled thinly at Jebi. "Will you speak, or do I need to remind you of what will happen to proven revolutionaries?"

"If you think threatening my sister is the way to get me to talk," Jebi snapped, "you should reconsider. I hope she's gotten far from you and your thugs."

"I'm going to leave you to think about the consequences of your actions," Hafanden said. He gestured at the automata, two of which repositioned themselves directly in front of Jebi's cell, staring imperturbably at them. "I will speak with you later."

With that, he and Vei strode down the hall and away from the cell.

"CAN EITHER OF you talk?" Jebi asked the automata after Hafanden had gone.

The automata stared at them, their eyes flickering with that familiar faint light. They didn't answer, or make any sign that they'd heard or understood. On the other hand, they weren't tormenting Jebi the way some human guards might have been tempted to.

*Perhaps,* Jebi thought, *they are only as monstrous as we make them.*

*{They won't respond,}* Arazi said. *{When you study the glyphs and grammars, I learn them too. Their grammars aren't complex enough for conversation.}*

*{Too bad,}* Jebi said. *{It would be nice if I could bribe them to let me out.}*

*{I don't think money means a great deal to my kind,}* Arazi said.

They looked around the cell now that they weren't distracted by the presence of other people—by Hafanden, by Vei, by their uncertainty about Vei's motives. It was spacious, which they appreciated, with a straw mat and a thin blanket on the floor. There was even an old-fashioned chamberpot in the

---

corner. It occurred to Jebi that keeping prisoners in filth would have offended Hafanden's sensibilities, and they snickered.

Their moment of levity faded as reality set in. They walked up to the grille and tested the door. It rattled slightly, but didn't give. Jebi had no illusions that they could break out of the cell. Besides, they'd always been a wimp about bruises, to their sister-in-law's amusement.

"I've fucked up," Jebi whispered, not caring if the automata overheard them. "What do I do now?"

Would Hafanden leave them here to die of thirst or starvation? Jebi was suddenly, unpleasantly aware of how much they longed for tea, or water, or even the deeply mediocre broth that the kitchen sometimes served in the Summer Palace.

The automata didn't answer. Jebi hadn't expected them to.

{I don't suppose you hid the keys before they locked you back in,} Jebi said to Arazi.

{No,} it said. {Hafanden's soldiers retrieved those.}

So the escape attempt had been for nothing.

{There must be a way to rescue you,} Arazi said, and Jebi wasn't sure whether to laugh or cry. Sure, the dragon was a big, frightening war engine, but it was still a prisoner.

{Let me know if you come up with something,} Jebi said without hope, and sat down on the mattress.


JEBI LOST TRACK of time's passage. One would think that they'd be used to this timelessness by now; but it never grew *familiar*. The two automata who guarded it never moved. Another arrived at irregular intervals, bearing trays with weak tea and rice porridge. Jebi fell upon both, angry at themself at their pathetic gratitude. They couldn't even complain about the awfulness of the porridge, because it wasn't any *more* awful than what they'd gotten used to eating.

Through this time, Arazi kept them company. Jebi had to fight off their own irrational anger at the situation when they spoke to it. The endless hours without other humans wore on them, although they would have suffered worse without at least the dragon to talk to.

*{If you got free,}* Jebi asked it once, *{where would you go? What would you do?}*

*{I would like to go somewhere distant from all this talk of war,}* Arazi said after a pause so long that Jebi was afraid that they had offended it. *{Somewhere I can live without bothering anyone, among friends. Surely such a place exists, even for an automaton.}*

*{There are remote mountains, and I've heard of deserts in faraway lands,}* Jebi said. They weren't clear on the geography involved, although they remembered the map with its neatly planned conquests and targets on the wall of Hafanden's office in the Summer Palace. *{As for friends...}*

*{Yes?}*

Their heart ached as they thought of Bongsunga's mission, her determination to use the dragon against the Razanei. *{There are people who wouldn't be afraid of you,}* Jebi said slowly. *{But some of them would want to use you just as Hafanden did, like my sister. They wouldn't be interested in what you want for yourself.}*

Another, longer pause. *{At least you are honest with me,}* Arazi said. *{Is that what you want to do, if we escape together?}*

*{No, no,}* Jebi said vehemently, although they weren't sure

their own motives were as pure as they insisted. If someone threatened their sister, wouldn't they want to rescue her by whatever means necessary? Especially since Hafanden had already threatened her?

*{You were the only one who thought to give me a voice,}* Arazi said. *{I owe you for that, if nothing else.}*

That only made Jebi feel more wretched. *{I did it because I needed information,}* they said, compelled into honesty. *{I didn't think of it earlier.}*

*{Nevertheless.}*

Jebi's stomach seized up when they heard footsteps. What was going to happen now?

They didn't have to wait long to find out. Hafanden had returned. This time he was accompanied not just by two automata, but two guards—and no Vei.

*This can't mean anything good.*

"You have information I need," Hafanden said without preamble. "I will get it from you one way or another."

"Go to hell," Jebi said, unwisely.

"It's a pity," he said. "Your Razanei is excellent, your mannerisms almost perfect, exactly the sort of assimilation we wish to encourage in Fourteeners. But the truth is, these are desperate times, and I am running out of options."

"If you're going to kill me, do it already." They didn't mean it—they weren't brave like Bongsunga or Jia—but the words flew out of their mouth anyway.

Hafanden's endless fussy need to *explain* things was going to be the death of him. Or, more accurately, of Jebi. "Ordinarily I agree with Vei and my counterpart at the Ministry of Ornithology," he said. "But it's been a week."

Jebi's heart sank. That long? How could they not have noticed, even without sight of daylight?

"Guards," he said, "begin." And he nodded to the nearest one.

Jebi had ample opportunity to examine the two guards as they came forward. Both were large, sturdily built, the one on the left running toward fat at a time when few Hwagugin, except prosperous people like Hak, could afford that much food. Jebi had every confidence that Hafanden had selected them for their strength, loyalty, and aptitude for punishment.

"Last chance," Hafanden said as the guards unlocked the door to the cell. "I would prefer to deliver you back to your lover intact."

The mention of Vei broke something in Jebi that they hadn't known existed. When the door opened, Jebi charged at the guards, howling at the top of their lungs. They'd always wondered, in the past, what gave soldiers the courage to rush at the enemy in the face of bullets and blades. Maybe it had nothing to do with courage, and more to do with sheer aggravation.

Their dream of breaking past the guards and pelting down the halls and up the stairs to freedom lasted a second at best. Maybe less. They might as well have run at a brick wall. The guards caught them handily and flung them down so hard that they knocked the breath out of Jebi. For several long panicked moments, Jebi couldn't see or hear or think about anything but the brutal fact of pain.

The beating could have lasted anywhere from seconds to a century. Jebi screamed and struggled, to no avail. The guards were professionals, which prompted the question of how often they'd done this before.

By slow degrees Jebi became aware that the hitting and kicking had stopped. Their mouth tasted of blood and a ringing noise filled their head. They wished they'd taken the time, long ago, to ask Jia to teach them how to fight, but they'd never been interested in the martial disciplines. They were paying for it now.

*Who are you kidding?* they thought, wishing that something they'd always taken for granted—breathing—didn't wake waves of agony. *I would have had to spend hours on it, and those were hours I spent on learning how to paint.*

Hafanden's voice came to them as though from a distance of mountains and moons. "I will ask as often as necessary. Where were you planning to go?"

Jebi bit the inside of their mouth. Not like more blood made a difference at this point.

Either Hafanden's patience was wearing thin, or the guards were bullies. Jebi didn't see a practical difference. They'd scarcely had a chance to draw a shuddering breath, curled up on the floor, when the guards kicked them again, first in the ribs, then in the stomach.

Jebi retched, bringing up nothing but bile. It had been too long since they'd last ate. Too bad they hadn't feasted so they could puke all over Hafanden's fucking shoes.

"All right," Hafanden said, his voice even more distant, "one last thing. Because I feel you deserve to know."

They couldn't help themself. "Know what?" Jebi wheezed. It hurt to speak. It hurt to breathe. It hurt to do anything, or to do nothing at all. Perhaps this was the torturer's secret: the impossibility of escaping pain.

"Your sister," Hafanden said, then stopped.

Jebi had no patience left, either. "If you did anything—"
They coughed, choked, spat out blood. "If you *killed her*—"

"On the contrary," Hafanden said, his tone viciously
reasonable. "She's more useful to us alive."

Jebi discovered, to their dismay, that hot tears were leaking
out of their eyes. They longed to scrub them away, but they
wouldn't give Hafanden the satisfaction of seeing their
discomfort. "More useful how?"

*Don't talk to him,* a frantic voice in the back of their head
insisted. *The more you talk, the more you give away.* But it
was so hard to think past the mosaic of pain that had replaced
their body, and they had no resistance left in them.

"That is the question, isn't it?" Hafanden said, as though
Jebi had made some penetrating observation, instead of asking
him to explain what the hell he was going on about. "How
involved are you with her games, and for how long has this
been going on?"

"Look," Jebi burst out, "just do whatever you're going to
do and get it over with." They stopped, hacked out a cough
that also tasted like blood. At this rate, they were going to be
tasting blood for the rest of their life. "I don't know anything
about Bongsunga that *you* didn't tell me to begin with. It's not
as if we get along anyway."

They stopped short, appalled that they'd revealed something
so personal to an enemy. For that was what he was, in more
ways than one; what he had been ever since he blackmailed
Jebi into taking a position with the Ministry, and never mind
that he'd gotten them out of the rain.

"All right," Hafanden said coolly, "let's see how much you
knew about your sister's revolutionary connections."

Jebi's throat constricted in sheer atavistic terror. *What if he knows about the safehouse?* And what if currently Bongsunga occupied a cell elsewhere in the Summer Palace, or aboveground in the Ministry proper?

But that wasn't what Hafanden was interested in talking about—not yet, anyway. "Tell me," he said, "what do you know about her overseas connections?"

Jebi blinked stupidly. Overseas what? Then the memory returned to them, of that visit to the safehouse. Bongsunga had mentioned revolutionaries in exile. There'd been something in there about alliances with foreign powers, hadn't there? Jebi wished they'd paid closer attention, except it had been a hectic night, and right now they weren't in the best condition, either.

"Your sister and her friends," Hafanden said, in a voice so level that it made Jebi curl up in terror, "are so determined to overturn Razanei rule that they're willing to work with whatever Western powers smile and offer them money. For make no mistake—the Westerners are just as hungry for Territory Fourteen's resources, and they will be far less merciful than we have been if they 'liberate' you."

"*You're* here," Jebi said pointedly, "and the Westerners aren't. I've never seen a Westerner in my life." For that matter, they didn't have a clear idea of what Westerners looked like. They appeared occasionally in Bongsunga's detective novels, either as exotic courtesans or equally exotic hypercompetent villains, although Jebi had their doubts about the accuracy of the descriptions—did humans really come with orange hair, for instance? And presumably there were real live Westerners who chose career paths other than those.

Hafanden looked grim. By now Jebi had recovered enough

that they could peek up at his face. The angle only made him look more imposing, and Jebi couldn't help but flinch at the sight of his cane. They bet it made a great impromptu weapon.

"I hope you never have cause to meet a Westerner," Hafanden said. "Because if you do, then I will have failed in my duty."

Jebi couldn't conceal their confusion.

"This may be difficult for you to believe," he went on, "but as a Fourteener you are one of my charges. The duty of the Ministry of Armor is to *protect*. That includes you, believe it or not."

"So you weren't going to kill me after all?" Jebi shot back.

A flicker of irritation crossed his face. "Is that what you think of me?"

"I know you had Issemi killed!" *Great,* Jebi thought a moment later, *he doesn't even have to have you tortured. Just give away everything you know, why don't you?*

Even so, the fact that they didn't have to keep their knowledge a secret anymore gave them a moment's relief, however illusory.

The guards looked at Hafanden. "Again?" one of them asked. "This one's insolent, for a Fourteener."

"No, that won't be necessary," Hafanden said with deadly confidence.

"Bongsunga's gone where you'll never find her," Jebi said, finding their way to defiance too late. They had no idea if any of it was true, or if Hafanden would fall for the bluff. "You can send your automata and your thugs after her. It won't do a bit of good. If you think threatening her is going to make me cave to your demands, you can think again. You might as well grind me up for your paints for all the good it'll do you."

To Jebi's horror, Hafanden started to laugh. He bent over the cane, wheezing. They were almost *worried* for him, which was ridiculous considering that he'd had them tortured.

"Is *that* what you've been thinking all this time?" Hafanden demanded.

"That's what you *let* me think," Jebi said, resenting the incredulous note in his voice. After all, wasn't that what he'd done? Threatened Bongsunga in order to recruit them?

He shook his head in amazement. "I'm more used to dealing with devious minds... You have it exactly backwards. I didn't threaten your sister in order to recruit you. After all, I could have my pick of artists. Willing ones, even.

"No," Hafanden said as horror gnawed at Jebi's stomach, "it's the other way around. I had you brought in as a favor to Ornithology. *You're* our leverage on your *sister.*"

# Chapter
# THIRTEEN

THE HOURS CRAWLED past. Jebi huddled miserably in their cell, unable to think about anything but how badly they'd fucked up. If only they hadn't gotten the damnable name certificate... if only they hadn't taken the Ministry of Art exam and then quarreled with Bongsunga... if only they hadn't accepted the job with the Ministry of Armor. Jebi wasn't under any illusions that Hafanden would have let them go, but they should have made a better effort to escape.

The only consolation was that Jebi trusted Bongsunga's common sense. Bongsunga wouldn't return for them, blood tie or no blood tie. She'd know that the Razanei couldn't be trusted to release their hostage, and that the best course of action would be to stay free and continue to work against them.

Still, Jebi couldn't help wishing that their sister would come to their rescue after all.

{I'm here,} Arazi whispered to them. {I won't let anything happen to you.}

{Any luck with your chains?} Jebi shot back, letting their bitterness seep into their tone.

Another of those nuanced silences. Then: {No.}

Jebi slumped. They'd known the answer; why torment them both with the question? {Thanks anyway,} they said dully.

Their entire body hurt, although they didn't think anything was broken. Jebi, always a coward about injuries, didn't investigate closely. Hafanden's goons could have done permanent damage if they'd wanted to. Jebi knew from talking to Jia, once upon a time, that people trained in such things could work you over without doing anything irreversible.

A small eternity of tepid meals later—the same kitchen offerings of porridge and small side dishes, pickled or fermented for the season—Jebi realized they were running a fever. They blinked blearily at the cell walls, which they didn't recall looking so blurry earlier. And their head ached miserably, which they hadn't noticed before because everything *else* hurt so much.

Jebi wanted many things at this point. They wanted to go back to their room in Bongsunga's house, assuming the Razanei hadn't confiscated it on some pretext, and huddle in their old room. They wanted Bongsunga to bring them porridge that actually tasted good, not that they could tell good food from mediocre at this point.

Hell, since they were malingering in the land of impossible fantasies, why not go for broke? They wished the fucking

Razanei had stayed home, or invaded someone else. They weren't clear on who that someone else would be, given their shaky grasp of geography, and maybe wishing the Razanei on some other innocent country was just cruel. Anything so that they wouldn't be stuck in this fucking cell.

*If the Razanei hadn't come, Vei would never have been born,* a traitorous voice whispered in the back of their mind. Although Vei had to have been born years before the invasion, given her age, during the uneasy last years of the Azalea Throne, when certain factions had gotten in bed with Razanei visitors.

*Vei did nothing to save me,* Jebi retorted inside, and then felt even more traitorous. Doubt gnawed inside them: had Vei known about Hafanden's last visit? Sanctioned it, even? Or simply refused to intervene?

Rationally, Jebi understood that Armor's duelist prime could hardly defy its deputy minister, at least not openly. All the same, Jebi resented her for not trying harder; for not being here when they needed someone in their corner. And never mind that stealing Vei's keys was how they'd gotten into this fix in the first place.

They settled into a miserable half-sleep, pricked through by unhappy dreams. Some of them concerned a simpler time, before the Razanei came, when they'd only been a teenager— just on the verge of adulthood. They hadn't cared about the rumors of the Razanei armies; had thought them exaggerated gossip, despite their sister-in-law's insistence otherwise. Other dreams concerned Arazi and its endless pacing, the dismal musicality of its chains.

Jebi drifted back awake, or more accurately, half-awake.

They wondered, in a fit of confusion, what had happened to the art supplies they'd left with Hak. For that matter, had Hak been in on the scheme from the beginning? Jebi couldn't believe it of her, despite her involvement with the antiquities trade, but perhaps that was simply naivety on their part.

More time passed; waves of nausea joined the pain. Periodically an automaton entered the cell to empty the chamberpot. Jebi wondered if they disliked being stuck with menial chores; not like Hafanden would have asked them. Even the Hwagugin servants who staffed the Summer Palace had a choice not to serve at all, however unpleasant the alternative.

Jebi contemplated the universal unfairness of life, which let horrible people like Hafanden wander around torturing artists who just wanted to be left alone to paint, to say nothing of well-meaning pacifist dragons. They wondered if the mae-deup charm they'd given Vei had brought *her* any luck. The one Jebi had kept hadn't done them a lick of good.

Out of boredom or frustration or maybe both, Jebi spat into a corner of the cell where some dirt had gathered and began mixing it into (admittedly disgusting) mud. It wasn't much to work with, for which they had Hafanden's high standards for cleanliness to thank. But working with earth pigments wasn't new to them. And it wasn't as if they were spoilt for choice.

{Water is water, wherever it comes from,} Arazi said philosophically, which only made Jebi think of any number of jokes involving piss and bad rice wine.

Jebi daubed a crude depiction of the moon and one frolicking winged moon rabbit before running out of mud. Now that they had something to do, they decided they ought to give the project more consideration. Just because this particular art installation was unlikely to have a human audience—they imagined Hafanden would simply let them die here of old age, since Bongsunga wasn't going to show up—didn't mean they didn't have *standards*. If they were going to decorate their miserable, overly bright cell, they wanted to do it right.

{*I'm watching,*} Arazi said. {*Paint for me.*}

{*Yes,*} Jebi said, cheering up at the thought of a sympathetic audience.

The moon was a done deal, or anyway, Jebi didn't have the heart to scrape it off and redo it. So they'd have to plan everything else around it. They'd never done three walls quite like this, and moreover the grille that separated them from their captors meant that no one would be able to get a clear view of the artwork unless they came *into* the cell. Jebi couldn't imagine that anyone would do that voluntarily.

*At least I'll leave some entertainment for the next person to die of old age down here,* Jebi thought, working up some macabre cheer. Besides, as much as they didn't *want* to be here, the challenge of making this place more interesting was starting to appeal to them, and they wanted to show their best work to Arazi. No wonder people said artists had no common sense.

First Jebi gathered the dirt into a pile. There was more of it than they had realized, perhaps because feverish people had better (worse?) things to ponder than a little harmless dust. Bongsunga had higher standards, but then, Bongsunga wasn't the one who went around with random stains on their clothing after accidentally spilling lamp black or vermilion. Jebi estimated the amount of mud they had to work with. Normally they preferred denser, more elaborated styles of art, but they'd have to compromise and make more use of negative space.

The more they thought about this, the more they liked the idea. The night sky might be full of stars and celestial attendants and the occasional paragliding moon rabbit, but they'd heard an astrologer explain once that vast distances separated these celestial bodies from each other. It seemed incredible to Jebi that the stars were suns so far away that they only appeared as pinpricks of light, and they weren't clear on what kind of distances were involved. Bongsunga would have been able to unpuzzle it; she'd always had a good head for math. Jebi wondered if knowing the figures made the sky's spectacles more or less wondrous.

Jebi thought longingly of a time when they'd been able to go up onto the roof of their old house with Bongsunga and cling precariously to the roof-tiles and stare up at the shimmering expanse of the night sky. They hadn't done that in years, not because they'd gotten any worse at climbing but because of the Razanei curfew. The Azalea Throne's government had had one too, but they'd been lax about enforcing it. They supposed, among other things, the Razanei had a justifiable fear of rooftop snipers, especially during the early years.

Jebi closed their eyes and tried to visualize the sky during the first brisk nights of spring, around the time of year when the forsythias would bloom yellow all throughout the city. They imagined the scatter of constellations as four-petaled forsythia blossoms, whimsically adrift in the sea of darkness. Arazi's earlier words came back to them, and its wish for somewhere to live peacefully. Why not the moon?

Hafanden might have plans for a moon base and there

might even be Westerners there already—no, that didn't make sense. Jebi didn't have a clear idea of how the logistics would work, but surely the Razanei had the moon under surveillance with whatever telescopes they'd built. Their heart thumped painfully as they remembered the news of the Razanei moving to secure the famous Hwagugin observatory, oldest of its kind on the continent. At the time Jebi had dismissed the news as uninteresting, reckoning the Razanei had some military use for the high ground. They'd been thinking of ordinary guard posts, rather than observing the *moon*.

*I can make it real here, even if it isn't real outside my cell,* Jebi thought, eyes still closed. A three-wall panorama depicting a journey from the earth below through the sky and finally to the moon. Yes. That would work. They could borrow some compositional elements from those hoary old paintings of the Eight Immortals flying through the air or meditating on mountaintops. After all, who would criticize them?

Then, because Jebi didn't trust themself to keep everything in their head while they were borderline feverish, they scratched out preliminary sketches on the floor. They were hard to see, even in the ubiquitous light, and Jebi stepped on their own drawings more than once. But the act of producing the sketches, however tenuous, helped fix the planned images in their mind. Saving grace: Jebi's jailers had, at least, given them adequate water, even if it pained them to pour it onto the dirt.

They considered improvising a brush from a rag torn from their clothing, or their hair. But fingers were more direct, and besides, while Jebi had learned how to make their own brushes, they doubted that their extremely greasy, tangled hair would make for good brushes even if it had any appreciable length. Granted that they were shaggier than usual—how fast did hair grow, anyway?—but that didn't help with the greasiness. They tried not to think about how they reeked after this long without a bath.

*{I can't smell you, anyway,}* Arazi said, which it probably intended to be comforting.

Jebi choked back a laugh. *{Thanks, I think.}*

They began painting, taking frequent breaks. Sometimes they fell asleep next to the mud and had to rewet it from their dwindling supply of water. They became familiar with grit in their mouth and the unappetizing taste of dirt. At least the automata didn't make wisecracks about their endeavor.

Jebi had just paused for the—third? fourth?—time to admire their handiwork when they heard the footsteps behind them. *Fuck you,* they thought, their back resolutely to the grille. Whoever had come—assuming it was anyone human—could wait. The automata wouldn't care one way or the other. After all, it wasn't as though Jebi had the strength to resist them.

*This might be my best work yet,* Jebi thought, *and only Arazi will ever appreciate it.* And maybe the other automata as well, if they possessed higher virtues like a love of aesthetics.

*'Higher virtues,' who am I kidding? It's not as if human beings have shown any great moral superiority.*

The triptych spread across all three walls. Jebi had planned the composition so that it struck the viewer with full force from this exact vantage point, not something they had much prior experience with. Going to jail could open up new artistic horizons! Even if they would rather have skipped the being-in-jail part of the experience.

In the first part, moon rabbits and hawks soared above the peninsula's mountains, with a tantalizing glimpse of the sea along the southern coast. Jebi wished for one heartstop moment that they could fly—that ancient dream—and see what the world looked like from above. Alas, imagination would have to suffice.

In the second, a dragon that resembled Arazi soared amid celestial attendants tossing balls back and forth. Jebi didn't have any idea why celestial folk would play games all day— it sounded boring, honestly—but maybe a mere earthbound mortal like themself wasn't meant to understand. Or maybe it was that the artists who painted such things preferred not to challenge whoever had first come up with the visual trope. They'd included two tiny figures on the dragon's back, waving at the celestial attendants.

In the third and final part, Jebi had depicted a moon-colony based on Arazi's wishes, with fanciful architecture with elongated walls and elaborate roofs hinted at by frenzied smears of mud, cities opening up layer after layer like a chrysanthemum in full bloom. None of the cities had walls. On a peaceful moon, none should be necessary.

"Tsennan," said a baffled and all too familiar voice, "*what are you doing?*"

"Go 'way," Jebi mumbled. They'd meant to sound more authoritative, but their scratchy throat made that impossible.

Vei persisted, though Jebi was convinced that she was a figment of their imagination. Why would Vei come back, except with Hafanden, to torment them with their helplessness? Or even worse, to confirm that Hafanden had captured Bongsunga after all.

"Tsennan, look at me."

Jebi refused. The longer they could avoid looking at Vei, the longer they could deny that she was here. *It's a dream, it's a figment, it's a ghost mirroring my own hopes back to me.*

"All right, *don't* look at me," the figment-who-couldn't-possibly-be-Vei said, starting to sound exasperated. "It'll be harder to get you out of here, but I suppose I can manage. It's too bad I can't knock you out and *carry* you out of here, but unlike the authors of those dreadful novels where you're kidnapped and held captive by the strangely suave and attractive leader of the local bandits, I happen to know that concussions are nothing to joke about, and you've already had one."

All right, *that* convinced Jebi this was Vei. The only part of the diatribe that Jebi grasped, however, was the bit about being knocked out. They weren't going to stand for that, whatever Vei's motives.

Just as Vei unlocked the grille, Jebi whirled and charged Vei, shrieking like an offended magpie. Vei sidestepped out of sheer habit—Jebi had managed to forget how swift her reflexes were—then cursed under her breath as Jebi tripped over the uneven ground and smashed into the side of the opening.

"Fuck," Jebi tried to say. They tasted blood.

*{I think she's trying to help,}* Arazi ventured. *{Maybe you should let her.}*

Vei caught Jebi and propped them up. "That was not your wisest move," she said. "Tsennan—I'm sorry: Jebi."

"Doesn't matter," Jebi muttered, and spat out the blood. For a macabre moment they wondered if they could incorporate it into the installation.

Vei had read their mind, or knew enough about the unsavory habits of bored artists, because she said, "We don't need any more marks in the prison cell! And look, I managed to sneak out the last of the Phoenix Extravagant and all the rarest pigments I could gather up."

Jebi struggled, although they gave up on the shrieking on the grounds that they didn't want to get punched in the mouth and lose a tooth. It was a miracle they hadn't misplaced one already. Unless it had happened and they hadn't realized it.

"Quit that!" Vei said, her voice rising. "I would prefer to do this peacefully."

"You can slice me in half just like you did that poor duelist," Jebi yelled, "but my sister will never surrender to you Razanei bastards!"

"I may literally be a bastard," Vei said, and Jebi was sure they hadn't imagined the way she stiffened momentarily when they spoke the word, "but I'm *half*-Razanei, and I have *opinions*, thank you very much. Would you *stop that* and let me help you get out of here?"

Jebi slumped in her arms, and Vei cursed again, strong as she was; Jebi was not exactly well-balanced at the moment. "Why would you do that?" Jebi slurred.

"I'm not going to let the deputy minister 'disappear' you."

"It's a bit late for that."

"And I'm not going to let him use you as bait, either. We've got to get out of here before one of the guards realizes that I'm abusing my authority."

Jebi's imagination inconveniently supplied visions of much more pleasurable ways that Vei could 'abuse' her authority. They grimaced, which Vei naturally misinterpreted.

"It may sound incredible to you," Vei said, "but you are not the only one who has qualms about the Ministry's actions."

"Which ones?" Jebi asked pointedly. "How long have you known about the deputy minister's plans?"

"Since the beginning," Vei said. "But it would have hardly made sense for me to cut him down the second I found out!" Her exasperation was showing again. "Think about *strategy* for a second."

*{She's making sense,}* Arazi said, *{if you think she's telling the truth.}*

*{Why,}* Jebi said, *{do you think she's telling the truth?}*

*{I do.}*

Jebi gaped, partly at Vei, partly at the dragon's assured tone. "What does baduk"—what was the Razanei word for it again? they were having trouble thinking—"I mean, what does go have to do with anything? Or soldiers and supply lines?"

"I didn't realize artists were so literal," Vei said dryly. "I could have gotten rid of Hafanden, and then I would have been executed for my trouble—I'm excellent with a sword and a passable shot with a rifle, but one of me isn't going to do much good against an army. And then the minister would have appointed another deputy minister, and the whole program would have gone on with scarcely a hitch. I needed a way to take it down forever."

"Yes," Jebi said, their mouth puckering, "you've done so much to—"

Vei continued speaking as though she hadn't heard Jebi, without raising her voice. "The plan went bad when Hafanden turned on Issemi. We were going to sabotage the entire production run of war-dragons. But Hafanden isn't stupid, and he insisted on a test, and—well, you know what happened."

"You were her friend, after all," Jebi said, finally understanding. "But why didn't you *tell* me?"

Vei switched to speaking in near-perfect Hwamal, with only the faintest hint of a Razanei accent. "You wouldn't," Vei said with delicate precision, "be the first Hwagugin to pledge loyalty to the Sun in Glory. For money, or for convenience, or hope of a new beginning. For a thousand reasons. I'm not one to judge. I couldn't be certain of your loyalties—and then I *was*, but Hafanden was there."

"I had to scotch it all by getting caught," Jebi said. If only— but they hadn't known, either.

"There's more," Vei said, "but I recommend getting out of here first and worrying about details later."

Jebi balked. "Only if you get Arazi out too." That had been the original plan, after all.

Jebi's heart swelled when Vei, instead of arguing, nodded briskly. "That complicates the op—"

"It's so sexy when you talk military," Jebi rasped, even though they didn't have any *current* amorous intent. Especially when their whole body hurt this badly. Maybe attempting to ram Vei hadn't been their brightest idea, especially since it had resulted in crashing into unyielding metal instead.

"Come *on*," Vei said. "We only have so much time, as much as I would like to keep holding you."

"You would?" Jebi didn't realize they had said that out loud until the corners of Vei's mouth rose in a sudden rare smile, and then their heart lifted at the same time that heat rushed to their cheeks and the back of their neck.

"Don't get any ideas," Vei said, "but I'm going to bind your wrists. You'll have to carry the bag—if we move quickly, no one will ask why you have it, and I'll be out in front. You have to look like my prisoner. You should be able to undo the knots with a sharp tug, but don't do it unless we have no choice but to run. Got it?"

"Got it," Jebi mumbled.

Vei passed over the bag, then secured the knots with professional efficiency, making Jebi wonder where she'd picked up that particular skill, and whether it was something they could explore later, after they'd escaped the Summer Palace and its hideous secrets. Then she unsheathed her sword. "It's nonsense, going around with live steel like this," she said, her mouth twisting, "but it will make for excellent theater. I'll prod you with the tip to let you know where to go."

Jebi didn't like this part of the plan, even if they knew, rationally, that Vei had unparalleled control of her blade and wouldn't so much as part a thread of their clothes by accident. The delicate touch of the swordpoint guided them out of the prison complex, away from the cell that they had so painstakingly decorated. *Let Hafanden and Shon try to reduce that in a mortar after I fetch up dead.*

They passed a number of guards, none of whom questioned Vei. And why would they? She was the Ministry of Armor's duelist prime, answerable only to the deputy minister himself. The unsheathed steel helped, a naked threat.

For her part, Vei didn't speak; didn't explain herself. It would only have invited questions. Jebi wished she'd say something, or walk more loudly. They could barely hear her footsteps. It made them feel as though they were being ushered to the gates of the underworld by a ghost.

After a lot of painful trudging, with only the pinprick pressure of the swordpoint at their back, Jebi recognized the labyrinthine route that led to Arazi's separate prison.

*{I will be ready,}* the dragon promised. *{Not like last time.}*

Jebi's heart ached. *{My ineptness wasn't your fault!}*

*{Still.}*

One of the guards to Arazi's cavern frowned at Jebi. Then his gaze slid past their face, presumably to Vei. He shook his head minutely when the other guard glanced aside, clearly bored with the proceedings.

"I have important business here," Vei said, her voice even.

Jebi admired her sangfroid and wished they didn't want so badly to piss themself. *I can endure until we get out of here,* they told their bladder.

"Of course, Duelist Prime," the guard said. "I wouldn't dream of standing in your way."

Jebi risked turning to look back at Vei. The sword's tip pressed into the small of their back. They couldn't tell if it had pierced skin or not; they expected she kept her blade as sharp as night.

Vei's countenance revealed nothing. "Then let us through."

The doors opened, and the clanking music of Arazi's chains came to them as from a great distance.

Helplessly, Jebi walked into the cavern, followed by Vei.

The doors slammed shut. And Hafanden was there, waiting for them.

*Chapter*
# FOURTEEN

JEBI'S STOMACH PLUMMETED. They thought about running, despite knowing that Vei would then have no choice but to cut them down, unless she wanted to die too. Why hadn't they anticipated this turn of events?

Or—had Vei led them into this trap? But why? After all, Jebi had already been imprisoned. It wasn't as if they'd had any opportunity to escape.

Jebi turned slowly to face Vei, struggling to hide their dismay.

Was it their imagination, or was Vei's face paler than usual? She tipped her chin up, her gaze fixed not on Jebi but on Hafanden.

Jebi reoriented themself to face Hafanden. This time they noticed his attendants, some of them human guards, some of them automata. And then they realized that Vei wasn't looking at Hafanden, but at a *specific* automaton.

"The hell?" Jebi whispered, staring at the one that didn't resemble the others. It was shorter, about their height. No— *exactly* their height. Their build, with limbs carefully sculpted to resemble theirs, modulo the fact that Jebi had lost weight during their imprisonment.

And its mask—unlike the traditional masks with their alien motifs, it had been painted in the realist style, to resemble Jebi themself. Or an idealized version of them, anyway; Jebi was sure their skin didn't currently have that fresh glow, or their mouth that bland, untroubled curve.

It would have been trivial for the artisans in the workshop to concoct this. Jebi could have done it themself if it had ever occurred to them. And they knew by now that the mystical pigments that controlled the automaton's behavior had little in the way of conventional color. A painter could have simply applied the mystical pigments beneath the normal ones.

Jebi started to shake; hated themself for showing weakness in front of Hafanden. "I've become a liability, haven't I?" they said. Even so—"That automaton isn't going to fool my sister."

Jebi had almost said *thing*, derisively, but an odd qualm stopped them. After all, no one had given the automaton any choice in this farce. It was even more a prisoner of circumstance than they were. Jebi could speak and rebel; the automaton could only act as its grammar directed.

*If only I could free you,* Jebi thought. Would it help them? Run amok? Something else?

"Not from close up," Hafanden was saying, and Jebi forced themself to focus on his words. To their aggravation, creases lined his face, as though he only wanted to go back to bed; as though this was a sacrifice on his part, a kindness to them.

"This is a travesty," Vei said crisply. "Automata should never *replace* people."

"Under ordinary circumstances I would agree with you," Hafanden said as though they were debating literature or philosophy over dinner. "But the situation has forced my hand."

Behind them, Arazi came to a halt right behind Hafanden. Hafanden paid it no heed.

*{If he comes within reach—}* Jebi said.

*{I can knock him aside,}* Arazi said, but it sounded uncertain. *{I don't want to injure him.}*

"Your sister's alliances are even more far-flung and dangerous than I had originally believed," Hafanden added, "based on the latest briefing I received from Ornithology. It's imperative that she be brought in so that we can untangle her connections."

Hot tears slid out of the corners of Jebi's eyes. *I can't let this happen,* they thought. But what were they going to do? Grab Vei's sword and swing at Hafanden? They didn't have the faintest idea how to wield a blade, let alone get past all the guards.

Hafanden shook his head. "It's not your fault," he said, almost gently.

Jebi gaped at him.

"You're acting to protect your family," he said. "It's a natural impulse. I'm convinced you think this is for the good of Territory Fourteen. You're mistaken, of course. You're used to thinking of what's in front of you, not the broader picture."

Jebi wished he would stop condescending to them. Just because they weren't immersed in matters of national security didn't mean they were *stupid*. But an idea had occurred to them. They didn't know if it would work. On the other hand, they didn't have much to lose.

Hafanden nodded curtly at Vei. "I'm sorry it's come to this," he said, as courteous as he had to be and no more, "but I require you to execute the artist Tesserao Tsennan. If nothing else, we can make use of their creations in the next phase of the project. Their stubbornness ought to result in *some* form of usable pigment, even if it's not the Phoenix Extravagant we've had such difficulties sourcing."

"A loyalty test," Vei murmured, her mouth twisting.

"It is your last chance to redeem yourself in the eyes of the Ministry."

"And a chance at ritual suicide afterward, I assume, to cleanse my family's name," Vei said.

Now or never. Jebi didn't want to find out if Vei would carry out the order or, worse, throw away her life in some brave but foolhardy last stand against Hafanden's entourage. Instead, they barreled into Vei, yanking their hands against the bonds.

As Vei had promised, the knot gave way. They didn't intend to give Hafanden enough time to think about what that meant, though. Vei didn't backhand Jebi, but froze.

Jebi dragged her closer and hissed in Vei's ear, "*Get rid of the masks!*"

Vei exploded into action so quickly and dazzlingly that Jebi saw nothing but a succession of liquid silver arcs, the deadly steel moving from one target to the next. Jebi staggered backwards and landed badly, barely catching themself against the rough ground of the grotto. Sobbing with renewed pain, they looked up just in time to see the result of Vei's defiance.

Shattered fragments of masks fell away and landed on the floor. Vei was *still moving*, how did she *do* that?—Jebi would have stopped in the middle to get their bearings and figure out what was happening. Which was why they'd never have made it as a soldier, while Vei was demonstrating the skill that had won her the position of duelist prime.

Hafanden pointed with his cane. The gesture needed no translation. The guards bulled forward, to no avail. None of them rivaled Vei's unbelievable speed. She cut one down while he was still reaching for his weapon. Then another, and another.

The automata marched to the wall and stood there, leaving Hafanden exposed. One of the remaining human guards blanched and attempted to run, as though the automata had threatened her instead of becoming inert. Vei killed her too, as efficiently as a crane spearing a frog.

Jebi blinked in dazzlement. They'd believed that removing the masks would render the automata inert, but apparently that wasn't the case. Perhaps giving a mask gave the gift of life, after which the masks were redundant—or used solely to restrict their actions.

In a matter of moments, Hafanden stood surrounded by corpses. Jebi gagged at the stink of blood and entrails, and other things they didn't want to name. They'd *painted* duels and battlefield scenes before, but a painting didn't include the *stench*. How Vei dealt with it, they had no idea.

Jebi had seen life-size paintings done in the new realist style, so vivid that they could have passed for reality. But for them, the evidence of their eyes wasn't what distinguished art from truth. It was the other senses: smell and taste and touch.

Jebi wouldn't have blamed Hafanden for running. They would have fled in his situation. But Hafanden stood unmoved, as though he refused to acknowledge that he'd made an enemy of a whirlwind of steel.

As it turned out, he was right to. Vei blurred to a halt past him, pivoted neatly. She pointed her sword at him. It was clear that she could have cleaved him in half without raising a sweat.

"I want safe passage," Vei said, "for myself and my guest."

"You won't last long out there," Hafanden said. "Do you think the Fourteeners will welcome you because you saved a collaborator?"

Vei's expression didn't change. "That's my problem."

"Just kill him and let's get out of here," Jebi croaked. After all, they couldn't imagine that Vei could go back to working for the Razanei government. Not after she'd just murdered Hafanden's guards, people she had worked with for years.

"Was your oath to the Ministry false from the beginning?" Hafanden asked, his voice low.

Jebi bit their tongue instead of groaning. Too bad they couldn't snatch the sword away and run Hafanden through themself—in their condition, even given the man's dependence on his cane, it was an open question as to who'd prevail—but they knew Vei well enough to realize that they'd alienate her forever. Her honor meant something to her, even though she'd already turned coat.

*I need her to get out of here, anyway,* Jebi thought, although they knew the real reason they weren't about to betray their lover. Or more than they already had, anyway; they were starting to lose track.

Hafanden closed his eyes for a long moment, opened them. Gave Vei a searching look. "You can run," Hafanden said, "but you can't go far. And I know what you know."

"That may be the case," Vei replied, with that old-fashioned courtliness upon her, like a vassal to a lord in the storybooks. "What you know of me, Deputy Minister, is not the sum of who I am."

"I never thought otherwise," he murmured.

"Safe passage," Vei said, implacable. "Sworn on the blood of your ancestors. Or I will run you through here and now, and take my chances that you'll stop protecting those artists you find worthy." Her voice dipped contemptuously on the last word.

"Fine," Hafanden said. "I swear it on the blood of my ancestors." And he leaned on his cane and waved them off with despicable calm.

"Your first mistake was coming down here yourself, you know," Vei said. She wasn't done yet. "The keys."

"Which ones?"

"Don't play coy, Deputy Minister." Vei nodded at Arazi.

*{Now,}* Jebi said.

Arazi brought its great head down before Vei, equal to equal.

"We're not going to be able to smuggle the dragon out in pieces," Jebi said. "There won't be time." Sooner or later someone would realize that Hafanden hadn't been seen in some time and come looking for him.

Hafanden's mouth tightened. Then he handed over a key ring. "You'll regret freeing the dragon," he warned Vei and

Jebi. "Whatever you think you've done, you can't trust that thing loose."

Ignoring him, Vei unlocked the dragon's chains. It took longer than Jebi liked, and they couldn't help fretting, wondering if Hafanden had signaled reinforcements, oath or no oath, and they would all die in the earth's womb after all.

Arazi held still the entire time, until the last of the locks clicked free. Then it shook itself like a cat waking from a long sleep, and arched its neck toward Hafanden. Hafanden, give him that much credit, didn't flinch.

"I have prepared for this," Arazi said, this time out loud, in a voice like the music of metal on metal.

Before Jebi could ask what the hell it meant by *prepared*, the entire dragon collapsed in on itself, like an avalanche. Jebi's hands flew up to their mouth as they swallowed a sob. "Arazi, *no*," they gasped.

Vei's fingers dug into Jebi's arm. "Wait," she said.

To Jebi's astonishment, the dragon's individual components reassembled themselves into several disparate mechanical spiderlings. Jebi was torn between fascination and queasiness. They'd never stopped to think about the implications of Arazi's machine nature. A *human* couldn't have reshaped themselves like this, puzzle-fashion; but apparently Arazi's design, or some cleverness of its own devising, allowed it to accomplish this.

"Arazi?" Jebi whispered. "Are you still there?"

"We are following," a multitude of voices said; one for every one of the spiderlings.

Jebi tried, and failed, to suppress the shiver that crawled down their skin. *Sorry,* they thought guiltily. They'd never liked spiders. But they could apologize later. *{Why couldn't you do this earlier?}*

*{The chains,}* Arazi said. *{You didn't think they'd use ordinary chains to hold a magical creation, did you?}*

"We need to get out of here," Vei said crisply. "Follow me." In an undertone, she added, "Hafanden will already have raised the alarm. We'll have to move quickly and leave no survivors."

Jebi quailed at the finality in Vei's tone. "There's no other—" They swallowed the rest of the sentence. What had they expected? That they'd be able to foment revolution without getting any blood on their hands?

The first part of their escape went easily—too easily. Hafanden had denuded most of the Summer Palace of its guards. This only meant, as Vei remarked, that the guards were gathering elsewhere to ensnare them.

The spiderlings—Jebi scrabbled for a better word, then decided it was a problem for a less hectic time—threw uncanny, many-angled shadows against the walls of the corridors and the rough-hewn floors. It seemed, at times, that the shadows wove a calligraphy both ancient and new, describing wonders and terrors from an age just out of their reach. Jebi told themself to pay less attention to their imagination—difficult when their head ached and the fever still burned within them—and more to Vei, who was leading the way.

Under other circumstances, Jebi would have gladly leaned on Vei. She was strong enough to support what was left of Jebi's weight. But this time Vei had her sword out in earnest, and Jebi didn't want to foul her sword arm when they ran into more of Hafanden's people.

Jebi tried several times to count the junctures and turnings and stairwells before giving up. They could have blamed the distracting clattering notes that Arazi's spiderlings made as they skittered in Vei's wake, but the truth was they could have been in the shade of a willow in a perfectly landscaped garden with the breeze blowing and they would have gotten distracted anyway, given their current condition. After the— fourth? fifth?—time the entourage turned left, Jebi gave up and focused instead on staying upright.

At last, perhaps nearer the surface world, perhaps not, they encountered guards.

"It figures he'd pick this bottleneck," Vei muttered, perhaps for Jebi's benefit. Jebi had no idea how tactics and terrain worked other than very basic concepts like *keep the high ground*, which everyone knew from childhood play, and *if the enemy has you surrounded, you're fucked*, a basic principle in baduk, which the Razanei called go. In particular, they had no idea how to *apply* maxims like those to real-world situations, unlike Vei.

The guard captain—Jebi recognized the insignia, even if they couldn't quite place their face—saluted Vei ironically. Jebi was more concerned about the troops backing them up. Ordinarily Jebi was good at estimating the number of people from a glance, but their head ached so much. Twenty? Fifty? Something in between?

"I request your surrender, Duelist Prime," the captain said. "We've sent to the military for reinforcements. You can't hope to escape."

"Hope, no," Vei said with an equanimity Jebi wished they shared. "Plan, yes."

*It would be nice if you'd divulged this plan to me,* they thought.

Still, just because Vei had plans of her own—whatever they were—didn't mean Jebi couldn't contribute. While Vei and the captain exchanged words that Jebi could hardly puzzle out, mostly because they'd never had a head for military jargon, Jebi knelt and scooped up some of the dirt. At least there *was* dirt, here in one of the less-used passageways.

*I am going to look very stupid if this doesn't work.*

What the hell. Very stupid was better than very dead if they didn't help. Considering that Vei was facing off against cold steel on their behalf, they would never forgive themself if they let the guards cut her down.

A flicker at the edge of Jebi's peripheral vision and shouts told them that the fight had begun, but they had no attention to spare for specifics. Besides, they knew from experience that Vei moved in a blur and didn't *stop* moving until everyone was down. It wasn't as though Jebi could call out useful tips; everything they knew about the sword arts could be written on a pimple.

It took all their self-control to let the clamor of battle fall away around them. Jebi dug in the bag for the mortar and pestle, and the precious supply of Phoenix Extravagant. They spat into the mortar, mixed the spittle with the pigment and scraped chunks of dirt. Who had known that their recent adventures in mud-painting would serve as practice for battle art?

Visualizing the glyphs in their mind before setting fingers to the wall's cool surface, Jebi began painting. They didn't have access to the wider variety of pigments in the workshop anymore, but they had the few rare pigments that Vei had liberated, and they knew that dirt didn't come from nowhere. The life of everything that lived and moved eventually returned to the earth; they'd even heard stories of ancient creatures trapped in the earth. They'd seen traces of those fossils in the excavated passageways. Surely some of those long-ago creatures' virtue haunted the dusty leavings? It was worth a try, anyway.

Jebi's experience with the combat-oriented glyphs was more theoretical than practical, despite their sessions with Nehen. They'd never liked the idea of writing grammars to harm people—and who *else* would they be targeting but people, since the other side didn't have automata of their own? They didn't want to kill anyone, just scare the guards off and deter them from following them and Vei and Arazi.

Jebi ran out of mud; made some more, grimacing at the taste of dirt, the texture of grit between their teeth. But Vei was still fighting—they heard another shout, recoiled—and they had to do their best. Was that thud a body falling? Or something else?

*—don't think about it don't think about it don't think about it—*

More mud. More glyphs. They had to connect them in particular ways, arrange everything with the same care as a geomancer arranging furniture to ensure a building's good luck, or plants for a garden's fortunes, or even a nation's. Connect the pieces, and build in a break—suggest an eruption.

*This isn't working*, Jebi thought as they dragged their fingers across the stone to complete the last curve. *I've fucked it up.*

And then the earth trembled.

Even though Jebi had hoped for this, they mistook the shaking for the unsteadiness of their own limbs at first. Then the tremors increased in intensity, and they knew their art had summoned the magic they required. They'd called for rupture and breakage, the hard sharp spill of cracks in the otherwise stable earth.

Vei kept her balance—Jebi spotted her an impossible distance ahead in the passageway, a wake of bodies behind her like a fanciful train. *Like a red peacock,* Jebi couldn't help thinking. The phrase kept repeating itself in their head, a refrain that wouldn't go away. They slumped against the wall, spent; saw blood on their hands. They must have scraped the skin off their fingers without realizing it—not much of an injury, but it had already been a taxing day, and the smell of all those bodies made them feel faint.

The Razanei reacted much more frantically, although Jebi heard their cries as through a curtain of mist. It took Jebi another few moments to recognize the word they were shouting to each other, one they'd rarely heard: "Earthquake!"

*I outsmarted myself,* Jebi thought as the walls buckled and the Razanei trampled the dead in their haste to get out of the way. The Razanei dreaded earthquakes, even built their temples and dwellings to withstand them. Jebi knew that much from the novels. But despite its proximity to Razan, Hwaguk was geologically stable; Jebi hadn't heard of any earthquakes in Hwaguk even in the oldest lore and legends.

Maybe, given the Razanei's alarm, *they* should run, too. If this was a sensible application of magic, as opposed to a fucking dangerous one, the Razanei would have been using it all along. After all, what if the entire Summer Palace collapsed and buried them alive? Arazi would survive, but Jebi found themself hyperventilating at the prospect of being entombed in this of all places. Dying with the stink of corpses in their nostrils. What a way to go.

Vei had grasped the peril while Jebi was still dazed, and dashed back for them. "Tell Arazi to follow us," she said. "We have to get out of here before this place collapses!"

Jebi was wracked by a coughing fit triggered by the dust in the air, but Arazi seemed to get the idea. The spiderlings scampered over the heaving floor and up towards the surface, visible as a faint sky-colored gash in the ceiling, with an agility that Jebi could only envy.

Vei grabbed Jebi's arm and dragged them. Jebi twisted their ankle on a protruding chunk of rock that hadn't been there one second ago, whimpered. Before their dazzled eyes, the Summer Palace was falling apart.

Jebi hobbled as fast as they could, still coughing and spitting out dirt. As they scrabbled past the tumbling walls they thought they heard the keening of a long-ago dragon from the deeps. But they broke through to the surface and its sweet chilly air, and collapsed in relief when they'd gotten clear of the artificial earthquake.

Chapter

# FIFTEEN

"WAKE UP," JEBI heard a soft, worried voice saying over and over again.

*Don't wanna,* they thought, refusing to squeeze their eyes open. Their head hurt as though someone had split it with an axe. The axe would have been preferable. If they'd died, they wouldn't be in pain. Jebi had the impression that the honored ancestors didn't go in for trivial inconveniences like headaches.

Firm, strong hands propped them halfway up. Jebi groaned in protest.

"Now I *know* you're awake," the voice said, coming into focus. Vei. "Come on, Jebi."

"I don't have any projects due right now," Jebi mumbled, which might or might not have been true. "Lemme get some more sleep."

"*Jebi*," Vei said again. "I need to know you're all right."

"Be all right if you let me sleep."

"I need to know you're all right."

Their escape from the Summer Palace returned to them in fragments and snatches. The flash of steel, the mud paintings, the waking of the earth. The way the whole complex had collapsed like a giant's fist had closed around it.

A different voice interjected, "Maybe they'd like something to drink."

"Yes, Ajummae," Vei said, her voice revealing exhaustion.

Jebi's eyes flew open at the intrusion. *Where are we now?*

Vei had installed them in a spacious room with the view of the exit obscured by a set of folding screens. The screens featured a lattice motif that Jebi had seen in older Hwagugin homes, not the flowers and butterflies that were popular today. "What?" they asked intelligently.

The ajummae in question was a middle-aged person whose asymmetrical haircut, however old-fashioned, indicated they were a geu-ae like Jebi, or didn't mind being mistaken for one. Jebi couldn't remember the last time they'd seen a person of that age in clothes quite so colorful. Their jacket featured stripes of red, yellow, and green, in the style for the young.

"Who are *you?*" Jebi demanded. Their hands flew to their mouth. What was wrong with them? Besides the headache, anyway.

"You're probably disoriented," the ajummae said with the kind of brisk kindness that Jebi associated with older relatives. "I'm Namgyu, one of Vei's parents. Her mother is preparing some food for your journey, and Captain Dzuge Keizhi is out looking for signs of Armor's watchers. He was grateful for a break from his paperwork, anyway."

"The automata—"

Vei restrained Jebi from sitting all the way up, which was just as well, because the headache was suddenly throbbing with renewed ferocity. "We don't have much time," she said, "but I came to my father's manse for help."

Jebi squinted blearily at her. "I didn't know you were still in touch with your father." That must be the Captain Dzuge whom Namgyu had referred to. They'd assumed that Vei must be estranged from him, since she'd never mentioned him before.

Vei shook her head. "Who do you think taught me the art of the sword? He's retired now due to a battle injury: lost most of one leg to gangrene."

"I'd never thought about it," Jebi admitted. But that was true: swordplay at Vei's level wasn't something one picked up by studying on the weekends, or taking lessons from itinerant swordmasters. You needed real expertise.

"One of my first memories is of my father letting me try to lift his sword," Vei said, tranquil. "I couldn't, of course. Then he had one of his retainers bring a wooden practice sword for me. I was so disappointed that I wouldn't get one with an edge yet. Then he had them bring out a chicken, and he killed it right in front of me. There was so much blood."

"Did you eat the chicken?" Jebi asked, because tact was not a thing that happened when they had a headache.

"Of course," Vei said. "Soldiers know not to waste food. It was a stringy old bird, but that wasn't the point. He wanted me to take the blade seriously; to know that killing is something you can't ever take back, and that I'd have to learn it anyway. Because I was an officer's bastard, and I had two Hwagugin parents."

Jebi noticed, even in their current state, that she didn't say *Fourteener*.

"I'm the third," Namgyu said, their eyes crinkling, "although that part is less well known." They raised their voice. "Hyeja, do you need help with the food?"

"It's just about ready," an alto called back.

"That's my mother," Vei added, helpfully. "Sorry you have to meet my family all at once."

"There aren't more?" Jebi asked.

A woman with a deceptively youthful face entered with a tray of porridge. This smelled good—especially after what they'd served in the Summer Palace—with savory hints of chicken. She affected Western dress, an elaborate satin gown trimmed with ribbons and ruffles, and necklaces of baroque pearls.

Bongsunga would have had words for people like Namgyu and Hyeja, none of them polite. For their part, Jebi noticed the way Namgyu's eyes softened as they regarded Hyeja, and the other way around. It didn't take very close observation to sense the love they had for each other. If that affection encompassed Vei's father as well, it was an unusual arrangement, but not one unheard of, at least in Hwaguk.

Hyeja set the tray down on the table next to Jebi. She must have guessed the direction of their thoughts, for she said, "If you're wondering if this is acceptable in Razan, the answer is no, not under terms that we would have found livable. The officers and nobles take concubines as they choose. But lovers as equals—that would be hard to explain. It's one of the reasons the captain decided to stay with the occupation."

"I wasn't planning on asking," Jebi lied.

Hyeja's eyes crinkled. "Eat. I've packed up some food for you and Vei to take on your journey."

"You should leave too," Vei said. "Once word gets out of what happened, you're not going to be any safer than Jebi and I are."

"I can't," Hyeja said. "Suni's baby is due any day now. I promised I'd be there for them."

"You're a midwife?" Jebi asked. They wouldn't have guessed it from Hyeja's attire, but they assumed that she didn't dress in such elaborate clothes for work.

"Among other things," Hyeja said. "I'm a physician. I studied with some of the Western missionaries in Huang-Guan in my youth."

Jebi almost asked if she'd met people with orange hair; thought better of it.

"My family disowned me, of course"—Hyeja spoke of it as though it were a distant pain, hardly worth mentioning—"but I learned many useful remedies. I can't abandon Suni this close to the birth."

Vei frowned. "You're not required to give up your life for them, Mother!"

"Don't worry about me," Hyeja chided. "I have contacts in the Blossom District." It was the old euphemism for the Virgins' District. "I can disappear if I need to. As can your father and Namgyu."

Vei didn't look convinced, but she didn't argue further. Jebi had only a faint notion of how one argued with mothers, having lost theirs at an early age. Bongsunga had all but raised them, and they wouldn't have dreamed of arguing with their older sister in a similar situation.

"I want to see Arazi," Jebi said.

"You haven't touched your food," Hyeja said. "At least do that. I don't think your escape will be any less daring for having filled your belly."

Responding to the note of authority in her voice, Jebi picked up their spoon and began eating. The stoneware bowl had kept the porridge warm, and they savored the taste as it went down. This might be the last good meal they enjoyed in a while.

At this point, Jebi realized belatedly that they no longer stank, and that while they remained sore all over from the beatings and abuse, someone had dressed them in fresh clothes. They were too loose, but Jebi didn't care about details like that right now.

"Thank you," Jebi said around a mouthful of porridge. "For the doctoring."

"She's very good at it," Namgyu said with a sideways smile.

"If she's a physician," Jebi said, remembering just in time to keep their language respectful, "what do you do?"

Instead of being embarrassed by Jebi's lack of manners, Vei merely looked amused, with the corners of her eyes crinkling in that almost-smile she had.

"I'm a calligrapher and interpreter," Namgyu said. "There are a lot of illiterate people in the Virgins' District, and they need someone reliable to read contracts, or write them, in Razanei or Hwamal. Sometimes other languages. My prices are high, but I've lived here all my life. They know they can depend on me."

"I see," Jebi said, impressed, especially at the mention of other languages. They had a fuzzy impression that other nations had other tongues—Huang-Guan reportedly had several spoken ones, although only one writing system, which sounded confusing—but had only rarely met people claiming to speak them. For that matter, Jebi had no way of telling jibberish from the genuine article.

Then they tucked their head down and finished the bowl of porridge, even though the act of swallowing hurt. *It's free food,* Jebi reminded themself. They had no resources in the outside world. As little as they liked depending on someone else, they didn't have any other option.

Vei had risen and was talking with her mother in a low voice. Jebi took the opportunity to examine the two at their leisure. Vei had inherited something of her mother's fineness of features, especially around the eyes and nose, although her cheekbones and jaw must come from elsewhere in her heritage. The lithe build that Jebi had gotten to know so well—that, too, came from Hyeja.

Jebi suspected, from what Hyeja had said about being disinherited, that she came of one of the old families of scholar-aristocrats, rather than the merchant and peasant stock from which Jebi and Bongsunga were derived. They couldn't imagine defying their family outright, to leave the country no less—except they had done it themself, hadn't they? Starting with that damnable name certificate.

Jebi had gotten around to wondering what kind of Razanei officer allowed his feelings for two Fourteeners to sully his name when the man in question strode into the room. Vei straightened, although Jebi had not previously noticed that she had relaxed, even slightly. So did Hyeja. Only Namgyu remained calm, as though nothing unusual was happening.

Captain Dzuge would have stood out as a soldier even in ordinary clothes. Jebi had to prevent themself from flinching from the blue uniform, neatly pressed, with its gold buttons. He had massive shoulders and moved ably on his crutches. His motions reminded Jebi not so much of Vei, although they saw the resemblance in the triangular shapes of their faces, as Jia. Jia had had the same sense of vitality.

"I got word from one of my contacts," Dzuge Keizhi said in a raspy tenor. "They're mobilizing the military. You left one hell of a trail behind you, daughter mine. They're going to send someone to question me soon."

"I'll be out of your way," Vei said, and bowed. "My companions, too."

He gestured impatiently. "I'll buy you what time I can."

"You should plead ignorance if you're not going to go into hiding," Vei said. "Say that Mother and Ajummae took me in, and you can't find them."

"You shouldn't be worrying about this," he returned. "We can take care of ourselves. Get out of here."

Vei hesitated for a moment, then bowed to each of her three parents in turn. "I will send word when I can."

"You do that," Hyeja said. "You know where to go?"

"Of course, Mother," Vei said.

*We do?* Jebi wondered. They submitted to Vei helping them up, then strapping them to a wooden frame with a judiciously calculated weight of bags. Any more and they would have staggered. Vei bore a less encumbering rucksack, but that made sense: she was responsible for their defense.

Vei led Jebi out into the courtyard, where Arazi had reassembled itself. The dragon's masked head was poorly concealed amid the branches of a well-established plum tree. Even so, Jebi knew—how they knew!—that Arazi wasn't standing at its full height; it had ducked its head down so that it rested lower than its withers.

"Arazi?" Jebi asked softly.

"I had a chance to talk to it earlier," Vei said, bowing almost as politely to the dragon as she had to her parents. Parents outranked allies.

Jebi hobbled up to the dragon and saw, in the mid-afternoon light filtering through the trees—how many trees *did* the captain keep in this luxurious manse, anyway?—that they weren't the only one going around with extra gear. Someone had rigged the dragon with a set of foot- and handholds leading up to... a set of saddles? The whole setup looked precarious. "Um," Jebi said, peering up.

"We have to outpace our pursuit," Vei said.

"Where are we going?" Jebi demanded.

Vei smiled tightly. "My other parents have contacts in the Hwagugin community. I have a good idea where one of the revolutionaries' biggest recruitment camps is. We'll land there and try to find some higher-ups to give our information to."

"They'll want to seize Arazi," Jebi said, feeling as though a fist had closed around their chest. They gazed at the dragon, imagining it chained up again.

"They can try," Arazi said, tranquil. "You will tell them what you know, and then we will continue on our way."

Jebi didn't think it would be that easy, but far be it for them to dash Arazi's hopes, or Vei's either, for that matter.

"I'll go up first," Vei said. "Are you feeling steady enough to ride?"

Jebi squeaked. "Ride?"

Vei's mouth quirked at the corners. "Can you think of anything likely to be *faster* than a dragon this size? Especially since Arazi assures me that it can fly."

{*I can definitely fly,*} Arazi said with disturbing confidence.

{*Have you ever tried it?*}

{*I'm a dragon. I can fly.*}

"Um," Jebi said. "Are you sure those are secure?"

A voice called from the highest story of the house: it was Namgyu. "I can see the blues," they warned.

"My mother and my ajummae rigged the harness," Vei said. "It will hold. I'll go up first. I obtained a pistol in case of emergency, but to be honest I doubt it will do us much good. Our best hope is speed. We're certainly going to be conspicuous."

Jebi forced themself to watch as Vei clambered up to her seat. She waved with entirely too much cheer once she was settled. "Now you," she called down.

During their misspent childhood, Jebi had occasionally climbed trees and roofs. There was also the time they'd gone over the wall to their neighbor's house before one of the servants caught them at it and shooed them out, back when they'd been little. They would have gotten away with it if they hadn't ripped their pants in the process; Bongsunga had snitched on them when she saw them trying to mend the tear on the sly. Years had passed since those escapades, however, and Jebi didn't trust their sense of balance after their recent adventures in the Summer Palace.

*If I fall off, I will look like an idiot,* Jebi thought, deciding that fear of humiliation could be as powerful a motivator as anything else. They squeaked once when Arazi shifted, then realized that it was compressing itself to reduce the distance between the foot- and handholds. "Thank you," Jebi muttered; they were now even more embarrassed, but that was no reason not to be gracious about the help.

Jebi made it to their seat behind Vei and fitted themself awkwardly into it. Hyeja and Namgyu had a good sense of human anatomy and the amount of flexibility that could reasonably be expected of someone who had recently undergone minor torture. Jebi's legs ached as they straddled the dragon's back—they'd never realized before just how broad its vertebral pieces were—but they could endure.

Jebi looked first to the left, then to the right. They didn't see much beyond the elaborate winter landscaping of Captain Dzuge's garden and glimpses of the neighboring manses, which featured similar vistas of carefully arranged trees and rocks that had probably been imported from Huang-Guan for their picturesque qualities. What the view from this vantage point didn't reveal, but they and presumably Vei also knew, was that the roads of the capital were all narrow, except for the two big thoroughfares that quartered the city—one north-south and the other east-west—to connect the four gates at the city's boundaries.

*{Are you really going to fly?}* Jebi asked.

A strange chiming drifted back toward Jebi. After a moment, they realized the dragon was *laughing.* "Going through the city would be a bad idea," it agreed. "But in this form, I am a creature of *storms,* and the sky is my element."

Jebi clung to the saddlehorn as Arazi maneuvered itself out from under the cover of the trees. Like a snake, its multitude of articulated parts gave it alarming flexibility.

Arazi gathered itself, thrumming with tension, then leapt *over* Captain Dzuge's house. In spite of their best intentions, Jebi screamed, convinced they were going to crash into it and bring the whole structure tumbling down on top of them. They had already sworn never to repeat the earthquake trick.

Instead, Arazi gained altitude, tensed again, gained more altitude. The wind cut into Jebi's face, forcing tears from their eyes. Jebi squeezed their eyes shut, wondering if they were imagining the whole thing. Distantly, they heard Vei laughing in delight.

After several heartstop lurching moments, Jebi peeled one eye open, then the other. The city spread out beneath them, the trees no bigger than toothpicks. Jebi hoped devoutly that Arazi wouldn't go any higher. They didn't think their nerves would endure it if they left the sheltering earth behind altogether.

"—more!" Vei shouted at them, craning her head back.

"What?" Jebi shouted in response.

"It's cold!" Vei said, which Jebi could understand only by reading her lips. "Should have bundled you up more!"

Jebi mimed that they were fine, more to reassure Vei than because they believed it.

They nerved themself to look down again. The hell with flying dragons as war machines; Jebi could see all sorts of applications in surveying and reconnaissance. Which Hafanden had already thought of, no doubt. One could make spectacular maps from this top-down view, instead of the traditional three-quarters view that the cartographers of both

Hwaguk and Razan favored. Jebi could think of whole new
conventions for traditional subjects, like the Eight Immortals
meditating on their mountaintops. Would it be heterodox
to paint them from above, looking down on them from a
superior vantage point, rather than from below the way all
the old paintings had it?

Then they saw the fire.

"We have to turn back!" Jebi yelled at Vei. "They set your
father's house on fire." But the wind tore their words away.

*{Arazi, tell her!}* Jebi said, desperate to catch Vei's attention.

From this distance they could barely discern what color
the swarming figures wore, some dark color. It had to be the
Razanei military's blue. And while Jebi hadn't seen much
beyond the barest glimpses of the neighborhood, they could
identify that plum tree.

In a more fanciful mood, Jebi would have likened the scene
to a whimsical candle or lantern set alight. It was hard to
believe that something that looked so small was real; that
they'd woken up in that house not so long ago. They didn't
subscribe to the realist schools of painting that had invaded
from the West; they preferred the more usual convention that
portrayed *more important* things larger than *less important*
things, the way any sensible person would.

Arazi slowed, circled, and tears started up in Jebi's eyes
again. This time they couldn't blame the wind, or the cutting
chill of the air.

"We have to help them!" Jebi shouted. "They're your *family*,
Vei."

They couldn't let Vei turn her back on her own parents the
way Jebi had turned their back on Bongsunga.

Arazi banked, began veering back toward the house.

Vei shook her head emphatically. Jebi glimpsed her face as she gazed down at the scene. Could she tell who was winning, or whether her parents had gotten away? Numbers didn't mean everything, in a fight; Jia had said that so often that it had to be at least partly true.

"How can you be so heartless?" Jebi cried.

"*Go*," Vei said to Arazi.

After a reluctant pause, the dragon banked again and resumed its flight away from the burning house. The flames leapt higher, blazing orange and red. Jebi wondered if the fire brigade would arrive early enough to prevent the entire district from burning down.

*I can't believe they did that,* Jebi thought, staring down despite the strain in their neck and their aching eyes. They almost didn't notice the way the wooden frame dug into their side, the way they were twisted around to look behind themself. Even during the initial conquest, the Razanei had scorned to use fire. It was self-interest: the moment they consolidated their hold on the peninsula, they came up with flimsy pretexts to seize the nicest houses and parcel them out to their officers and functionaries. Captain Dzuge's house would have been one of those, and however well he seemed to get along with his two lovers, Jebi couldn't help but wonder what had happened to the house's original owners, and how they would feel when they heard that it had burned down.

*Who am I kidding?* Jebi asked themself. They'd accepted the captain's hospitality; brought danger to Vei's family. Never mind that Jebi hadn't been conscious at the time. They had to make sure that the sacrifice meant something.

# Chapter
# SIXTEEN

THE FLIGHT AWAY from Administrative City Fourteen lasted minutes, hours, days. Jebi had a good sense of passing time when they weren't trapped underground, and also a good sense of how long it took to walk from one point to another. What they did not know was how fast travel by flying dragon was. The landscape sped by beneath them on a scale that Jebi could only have dreamed of in times past.

The Summer Palace and their confrontation with Hafanden evanesced like a dream in the first moments after waking, up here. The sun beat against their back like a sentinel's lantern. The wind scraped their skin raw. Jebi was wearing gloves, but even the scarf they'd wrapped around their face did little to ameliorate the effect. They wanted to ask Arazi to slow down, but knew they didn't dare linger. Their best hope of safety lay in reaching the rebels' recruitment camp as quickly as possible.

They'd left the city far behind. Jebi remembered spotting the West Gate far below, the white peak of its roof standing out from the surrounding buildings, and from the worn wall that zigzagged to either side. The road leading to it curved like a restive snake, following the river that bisected the city.

*I may never see the city like this again,* Jebi said, entranced by the idea. It was like seeing a particular moment in time, amber-trapped. Even if Arazi took them on another flight like this one, there was no guarantee that the city itself would remain intact. Not after everything Jebi had learned about Hafanden's plans.

"My father once asked if all these mountains had names," Vei said as Arazi sped onward, exaggerating her speech so Jebi could read her lips more easily. "Razan is mountainous too, in places, but he comes from the plains on one of the larger islands."

Jebi had difficulty envisioning this. "The islands are big enough to have plains?"

"The two largest ones are," Vei said. "They're more varied than you'd think, according to him. He told me stories of his travels as a younger soldier... he didn't see as much of Razan as he would have liked. And then he ended up settling here."

"Did he ever miss Razan?" Jebi asked, because they would have, in his place.

"This is his home now," Vei said, which didn't answer the question.

By now Jebi had recovered enough tact not to press further, and besides, having to gesticulate and read lips made conversation taxing.

Was it possible to love a country you hadn't been born in? Jebi didn't know the answer to that. They'd hardly ventured past the walls of the capital, although they knew most of the jokes about Hwaguk's old provinces, like the one about how the farmers of Ggensang Province were so taciturn all they said all day, every day, was "Good morning," "Give me lunch," and "Goodnight."

Bongsunga had spoken of connections abroad, and rebels who had gone into exile, either because Hwaguk was no longer safe for them, or because the Razanei had driven them out. What if Jebi, too, had to leave their homeland? And what if Bongsunga had done so already?

*Forgive me,* Jebi thought, staring down at the distance-blued earth: scarves of snow, and sunlight glinting on the ice, and the darker ribbons of roads cutting into the expanses of white. *All those years I could have painted more landscapes.* They'd never put in more than required for basic proficiency, especially considering that more 'intimate' subjects were more in fashion right now, from portraits to creepily detailed depictions of people's offices and kitchens. Jebi had never forgotten the one that lingered lovingly on the chef's knives, giving them pride of place, and blood dripping from the biggest one. There was a story behind that painting, and Jebi hoped they never found out what it was.

They pulled their mind away from the visuals spread out tapestry-fashion beneath them and rehearsed what they would say to the rebels. What *did* one say to persuade rebels not to kill a Razanei duelist on sight? They weren't sure whether it would be better if Bongsunga was at the camp or not. After all, Vei had killed Jia—that fact hadn't changed. They didn't want to get Vei killed, but they couldn't in conscience keep it a secret from their sister, either.

"There it is," Arazi sang out, vibrating with eagerness, or perhaps dread; it was hard to tell. "They haven't spotted us. I see at least six lookouts on the perimeter." It slowed as it spiraled downward.

Jebi startled at the dragon's spoken voice. It sounded just like its mental voice, except with stronger metallic overtones. "How do you know they haven't spotted us?" they asked. And: "How good is your eyesight, anyway?"

"Eyes of Hawk," Vei said reminiscently. "That's what Issemi told me. We ran out of *that* pigment very quickly."

Jebi swallowed their queasiness and asked, "How do you get 'eyes of hawk' out of a human artist?"

"She didn't," Vei said. "Not an artist the way you're thinking, like a painter or potter. A falconer."

Jebi blinked. "I didn't realize any of the old falconers had survived the invasion." Or that any still lived other than in countryside retreats. The sport had more or less died out in the final decades of the Azalea Throne's reign.

"It took a lot of hunting," Vei said, with a careful lack of specificity.

Arazi veered left suddenly.

"Archers," Vei breathed. "*Now* they see us. Too bad they couldn't have kept their eyes down a little longer."

"Bongsunga sent us!" Jebi shouted before it occurred to them that this particular camp might be unfamiliar with their sister, or worse, that Bongsunga had used some assumed name for her revolutionary activities. "We're allies!"

"I'm going to land," Arazi said.

Jebi couldn't see the arrows, although they heard the buzzing as they whizzed past. It did nothing to make them feel better about this course of action. Then again, what had they expected? A welcome party with honey-ginger cookies and rice wine?

It took Jebi several moments to understand that the rebels had them surrounded. Rather than approaching Arazi closely, they stood well back. Most of them were archers, and Jebi's stomach plummeted when they saw that the arrows were aimed at themself and Vei. It made sense: Arazi's metal construction was plainly visible and it would take one hell of an arrow to blow apart its joints. Maybe one of those gunpowder-propelled ones from the hwacha of old, if any.

"Who's your leader?" Vei called out.

"We'll ask the questions," responded a woman with one eye. Jebi couldn't help staring in fascination, because they didn't feel the need to pretend politeness. *She* didn't wield a bow; didn't wear any obvious symbol to set her apart from the rest of her squad. But the hard lines of her face told Jebi that she knew suffering, and wasn't afraid to inflict it, either.

Vei bowed, equal to equal.

The woman's mouth tightened. "Did you come here in a straight line?"

Arazi answered, using extremely polite verbs: "No. I took a roundabout path"—not that Jebi had been able to tell, dazzled as they were by the clouds and the sun and the landscape below—"and I would have known if anyone was following me."

The woman didn't jump, or flinch, or give any sign that Arazi cowed her. Jebi's respect for her increased. "Are there other automata that speak?"

"Not that I am aware of," Arazi said, still polite.

She shook her head, considering them. "It's true that people rarely look up if they're city folk," she said. "But out here in the country, we watch for birds. And you cast a bigger shadow than any bird that's been seen in these parts."

The archers' aim remained steady.

Jebi's bladder reminded them that it was very full, what with the porridge they'd had earlier, and their nerves. This wasn't some hasty assortment of quasi-bandits. Jebi knew, again from Jia, that archery wasn't something you picked up overnight. It took years of training to become proficient. They bet that everyone with a bow in hand would hit what they aimed at.

"Bring them in," the woman said at last. "I'm Han." It meant 'one.' As she only had one eye, Jebi figured it was not her real name.

Vei opened her mouth.

"I don't want to hear from you yet," Han said, terse but not unfriendly—quite. She made a string of signs at the archers. Two of them covered Vei and Jebi—their confidence didn't reassure Jebi—while the others dispersed, perhaps to check for other intruders. Others relieved Vei and Jebi of their packs, and Vei of her sword.

They trudged for a long time through the scrub and snow. Jebi's legs shook, and they wanted nothing more than to lie down somewhere warm and surrender to a massage. But Vei gave no indication of anything as ordinary or human as fatigue, damn her, so they wouldn't either.

Jebi's eye picked out features in the landscape: rocks of unusual shape, wind-blasted trees bent over like an old gran, narrow footpaths along the contours of the hills. A few confused flowers bloomed in the lee of one rock, their color already faded. Jebi paused for a second, struck by the image, before the bulkier of Han's guards gestured for them to hurry up.

At last they reached a campsite in the shadow of a hill. Jebi's hopes for a cozy fire were dashed; they saw no such thing. But the rebels had to keep warm somehow.

"How well can you hide yourself?" Han asked Arazi.

In answer, Arazi crouched down into a remarkably compact package, like a cat squeezing into a box.

"I have questions for you two," Han said to Vei and Jebi. "Will your mount wait outside?"

Jebi conceded that they couldn't reasonably ask Han to allow Arazi inside any of the tents. Besides, did they want Han to know that Arazi was a free agent? They glanced uncertainly toward Arazi, who rested its head on its forepaws and appeared quiescent. Jebi reflected that the usual signs of mood with an animal—like a cat's ears or tail, or a dog's expressions—told them nothing about the dragon's mood.

{If you need escape, let me know,} Arazi said in an anxious tone at odds with its pose. {I am hoping that they'll underestimate me if I lie here quietly.}

Han ushered them into the largest tent, hidden under a layer of sod and carefully cut brush. To Jebi's relief, the tent's interior featured a brazier. Han hustled them in and closed the tent after them. "I heard Bongsunga's name," she said. "Who has claim on her?"

Vei nodded at Jebi, who swallowed and said, "Me. I—I know her." Maybe it was best not to give away the exact relationship yet.

PHOENIX EXTRAVAGANT

Han grimaced. "Really."

*Fuck.* Jebi hadn't stopped to consider that the rebels would have factions and divisions and quarrels of their own. They'd assumed that anyone who knew Bongsunga would be her ally, or a friend.

"Please," Jebi said in a rush. "I don't know what your quarrel is with her, but I have important information about the Ministry of Armor's plans. Bongsunga is—is the one I know."

"How did you come by this information?" Han demanded. "Especially since you're traveling with Armor's duelist prime?"

They should have realized that a rebel leader would keep track of the duelists prime. Jebi tried to take heart from the fact that Han had recognized Vei and hadn't ordered her executed immediately. Although maybe she meant to torture information out of the two of them first. They gulped.

They didn't enjoy the prospect of confessing the truth to this woman, but they didn't see any good alternatives. "I'm an artist," they said. "I used to work for the Ministry of Armor."

Han's eyebrow rose. Jebi couldn't help staring at the scarred expanse of skin where the other eyebrow should have been, and at the empty socket. "Armor," she repeated. "Damnation. It's consistent with the reports, at least. And you—" She jerked her chin at Vei. "What are *you* doing here, Duelist Prime?"

"I have forfeited that position," Vei replied, "in escorting the artist here."

Han's mouth twisted. "We don't have any way to verify that claim out here, and you'll have outpaced our usual sources. Very well done."

"You can hold us as long as necessary," Vei said, and Jebi's heart sank. "But Armor will be sending people after us. If you

248

want to act on this information, you should do so as quickly as possible."

"You're Bongsunga's younger sibling, aren't you?" Han said, her eye narrowing as she studied Jebi's face. "I assume you're not normally that scrawny, but the eyes and the bone structure are the same."

Jebi didn't see any sense in denying it. "I'm Gyen Jebi, yes," they said. "Please. I don't know what your issue is with my sister, but she should at least be able to verify my information."

"Sit down and start talking," Han said.

Jebi sat and took a deep breath to settle their nerves. Then they squared their shoulders, shrugging off Vei's steadying touch, met Han's eye, and began.

Han listened patiently, frowning only a little. Jebi hesitated only once, when Han asked how they had stolen Vei's keys. They could have equivocated, but they suspected she was not a good person to lie to.

"I was sleeping with her," Jebi said, ducking their head in Vei's direction. They didn't know whether to be embarrassed or defiant. Maybe both.

"*I* have a question," Vei said when Han didn't respond to that. "You had plenty of opportunity to have me killed. Why didn't you?"

"Because it's fucking annoying getting information out of a corpse," Han replied, "and it was clear that you'd come willingly. It's a risk having you here, but everything's a risk in this business."

A bird called once, twice, and then again.

"That's not a bird," Vei said a half-second before the thought occurred to Jebi. "A crane, at this time of year?"

"Indeed," Han said. She lifted the tent flap, poked her head out, and signed instructions. Jebi desperately wished for a translation.

Han signed some more, then moved aside to let a newcomer in: Bongsunga.

Jebi gaped at their sister. She'd dropped weight too, not as dramatically as Jebi themself, but her cheekbones stood out sharply against the planes of her face. She'd wrapped herself in a practical dun coat that would be hard to spot against the sleeping winter earth, with slits up the sides so she could walk more easily. Jebi spotted a lump under the coat that had to be a weapon.

"You heard all that?" Han said to Bongsunga, speaking deferentially.

"I did indeed," Bongsunga said. She spoke to Han as though to a subordinate, and Jebi started to wonder what was going on. "We'll have to act on this soon."

"Wait a second, Bongsunga," Jebi protested. "We came here for help, not to—"

Bongsunga looked at Jebi, then shook her head. "Family is important," she said, "but the nation is more important still. There is a hierarchy to these things."

"Arazi, run!" Jebi shouted.

*{Not without you,}* the dragon said, to Jebi's dismay. *{Besides, I want to hear more about what your sister has to say.}*

Bongsunga grabbed Jebi and clamped her hand over their mouth, a display of aggression that shocked them so much that they went limp. She'd raised them; had taken care of them for years. How could they possibly fight her?

Vei tensed.

"I wouldn't," Bongsunga said, letting go of Jebi.

Jebi sprawled on the tent's floor, knocking against one of the poles in the process. They cringed away from it, afraid of bringing the whole thing toppling down on everyone. A tent was unlikely to smother people, but they had a terrified flashback to the earthquake they'd caused in the Summer Palace.

"Arazi and I," Bongsunga said, pronouncing the dragon's name with care, "have been negotiating."

Jebi's stomach twisted. "You're going to go to war."

"Do you see a better way to get rid of the Rassanin?" Bongsunga demanded. "They have to be stopped *before* they manufacture an army of *flying* automata along with the human-shaped ones. If they're able to secure enough metal for their factories and pigments for their artists, they'll roll over everyone who stands in their way. We have the chance not only to free Hwaguk but to prevent the spread of the Rassan Empire. Or did you think you could *shame* them into a retreat?"

"I don't know what I thought," Jebi admitted. "Arazi, is this true? Did you make a deal?"

The space behind their eyes ached with an incipient headache. When had their sister become the enemy? Or perhaps 'enemy' was the wrong term for it. Bongsunga had chosen to represent something bigger than herself. Jebi didn't understand how that could supersede loyalty to family, but then, Bongsunga had always had her eyes on the bigger picture. If they were honest with themself, her pragmatism had given Jebi the freedom to pursue art, in a time when few Hwagugin artists saw prospects. Perhaps they should, instead, show gratitude to her for thinking about the nation as a whole.

Arazi snaked its head into the tent. Jebi, still flat on their ass, yelped. "Sorry," it said, the lights of its eyes dimming slightly. It nudged them with its muzzle like an apologetic dog. "I did indeed talk with your sister." It added, *{She's so different from you! I see why you don't always get along.}*

The reassurance should have made Jebi feel better. Why, then, was their stomach knotting up? "That's good," they said, voice cracking with strain. "I thought—I thought you were a pacifist."

"No wonder Deputy Minister Hafanden was so furious," Han muttered. "All that wasted potential..."

*Fuck you,* Jebi thought.

"Your sister has convinced me that it's too late to carry out a coup bloodlessly," Arazi said. "I am not willing to stand aside while others die. I can always be put back together; the same is not true of you meat people."

Jebi had never thought of this before, even though they'd witnessed Arazi taking itself apart. Surely there existed some point of dissolution beyond which even the dragon couldn't come back. They hoped never to find out.

"Be fair, Jebi," Bongsunga said. "It's not as if we have the resources to *force* your dragon to do anything it doesn't want to. I don't think all of us working together could tie it down."

"Arazi isn't *my* dragon," Jebi shot back. Vei's hand grasped their shoulder and squeezed, this time in warning.

"Fair enough," Bongsunga said, and nodded an apology at Arazi. "It has agreed to provide transportation for our cadres. We're hoping that a series of rapid strikes will demoralize the

Rassanin troops to the point where we can present them with our demands."

"That won't work on the deputy minister," Vei said, her brow creasing. "He's a true believer, committed to the cause. He's not going to let a few logistical obstacles get in the way."

"If you can't go through an obstacle, you have to go around it," Bongsunga returned. "We bribed an agent in Armor—not at the underground complex, but one of the couriers who relays reports to Rassan. Hafanden may be a fanatic, but the *minister* is, by all accounts, a practical woman. And Hafanden has hidden the extent of his misadventures from her. Once she finds out, she is likely to replace him. The ensuing confusion will weaken Armor at a critical juncture."

Jebi was impressed by this, and not in a favorable way. "You're relying on someone staying *bribed?*" they demanded. "How do you know they won't report the incident and pocket the money?"

"Multiple agents watching each other," Vei said unexpectedly. "It's how I would do it."

"You're military too," Bongsunga said, slanting Vei a considering look. "You could be of use to us, given your familiarity with Armor's emergency protocols. If you chose to be." Even Jebi could hear the implicit threat.

"I've made my choice," Vei said, with a formal half-bow. "But my loyalty is not to you, but your sibling."

"Jebi's my own blood," Bongsunga said with chilling certainty. "It will do."

"They're more than blood to me," Vei said, which Jebi would have found romantic under other circumstances. "I will tell you what you want to know, under one condition."

"You're not in a position to dictate terms."

Vei's eyes narrowed. "Any pigments you recover must be destroyed," she said. "The process used to make them is monstrous. The religious rite from which it's derived has been perverted in ways that even the old Razanei priests would never have tolerated."

"Agreed," Bongsunga said.

*Is she lying?* Jebi wondered, hating themself for the thought. But Vei was good at reading people, and she seemed convinced. *I'm imagining things,* Jebi thought. They wanted to return to a simpler time, when all they had to worry about was matching hues after running out of gamboge from a particular supplier, or helping Bongsunga with cooking and dishes and laundry. They didn't enjoy intrigue. But they'd gotten themself involved, and it was up to them to see everything through.

"First order of affairs," Bongsunga said, "now that that's settled. We need to move camp before we're located. My scouts haven't spotted any blues yet, but that doesn't mean they aren't out there."

"'My scouts,'" Jebi repeated. It confirmed what they'd guessed earlier. "You're in charge of this encampment, then. Not Han."

"Han ordinarily is in charge of this camp," Bongsunga said. "But she's good at following orders when she has to."

"How long," Jebi said, "have you been in this deep?" They didn't imagine that people vaulted up the rebels' chain of command in a matter of months.

"I signed on two days after Jia died," Bongsunga said. She stood straight-backed, her eyes like black ice.

Jebi did the math. "Almost *ten years?*" they said, their voice rising. "And you never—?" They checked themself. What would they have said to Bongsunga, after all? They'd been seventeen. Had hardly known what to say to their newly widowed sister. "I didn't... I didn't think the rebellion went back that far!"

"It went back further," Bongsunga said, "if you'd ever shown interest."

Jebi bowed their head at the rebuke, and stared blankly as Bongsunga began to give orders to break camp.

# Chapter
# SEVENTEEN

THE NEW CAMPSITE gave Jebi the impression of a temporary fortress, which was probably the intent. They had expected Bongsunga to lead them into the forsaken woods that still blanketed the wilderness of Hwaguk, and this was in fact what happened. Jebi had ambivalent feelings about the woods, because they'd grown up in the city, and in all the folktales, either tiger-sages or regular tigers prowled among the trees looking for delicious children. They did not want to take the chance that they might smell delicious, even though they'd had a bath recently.

Palisades surrounded the camp, which looked as though it had endured for longer than a mere few days or even weeks. Jebi couldn't imagine that anyone would be stupid enough to run up to a bunch of sharpened sticks. On the other hand, automata might be sturdy enough not to *care* about sharpened sticks.

When they expressed this thought to Vei, she said, "It's meant to encourage a thinking opponent to channelize their attack down that passageway—see? And then the defenders can attack them with arrows or rifles."

"We're not allowed to own—" Jebi began, then shut up. Why would rebels care about the Razanei administration's rules about armaments, other than as impediments to be gotten around?

Bongsunga called out a garbled-sounding passphrase, and a voice responded from within. She turned to Arazi, who had obligingly allowed the rebels to use it as a beast of burden for a great many of the tents, packs, cookpots, and so on, to the point that Jebi wondered if this had been an intended secondary use of the automaton. Would Hafanden, with his obsessive focus on Arazi's thwarted capacity for destruction, have thought of something so practical? Or would he have insisted on using Fourteener laborers instead?

Jebi was about to ask Vei when Han gestured for Jebi and Vei to follow her. The last thing Jebi wanted was to disappear into a dingy hillfort, but they didn't see that they had much choice.

"Arazi?" Jebi said, because they didn't like the thought of the dragon being left exposed on the outside.

"There's space inside," Han replied, "if it can hunker down."

*{That's no problem,}* Arazi said, doing exactly that. It did occur to Jebi that it would almost certainly fit in whatever nooks and crannies could be found, if it disassembled itself into spiderlings again, but if Arazi hadn't volunteered that

information, it had good reason. Jebi felt disloyal keeping
secrets from their sister and her lieutenant. Then again, that
went both ways, didn't it? And besides, it wasn't their secret,
it was Arazi's.

Jebi watched in bemusement as Arazi snaked into the
hillfort, following a grubby rebel whose expression suggested
that he was afraid that it might eat him if he offended it. If
they hadn't witnessed it themself, they would have doubted
that the dragon could squeeze into so little space.

*{I won't eat him,}* Arazi assured Jebi, *{unless he asks me to.}*

Jebi wondered how literally to take the sentiment, then
decided they didn't want to know.

Vei rested her hand on their shoulder, more of a warning tap.
Jebi looked at her, then followed her gaze to where Bongsunga
had lifted a hand in greeting to a strange, tall person with
ruddy hair. "A Westerner," Vei breathed in their ear.

"That's impossible," Jebi said, even though Hafanden had
warned them of their sister's allies. Jebi hadn't expected to
see one wandering around Hwaguk. The person, despite being
bundled up in the same grubby felt coats as the other rebels,
stood out like a hoopoe amid a flock of magpies. Even their
horsehair hat—traditional Hwagugin wear for elders—and
the scarf wrapped around their neck did nothing to disguise
the flyaway locks of that hair. Quite aside from the outlandish
orange-red color, their hair formed even more outlandish coils.
Jebi wanted to ask if they were wearing a wig or they'd done
something special to get their hair to do that... *any* of that.

Vei nudged Jebi. "You're staring," she mouthed.

Jebi hastily pretended to be looking over the orange-haired
person's shoulder at a completely jejune weapons rack. Or at

least it would have struck someone like Jia as jejune; it made Jebi's skin crawl. They supposed they could hardly expect rebels to march naked into battle like monks plunging into ice water to prove their resilience. The old stories also said that fully trained battle monks could shrug off arrows as though their skin were made of stone. Jebi had their doubts, but with monks, who could tell?

Bongsunga had noticed their staring. "Jebi," she called out. Jebi jerked upright and automatically walked over to her and bowed, trained by a lifetime of conditioning. "I'd like you to meet someone."

*The feeling isn't mutual,* Jebi thought, wondering if the orange-haired personage was hiding any other anatomical oddities or defects beneath that coat. Maybe that was why Western dress, as imported into Territory Fourteen anyway, featured such absurdly full skirts or coats and ruffles—to disguise such unnatural features.

"You must be the younger sibling," the person said, and Jebi's mouth hung open for a second before they remembered to close it. The Westerner spoke Hwamal, which wasn't a complete surprise; presumably even foreigners could learn the language if they applied themselves. But instead of garbling the pronunciation—a prejudicial expectation, to be sure—they had a faint but definite Huang-Guanin accent.

"You may call me Red, if you like," the Westerner went on. "I will be leading the mission."

"Red?" Jebi asked, because curiosity overcame them. "But your hair is orange." Unless it referred to something else?

"Red for the blood of my enemies," they said, winking disconcertingly. "No, actually, it's because my hair color is called 'red' among my people, even though it isn't, from a painter's standpoint."

Jebi suppressed a twitch. How much had Bongsunga told this person about family matters, or was that just a figure of speech?

Vei, less distracted by trivialities, was studying Red intently. "What's the mission?"

"The manufactories are heavily guarded," Red said. "Our saboteurs have had a hard time getting through, and our earlier leadership just made things worse by putting the Razanei on alert. We've limited ourselves to keeping watch, for now."

"Then—" Vei asked.

"Less well guarded are the expeditions of archaeologists and art collectors," Red went on. "They have a few guards to protect themselves from bandits and petty thieves, but they've been relying on secrecy most of all. After all, marching around old temples and tombs with squadrons of blues or automata would only signal that they're protecting something important."

"Quite correct," Vei said. "But it's not a strategy without its risks."

"You and your lover are to assist us in the raid," Red said.

Vei stilled. "I am a master of the sword," she said. "Return my sword and take me, but leave Jebi in camp. They don't have any martial training that I've ever been able to discern."

The words would have stung, but Jebi had learned that they had no business getting into a fight. Perhaps they should have asked Vei's father for a quick lesson. Unfortunately, they also knew that fighting, like painting, wasn't something you picked up overnight. And besides, Vei was trying to protect them.

They fretted that it looked bad for Vei to argue with someone the rebels trusted, orange hair or no, but Vei knew what she was doing.

"Hardly," Red returned, and there was more than a hint of iron in their voice. "Your lover"—Jebi was starting to hate the epithet, as though that *defined* them—"may be no duelist of renown or marksman, but they were instrumental in the cave-in that destroyed the Ministry of Armor and the surrounding gardens, weren't they?"

*The gardens?* Jebi thought faintly. They hadn't had a chance to survey the extent of the damage. Just how much of the complex *had* they destroyed?

"How did you find out about that?" Jebi demanded.

"Word got out from the survivors," Red said with suspicious lack of specificity.

If the gardens were ruined, how many survivors had there been? They hadn't spared the other artists any thought—until now. Mixed nausea and guilt speared through Jebi's gut as they thought about Shon, the lovers Tia and Mevem; hell, all the staff who'd only been guilty of accepting shitty menial jobs in service to the Razanei so they could feed their families.

*I was desperate,* Jebi thought; but that was no excuse.

Red and Vei were still arguing.

Vei: "Freak accident."

"Accident nothing," Red retorted. "Hwaguk has rainfall and seismology records going back *continuously* 767 years; even longer, in the former case, than Huang-Guan. The capital is sited in an unusually geologically stable location on a generally geologically stable peninsula. That was—" They used a term that Jebi couldn't unpuzzle, although it had the singsong sound of Huang-Guan's language. "And your 'painter' is the source of that power. They can damn sure invoke it on the rebellion's behalf."

"What's it to you?" Jebi demanded, because they were tired of being talked over like an adolescent at a matchmaker's meeting. "You're a foreigner, what do you care?"

Bongsunga's gaze cut sideways in warning or rebuke. But Red nodded as though they'd fielded the question many times before. Probably had, and suddenly Jebi felt like a boor.

"The Western lands aren't a monolith," Red said, their voice thick with suppressed emotion, "whatever you may think."

Jebi bit the inside of their mouth to keep from shouting that they barely had any *idea* what the world looked like outside of Huang-Guan, Hwaguk, Razan. While they'd glimpsed the map that Hafanden used to keep on the wall of his office, who knew how accurate it was?

"I come from a people who lived on the uneasy border between two nations," Red continued. "They were divided and swallowed up by war. I ran; went into exile. I was going to be a priest. I loved studying books and medicine. But it takes more than books and medicine to survive, so I turned mercenary until I found a second home."

"Do you feel welcome here?" Vei asked.

"I'm homesick sometimes," Red said. "But this is home now, and I will fight for it." They raised their chin. "Will you help with the mission, or not?"

"I can do it," Jebi said before Vei could stop them. "I'll stay out of the thick of the fighting. I'm not completely stupid." That was not entirely true, but Vei didn't mention the many stupid things that Jebi had done in front of a stranger. Partial stranger. "I'll need my supplies from the bag." The pigments, in particular.

Their stomach roiled at the thought of killing people, but maybe if they created an earthquake some distance away, it would scare the Razanei off without hurting anyone. They kept this plan to themself, since they were sure Bongsunga had no such compunctions.

Vei lifted one shoulder, let it fall. "It's your choice," she said, resigned. "I will keep the hostiles from touching you. I will cut down anyone who so much as stirs a hair on your head."

Jebi was torn between saying *You are embarrassing me* and *I am going to take up my brush and make a painting of you that they will talk about for the next 10,000 years.* They said neither.

Vei added to Bongsunga, despite Jebi's vexation, "I expect you will cut us down if we stray from the mission. It's a loyalty test, isn't it?"

"I wasn't trying to make a secret of it," Bongsunga said.

"I'm *family*," Jebi said, not because they thought it would change her mind but because they had to say *something*.

Bongsunga said, "The name certificate." That was all.

"You must be very certain of Red's loyalty," Jebi said, because it was someone else's turn to be talked over for a change.

Bongsunga and Red looked at each other for a long moment, and then Jebi knew what they were to each other. The last time Bongsunga had looked at someone like that had been while Jia still lived.

"Don't make me regret this," Bongsunga said.

Jebi didn't know whether she was addressing them or Red; didn't want to know.

\* \* \*

*THIS WILL BE easy,* Jebi thought while the squad assembled. *All I have to do is follow orders.*

Arazi emerged from the fort in short order, which made Jebi wonder why they'd crammed it in there in the first place. Then they saw that the rebels had rigged the dragon with a more elaborate version of the harness that Vei's parents had improvised. Arazi knelt like one of the tame jaguars in an imported tapestry Jebi had seen years ago, and three rebels clambered up to take their seats upon its back.

"Now you," Red told Jebi, "and the duelist after." A stony-faced rebel handed Vei's sword back to her, with a scowl that implied that she had better be careful who she hacked up with it.

Jebi did as ordered. Climbing up was less nerve-wracking than the first time. They figured out as they strapped themself in that Red wanted Vei behind Jebi to keep her from cutting down an actual useful rebel in front of her. Significantly, Red took the last seat, right behind Vei's.

*I should have bought a lot more mae-deup charms for luck,* Jebi thought as Arazi sprang into the air with no more difficulty than when it had been carrying only two people.

Arazi flew lower, barely skimming the treetops. Jebi couldn't decide whether the thought of plummeting to their death on the first flight, or crashing into pine trees on this one, intimidated them more. Maybe the dragon thought they'd avoid being sighted by scouts, especially if they were primed to check the sky. Woods-wise people kept an eye on the patterns of migrating birds in all the stories Jebi had ever heard; presumably *unexpected incoming dragon* was the kind of thing one wanted lookouts to warn one's soldiers about.

This time, instead of admiring the landscape and thinking about the pigments or brush techniques they would use to paint it, Jebi tried to view it as a soldier might. Features that had previously appeared picturesque or charming took on a more ominous cast. Ridges behind which enemy soldiers might be hiding, for instance, or half-frozen rivers over which it would be difficult to retreat. They kept their observations to themself, not least because the battle-hardened rebels would have found their attempts at reading the terrain comical. Even Vei might have cracked a smile; if it had just been the two of them, Jebi would have exaggerated their uncertainty, just to see it.

At one point Jebi leaned to the left to get a better view of a dappled boulder, so perfectly in harmony with the surrounding contours of the hills that they suspected someone had moved it there for the aesthetic effect. Vei grabbed their arm and gently but firmly hauled them back into line.

"We're almost there," Red said at the same time, almost inaudible over the hiss of the wind. "See?"

Jebi didn't see anything remarkable at first, until Vei pointed it out: an unnaturally symmetric hill. It must be a tomb from one of the old dynasties, back in the days when people believed in interring the highest of the scholar-aristocrats, and the occasional conquering general or favored entertainer, with miniature grave goods for the life beyond. The oldest and most valuable of those artifacts, like the ones Hak had displayed at that party, had by now vanished into the lairs of thieves or collectors. Only in the last several decades had people become interested in the symbolic and generally nonfunctional tokens of clay that the less prestigious tombs contained.

Beyond the hill Jebi spotted an encampment not much different than the rebels', except better organized, with the tents forming neat rows. The Razanei influence, they expected. Even Bongsunga's hillfort had lacked this obsession with right angles.

Arazi circled just out of sight. It couldn't hover in place, like a dragonfly. "The approach?" it asked, weirdly audible like a chiming of metal despite the softness of its voice.

"Take us straight in," Red said, "right in the center of the camp. They won't be expecting that."

*Neither was I,* Jebi thought faintly.

Arazi dived like a stooping hawk, so swiftly that Jebi's eyes swam. It landed in an explosion of dust and dead leaves right in the center of the encampment, crushing two unfortunate tents in the process. Jebi trusted that no unlucky camper had been caught inside. The impact jolted up through the dragon's metal limbs and jointed vertebrae and all the way up Jebi's own spine, causing their teeth to chatter unpleasantly. They were going to have a bruised tailbone for the next week.

The guards below, dressed not in the blue uniforms of the Razanei army but the shabbier patchwork wear of mercenaries, shouted in comical dismay. They ran around, getting clear of Arazi's viciously swinging tail—Jebi was sure it missed them on purpose—while fumbling for their weapons. One, better prepared than the rest, unsheathed their sword and swiped it at Arazi's hind leg, only to swear viciously when the blade broke.

"Disembark," Red ordered. "That includes you, artist."

Jebi would rather have stayed safely on Arazi's back, for values of 'safe' that included getting slung around like a sack of rice. But despite their personal preference for strategic cowardice, it would have been ungracious to refuse to join the others in their fight. Even if they wouldn't, strictly speaking, *be* fighting.

Besides, if some stray bullet took Vei out and they weren't at her side, they would never forgive themself.

Arazi, considerate of people climbing down, stilled and lashed out only with its tail. The guards recognized the opportunity and regrouped, this time directing their attacks against the dragon's joints. Perhaps they weren't as stupid as Jebi had assumed, just befuddled by an unexpected situation.

Jebi, distracted by the fighting going on around them, lost their grip on a handhold and fell a meter to the ground. They bit their tongue when they landed, and tasted blood. At least they hadn't landed on their neck—they were reminded of all the gruesome stories Jia had loved to tell about people who died or became paralyzed after bad falls from horseback—but either they'd twisted their ankle or broken it. They dragged themself underneath Arazi, the only shelter anywhere in the vicinity, and dug in their pack for the precious pigments.

Vei, more dextrous as always, had not only disembarked safely but had leapt from the second-last foothold and launched directly into an attack. If Jebi hadn't been miserable with pain and the conviction that they were two breaths away from dying, they would have admired the sheer elegance of her movements. They were struck silent by the way Vei's sword described gleaming arcs that ended in lethal sprays of red.

All of Red's squad had successfully dismounted Arazi and

had joined the fray. Jebi paid them little attention, although Vei would later tell them it would have been an excellent opportunity to assess their fighting skills. Excellent opportunity for *Vei*, anyway; Jebi couldn't tell a good fighter from a bad one except by reading commentaries, most of which made abstruse references to fighting forms and techniques in jargon so thick it would have put sailors to shame.

Vei paused, which was so unusual that Jebi gaped at her. Without turning, she said, "Jebi, are you still there?"

"Watch your back!" Jebi yelled. They'd caught a glimpse of a blur just beyond one of Arazi's legs while they were setting up to summon an earthquake, a process that took more time than they liked.

Vei whirled too late. An arrow whistled by and embedded itself in her right shoulder. Vei was right-handed. Jebi's throat went raw with pain, and only a moment afterward did they realize that they'd screamed her name as they ran toward her. The injured ankle gave away, and they landed sprawling in the dirt at Arazi's feet.

Jebi didn't see what happened in the next several moments, although they heard more shouts, several clanks—sword on sword, sword on dragon, something else?—and some thuds of the kind that suggested people had either been knocked out or outright killed. Sobbing at the agony in their ankle, they forced themself up to a kneeling position. If Vei was dead—

Vei was standing over them, having switched her grip so she was wielding her curved sword left-handed. More or less left-handed. It was a two-handed sword. Jebi wasn't clear on how that worked, either. Vei had not done the thing they always did in the epics and yanked the arrow out by its shaft to fling at her enemies, or even better, stab one, and Jebi wondered why.

*Should there be this many guards?* Jebi thought.

"No, wait, stop, we can talk this over!" yelled a shrill voice.

Jebi didn't recognize the newcomer at first. Sheer nervous sweat was fouling their eyesight. After wiping it away on the sleeve of their coat, they squinted at Vei. A short plump woman ran straight at her.

Too late Jebi identified her. "Vei, no, stop!" they cried. "I know her!" They reached out to grab Vei's leg, to keep her from doing the inevitable thing, but as always she was too fast for them.

Vei saw the figure running toward her as a threat either to herself or to Jebi, even if Jebi did not. If she'd heard Jebi's entreaty, she was either too focused to acknowledge it, or disregarded it as unimportant. In a single practiced motion, she beheaded the woman.

Jebi began to cry as Hak's body staggered several more paces only to come crashing down before them. In death, three fox tails sprouted from her backside. Her head, mouth still open in a surprised gape, rolled to a stop nearby.

"She was my friend," Jebi said to Vei's back. "Her name was Hak, and she was my friend."

# Chapter
# EIGHTEEN

*I CAN'T BELIEVE it,* Jebi thought for the—twentieth? thirtieth?—time that evening, back at the encampment. They sat inside a tent with two guards outside, personnel that the rebels could ill spare; but they didn't care about that. The encampment lacked prison cells, for which Jebi would have been grateful under other circumstances. The guards had, mercy of mercies, spared Jebi a single lantern. Its light brought them no comfort.

They had asked after Vei some time ago. The guards refused to answer, so they hadn't pursued it further. Besides, they weren't sure how much they wanted to talk to her, considering what she'd done.

"I can't believe it," Jebi said, this time out loud.

"Shut up in there," one of the guards called back, words that made as much sense as the language of rocks.

*{Jebi,}* Arazi was saying. *{Jebi, shall I come for you? We can fly away from here.}*

*{It doesn't matter,}* Jebi said dully. *{Hak is dead. She was my friend, and she's dead. I can't leave her body with the rebels. Someone has to do the rites. And if you fight them, more people will die. I don't want that.}*

The mission had, according to Red, gone off without a hitch. Jebi had overheard them reporting in to Bongsunga earlier—heard without comprehending anything but the fact that Hak was dead. They'd hugged their knees and tried not to retch at the memory of the gaping severed head, the limp fox tails.

Jebi remembered an earlier conversation they'd overheard. *Even for a loyalty test, that was cruel.* Vei's voice, low and hard, like forged steel. *At least, I assume you picked that expedition on purpose.*

They tried to remember Bongsunga's response; couldn't.

Jebi closed their eyes and tried not to hyperventilate. This would be a great time for a meditation exercise if they could calm down enough *to* meditate. Breathe in. Breathe out.

They suppressed a shriek when something cold and wet came in contact with their left hand. Jebi scooted back instinctively and flailed about, although they didn't want to catch their captors' attention, either. They hoped it wasn't a leak in the tent, if it had started raining or snowing? They hadn't seen much in the way of clouds, and given the dead, chilly stillness of the air, they didn't think a storm could have moved in that quickly.

There was a blur of gray, and the startling softness of fur against their skin. A cat crouched in the corner of the tent, ears laid back slightly, staring at Jebi with pale green eyes. The green would not have been remarkable anywhere else, but here they formed unexpected spots of color, like the first buds of leaves in spring.

"—half a mind to put it in the cookpot if I see it again," one of the guards was saying outside the tent. "Been a while since we had meat. Just endless bowls of millet and beans."

"Probably diseased," the other guard opined. "Besides, I hear that if you offend a cat and it gets away, the council of cats will get together to curse you. My gran said that and everything they told me about foxes was true, why not cats?"

The first guard scoffed. "Your gran was..."

Jebi lost interest in the conversation and held a hand out toward the cat, moving slowly so as not to spook it. Perhaps it was selfish considering they'd had a good meal less than a day ago, but they didn't want the cat to be caught by hungry rebels. Besides, they doubted the poor thing had much meat on its bones. Its gray tabby coat, however soft-looking, didn't hide its thinness.

"Stay there," Jebi whispered, although even they knew that cats, unlike dogs, didn't take orders, except maybe from tiger-sages. And probably not even then. "I don't want them to put you in the stewpot!"

Then they raised their voice: "Can I get some food in here?" They wished the hint of a whine was deliberate, but they were getting hungry. Horrifying, considering they'd just witnessed the death of one of their best friends.

"Shut up," the first guard said, while the second said, at the same time, "They're *her* sib, maybe we better treat them good."

It occurred to Jebi that if everyone was eating millet, the kind of food that would sustain a cat would be in short supply. The hunting must be terrible around here, considering how thin it was. Perhaps it was hanging around camp in hopes of scraps.

While the guards discussed the matter, ultimately deciding to kick up the problem to some superior, the cat busied itself making a nest amid the rags and blankets that occupied the corner. Some time later, one of the guards thrust a bowl in through the tent flap so roughly that some of the contents slopped over the side. They flung in a spoon after, but no chopsticks. "Make the most of it," the guard said, and let the flap fall.

"Thank you," Jebi called out, hating the way their voice quavered. They crawled over to retrieve the bowl and its contents. Millet and some foraged roots that looked tough and nasty, although the cook had included a couple thin scraps of meat. Jebi spooned it up and nibbled cautiously. At least it was warm. Some kind of bird—the gamey taste suggested someone had gone hunting.

The taste of meat reminded Jebi that their stomach was, in fact, starting to grumble. But the cat looked hungry, too. With a sigh, Jebi picked up the scraps of bird meat and placed them halfway between themself and the cat, whose bright eyes regarded them with great interest.

"That's right," Jebi crooned. They didn't care if they were wasting the guards' grudging generosity on a cat. Someone might as well have a good day today, for pitiful values of 'good.' They continued to make coaxing noises as they retreated to their side of the tent.

Jebi closed their eyes on the grounds that it might make the cat feel more secure. They didn't actually know much about cats. They'd seen strays around the city, of course. Bongsunga lacked any soft spot for animals, so they'd never attempted to feed one, although Hak and some of her well-to-do friends would occasionally leave out scraps in the winter.

The reminder of Hak's unthinking kindness brought tears stinging hotly to Jebi's eyes. Maybe they'd imagined the whole horrible incident and they'd wake up tomorrow in their bedroom, hungover from too much rice wine at one of Hak's parties, and Bongsunga would scold them as they staggered to the kitchen to brew tea for the headache. Then they'd show up at one of the art stores or the butcher's, and exchange a few friendly words with Hak, and everything would be back to normal.

Jebi's fantasy collapsed as the sounds of bickering resumed outside the tent. To distract themself, even though they really should pay attention, they watched the cat. Its eyes stared unblinkingly back at them.

"Don't make me regret wasting perfectly good meat on you," Jebi entreated it.

The cat continued to stare. Jebi was starting to feel offended at wasting a good deed on a *cat*, of all creatures, when they realized that the cat, still staring, had slipped out from beneath the rags and was approaching the food. Jebi held their breath, not wanting to scare it away.

The cat sniffed the meat. For a bad moment, Jebi thought it was going to reject the food for inexplicable cat reasons. Maybe it came from cat aristocracy—if there were tiger-sages, surely there could be cat-aristocrats—and demanded only the choicest of meats, which would explain why it looked half-starved. And never mind that most animals that didn't belong to Razanei officials or soldiers were going to be half-starved at this time of year.

Then the cat bolted down the meat so quickly that Jebi almost missed it, and mewed. Jebi couldn't tell for sure, but they thought it had warmed toward them. Its ears were pricked forward, and it blinked slowly.

"—hear that?"

"Even if it's damn poor meat, I could make mittens from its hide. Mine have holes in them and I'm going to get frostbite at this rate."

The cat mewed again.

Jebi groaned and dived for the cat—they had to protect it from being skinned—but it easily evaded them and slipped out through a rip in the side of the tent that they hadn't noticed earlier. With any luck, it would stay out of the stewpot another day.

"—definitely a cat."

One of the guards kicked the side of the tent. Jebi groaned in protest as the boot connected through the canvas. "There a cat in there?"

"I heard one go by," Jebi lied. "Haven't seen one, though."

"Well, let us know. There could be more of that meat if you liked it."

*Are cats cannibals?* Jebi wondered, gorge rising at the thought that their millet stew had contained cat meat. It had *tasted* like bird... "Uh, was that meat—?" *Shut up, shut up,* another voice inside their head insisted, *do you actually want to know?*

"Oh, that," the second guard said, still sounding friendlier. "That's from yesterday's hunt. Some unlucky bird. You're lucky there was anything left at the bottom of the cookpot."

Whew. "Thank you," Jebi said, as servilely as they could manage, That reminded them that they should eat the food provided. They didn't know whether they'd get another meal anytime soon.

The millet was insufferably bland; Jebi guessed that the rebels were rationing salt. Jebi forced themself to chew the roots, bitter as they were, and choke them down. They hoped the roots weren't poison—some of the traditional remedies were dangerous in higher doses, and Jebi didn't have the expertise to tell beneficial roots from bad ones—but surely the rebels had easier ways to do away with them if that was their intent.

Jebi was in the middle of picking grit out of their teeth—something everyone was used to doing, even in the city, and even if the household's cook was as meticulous about picking stones out of grain as Bongsunga—when someone opened the tent. A burst of cold air swirled into the tent, and Jebi shivered, wishing their coat provided better protection against the weather. Outside, night had fallen; the single lantern hanging from the tentpole shone like a fettered star.

Bongsunga entered and sat, as self-assured as a queen. "There's good news and bad news," she said without preamble. "I assume you want to hear the good first."

This reminded Jebi of the time one of their hired art instructors had sent a letter to Bongsunga giving insipid praise for Jebi's willingness to work hard on holding a brush correctly and slagging everything else. It hadn't taken her long to fire that one for 'aggressive uselessness.' Alas, Jebi didn't think any such joyous outcome awaited them here.

"Sure," Jebi said warily.

"It was a loyalty test," Bongsunga said—not exactly Jebi's idea of *good news*—"and your lover passed."

Jebi opened their mouth to opine that Vei, brilliant, beautiful Vei, had *of course* taken down five times as many of the enemy—her own people—as any of the rebels, then shut it. After all, the 'enemy' had included poor unlucky Hak. "The bad news?" they asked after it became clear that Bongsunga was waiting for a response.

"You didn't."

"Oh," Jebi said stupidly, even though it should have been obvious. "So sorry to be a disappointment."

Bongsunga yanked a strand of her hair, and for a moment she was the sister Jebi remembered. "I tried to keep you out of this," she said. Jebi thought at first she was referring to the raid. "I tried *so hard*. You wanted art, so I gave you art. I would have been happy for you to *keep* doing art and stay uninvolved with the bloody work of resistance."

Jebi grimaced. "And then I had to go blow it all to hell by working for the Ministry of Armor," they said.

"Perhaps," Bongsunga said, grudging, "this wouldn't have happened if I'd been more open with you in the first place. I didn't want you to worry..."

"It was Hak," Jebi said. "I couldn't say nothing. It was Hak." They'd known her since they were both art students. She'd said that even gumiho had to change with the times and learn respectable professions. They still remembered how proud she'd been of her one experiment in sculpture, with some low-quality clay a client had donated to the instructor. A rotund, happy pig. The memory of the clay pig—lumpy, slightly lopsided, and too cheerful for its own good—made Jebi tear up all over again.

Bongsunga went quiet for so long that Jebi almost thought that she had left the tent and only her afterimage remained, like a reproachful ghost. But no: she was only thinking things through, the way she did sometimes. At last she said, "You know what she was involved in."

"It's not a crime to be an art collector!"

"*Think*, Jebi. She was putting art in the hands of Rassasin collectors. To be destroyed. And you know for what cause."

"You don't know that *she* knew." Jebi doubted that Hafanden would have entrusted that kind of information to a mere collectibles broker. If nothing else, surely Vei would have known if that had been the case.

"She never," Bongsunga said with frustrating finality, "*asked*."

"There could have been perfectly innocent reasons to collect our art!" Jebi realized how that would sound the moment the words escaped their mouth.

Bongsunga just looked at them. "Yes," she said. "*Our* art. Our art, leaving our country. One more resource they're plundering from us."

"Oh, come on," Jebi protested. "We've been exporting art for centuries. Most artists would be happy to find a following overseas. Getting paid is getting paid." Even if the person doing the paying had *orange hair*, but they weren't about to say that to their sister.

"It's not the same," Bongsunga said, her mouth puckering.

"They're interested in our art because it's 'primitive' and 'exotic' in comparison to 'refined' Rassanin art. And that's before you consider its *destruction*."

Once Jebi wouldn't have cared. After all, they'd entertained similar opinions about some of the wilder Westerner art they'd viewed. Had even obtained one or two badly printed copies for amusement value, to discuss with friends.

But perhaps there was something to what Bongsunga said. Would Hafanden so casually destroy art he valued? Razanei art? They couldn't see him doing it.

"So I failed," Jebi said. "I'm not sorry."

Bongsunga's lips compressed for a second. "I didn't think you'd be," she admitted. "I will have to keep you under guard." Mercifully, she refrained from adding what an inconvenience this would be. "But you are in a position to do us a great favor."

"Which is?" Jebi asked, wary all over again.

"We recovered some of the artifacts that the expedition had excavated," Bongsunga said. "I'd welcome your help cataloging it."

"Of course," Jebi said. Then they thought to ask, "What are you going to do with it?"

Bongsunga smiled grimly. "Move it where Rassan can't get at it."

"Sell it to the Westerners?" Jebi said, before they could stop themself.

"It's not selling," Bongsunga said. "Those of our people who have found refuge outside of Rassan's sphere of influence can keep these works safe until we can return them to the country. A free country, I hope."

Something didn't add up. What prevented these so-called patriots from selling everything off for a profit? Assuming Westerners also found Hwagugin artwork charming, a big *if*. "What," Jebi said slowly, "are you going to do with all that art? Make your own automata?"

Bongsunga looked at them steadily. "I wanted to keep you out of this," she said.

The fact that she wasn't even trying to deny it only hurt worse. "How long have you known?" Jebi asked. "About the automata and the horrible pigments?"

"Not as long as you might think," Bongsunga said after a telling pause.

"Really."

"The only reason I even took notice of Armor's activities in this area," she said, "was because art always reminds me of you. No matter what kind it is."

Had this come from anyone else, Jebi would have been offended—-their art was not *interchangeable* with everything else out there—but this was Bongsunga. For all her support over the years, she'd never been able to distinguish art styles except in the crudest terms. She couldn't even tell different schools of calligraphy apart. Jebi accepted that not everyone had the eye, or the patience to develop it.

"Fine," Jebi said, which came out about as hostile as they felt. "Show me the things you want appraised."

Even then Bongsunga hadn't finished with unpleasant surprises. "I feel obliged to warn you," she said, "that if you try to escape—"

Jebi had a very good idea of their sister's ruthlessness. In a play, they would have found it admirable. In life, they found it inconvenient. "Save it," they said.

Bongsunga preceded them out of the tent. The guards didn't snap to or salute, which disconcerted Jebi after their stint with the Ministry of Armor. They did, however, straighten and murmur respectfully to Bongsunga as she passed.

Arazi had hidden itself cleverly beneath the tops of the palisades by coiling in on itself like a spring. The effect would have been comical if Jebi had been in any mood for humor. *{Jebi?}* it asked, its voice dissonant with worry.

*{I'm all right,}* Jebi said, not because it was true but because they didn't want Arazi to worry about them. *{She won't hurt me.}* As long as they behaved, anyway.

*Which dead artists made you possible?* Jebi thought as they considered the dragon's involvement. Would the artists mind, if they'd died of natural causes—or, perhaps, ascended like the Eight Immortals of old—rather than being murdered for the Razanei's convenience? Despite the dragon's unnatural origins, it had never acted with anything but a thoughtfulness that put Jebi themself to shame.

*{I'm here and watching,}* Arazi said to them as they passed, even so.

Bongsunga had not a tent but an alarmingly spacious building to herself at the heart of the encampment. The encampment must have been built around one of the older hillforts. Bongsunga exchanged a few words with the guards before motioning Jebi to enter. A damp, mildewy curtain covered the door.

Jebi, who'd shivered in the short distance from tent to building, gratefully sidled toward the largest of the braziers that heated the space. The building smelled of rust, grease, and an overabundance of incense, an indulgent remedy for smells among people with uncertain resources. Maybe the rebels had purloined a shipment of the stuff from some Razanei officials.

"Here's the art," Bongsunga said abruptly.

Jebi turned their attention to the crates stacked against one of the walls. Some of them sported dents—or, more alarmingly, flecks of mud and splotches of caked dried blood. It didn't make them confident about the contents. Not for the first time, they became aware of art as *fragile*. Burn it down or tear it up, and no one would ever know that it had existed or what it had looked like, except perhaps in some critic's passing diatribe or a scholar's pamphlet.

Aware of their sister watching, Jebi opened the first of the crates and leafed carefully through the artworks. This one contained a mixture of silk scrolls and paper. At least none of the former were the old, elaborate kind that could extend for meters and meters, depicting a panorama of idealized landscapes along with commentaries; the one table in the building wouldn't have accommodated such a thing.

"The signature chops are right there," Jebi said, disgruntled. But only a little, because among a gaggle of lesser-known to downright unknown students of that one school that liked to insert gratuitous crickets in the borders was a particular artist who would go on to found a completely different and much more famous school.

"Go on," Bongsunga said.

Jebi sighed and commented on the conditions of the scrolls and paintings as well as the artists. This included some pointed suggestions on better storage methods if Bongsunga meant for the works to survive any kind of journey intact. "You should at least," Jebi said, "scare up some cases for the loose scrolls, or it's going to be a mess in there. Rat's nests and all."

"Jebi," Bongsunga said, "does it look like we have an excess supply of scroll cases back here?"

"I'm just saying." The next crates weren't much better— pottery packed in straw to keep it from breaking. At least in theory; one of the vases had a hairline crack at the lip. Jebi conscientiously pointed this out, too.

"The duelist said the same thing," Bongsunga admitted grudgingly after Jebi suggested more straw.

Jebi blinked. "You asked Vei?"

"She mentioned she'd had a collection, before the earthquake. I thought I'd check her 'expertise' against yours."

"In some regards I expect she knows more than I do," Jebi admitted, hoping Bongsunga didn't hear the faint note of pride they hadn't managed to suppress. "She would have seen a great many examples."

Bongsunga's eyes narrowed. "I'm sure she did. It's funny that someone with that kind of expertise in the sword has a sideline in art."

"Is it really?" Jebi countered. "Even master duelists are allowed to have hobbies."

"Why, you've seen her train?"

Jebi shrugged because it beat gushing over something they comprehended only dimly. "Saw her duel once. It went by so fast I couldn't tell you what happened. I mean, you've seen her fight."

Hak's severed head flashed in their memory again, and they fell silent. If they closed their eyes, they were afraid they'd see her staring reproachfully at them. *You should have stopped her,* she whispered.

"How is Vei?" Jebi asked, with a pang of guilt for not having questioned Bongsunga sooner. "I saw an arrow wound..."

"You didn't think we'd leave her languishing in a tent to die of infection, did you?"

Jebi responded with a pointed silence.

"All right," Bongsunga conceded, "we haven't given you much chance to trust us. But it's true. We have a physician in camp. He's proven reliable," she added, which instantly made Jebi distrust him.

In an ideal world, Jebi would have rushed to Vei's side to nurse her back to health, despite their grief. In reality, they had no idea how to treat an arrow wound. "He can do something about the arrow?" they asked. If Vei's life was in their sister's hands, they should do everything possible to cooperate with her.

"He said it was smart of her not to yank it out the way they do in the paintings," Bongsunga said, which made Jebi think not only of the splendid pieces of art they had seen which depicted exactly that, but of offending pieces they had painted themself.

"Why," Jebi said, "what's wrong with doing that?" Especially if everyone thought it looked impressive?

"The arrowheads," Bongsunga said. "They tear up the wound on the way out. Jia had some scars she'd gotten that way, from bandits."

Jebi looked at her thoughtfully. For the longest time, they'd been afraid to bring up Jia's name, knowing that the wound still festered. But here was their sister, talking about her from a bygone time. And healed of her grief, apparently, enough to enter a new relationship. How long had she known Red? "I suppose," Jebi said, "it was some asshole painter like me that gave her the idea."

Bongsunga blinked, then the corners of her mouth twitched. "That's right," she said, a rare concession to humor. "Some painter like you, I'm sure."

Jebi let out their breath. The job Bongsunga did might have changed her, but she was still their sister. "Please let me see her," they said.

"I will," Bongsunga said, "if you'll tell her we could use her help planning the next strikes."

"It never stops, does it?" Jebi said in wonder. "You're *always strategizing*."

The wrinkles around her eyes deepened momentarily. "Jebi," she said, "this is like when you were four and you thought laundry magically happened."

Jebi opened their mouth to protest that they'd helped with the laundry, then remembered that 'helping' had consisted of running around shrieking with glee while pulling underclothes off the line and flinging them about. In retrospect, it was a wonder that their mother—or Bongsunga, always the responsible elder—hadn't strangled them. "Right," they said, chastened. "I suppose revolution is work, too."

This was close enough to assent that Bongsunga led them out of the tent and toward another. This one smelled of incense, or maybe herbs. Something bitter and medicinal, which left an unpleasant almost-aftertaste in the back of Jebi's throat.

Within the tent lay four people on closely packed cots. Jebi recognized one as Vei and cried out to see her hair shorn. "Was that necessary?" they demanded. "It's not like the arrow hit her in the *head*."

"Jebi," Vei said, her voice shockingly weak. "Jebi, is that you?" Someone had wrapped a coarse robe around her, and grubby bandages covered the arrow wound.

Jebi carefully picked her way to Vei's side. "It's me," they said, resisting the urge to squeeze Vei's hand and instead stroking her arm and feeling helpless. "Your hair, Vei."

"I insisted. It was only going to get in the way. Less to keep clean in the field." She didn't sound fussed about the loss, even if Jebi already missed running their hands through the long locks.

Bongsunga cleared her throat. "You could have died," she said. Jebi wondered at the roughness of her voice, the intimation of suppressed emotion. "Even injured, though, you may be of use to us."

"You have shown a great deal of tolerance for someone of foreign blood," Vei said quietly. "I'm not unwilling to be of assistance. But why? Why ask for what you can take?"

Bongsunga's lip curled. "Because even revolutionaries have to follow rules," she said, "or there's nothing worth rebelling for. It won't surprise you that there are disagreements among my people as to the best way to resist. Some people want to burn everything down and seize what remains for themselves. Others would as happily conquer Razan in turn and do to you what was done to us. We're divided, and *that* isn't Razan's doing. We did that to ourselves, and we will be paying for it well into the future. But here, now, I have my people and I set my own rules; that is one of them."

"Appreciated," Vei said. "I am amenable."

Jebi let out their breath, and sat down to listen while Vei and Bongsunga strategized.

# Chapter
# NINETEEN

IN THE DAYS that followed, Bongsunga conferred every hour with her scouts. She did not drill with her troops, which surprised Jebi at first. They'd had some notion that revolutionary types respected strength above anything else, or arm-wrestled for leadership positions, like bandits did in the stories (real bandits, Jebi had no clue). On the other hand, Bongsunga allowed them to watch her playing baduk against some of the other rebels. Jebi followed the game well enough to tell that she always won.

Bongsunga had shifted the crates of artwork to a tent, where she confined Jebi during most of their day. Jebi poured all their frustration with the situation into the cataloging that they'd agreed to do, this time recording everything on the water-stained paper that she'd provided. A single guard paced around the tent. Jebi's two attempts to talk to him had revealed that either he was deaf or he had orders not to respond to a word they said; either way, no help there. Even when they had to use the latrine—located, to Jebi's relief, a sanitary distance away from the rest of the camp—the guard accompanied them and watched.

Jebi, not being entirely naive, had refrained from telling Bongsunga about Arazi's ability to speak mind to mind with them. Arazi entertained them during their work by telling stories about the rebels and their pastimes. *{I want to gamble too,}* it added, to Jebi's alarm, *{but I don't have any money.}*

*{Given your luck, you probably shouldn't,}* Jebi said.

Its attention had moved on to other matters. *{Everyone has such different hair!}* And it was off burbling about its latest enthusiasm.

On the third day, Jebi satisfied themself that they couldn't simply sneak past the guard, or at least, they didn't want to risk having him pound them into the dirt unless they had no other option. Jebi studied his bulky physique, muscles all the way down, and concluded that they couldn't be guaranteed that the biceps were for show. Vei would have been able to tell; but they couldn't confer with her in anything resembling privacy, either.

*{Arazi,}* Jebi said as they used an old, shitty brush someone had scrounged up to remove caked mud from one of the vases. A nice piece, slightly asymmetrical in what Hak would have touted as "peculiarly Fourteener charm." Thinking about their dead friend brought the grief back, but they couldn't afford to mourn. *{Arazi, are you busy right now?}*

The dragon didn't answer.

*{Arazi?}*

The dragon continued not to answer.

Jebi buried their face in their hands and moaned. The guard kicked the side of the tent in warning—not the side with the stacked crates, thankfully, although how would he know they hadn't *moved* them out of spite—and Jebi chewed on their lower lip. They didn't know how to concentrate on art cataloging when they needed to escape an entirely new prison. What if Arazi, seduced by the charms of revolutionaries and their hairstyles, threw in with Bongsunga after all?

Jebi set the brush down and stared sightlessly at the vase. It was snowy white with a fine pattern of combed lines zigzagging down one side, not a design motif that they'd seen elsewhere. But then, pottery wasn't their area of expertise. They resented that Bongsunga seemed to consider all forms of art faintly interchangeable. Were swords and spears interchangeable? They bet not.

Why did it matter so much to them? Arazi could make up its mind for itself. In particular, why did the idea of the dragon taking up with their sister bother them so much? After all, Bongsunga's distrust of the Razanei regime had proven wise. Jebi could no longer claim that life under the Razanei was no different from life under Hwagugin rule.

That night, as Jebi slept on a pallet in the tent with the precious artifacts, they thought they heard Arazi calling their name. But they were tired, so tired, and they fell asleep even as they mumbled, "Later."

They woke shivering in the middle of the night. The brazier had gone out. They ventured out, only to almost get kicked in the shin by a different guard.

"Latrine?" the guard asked brusquely.

Jebi started to say no, then realized that was a yes. "Also my brazier went out," they added, hoping the guard would think that letting them die of hypothermia wouldn't endear her to Bongsunga.

The guard grunted. After the trip to the latrine, she grudgingly relit the brazier.

"Thank you," Jebi said, which received another grunt.

They were wide awake now, thanks to the cold. {Arazi?}

This time the dragon's sinuous voice responded. {I'm here,} it said penitently. {I have been much occupied.}

Jebi's trepidations only grew. {Occupied doing what?}

{Drills with the soldiers,} Arazi said. {Including flying drills to figure out who's afraid of heights, and who's likely to vomit during ascents, descents, and turbulence. There has been much vomiting! I am told it is very smelly.}

{Like at sea?} Jebi asked, distracted by the image of green-faced rebels clutching the dragon's harness, then realized neither they nor Arazi knew anything about nautical endeavors except from stories. {I suppose the weather's unpredictable.} They'd had some awareness of the wind whistling through the camp, but hadn't paid much attention to it other than to wish that they had extra braziers, and never mind the fire hazard.

{I suppose?} Arazi said, dubious in turn. {I've never seen the sea. But you didn't call to me because you wanted to talk about the sea.}

{Not exactly,} Jebi said. {I was—I was going to ask for your help escaping. Although I realize that it's up to you, and I don't know how to get Vei out.}

For the first time, Jebi had an uncomfortable insight into the mindset of people like Hafanden, or, for that matter, the unnamed Razanei who had come up with the concept of an army of automata in the first place. It must be so convenient to have soldiers who would obey your every command, unlike fallible, or lazy, or malicious human beings who had minds of their own.

Except Arazi had a mind of its own, too, when allowed to express its thoughts.

Luckily for Jebi, Arazi's pause was only momentary, or they would have held their breath in an agony of suspense. {I am no expert in the ways of siblings,} it said, gently ironic, {but I take it that you and your sister have disagreements over the proper way things should be done.}

{That's putting it mildly,} Jebi said. Miserably, they wondered when their family affairs had become so complicated. {You can do what you want—I mean, not that you need my permission. I just want to paint. But sometimes I wonder if Bongsunga isn't right, and fighting for Hwaguk's freedom is more important.}

{Your sister wants you to make another earthquake?}

{She hasn't come out and said it,} Jebi said, {but I know she's thinking it. Even if we're almost out of Phoenix Extravagant and the other pigments I need.} They'd considered using an earthquake to escape, but they couldn't think of a way to do it that wouldn't destroy the camp, and they weren't that desperate yet.

{You should talk about it.}

{I should,} Jebi agreed. Maybe tomorrow.

*     *     *

IN THE MORNING, Jebi reinventoried all the crates. Some of the rebels had gotten into a brawl next to the tent. Everyone had heard Bongsunga upbraiding them, even Jebi.

Most of the contents hadn't shifted too badly, and the few metal or stone pieces—a scratched-up bronze mirror, a handful of the ubiquitous comma-shaped jades, a jewelry box depicting two pheasants—had survived intact. But several of the paintings had new rips in them, which Jebi recorded in their most sarcastic handwriting, and no less than three of the ceramics were broken, one of them beyond repair.

The sounds of shouting and—a riot?—interrupted Jebi's concentration after lunch. At first they dismissed it as a fancy, or perhaps some inexplicable drill involving lots of cadence. Jia had explained to them about cadence once. It had sounded like so much nonsense. In retrospect, it was a miracle that Jia hadn't retaliated by mocking Jebi's expertise in painting.

The shouting grew louder. Jebi thought they heard a familiar voice bellowing to be heard, in Razanei-accented Hwamal. Could it be—?

Jebi timidly ventured out of the tent, only to be greeted by the guard's frown. "Are we in danger?" they asked.

"Get back in there," he said, "it's none of your affair."

"If it's something I can help with—" Shit. Had Bongsunga mentioned their ability to call earthquakes? And if so, would it antagonize the guard further to tell him of it? Assuming he believed them in the first place.

Fuming, Jebi allowed the guard to herd them back into the tent, where they listened to the commotion. They were about to try sneaking out, even knowing it was a terrible idea, when

Bongsunga appeared, her face flushed. She'd been running, Jebi guessed, recognizing the dangerous spark in her eyes.

"What is—" Jebi began to say.

Bongsunga shook her head impatiently. "Come with me," she said, and didn't wait for an acknowledgment.

The guard prodded Jebi into following, although they didn't need the encouragement. Surely the camp hadn't come under attack, or Bongsunga wouldn't be wasting time fetching them?

In the center of the camp, a circle of rebels surrounded—two? three?—figures. Jebi couldn't see over their heads or, more importantly, their spears, bows, and rifles, leveled at the newcomers. Toward the entrance of the camp, Jebi saw two horses—no, three. The third had collapsed nearby. Jebi didn't know much about horses other than what they'd picked up from Jia, who'd served in the cavalry, but they recognized a dying horse when they saw one. It had an elaborate saddle of a type Jebi had never seen before.

"They claimed to know you," Bongsunga said without preamble, "and Vei. Since Vei is in no condition to come out and verify their identities, and I'm certainly not taking strangers to the invalids' tent, it has to be you."

"Thanks?" Jebi said dubiously.

The guard shoved them forward, and the circle of rebels parted to let Jebi through. They'd been right the second time: three people. Three people, each of whom they'd met before, however briefly. Vei's parents.

"I know them," Jebi said, resisting the urge to sag with relief. Not least because they had no guarantee that Bongsunga wouldn't order Vei's parents killed. They pointed to each in turn as they named the newcomers: "Captain Dzuge Keizhi.

Hyeja, a physician. You always find those useful, don't you?" they added, unable to resist needling Bongsunga. "And Namgyu, a calligrapher and translator."

Bongsunga eyed the three without fear, which made Jebi worry all over again. Vei's father had surrendered his sword, not that Jebi thought they considered him a real threat; the rebels had allowed him to keep his crutches. Jebi couldn't imagine why they were here, or how they had found Bongsunga's camp.

"Explain," Bongsunga said, "why you are here."

"You think your experiments in dragon-borne troop transport haven't been noticed?" Captain Dzuge said grimly. "Even after we went underground—a narrow escape—all I had to do was triangulate the reports to locate your base. I still have some friends in the service."

Jebi flashed back to the image of Vei's parents' house, burning, and the blues closing in.

"It won't matter," Bongsunga said. "We're ready. And you haven't answered the question."

"I haven't indeed." His Razanei accent thickened, although no one remarked on it. "I came to warn you that the Deputy Minister of Armor is working with Ornithology and the military. They're planning a raid to recapture your dragon. I assume it's still here."

Arazi's head snaked out of nowhere to peer *over* the circle of rebels and down at Captain Dzuge. "I will not permit it," it said. "I will not work for the deputy minister."

"He believes otherwise," Captain Dzuge said grimly. "That's the warning. We rode several horses to death bringing word. I hope you can do something with it."

"You're a deserter, then," Bongsunga said, as if *that* was the most important point.

Captain Dzuge's mouth crooked. "I think my loyalties burned down with my house. There are limits to what I'm willing to tolerate."

"You're a captain," Bongsunga said. "That's not a trivial rank to give up so easily."

"Even a Razanei captain," he said, "may have principles. Let's be clear. I'm not here for *you*. I'm here because my daughter came this way, and because she's made certain choices. That's all it is."

"I appreciate your honesty," Bongsunga said. "How many are coming this way, and how soon?"

"Three days at best, more likely two," the captain said. "I would either reinforce your defenses—which, sorry, aren't going to stand up to the new tanks they've been testing—or I would evacuate the hell out of here. Your choice."

"And these people?" Bongsunga asked, gesturing at Hyeja and Namgyu, who were huddled together. Jebi was relieved to see that Hyeja had ditched the extremely conspicuous Westerner dress, with its lace and ruffles, in favor of something one could actually sit a horse on.

Captain Dzuge kissed first Namgyu's hand, then Hyeja's, courtly as a figure out of legend. "Family," he said simply. "They're of your people. Do with me what you will; but keep them out of harm's way, if you can."

An ugly mutter of *collaborators* went around the circle. Bongsunga raised her hand, and everyone stilled. "They will have my protection," she said, "in thanks. But you should have left them hidden elsewhere if you wanted *safety*."

Chapter

# TWENTY

"WE NEED INTEL," Bongsunga said. "Arazi, if you would be willing—"

"I did not want to fight," the dragon said with a metallic sigh, "but I don't want to see you slaughtered, either. I can at least tell you what I see coming."

"You're not going to be able to conceal yourself from their scouts," Captain Dzuge said. "If you can see them, they can see you."

"Then perhaps I can scare them away," Arazi said. "The fewer there are, the better for you, yes?"

Before anyone could respond to this suggestion, it sprang up into the air. Jebi stared after it, both longing and envious. If only it had *wings*, like a crane or a dragonfly; there was something uncanny about the way it simply willed itself into the air. But then, given its origins, perhaps that was no stranger than anything else about it.

Bongsunga began giving orders in a jargon that meant little to Jebi. They stood uncertainly in the middle of the camp as the rebels snapped to, some heading toward the walls and others moving mysterious barrels and bales. It was not unlike sitting amid one of those wire puzzles that Bongsunga had liked to foist off on them to keep them occupied when they were smaller. Back then, the puzzles had never lasted long— Jebi excelled at figuring out how to rotate or flip the pieces— and they'd always been scolded for taking them apart out of boredom. Here, they had no idea what the shape of the action added up to other than *bad news*.

Dzuge Keizhi was escorted by two squinty guards to follow Bongsunga, presumably so she could question him about what he'd seen on the way. Or maybe so the guards could keep an eye on him. Or execute him, or—*Quit catastrophizing.* He'd known the risks in coming here; Jebi could only hope that he had a backup plan, just in case.

Namgyu and Hyeja insisted on seeing their daughter. Since no one else took them seriously, Jebi offered to guide the two to the invalids' tent. "Vei's hurt?" Namgyu demanded. "How badly?"

"Arrow to the right shoulder," Jebi said. "The surgeon cut it out. I don't know how she's doing now." It figured that the only reason they could slip in to see Vei was that everyone else was distracted by an impending attack.

Namgyu and Hyeja exchanged glances. "We can be of help here," Hyeja said.

They stopped in front of the tent. No guard, although a

youth was just outside, fumbling with a... tent? Tent poles?

"Are you here to help with the inevitable flood of wounded people?" the youth snapped without looking at the three of them. "If not, get out of the way."

"You're setting up more tents, aren't you?" Hyeja said. "This one's full?"

"What do you think?"

Jebi was impressed by Hyeja's ability not to take offense. Instead, she helped the stranger wrangle the tent. Wordlessly, Namgyu assisted.

*Go,* Namgyu mouthed to Jebi. They sneaked into the tent while the assistant was distracted, wondering why Vei's parents weren't following; or maybe they really did believe in the importance of extra tents for incoming casualties.

The smell of burning herbs—presumably because incense was dear—did little to cover up the stench of piss and suppurating wounds. To Jebi's relief, Vei was already standing, leaning heavily upon her sword. Jebi's reaction changed swiftly into dismay when they took in how wan she looked, and how matted her shorn hair.

"What are my parents doing here?" Vei hissed.

Jebi gave her the least garbled explanation of the situation they could put together in five seconds.

With a visible effort, Vei tied her scabbard around her waist—she was almost as dextrous with her left hand as she'd been with her right—and strode out of the tent. Jebi wondered how much pain she was in, but she knew asking would do no good; Vei would never admit to any of it.

"Where's Father?" was the first thing Vei asked, which Jebi considered a cold greeting for one's parents.

If Namgyu or Hyeja took offense, they didn't show it. Hyeja said, "You know how he can't keep himself out of this military nonsense."

"Mother," Vei said with an exquisite patience that must have been honed over years of daughterhood, "you know how he likes to stay involved in soldiering, even if only by giving advice."

Hyeja made an extremely obscene gesture. Vei's mouth twitched.

Both Hyeja and the youth agreed, wordlessly, that despite her thinness, Vei was able-bodied enough to help with the tents. For the rest of the day, Jebi assisted too, moving cots and changing bandages as ordered. Not work they liked, but work that had to be done.

{Be careful,} Jebi urged Arazi, wondering how far away it was.

{I am always careful!} Arazi answered with an enthusiasm that only made Jebi more nervous.

The next morning, a shadow blew over the encampment. People yelled and scattered as Arazi fitted itself to the available space, landing in a series of staggered coils. "Two tank divisions are on the way, with their accompanying human and automaton infantry troops," it said. "Someone tell Bongsunga, please."

One of the younger rebels ran toward Arazi as though she hadn't heard it correctly, hesitated partway there, then nodded and ran off in another direction entirely.

Jebi spent their time waiting for the tanks with Vei. They wanted to tell her how much they admired her bravery, and the fact that she cared about saving artwork, and her tireless diligence in helping with the invalids when she was halfway one herself. But the moment was never right, and the words went unspoken.

The attack came with little warning. Jebi was outside when they heard at first a hawk-screech in the air, and made the mistake of looking up. Arazi swung its tail and knocked them flat, as well as everyone standing near them—Vei, Vei's parents, the youth, quite probably the tent and its suffering invalids as well. Jebi cursed, or would have if their mouth hadn't been full of dirt. Their attempts to get up and see what had happened were foiled by the dragon's tail holding them down.

*That tears it,* they thought, more pissed off than anything else. *Arazi is unstable, or Hafanden figured out how to reprogram its loyalties from a distance somehow, or—*

The world exploded in a haze of fire and red and heat. Jebi screamed. Their skin hurt as though someone had scorched it.

Only when their hearing started to come back, several eternities of riotous pain later, did Jebi realize they had been temporarily deaf. A persistent ringing noise filled their ears. Through it they could hear Bongsunga rapping out orders— thank all the small gods and spirits she had survived that.

"—fireworks?" she was asking.

"Some new kind of incendiary shell," Red replied, and coughed wetly. "We can't afford to be hit by a second one. We're lucky it wasn't a direct hit. Fell short by a good two hundred meters and look what it did. The front gate's hanging on by a thread. I don't think we can shore it up in time for the next—"

"I'm not a sniper," Bongsunga interrupted, each word

coming out harshly, "but I've known some. The next shot won't fall short. It'll go *beyond* us. And then the third will nail us, once they've determined the range. That's how I'd do it. Shoring up the gates? You're fucking right we don't have time." It was the first time Jebi had heard their sister swear so openly. "We need to evacuate."

"We'll be sitting ducks out there—"

"We're sitting ducks if we *stay put*. Get everyone moving *now*."

"Arazi?" Jebi wheezed, and was pleased to discover they could speak again, even though their back was a mass of bruises. "You can let us up now."

"Are you all right?" the dragon asked anxiously. "I couldn't think of a faster way to shield you."

"A warning," Jebi said, "would have been appreciated."

Vei shook her head, and Jebi looked at her with renewed alarm. Her wound was bleeding again; red showed livid on her bandages. "Wasn't time," she said. "Come on, you heard the evacuation order. We have to get the invalids out of here."

"*You're* about to be an invaild again," Hyeja said, saving Jebi from having to say it. "But you can walk, so you can help."

"Mother," Vei said, her patience slightly less exquisite this time, "I'm an invalid with a sword and the knowledge of how to use it."

Jebi did not see what good a sword would do against fireworks that landed on people and exploded, or however incendiary shells were supposed to function. But they recognized that the weapon comforted Vei. Perhaps that was what mattered, in a situation like this.

"There isn't time to run this by your sister," Vei said, and Jebi knew then that they weren't done. "The earthquake. Can you make one last one, if we go to where the tanks are?"

Jebi squeezed their eyes shut. They should have known this was coming. But what was the alternative? Forcing Arazi to kill people, the one thing it didn't want to do? The least they could do was defend their own people, since they had the ability. Not just their people, but their sister.

"I need my pigments." Especially the last of the Phoenix Extravagant.

Vei set off at a run and returned an agonizing number of minutes later, breathing hard, with the bag that Bongsunga had confiscated.

"Arazi," Jebi said, "can you get us closer to the tanks?" Their teeth chattered. They did not want to get closer. In fact, turning tail and hiding behind some sheltering boulder sounded like an excellent idea. Jebi didn't have any attachment to heroism or bravery; that had always been Jia's domain, and look where that had gotten her. Heroism had almost gotten Vei killed. At the same time, they couldn't run away and let the Razanei wipe out the rebels.

"Yes," Arazi said. "Hurry."

Vei hoisted herself up more or less one-handed, which would have impressed Jebi more if they hadn't worried that she would faint dead away and leave them to do this alone. Jebi clung to the dragon's spine, so as not to encumber her if someone tried to fight them from the air. They realized what a stupid idea it was the moment it occurred to them. Still, in principle, Hafanden *might* have another dragon under his control that Vei didn't know about.

Arazi slung itself skyward. Jebi gulped as the ground tilted alarmingly beneath them. As they ascended, Jebi saw the next artillery shell arcing toward the camp. No—not *at* the camp exactly. They had a good eye for curves, could extrapolate the parabola's landing position. It would impact the ground *beyond* the hillfort, just as Bongsunga had predicted.

They'd expected the shell to look like a captive star, or a fist of fire, or a malevolent whirling mass of glowing colors. It was none of these. It resembled nothing so much as a dark cylinder of metal, pointed at one end—an elongated bullet, if bullets *exploded* on impact.

With a roar like an entire ensemble of drums, Arazi launched itself toward the shell.

"Don't!" Jebi screamed, because the only thing worse than getting exploded on was *charging into* the thing that was about to explode.

Arazi would not be deterred. It accelerated, true as an arrow loosed by a master archer. Jebi looked down, because that was better than looking *at* the shell, and saw its shadow speeding over the ground like a snake of deadly intent. For a heartbeat Jebi envisioned the scene as from the outside, heaven and earth rushing toward each other.

Then, because they'd never learned the trick of bravery, a scant moment before the impact, they squeezed their eyes shut. *We're all dead,* they thought, incredulous and not a little regretful. *I didn't want to die already.*

"Hold on!" Vei shouted at them.

Jebi's grip tightened reflexively on the cantle of the saddle. That was all that saved them from tumbling ass over heels and plummeting to the ground below when Arazi swerved and knocked the shell aside with its shoulder, like the world's narrowest and fastest ox.

Fragmented impressions of fire and smoke shattered Jebi's world. They couldn't breathe; made the mistake of trying, and coughed and hacked as they half-swallowed, half-inhaled dust and ash. The dragon continued to fly. Only later did Jebi work out that it had swerved away from the shell's path, so as to gain the greatest distance possible before the damn thing exploded.

"Jebi!" It was Vei again. Her throat sounded raw. "Jebi, tell me you're alive."

"I'm alive," Jebi croaked. They forced their eyes open one at a time and regretted it instantly. "How are we alive?"

"Arazi rolled to shield us," Vei said. That explained the weird way the ground had rushed toward them earlier.

"There they are," Arazi said warningly.

"They'll bombard *you*," Jebi said, dismayed. "Won't they?" At least, they couldn't imagine that the tanks would leave Arazi unmolested.

From up here, the tanks resembled cannons mounted on wagons, except they had caterpillar treads in place of wheels. Jebi fixed the image in their mind even as they recoiled: sure enough, several of the cannons were reorienting to aim at Arazi.

"I am faster than they are," the dragon said, not smug so much as grimly sure. "You will have to work quickly while I distract them."

Jebi and Vei scrambled down from the dragon's back from behind the cover of a hill. "That won't hold them long," Vei remarked. "They can lob their projectiles *above* a hillside, hit things behind. But they're not going to swat us with tanks; we're too small."

"That's good, right?" Jebi asked, anxious.

Vei tugged on their arm with remarkable strength considering that she was using her left hand. For the first time Jebi noticed that she'd also tied her scabbard on the opposite side, presumably for a left-handed draw. What the hell kind of paranoid person trained ambidextrously? They'd only sketched left-handed when one of their instructors insisted it would free them from their preconceptions. Interesting but ultimately unusable results. Then again, they didn't work in a profession where you could reasonably expect to *lose* your hand—or arm, or head—if you fucked up.

Vei hustled them farther away from the encroaching troops. "They have *infantry*," she mouthed. "Who will be more than happy to sieve us with bullets if we stick our heads out. Arazi is going to draw their fire"—the dragon hissed its assent—"and I'm going to protect you from anyone who makes it this far."

*I'm not sure this is a good idea anymore*, Jebi almost said. Then they looked into Vei's eyes, as dark as the inner heart of a sword. "They won't stand a chance against you," Jebi said recklessly, and kissed her. They'd been aiming for her mouth, but got her cheek instead when Vei angled her head.

"Go," Vei said, and drew her sword.

Jebi pulled out the Phoenix Extravagant and other pigments that Vei had helped them smuggle out of the Summer Palace. They would have felt safer if Vei had stayed at their side, but she ranged out ahead like a gyring falcon, crouched low so as to avoid silhouetting herself as she crested the hilltops. For their part, Jebi poured out a small measure of water from a canteen and got to work mixing crude paint with the materials they had on hand. For the rest of their life, they would never be able to look at something so simple as a plot of dirt without envisioning it as a mask, a monster, a martyr.

They hated this part, where they had to look at what they were doing and couldn't check on Vei. Where they could *hear* the artillery barrage. They'd never attend a fireworks display again without the sound of explosions making them jump or dive for the nearest cover. War was beautiful at a distance, when one read about it in the sagas and histories, or illustrated it with an eye to the prettiest vantages or formations. Close up, war reminded Jebi of nothing so much as a fist to the stomach, except one had a better chance of surviving the fist.

{*I won't desert you,*} Arazi said. Jebi almost jumped out of their skin. The dragon had chosen to make itself multiple fast-moving targets, disassembling itself into spiderlings as it had once before. Two spiderlings had backtracked toward Jebi. {*I don't think they know where you are yet.*}

The possibility that someone had tracked the dragon back to their position hadn't occurred to Jebi. {*Thank you,*} Jebi muttered, grateful but distracted. They didn't want to be caught in the earthquake this time; was there a way to limit its area of effect?

They heard shouts, screams, the percussive boom of more artillery fire. Rifle reports. Maybe someone of a more musical bent would have found some kind of beauty in the sound, like the world's most destructive drum ensemble. Jebi wished they'd brought lint to blot out the noise, because at this rate, the ringing in their ears would never go away.

Heedless of the damage to their skin, Jebi scraped away at the hillside to expose a minimum of bare rock beneath the thin layer of topsoil and gravel and the clinging roots of stubborn weeds, none of which they could name. Then they brought out their brush—the poor thing would have to be disposed of and replaced after this, they hated wasting a good brush like this—and commenced painting.

The glyphs poured from the bristles, coalesced like fast scars upon the grit-covered surface. They remembered the ones they'd painted last time as though branded across the sutures of their skull. Caught in the teeth of a trance, they almost replicated the ones they'd used last time; caught themself just in time, and modified the final boundary symbols in an attempt to confine the force of the earthquake.

Jebi had never studied the ways of earth and stone except in the unhelpful sense that any of their people knew the basic precepts of geomancy. Even then, they wouldn't have been able to tell a true geomancer from a charlatan other than by reputation. They had a sense that the forces of luck, good or bad, couldn't be confined, only redirected or harnessed.

They had never studied physics or engineering, except where it pertained directly to art—the foundation of color in light, for instance. They'd only paid attention to applications, rather than theory. In particular, they had no reason to anticipate that force artificially confined to a region of large but not infinite stability would pulverize the underlying rock and liquefy the soil.

The ground trembled and buckled beneath them, then stilled while Jebi was wondering what they had gotten wrong. With a disgusting slurping sound, the earth beneath the tanks opened up and *swallowed* them. Jebi was too far away to hear the screams, and yet they imagined them anyway. Forgetting everything Jia had once told them about avoiding ridges and making a target of themselves, they scrambled up for a better view.

The tanks were sinking slowly and inexorably into the mire that Jebi had created. Jebi gaped uncomprehendingly. The cracks in the earth opened, closed, opened again; but they were confined to a perfect circle, as though an invisible wall prevented them from spreading further.

Alerted by some unnamed instinct, or perhaps an intimation of shadow in the wrong place, Jebi looked up. Arazi's spiderlings climbed each other to form a pillar of gleaming metal, reassembling itself into dragon form. They hadn't seen the process before; were struck speechless with wonder.

"Jebi, *get down!*" the dragon roared.

Jebi blinked, then spotted a figure lying in the shadow of a barren forsythia bush. It was holding a stick. A familiar stick: Hafanden's rifle stick. Except he had pulled it apart, revealing—a steel barrel. No stick gleamed like that.

They stared at the barrel, transfixed with terror. *It's pointed at me,* they thought, wondering. *But my part is done.* And: *I should duck,* except they couldn't seem to move.

The earth belched and bubbled as the last of the tanks sank beneath the smothering mixture of dirt and pulverized stone.

Fire flashed at the rifle's muzzle. Too late, the dragon stooped, falcon-swift, landing on Hafanden.

Jebi felt nothing at first. Then the pain hit them in the gut.

"Jebi!" It was Vei. Jebi could only see her face in snatches, as though reflected in broken water. "I shouldn't have—Jebi, you can't, we have to get you to a—"

Jebi smiled at her, hacked up something that tasted like pungent salt water. Wondered why their gut was screaming in agony. "We did it," they said.

"You idiot," Vei scolded, "we're not supposed to *take turns* getting hurt."

By then Jebi had passed out from the pain.

*Chapter*
# TWENTY-ONE

JEBI WOKE ALL at once, as though they had surfaced from a bad swim. Which would have been especially impressive considering they had last gone swimming back when they'd been a child, at the age of eleven. "I've died," they explained to the blur in front of them. They'd never realized that the afterlife would be out of focus. Perhaps this was a hell reserved for artists.

"You were lucky the shot was fouled," said a dispassionate voice. "It'll hurt to walk around, but it's more pain than real damage, and I've stitched you up already."

Jebi racked their memory and came up with a name: Hyeja. Vei's mother, the Western-trained physician. Jebi had no idea what Western remedies entailed. Had she dosed them with weird foul-tasting medicines? Except native medicine already relied on weird foul-tasting medicines. To say nothing of acupuncture or exorcism, neither of which Jebi had extensive experience with. And besides, surely they'd have noticed if someone had stuck a bunch of needles in them, even therapeutic needles.

"What?" Jebi asked, and scrabbled for the rest of the sentence. They couldn't think of what to say. There had been... a battle? Yes. A battle.

*{Jebi!}* This time it was Arazi. *{You're awake. Thank the Dragon Queen.}*

*{I'm awake,}* Jebi agreed, although they weren't entirely convinced.

"Sit *down*," Hyeja insisted just as Jebi fought to free themself of the clinging blankets. As promised, it hurt, pain radiating from the bullet wound.

"Hafanden's after us," Jebi half-said, half-moaned. "We have to stop him." They tried to remember what had happened. Maybe falling unconscious hadn't been such a bright idea after all.

"You did it," Hyeja said, still calm. "The earth sucked down those war machines like a dragon with a powerful thirst. Two whole divisions, and nothing left of them but occasional fragments of metal and a vortex of quicksand. I don't think anyone's going to venture near the battlefield for the next four generations, for fear of bad luck."

*I did that?* The memories came back piece by agonizing piece. "I did that," Jebi said aloud. They wanted to throw up. They remembered their terror of the earth—the most *stable* element—caving in on them. How much worse would it be for people aboveground to have the very ground they relied on turn into a mire beneath them?

"—awake, then I should see them," a raised voice was arguing in the background.

"It's your sister," Hyeja said, her tone unchanging. "Do you want me to tell her to go away?"

"What?" Jebi said. "No, let her in." Their vision was still blurry. They hoped the effect was temporary, although this made it easier to notice blocks of color and value, like the trick their first art instructor had shown them of squinting to stop focusing on the piddling details of what they were drawing and instead seeing large shapes. It was useful, but they didn't want to do it *permanently*.

Jebi recognized Bongsunga not by her face, which they couldn't tell from anyone else's at a distance, but by the stiff-backed way she walked. They'd know that gait anywhere. "You're alive," they said, and then, because tact was still hard, "Where's Vei?"

"She's asleep," Bongsunga said. "Hyeja gave her a drug for sleep, because she was losing blood walking around like an idiot."

That sounded like Vei. "What happened after I—?"

"The dragon took out Hafanden," Bongsunga said. "I didn't see it, but Vei reported it to me. We recovered what was left of the body."

Jebi's gorge rose again. *{Did you?}* they asked Arazi.

A telling silence. Then: *{Yes,}* it said. *{Because either he was going to die, or you were going to die. I knew which I preferred.}*

Jebi bit the inside of their mouth at the undertone of anguish in the dragon's voice. *{I'm sorry it came to that.}* What else could they say?

*{He was the one who aimed at you.}*

"You slipped out without even telling me," Bongsunga said, causing Jebi to return their attention to her.

Jebi was reminded that Bongsunga rarely yelled. They would have preferred some honest yelling to this quiet intensity. "I couldn't stay behind and do *nothing*," they retorted, stung.

"You idiot," Bongsunga said, her voice even quieter and more intense. "You could have gotten killed."

"Everyone would have died if we hadn't done something about the tanks!"

Bongsunga grabbed Jebi's shoulders. Jebi yelped in pain, and she hastily let go. "You idiot," she was saying over and over. Jebi realized with a mixture of pale horror and embarrassment that Bongsunga's face was wet.

"You were worried about me?" Jebi choked out.

"You idiot," Bongsunga said one more time. "You're *family*, even if you have execrable taste in hobbies and dubious taste in lovers. Of *course* I worried about you. I was terrified that you'd fallen over dead in a ditch somewhere."

"I have to tell you something about Vei," Jebi said as the full extent of their deceit hit them. It was the worst possible time to tell Bongsunga about Jia's death. They should have told her earlier. But the time had never seemed right, and Jebi was beginning to realize that there was no such thing as a *good* way to break the news that one's lover had killed one's sister-in-law.

"You can see her in a—"

"No, that's not what I mean," Jebi said, desperate to get it out despite the rudeness of interrupting their older sister. "Vei was the duelist who killed Jia."

Bongsunga fell into absolute silence.

*I've done it now.* The second thoughts hit almost immediately.

Given Vei's condition, she'd hardly be able to defend herself if Bongsunga ordered her executed. Jebi should have waited until Vei had a chance to get safely away—but to where?

{*I'll protect her, if it comes to that,*} Arazi said. {*Assuming she needs it, anyway.*}

"I can't see your expression," Jebi said, which was true but had nothing to do with their stupefaction. "Everything's still blurry."

"Yes," Hyeja interrupted, "you will have to be careful as you heal from the wound in your gut, and you apparently never recovered entirely from an earlier concussion. But it should go away with time, assuming you don't do anything else precipitous." She did not say *stupid*, much to Jebi's relief.

"I already knew," Bongsunga said after Hyeja had finished.

"You already what?" Jebi demanded.

"Jebi," Bongsunga said, "I have been following the movements of all the ministries' duelists prime. I know their war records. Did you think it was a *secret?*"

Jebi gaped at her.

"It's not about forgiveness," Bongsunga said, her voice hardening, "or revenge. Vei has been useful to our cause. My personal feelings aren't important. I will say that the sooner I can get her *out of my sight*, the better."

Jebi bowed their head, taken aback at this glimpse of what Bongsunga's dedication to the revolutionaries cost her. *So I will have to choose between my sister and my lover.*

"The earthquakes," Bongsunga said abruptly. "Can you do that again?"

Would Bongsunga hold them here, and separate them from Vei, if they could produce earthquakes on command? "I'm afraid not," Jebi said. "You'd have to source more Phoenix Extravagant. I used up the last of it."

"I see."

"I won't do it again," Jebi added, their voice shaking. "Drowning in the earth itself—that's not a proper way for people to die. If you want to fight the old-fashioned way, fine. But I'm not summoning more earthquakes, and I'm not teaching anyone how, either."

"This is," Bongsunga said, "extremely inconvenient."

"You can't make me."

For a terrified moment, Jebi thought that Bongsunga would apply pain. It wouldn't take much, in the condition they were in.

"No," she said, "I don't suppose I can." The cool resignation in her tone chilled Jebi more than they cared to express. "But you can't stop our people from researching the matter, either. In any case, I have a funeral to arrange."

Jebi's mouth went dry; for a moment their tongue stuck to the roof of their mouth. They hadn't considered the practical matter of preventing the ghosts of the dead from hanging around to curse to the living. "How many people?"

"On our side, or theirs? The tank divisions and accompanying infantry would have accounted for a few thousand. On our side... the artillery barrage took out about forty people. It would have been a slaughter if your dragon hadn't intervened."

{*I'm sorry,*} Jebi said again, ineffectually.

The tent's entrance parted as a wedge-shaped metal head poked its way in. The dragon's gaze pinned Jebi's, its eyes burning lantern-bright. "I'm sorry people had to die at all. And that you got hurt."

"I was far away from the action," Jebi protested. "They weren't aiming giant explodey things at *me*." Never mind that Arazi had aimed *itself* at one of the giant explodey things. They didn't want to mention that in front of Bongsunga, who might have another attack of Overprotective Older Sister.

Arazi made a discordant jangling noise that Jebi interpreted as a harrumph. "Jebi," it said, "between firearms and archery, you could have died from a considerable distance."

Jebi spent this sentence trying to signal with their eyebrows that Arazi should avoid this line of argument. No such luck. "I didn't want you to," they said eventually. "You didn't have to do it for me."

The dragon nuzzled Jebi's shoulder with exquisite gentleness. "If standing on principle means that you lose the people those principles are meant to protect," it said, "what's the point? I oppose war; but I also oppose slaughter in all its forms. There wasn't time for a more peaceful solution."

Jebi nodded wordlessly, unable to think of a response past the lump in their throat.

Bongsunga cleared her throat. "There is going to be a funeral service tomorrow," she said. "Arazi has been helping dig the graves. Its strength is a great boon to us."

The lump dissolved long enough for Jebi to croak, "You have someone to find suitable grave sites?"

"You've been out for a while," Bongsunga said. "We contacted a nearby village where there's a geomancer. It took quite a sum to convince him to come out to where the earth itself turned to soup"—Jebi flinched at the reminder—"but he'll site the graves and speak the rites."

"I should be there," Jebi said, squeezing their eyes shut.

"If you insist," Bongsunga said.

"Will there—will there be a service for the Razanei too?"

The shadows across their sister's face shifted. Jebi was glad they couldn't interpret them clearly. "Of course," she said, "if only to keep their ghosts from haunting us."

"You shouldn't try to walk yet," Hyeja remarked as Jebi started getting out of bed.

"I want to see Girai Hafanden's body," Jebi said. "Before you dispose of him. Assuming you haven't already."

"Trust me," Bongsunga said, her face shifting again. "You don't want to. It's only—forgive me for being crude—so much mangled meat."

Jebi's mouth firmed. "I want to be sure he's dead."

"I advise against this," Hyeja said, "but if you are anything like my daughter, you'll just sneak out of the tent. I'll assist you."

"Fine," Bongsunga said. "But you're to rest again after, you hear?"

IN A WAY, blurred vision was a mercy. The rebels had laid out the dead in rows on the hillsides, guards standing watch to scare off the carrion-eaters and scavengers. Hyeja remarked, on the way, that she saw birds circling overhead.

Jebi, using an improvised cane, tottered by the rows until they reached the section that held the Razanei dead. Surprisingly few had been recovered from the battlefield. Or maybe not so surprising, considering Hyeja's description of the quicksand pit.

"It's going to be there until the hills grow old," Hyeja said as she guided Jebi through the graves. "At least you'd have to be drunk and wandering around the middle of nowhere at night to stumble into it."

"I don't want anyone else to drown in it," Jebi said, words scraping out of their dry throat. "I'm an artist, not a..." Their voice trailed off. *Not a murderer?* People had died, and by their doing.

"I've killed people," Hyeja said conversationally. "It's how Vei's father and I met, in fact."

"You what?" Jebi demanded, distracted from their own guilt—what she'd intended, of course.

Hyeja shifted slightly—smiling? scowling? "The Westerners have a law for their physicians," she said, "that they may never bring their patients knowingly to harm, unless that harm is itself in the service of healing. A law subject to a great deal of quarreling, as you might imagine.

"I was the most promising of my master's students, foreigner though I was to them. But I would not swear to this law, so they cast me out. I found a place with Namgyu in the Blossom District once I traveled back home. I once"—and this time Jebi was positive that she was smiling, however macabrely— "provided poison with which to despoil several supply depots some years before the invasion, when the Razanei were sneaking more and more troops into our country under various pretexts of trade and intrigue."

"I thought that was a myth," Jebi admitted. "Or anyway, it seemed just as likely to be some kind of ordinary food poisoning."

"There are many problems with poisoning that I won't bore you with," Hyeja said, which had the perhaps unintended effect of making Jebi intensely curious about the subject. "One of them is that, when you're poisoning people en masse, you're liable to get survivors because of inexact doses, or differing tolerances."

Jebi nodded.

"Captain Dzuge Keizhi, who was stationed in Hwaguk long before the invasion, thanks to an agreement with one of the factions who collaborated with Razan, was not one of the ones who was poisoned," Hyeja said, upsetting Jebi's ideas of how this story would go. "You see, he happened not to like the particular type of delicious rice cakes filled with red bean paste that I had so temptingly poisoned. But he had servants— all the officers did. And he'd given his shares to the servants, not realizing—and when everyone fell sick around him, he sent for physicians."

Hyeja's voice softened. "I came because I was a fool; I wanted to see my handiwork, and report back to the faction I was then affiliated with."

"You're a ghoul," Jebi exclaimed, finally understanding why Hyeja's physician teacher might have had reservations about their student.

"If you want to put it that way, yes," Hyeja said. "I have always been interested in all parts of the life cycle, and that includes its end."

She knelt then, and pulled off the sheet covering Hafanden. Jebi had expected more of a smell, but this was winter, and bodies wouldn't rot as quickly; small mercies.

Jebi bent down, putting their face close to the mangled corpse's so their eyes would focus. Despite the trauma to the head, Jebi recognized the stern lines of Hafanden's face, forever twisted in a rictus of agony. The entire back of his skull had been caved in. Jebi shuddered.

Jebi searched for words to distract themself from the violence of Hafanden's death. "You were impressed by the captain's generosity and repented your ghoulish ways?"

Hyeja laughed. "If that's how you want the story to end. I was thinking of ways to finish the job. He persuaded me otherwise."

Jebi didn't ask what form that persuasion had taken, because the answer would only have embarrassed them both. Assuming Vei's peculiar mother was capable of embarrassment, which they weren't sure of. "Have you poisoned other people since then?"

Hyeja made a contemplative noise. "Poison? No. Kill? Only after long consideration."

"I'm surprised anyone lets you treat them," Jebi said, which was the nicer way of saying, *I am never letting you get near me with your tools and medicines again.*

"That's legitimate too," Hyeja said. "But, you see, you can't understand the treatment of an organism without understanding the entire cycle, from the womb to the grave. And sometimes the best treatment looks like injury, but is necessary to save the organism."

"You sound too much like my sister."

"Yes," Hyeja said, "she would understand this."

It dawned on Jebi that Hyeja was, in the most roundabout way possible, counseling them about any possible regrets they had about Hafanden's death. "Listen," they said, wondering how to make this as little awkward as possible, "it's all right. He needed to die. He was coming after us. Now they'll have to appoint a successor, figure out how to restart his projects—if they even want to do so."

"You were about to throw up when you heard what state the body was in," Hyeja pointed out. "You're not Vei. She's inured to violence because it's a necessity of her profession. We don't usually, in this society, require our artists to think of people as assemblages of meat and bone and gristle."

"Why?" Jebi couldn't resist asking, their gaze drawn again to what remained of Hafanden. "Is there some society that does?"

"Some of the Western societies allow their artists to dissect corpses to improve their understanding of anatomy," Hyeja said. This sounded so outlandish that Jebi immediately dismissed it as a grisly but fanciful story that Hyeja had latched onto. "Not something that will ever catch on here, I suppose." She sounded *regretful*, and Jebi hoped that the woman never took up painting as a hobby.

"I've looked my fill," Jebi said, grateful to be able to escape by using the truth. "I suppose it's not really over. There will be another deputy minister after him. And reprisals. More people will die."

"Yes," Hyeja said, "but the revolutionaries have prepared for the eventuality." She replaced the coarse sheet that had covered Hafanden. "You should get back to the infirmary, such as it is."

"I want to see Vei."

Slight hesitation, then: "Of course you do. Tell me, what is my daughter to you?"

As if that hadn't been obvious. "Why," Jebi said, "does it matter?"

"I may be an eccentric," Hyeja said, "but I am still a parent. And I know what it is they say about artists, whether or not it's true." She might have studied medicine out of the country, but she would still know that artists were generally married to their profession. "What are your intentions?"

Jebi fought the urge to burst into hysterical laughter. Vei was unconscious, Jebi themself was recovering from a bullet wound, and Hyeja was concerned about *intentions*. "I'm not going to dump her for a succession of pretty lovers, if that's what you mean," Jebi said. "If—if she wants me, I want her. For as long as she wants me. I haven't asked my sister what she thinks, but"—and the words came out in a rush—"I don't care. I was never going to be carrying on the family lineage anyway."

Besides, Bongsunga had made it clear that if Jebi chose Vei, they were turning their back on the family anyway.

Hyeja said, "Your happiness matters more to your sister than you think, for all her strategizing and plans and duties. Of this I am sure."

"I'll find out, I guess," Jebi said.

HYEJA LED JEBI back to the one invalids' tent that had a guard, presumably because Bongsunga's people didn't trust Vei even after what she'd done. Jebi couldn't work up the energy to be offended. "Call if you need anything," Hyeja said. "I have work to do."

*I'm sure you do, and that you love it more than anyone is comfortable with*, Jebi thought. Did it matter if the physician had an unseemly fascination for the macabre as long as she got the job done? Jebi suddenly wondered how Hyeja's courtship with Captain Dzuge and Namgyu had gone.

Namgyu, for their part, sat next to Vei's pallet. Vei was sleeping fitfully, tossing and muttering unintelligibly in her sleep. "Namgyu?" Jebi asked, addressing the older person deferentially.

"Hyeja says our daughter will recover," Namgyu said, "although it will be a while before she recovers full range of motion in her sword arm."

"That's bad, isn't it?"

"Well," Namgyu said, "that depends on her plans, and yours." They smiled, although Jebi couldn't read the nuances of the expression. "The dragon has some thoughts, I hear."

One of Arazi's spiderlings clattered, and Jebi startled; they hadn't seen it in the corner of the tent. "You can be part dragon and part spider-thing?" they demanded.

"My tail doesn't need to be full-length for digging graves," Arazi replied. "I thought you would feel easier with an additional guard."

"I do," Jebi admitted. "Thank you."

Namgyu exhaled softly, then said, "I'd better see if Hyeja needs my assistance. If only in berating Keizhi for being a know-it-all."

Jebi reached down, and was rewarded by the spiderling nudging their fingers. "What's next for you?" they asked as they listened to the uneven rhythm of Vei's breathing.

Before Arazi could answer, Vei roused, perhaps at the sound of Jebi's voice. She did not, wonder of wonders, attempt to sit up, which had been Jebi's first impulse. "Jebi," she said. "And here I thought I'd be up before you were."

"Just stubborn, I guess. Is it—is it all right to—?" Jebi mimed a kiss, only to be interrupted by a fresh wave of pain. *Fuck you,* they thought at the injury, *I'm not going to let you prevent me from kissing the woman I love.*

Vei laughed weakly. "I don't think you can hurt me *that* way, Jebi." She lifted her chin, and Jebi met her lips with their own. It was a gentle kiss, since they didn't want to cause her pain. They couldn't see Vei except as a pallid blur, but they knew her body language; knew that her hesitant movements didn't just indicate injury—as if *that* had ever slowed her down—but uncertainty.

"I'm not leaving you, stupid," Jebi said.

Vei laboriously raised their right arm, cocooned in a bandage though it was, and waggled her fingers at Jebi. "I'm not much good for—" Heat rushed to Jebi's face, and never mind that they'd already *done* that together.

"There are other people in this tent!" Jebi reminded her.

"I doubt it's the first time they've heard such talk," Vei said, and only then did Jebi understand how badly the injury had shaken her.

Jebi pressed her hand against their heart. "I don't want to stay here," they said, forced to honesty. "But if you plan to, I will." They'd figure out a way around Bongsunga. Go into exile with Vei, if necessary.

"About that," Vei said, and Jebi's heartbeat stuttered in alarm. "Arazi and I have been talking, on and off."

"Oh?" Jebi said, not sure they wanted to hear this.

Arazi made a sound in between a chime and a sigh, drawing attention to itself. "After the funeral rites," it said, "I am leaving. I will only draw the Ministry of Armor's attention if I remain here."

"Of course," Jebi said, suppressing their sadness. "That... that makes sense."

"I wanted to ask you to come with me, you and Vei," it went on. "I don't enjoy being alone. I spent enough time being alone, chained beneath the earth."

Jebi's breath caught. "Vei?"

"I was going to say yes," Vei said, squeezing Jebi's hand. "I won't pretend that it won't be hard to leave. But my mother was very clear about the damage to my arm. Until I become as good left-handed as I was with the right, my dueling days are over."

"Oh, no, no, no, that can't be true," Jebi said, because even they had some idea of what dueling meant to someone like Vei. "You can fight left-handed. You're better left-handed than most dueling masters are. You can't give it up. And won't you miss your family?"

"It's not just that." Vei stroked Jebi's fingers, coaxing them to relax one by one. "My father told me once, when I was young, that no one wins a war except the crows. I didn't understand him then, but it makes more sense now. What was it the sage said, thousands of years ago? That if you have to take to the battlefield you've already lost. Everyone loses— parents, siblings, children, cousins. Innocence, always.

"There's a second war coming, Jebi, and this is just the beginning. Your sister is ready for it. I've been talking to her while you were unconscious. She's been preparing for the conflict ever since I cut down her wife." Vei's voice was almost steady as she said this. "But so many people aren't ready for this, Jebi. Artists. Charm-sellers. Grocers. Tailors. People who just want to get by, and who won't be given a choice when the guns begin to speak again."

Jebi's hand trembled, and they stilled it with an effort. "What's our part in this, then?"

Bongsunga spoke from the tent's entrance. Jebi startled, even though the sudden draft should have alerted them to her arrival. "We can't leave Hwaguk's artwork where Girai Hafanden's successors will destroy it," she said. "But we can't destroy it ourselves, either. It would be a betrayal of those artists and their work." Her voice softened fractionally on *artists*; she was looking directly at Jebi.

"What," Jebi said sarcastically, "you're not going to use it for Phoenix Extravagant?"

"Not *Hwagugin* art, no," Bongsunga said, betraying no reaction to Jebi's tone. "Razanei art will be good enough for that, when we can get our hands on it. There are old collections still, and the occasional imports."

"You can't," Jebi whispered, but their sister was still talking.

"Someone has to take *our* art away to a safe place until it can be repatriated. Someone who knows its value, and someone who's able to protect it from anyone who comes hunting it down. The Razanei will murder their own artists and burn up all their vaunted paintings too, to build their war engines, and that's something we'll have to address, but they can keep their fucking hands off *our people's art*.

"I can't spare many people. But you, and Vei, and Arazi—if you take the Hwagugin artifacts far away, to somewhere so remote that it isn't on the maps, you can have that space to recover. And hopefully my forces will be able to destroy any Razanei who attempt to track you down."

Jebi had an idea. "The moon," they said. "We'll take everything to the moon."

# Chapter
# TWENTY-TWO

THE FUNERAL SERVICE took place during a morning shrouded by mist. Not the best omen, but they wouldn't have a better opportunity, and Bongsunga said, a little fretfully, that she wanted it done with so that the rebels' next operations weren't dogged by ghosts. Jebi, who believed in ghosts the way most of their people did, considered this good sense, not just for reasons of superstition but because the deaths still didn't seem *real* to them.

The survivors gathered on the hillside, with its gashes of newly upturned earth. Jebi could smell it, despite the cold. Automatically, they inventoried the colors: the dark browns crusted with lighter umbers where the top layers of soil had dried in the pale winter sun, feathery touches of white where a light snow had fallen last night, the insipid desaturated yellows of dead grass and weeds. They could have painted the entire scene in ink and wash, rendered it unthinking with unhurried brushstrokes, papered over the fact that so many people had died.

Bongsunga gave a speech. She referred to earlier speeches and pamphlets that made the people gathered nod sagely, although Jebi had no idea what the references were and it would have been a terrible time to ask. They tried to pay attention to the words rather than the roughened contours of their sister's voice, but all they could do was stare at her— their vision had cleared up, thank goodness—and memorize her features.

Only someone who knew Bongsunga well would have noticed that she looked older. Jebi wondered how they hadn't seen it earlier. A Western painter would have pointed out the deeper lines around her eyes and mouth, or the deliberate rigidity of her stance. But Jebi believed that art was about the inner nature of things, and people. For the longest time, all they'd seen of Bongsunga was the grieving widow. Not until they'd taken up with the Ministry of Armor had they come to see that she'd found a purpose beyond that, and a new lover, and refused to let her grief bind her to the past.

*I will paint you,* Jebi thought, *as I see you here.* Above a grave, yes; but surrounded by the living. Death below, life above. The kind of spiritual balance that their third instructor had liked to natter about. As a child, Jebi had feigned interest. Now, they wished they'd paid closer attention.

Bongsunga finished her speech. Jebi couldn't remember a word of it. Then again, it wasn't likely that anyone would quiz them on its contents. Even if they did, Jebi planned to fake being overcome by emotion. It wasn't far from the truth, even if the emotion didn't come from the speech as such.

Vei patted Jebi's shoulder circumspectly. "You're going to miss her," she said.

Jebi's eyes pricked, and they turned away to scrub at their face. "That obvious?"

"Jebi, she's your sister. Of course it hurts."

"She can't come," Jebi said. "She's more useful to the resistance here." They didn't mention that they could have had a place with her—if they'd been willing to use the glyphs to kill, and to abandon Vei.

"That's not what I said," Vei murmured, but she left it there, to Jebi's relief.

Bongsunga went into Red's arms. People scattered into small groups of two, three, four. Jebi stared out over the graves, unmarked as was the Hwagugin tradition. Depending on the whim of the local weather, perhaps the small mounds would be washed into an indistinguishable flatness, and later visitors would only have whispers and ghosts to guide them in making their offerings. Perhaps not.

"I'm going to leave an offering to Hafanden," Vei said. "You don't have to—"

"Of course I do," Jebi said, and offered Vei their arm.

Vei leaned on Jebi as little as possible, which Jebi suspected had to do with her pride. They didn't say anything about it as the two of them walked companionably to Hafanden's grave. Or what Vei claimed was his, anyway. Jebi presumed someone—Arazi maybe?—had kept a record, but they hadn't been keeping track.

A shadow fell over them. It was Arazi. "You too?" it asked.

"I'm surprised you would want to do anything but piss on his grave," Jebi said to it. "If you'll pardon the expression."

"Believe it or not," Arazi said, very dryly, "I learned an extensive vocabulary from the Summer Palace's denizens. Also, I have concerns about rust, remember?"

Jebi kicked at the ground, remembered that the ground was *someone's grave*, stopped. Even if the someone was Hafanden, who'd had them tortured. To Vei, they said, awkwardly, "Do you miss him? I mean, you worked with him for years. It's got to be different for you."

They should have foregone the question instead of putting Vei on the spot. But Vei leaned more heavily on Jebi and sighed. "He believed very strongly in his mission. It was his strength and his weakness."

"I'm glad he's gone," Jebi said. "Is that a horrible thing to admit to? I just hope his replacement isn't even worse than he was." They considered. "To be fair, he could have been a lot worse. He might have had me beaten, but he wasn't... arbitrary about it." This last came grudgingly. But they were standing right over the man's grave. They didn't want to offend his ghost.

Vei made as though to kneel, and Jebi began to assist her. Vei smiled slightly and waved them off. "It's my arm that's injured, not my legs."

"Sorry, that was stupid of me," Jebi said, chastened.

Vei's mouth crimped. "There were other ministries that would have considered me for duelist prime, had I wanted them. Some of them in spite of my mixed heritage, some because of it. Not all Razanei are unreasonable on this point. But I'd heard rumors about what Armor was up to. I wanted to position myself to stop it. And so I went into Hafanden's service. I didn't imagine, all those years ago, that it would lead *here*."

"Maybe it's just as well that mortals can't see the future," Jebi said. "He needed to die, you know." And not just because of what he'd done to Jebi themself. Vei had given up her position in rescuing them. Even they could tell it pained her.

Vei stood, almost as graceful as she'd been before the injury. She shook her head. "Let's go. We have preparations to make."

"One moment," Jebi said. "There's a grave for Hak, too." Bongsunga had told them earlier, when they asked. "I want to say goodbye to her."

Arazi led them to Hak's grave, indistinguishable from all the others. Jebi closed their eyes and thought, *I'm sorry things ended the way they did.* Poor luckless Hak; perhaps the other gumiho in Hwaguk, wherever they were, would do better.

"Jebi," Vei whispered.

Jebi looked up, about to express their annoyance, and then they saw it: a nine-tailed fox, watching from a careful distance, its eyes glistening amber. Family, perhaps? Jebi had never before wondered who Hak had left behind.

"She was a good friend," Jebi said to the gumiho, and bowed to it.

The gumiho bowed back. "So were you," it said in a low voice. "Thank you for trying to save her."

Then Jebi blinked, and it was gone.

JEBI SAID GOODBYE to Bongsunga over one last private tea. Or perhaps 'tea' was more accurate; Bongsunga served yulmucha, really more of a thin sweetish porridge, but one that Jebi welcomed in the chill. The day had scarcely grown warmer by the end of the funeral service; a stiff wind had sprung up out of the west.

Vei had excused herself to say her own farewells to her three parents. This left Jebi looking mutely across the scratched-up table at their sister, wondering what to say. Even Bongsunga, who had spoken so eloquently at the funeral (and never mind that Jebi couldn't remember a word of it), sipped her tea and looked meditative rather than speaking.

Unable to bear the silence any longer, Jebi burst out, "I don't want to say goodbye to you again."

"I don't think you want to stay and join the resistance, either," Bongsunga said, uncharacteristically gentle. "Especially under the terms that I would require. You're not a fighter. There's nothing wrong with that. We need people to grow rice, and repair wheels, and paint the way the world is as well as the way the world ought to be. Jia teased you mercilessly; she meant well by it, but I should have asked her to stop."

"I didn't mind," Jebi said, mostly meaning it.

"Nevertheless." Bongsunga took a longer sip of the yulmucha. "Arazi has assured me that it can make trips back and forth to relay messages and ferry supplies to you. We don't have a great deal of intelligence about conditions on the moon, other than the fact that the Ministry of Ornithology believed that it was feasible to set up a base there. Still, I will feel easier knowing that you are adequately supplied."

Jebi nodded wordlessly.

"The air will be thin, perhaps to the point of nothing," she added, "at those heights. But Arazi has assured me that its enchantments will protect anyone riding it."

"That's good to know," Jebi said, although they had never thought about altitude sickness in connection with flight. How high was the moon, anyway?

"I have something for you," Bongsunga said. "A distressingly practical gift, which I'm sure you were expecting of me anyway."

Jebi was too disarmed by their sister's self-deprecating humor to have a response to this.

Bongsunga produced a tube of weathered wood. "We don't have many of these, but I think you will need it."

"What is it?" Jebi accepted the tube and fiddled with the end until they figured out how to open it. The contents, unlike the case, gleamed brightly: metal, not wood. "A spyglass?"

"You can gaze upon the celestials," Bongsunga said, "and perhaps more importantly, keep an eye out for any Razanei expeditions into the sky."

"Point taken," Jebi said, sighing. "We'll remain vigilant. Or anyway, Vei will. She's much better at vigilance than I am."

The corner of Bongsunga's mouth twitched. "I'm sure she can teach you."

"You are so brave," Jebi whispered, or tried to; their throat closed up.

"In the old days," Bongsunga said, "even the rulers of Hwaguk could not read the histories that the chroniclers wrote about their reigns, and during past invasions those records were always the first to be evacuated, until invaders burned them all down."

"Bongsunga," Jebi began. They had no idea where this digression was going.

"We don't have those histories anymore, except in excerpts mentioned in other scholars' letters," Bongsunga said fiercely. "But we still have the artifacts. They're not the whole nation's hoard—that's impossible—but they're a start. We'll gather more of them and send them for safekeeping. I like to think that we'll be able to restore them to their proper places within our lifetime. If not—well. They'll be safe as long as they need to be."

"Be safe," Jebi echoed. "*You* won't be."

"No," Bongsunga said, "but I made my peace with that years ago."

Jebi fumbled at their throat until they'd recovered the blue mae-deup charm. Miracle of miracles, they still had it on their person. "Keep it in memory of me," Jebi said. They wished they'd painted her, had a miniature to offer her, or even some whimsical cartoon of an upside-down dragon at the heart of a spiderweb. But the charm would have to do.

Bongsunga closed her fingers around it "Always," she said. "And Jebi—"

Their heart thumped painfully. "Yes?"

"Take care of that lover of yours," Bongsunga said. "I won't pretend I understand, or even that I approve, given who she is, but—" She stopped, picked her words over carefully. "If you make each other happy, perhaps that's what matters, not my understanding."

"Thank you," Jebi said, and fled before the conversation could become any more dangerous.


JEBI AND VEI prepared to leave the next morning, as false dawn brightened the horizon with ice-colored light. Jebi squinted skyward at the moon, visible as a quarter-moon. It seemed incredible that they'd be going there, even with a dragon's help.

Bongsunga's people had already burdened the dragon with an astonishing quantity of parcels. They must have improved the harness system and worked out how to balance the load while Jebi and Vei were recovering. Arazi stood patiently, the lights in its eyes flickering as Jebi and Vei approached.

"It will take all day at unimaginable speeds for us to reach the moon," Arazi said. "The enchantments that sustain me should sustain you as well. If not, then we turn back."

"I'm ready," Jebi said, casting one last glance over the camp. And what for? Soon they'd see it from above, too, the way no one but a bird should be able to see things.

"I, as well," Vei said. She pulled herself up, one-handed yet limber. Jebi hesitated, momentarily concerned that she would tumble from dragonback. They needn't have worried. Vei waved to Jebi from her seat once she'd secured herself.

Next it was Jebi's turn. *I will never get used to this,* they thought as they climbed up to their own seat, less gracefully than Vei had. Maybe they should worry about their own coordination instead of worrying about Vei's fitness. They did have the dreadful thought that Vei was going to want a *sparring partner* and that if Arazi wasn't going to volunteer, that left exactly one person.

"All buckled in?" Arazi inquired. "I would hate for you to fall off halfway there."

"Don't even joke about it," Jebi said. They were mentally revising all their sketches of dragonriders flying to the moon to include safety harnesses, something they'd never thought about before experiencing actual dragon rides. They also considered pulling out a sketchbook to jot down their impressions of the world below and the world above. Vei would—

"Jebi?" Vei asked. "Are you ready?"

"One moment," Jebi said, and squirmed until they managed to fish out their pocket sketchbook. They hoped they wouldn't drop their pencil; they didn't trust themself to attempt brush and ink mid-flight. "Ready."

Arazi vibrated with laughter. "You will have to show me your drawings once we arrive," it said. "The air will be colder the higher we go, although perhaps the stars and sun will light our way."

Most of Bongsunga's followers had come to see them off— or, more likely, to enjoy the spectacle. Not that Jebi blamed them either way. Vei lifted her chin, then waved to the well- wishers. Jebi belatedly did the same, narrowly avoiding dropping the sketchbook.

Arazi sprang into the air like a carp yearning heavenward, except, of course, it was already a dragon. The wind tore past them as though they were knifing into the heart of the sky. Jebi looked down: the encampment was already receding beneath them. In short order it was the size of a book, and then a speck, and then nothing at all.

The earth spread beneath them like a stitchery of gauze and shadow. Jebi sketched madly, using the flat of the pencil to shade areas rapidly rather than wasting time on hatching. They were struck all over again by how aerial perspective made landscapes look hazy from high up in the air, not normally a vantage point human artists thought about, even if they'd known about the phenomenon—impossible not to, what with all of Hwaguk's mountains—since childhood.

"Jebi," Vei called.

"I'm drawing," Jebi shouted back, captivated by the white-and-green-streaked crenellations that those selfsame mountains made, seen from above.

"*Jebi*," Vei said, and this time the wonder in her voice caught Jebi's attention. "Look around you."

They lifted their eyes and caught their breath involuntarily. Around them the stars shone like friendly eyes; one of them winked when Jebi gaped at it. The wind no longer felt as bracingly cold, and smelled faintly of quinces and cinnamon.

They'd always known that the heavens were home to the celestial court, but they hadn't expected to witness its wonders so directly. Celestial attendants and their moth-winged pets, from foxes to frogs, lounged upon the thin shreds of cloud and nebulae. The attendants fluttered their fans, smiling at them in equal wonder. One raised a shining cup in salute.

Vei's eyes had gone soft. Before Jebi could summon up any jealousy, she looked at them, and her eyes went softer still. "Jebi," she said, "I'd heard about the astrologers' reports, but I never thought I'd see this for myself. Not up close."

Jebi's pencil stopped moving. They didn't need the sketchbook to know that they would remember this sight for the rest of their life.

They didn't know then, or later, what impulse made them cram the sketchbook and pencil back into the nearest available pocket, and pull out the spyglass instead. They would never have forgiven themself if they'd dropped Bongsunga's gift, after all. It would have made so much more sense to wait until they landed on the moon. They didn't intend to snoop on the celestial attendants, as curious as Jebi was about them; it would have seemed rude to turn the glass on them.

Rather, Jebi lifted the spyglass to their eye and turned it toward the world below. Impossibly, they spied the curvature of the ocean, something they had never had to think about before. They'd always thought of the world as fundamentally flat, even though Bongsunga had explained otherwise to them long ago.

"Vei," Jebi said in a choked voice, "I see Hwaguk in miniature. The peninsula, like it is on the maps, but in different colors. And those splotches of islands over to the side—those must be the archipelago of Razan."

"There must be something else," Vei said. She'd gone tense in response to whatever she heard in Jebi's voice.

"I see it too," Arazi said; of course it did, with its falcon's vision.

For all their joy in greeting the heavens moments before, Jebi could not help but quail at the armada of great metal warships that was, even now, sailling for Hwaguk. "That can't be the resistance," they said. "Even my sister wouldn't have kept it a secret from me that we now have a fleet of metal."

"Let me have the spyglass," Vei said, and Jebi handed it over with an effort. She peered through it. She tensed further, her face gone white as despair. "I know those flags. Those are the Western nations and their banners. Once they subdue Hwaguk..."

Jebi didn't need her to finish the sentence. They'd fight the Razanei army first, and then turn to subduing the Hwagugin rebels. Hafanden had been right about the Western threat after all.

In appalled silence, Arazi, Vei, and Jebi continued into the sky, toward the welcoming arms of the moon.

# THE END

# ACKNOWLEDGMENTS

THANK YOU TO my editor, David Moore, and the wonderful folks at Solaris Books, as well as my agent, Jennifer Jackson, and her assistant, Michael Curry.

Thanks to my beta readers: Marie Brennan, David Gillon, Helen Keeble, Yune Kyung Lee, Mel Melcer, Vass, and Ursula Whitcher. Thanks also to my cheerleaders and alpha readers: Peter Berman, Pamela Dean, Eller, Elizabeth McCoy, and Sherwood Smith.

Special thanks to Marie Brennan for research assistance; to mecurtin, thistleingrey, and Ursula Whitcher for pointing me at resources; to Keaton Eagar and Lindsey Eagar for language assistance; and to the Metropolitan Museum of Art for its online essays on art history, which saved me 50 gazillion trips to the library. Thanks to Mom for fielding my weird questions and sending me books on Korean art, to Dad for passing me books on Eastern and Western philosophy, and to my sister Yune Kyung Lee for a lifetime of encouragement. Thanks as well to my husband Joseph Betzwieser and daughter Arabelle Betzwieser for their support, and my excellent catten Cloud for strict enforcement of 'typing breaks.' All those trips to cafes were not in vain!

The idea of magical pigments was inspired by the story of PO49 or Quinacridone Gold, the world supply of which ran out a couple of years back. You will take away my small stockpile of PO49 watercolors over my dead body.

# FIND US ONLINE!

www.rebellionpublishing.com

/rebellionpub   /rebellionpublishing  /rebellionpublishing

# SIGN UP TO OUR NEWSLETTER!

rebellionpublishing.com/sign-up

# YOUR REVIEWS MATTER!

Enjoy this book? Got something to say?

Leave a review on Amazon, GoodReads or with your
favourite bookseller and let the world know!